The dogs emerged into the clearing, racing toward us, and then they were on us.

There were two of them, white, big, and fast. Fighting a dog is no big deal. The fact is that one swift, well-aimed kick ought to end your dog problem real fast.

One swift, well-aimed kick almost cost me my leg. I didn't see the spiked collar it wore, and I sliced open my left leg at midshin.

The dog yelped as its ribs broke. It grunted as the air was forced from its lungs, and then it breathed no more.

I looked at Truck and Doc. The other dog lay several yards in front of them, its head a darkened mess.

I hurried to Doc. My leg gave out as I reached him.

There was a lot of blood. It flowed from the four-inch-wide wounds in Doc's chest, darkening matted fur.

We stared at Doc's body for a long time. Finally Truck looked at me. "No dream this me," she signed, trilling softly. Her eyes narrowed and she stood. "Hate dreams me! Understand you?"

"No, Truck. Understand I no."

She looked at Doc's body, at the bodies of our two opponents, then at the two moons in the sky. Truck looked at me. "Understand you no," she signed, and turned away.

Ace Fantasy Books by Steven R. Boyett

ARIEL
THE ARCHITECT OF SLEEP

The Architect of Sleep

STEVEN R. BOYETT

ACE FANTASY BOOKS
NEW YORK

This book is an Ace Fantasy
original edition, and has never
been previously published.

THE ARCHITECT OF SLEEP

An Ace Fantasy Book/published by arrangement with
the author

PRINTING HISTORY
Ace Fantasy edition/July 1986

ISBN: 0-441-02905-1

Ace Fantasy Books are published by The Berkley Publishing Group,
200 Madison Avenue, New York, New York 10016.
PRINTED IN THE UNITED STATES OF AMERICA

This one's for Adrienne—for
friendship and long talks.

It's also for Kerry

And the memory of Truck

Acknowledgments

Despite the enormous complexity and person-hours involved in the making of a motion picture, when all is said and done it is the director who receives the lion's share of the credit—or, as the case may be, of the blame. But a director is not the only person involved in the production of a motion picture, and at the end of the film the credits roll—and they ain't called "credits" for nothing. Therefore I, as director of this book, am rolling credits at the beginning:

Ken Mitchroney for visualization; Beth Mitchroney for llama-play; Doyle Pope for miscellaneous verisimilitude; Lisa Pianka, Larry Leker, and Nancy Lambert for cleaning and polishing; History of Science Professor Robert Hatch for conversations, extrapolations, and showing where to look for right answers; Stephen Jay Gould, Gene Bylinsky, and Carl Sagan for their lucid books on evolutionary theory and speculative evolution; Eugene Linden and Herbert Terrace for *their* books on communication with apes via Ameslan; Diane Duane for three-body problems; the Florida Speleological Society for anecdotes and information; and especially:

David Gerrold, for many kindnesses;

Melissa Ann Singer, for editorial virtuosity; and

Jessie Horsting, for How Things Work—and Why.

Lastly I should like to thank the coffee-plying staff of Coco's in Northridge, California, without whose caffeine pushing I could not have survived many a hyperkinetic evening.

Interpolated into the manuscript are four brief, slightly altered essays I wrote regarding the music of (in order of appearance) Tangerine Dream, Mike Oldfield, Brian Eno, and Peter Gabriel, and I should like to acknowledge their wonderful music for the imagery it has provided.

—SB—

"O God! I could be bounded in a nut-shell,
and count myself a king of infinite space,
were it not that I have bad dreams."

—*Hamlet*, Act II, scene ii, 263
William Shakespeare

The Architect of Sleep

1
Narrative of James Bentley

THE TELEPHONE RANG as I was chewing the final bite of the last American cheese sandwich I ever ate. The sandwich was utterly nondescript—single slice American cheese on a French roll painted with mayonnaise—so it was the perfect way to tie off a life fueled by microwave meals, Velveeta, coffee, and crackers. I swallowed this bite without knowing that it was a thing I should have savored, and I answered the phone on the third ring.

"Yeah."

"You know," said Nicole, "I really hate the way you answer the phone."

"Yeah? I was thinking of answering it with 'What?' from now on, but I decided that might sound a bit curt. What's up, Nicki?"

"There's a new Coppola movie opening tonight at the Plaza."

"Film. Coppola makes films, not movies."

She ignored me. "Eight o'clock. You drive, I'll pay."

"Why is it, Nicki, that we go out more now than when we were living together?"

"Because now it takes some effort for you to keep me around. Say hi to Albert for me. Bye." And she hung up.

I frowned, keeping the receiver to my ear and drumming my fingers on the rickety dining table until I heard a click and the dial tone resumed. I set the receiver of my antiquated princess phone back into its cradle and looked around for Albert. He sat curled in on himself in the corner beside the threadbare couch. "Your mother says hello," I told him. He made no reply.

I sighed and added my plate to the formidable pile in the sink. I stared at the dirty dishes at least a full minute, debating whether to risk life and limb and wash them now, or wait until tomorrow. If I wanted to go caving, make it back in time to shower, drive to Nicki's, and reach the Plaza Theater by eight o'clock, I'd better get a move on.

"Tomorrow," I promised the dishes—again.

It did no good for me to make sure the car keys didn't jingle when I picked them up—the second I touched them, Albert began to make a big show of playing with a sock in the middle of the living room to make me feel guilty.

I glanced at the digital clock Nicole and I had bought with green stamps a year ago. Two o'clock. Hurry, hurry, hurry.

I put two scoops of Jim Dandy Chunks into Albert's bowl. At the sound he abandoned his sock and trotted to his cracked plastic bowl. Unceremoniously he lowered his head and began to munch.

There is a sound effect they use in low-budget splatter movies, a horrible, teeth-grating sound of crunching bone. It is a recording of Albert eating his canine haute cuisine.

I picked up the phone again and dialed work. It was answered on the fourth ring.

"Seven-Eleven. Judy speaking."

"Judy, this is Jim."

"Jim?"

"I work for you. Eleven-to-seven shift."

"Yeah. Hold on a minute, will you?" The receiver clunked down and I heard her ring up a purchase. A minute later she was back. "Look, I need you to work tonight, if you wanted off. Eugene ain't gonna make it in the morning and I need a sub for him. You wanna work a double?"

I sighed. "No. I'll be in at eleven." I hung up. Shit. This meant dropping Nicki off after the movie—after the *film*—and rushing straight to work.

I went into the bedroom and grabbed my daypack from beside the thin mattress pad I loosely called a bed. Had I wanted to use the living room as a bedroom, the current bedroom could easily have been transformed into a walk-in closet.

I unzipped the pack and put in my contact-lens case, a small bottle of saline, two packs of matches, a coil of nylon rope, and my glasses, then carried it into the kitchen and threw in a packet of dried apples, a granola bar, and some high-caloric junk called "trail mix" I'd bought at an Albertson's grocery store. I zipped the pack, put it on, and automatically patted my butt, checking for my wallet as I always did before going somewhere. I decided to leave it home, because I could easily lose it in the cave.

I remembered that I was going to want to take a shower when I got home, and I turned on the water heater. To save money on my power bill I'd learned to keep it off until an hour before I wanted hot water.

At the front door I took a last look around. Albert was still making horror-movie noises in the kitchen.

"Hold the fort, bucko," I said, and I turned off the living room light and shut the door. I nudged it once to be sure the latch had caught, and I have regretted it ever since.

There is nothing so dark as a cave. With your light source off, you literally cannot see your hand in front of your face. I think you could pad the inside of a closet with black felt, sealing off all the places where light could get through, step inside and shut the door behind you, and it still wouldn't be half as dark as a cave.

You strain to see what's ahead in the inadequate beam of your light source, and after a time you experience a heightened awareness of hearing and touch. You feel your way along limestone walls that are sometimes wet and slimy, but more often rough and dry. Occasionally you hear the squeaks of bats or rats, though more often than not the most startling thing you find in a cave is cockroaches running across your boots in the dark.

If you've only seen caves in the movies or on television, then you haven't seen a cave. They aren't built to accommodate human beings; the ceilings will slope down until you are forced to crawl, the floors drop off unexpectedly. Usually there is no echo at all, not where I went caving—Florida isn't big on caverns, mostly just hollow veins in the ground. Central Florida is a good place for caving, though. Much of the state is tunneled through, and sometimes sinkholes collapse to create entrances to the tunnels, and you have a cave. Central Florida's also nice because that part of the state isn't too spoiled, unlike south

Florida. Last time I was there, anyway.

Tell people one of your hobbies is spelunking and you usually get a blank look, followed by a short pause and a, "Well, that's . . . interesting." People think there's something odd about a person who likes to traipse around in dark, wet holes in the earth. So maybe I wanted to return to the womb; I don't know—but until you have been in a cave, surrounded by the smell of the earth (which always made me think of coffee, though I never knew exactly why), and by the smell of lime, of moisture, and, vaguely, of decay; until you have been surrounded by the weight of it, the comfort of the sheer *volume* of earth around you—until you have done this, don't brush it off as just a quirky thing some people like to do. Sure, caving has its dangers—you can break your legs finding a drop-off the hard way, for one thing, or you can get wedged and die of hypothermia—but more people scuba dive in underwater caves, and *that,* as far as I'm concerned, is sheerest lunacy.

It was black inside Bat Cave, like being in space but with all the stars extinguished. I was outfitted like an intrepid little spelunker, with sturdy blue jeans, daypack, and lamp helmet. I was a few hundred yards into the cave, following a branch I'd never been through before—which was unusual, as Bat Cave was well explored and I had been in it many times. The branch began to narrow as I groped along, until soon I was crab-stepping forward.

Bat Cave was a pretty easy cave; the Speleological Society liked to use it to introduce neophytes to the arcane practice of going to and fro in the earth. It was also a popular cave with the frats, especially on Saturday nights—thus rendering Sunday spelunking a misery of crushed beer cans and used condoms. I remember one night I came to Bat Cave alone. You really aren't supposed to cave alone, but there I was, traipsing around with all my gear like a good little Boy Scout: two different light sources, heavy denim pants, and army surplus boots, the Intrepid Spelunker personified. As I was leaving the cave a group came in: eight guys, one flashlight. Shorts. Tennis shoes. "Little Sisters" in tow. At least one case of beer. I was glad it was dark so they couldn't see my reddened face.

I forced myself farther along the narrowing branch. Another half-dozen steps and my back and chest were touching rock.

It is a spelunker's terror to get wedged. It happens because of a common affliction among spelunkers: the urge to go Where No One Has Gone Before. Just a little farther, you think to yourself. If I can get past this, I'll find a passage no one's ever been in. So you push on, hoping the passage will widen within a few feet. Sometimes it does.

Sometimes it doesn't. Caught in rock like a fly in amber, you either force yourself out or you don't—in which case you pray. It happens most often to cavers out alone, those irresponsible types such as myself who prefer not to take along a buddy. In that, even fellow spelunkers thought I was crazy. But everybody has something they insist on doing alone, for whatever therapeutic, cathartic, or thought-gathering reasons. Mine was caving.

I moved my head to play the lamp beam around the passage as best I could. It looked as if it did indeed widen about three steps farther on. It would be tight, but I decided to chance it. I exhaled and began crab-stepping again, pushing and pulling with my hands as I did. A few scrapes and I was through. Good thing I'm built more along the lines of Ichabod Crane than Hercules.

I tipped up my helmet, wiped sweat from my brow, and breathed a long sigh that reverberated around me. I was in a small cavern, formed by a sinkhole who knows how long ago.

I readjusted my helmet and took a look around. The ground was hardened mud; as far as I could tell not even animal tracks were pressed into it. There were no Doritos wrappers in sight, no Miller cans or used prophylactics. Where no one has gone before? I smiled.

The beam of the helmet lamp paralleled my gaze as I looked around the wet limestone walls. It was cool in the cavern but quite humid, and I was covered in sweat. I sipped water from my canteen and chewed on a granola bar, taking care to put the crumpled wrapper into my pack.

I squatted and rested a few minutes, sweat trickling down my face, stinging my eyes. Well, no one said it was a picnic. I got up and began examining the cavern a little more closely. Off to one side something shimmered, caught in the beam of my helmet lamp. I widened my eyes and stepped toward the center of the cavern. There was a vague flickering in the air ahead of me, like the watery undulations of air rising in the distance from a sun-baked road. Since this was a cool cave and the shimmering looked to be about ten feet in front of me,

I frowned. I walked forward slowly, arms extended like Karloff's Frankenstein's monster.

I stopped when my hands began to tingle. I felt the sort of tension you can feel beneath high-voltage power lines, a sort of nervous agitation, a high-strung feeling of unease. I stepped forward again, and a coldness blossomed in my stomach. It spread, chilling my sweat, then was replaced by a heat that made me clammy. Pinpoints of light danced before my eyes, and there was a high-pitched ringing in my ears. I sank to my knees and hugged myself. I whipped off my helmet and tossed it aside, and then I vomited. It went on and on, the cavern walls throwing back the sound of my retching, and the reverberant splashing made me heave even more. My stomach continued to clench like a fist long after I had run out of things to throw up, and I felt as though my eyes were about to pop out of my head. The spasms grew less intense, until finally they were gone. I felt a sense of almost religious relief, and I sat back and shivered in the dark. I wiped my mouth and took a few small sips from my canteen.

Salmonella? I'd only had that cheese sandwich for lunch. Maybe the mayonnaise had gone bad. But unlike salmonella, this sickness had come upon me suddenly, with no warning. I hadn't felt so much as a grumble from my stomach until then.

I waited in the nightless dark until my breathing slowed and I felt sure I wouldn't be sick again. I decided I'd better find my way out; it wouldn't do to have food poisoning and be wandering around alone inside a cave. In the midst of my sick spell I had become disoriented, though, and wasn't sure which way to go. Stepping around the pool of vomit, I retrieved my helmet and shone it around. I found the exit and hurried toward it. The cave smelled awful.

I was past it before I realized what was wrong: the constriction was missing. The place I'd had to squeeze past to get into the cavern—it wasn't there; I had hurried from the cave unhampered. I was puzzled, but not enough to return and find out what was what.

The way out seemed longer than the way in had been, but before long I emerged, blinking in the sunshine. The grass was tall. Spanish bayonets grew in spiky clumps. The ground was wet and muddy, though there hadn't been rain in several days. Mosquitoes lighted atop my bare arms.

I set about looking for the trampled path I had followed to

within half a mile of the cave entrance, but I couldn't find it. In fact, none of the landscape looked familiar. There had been a huge cypress tree not a hundred yards from the cave when I had gone in. It wasn't there when I came out.

I thought of the missing constriction in the cave. Had I stumbled upon another passage out? It was possible.

It was past noon and the sun was westering. I turned my back to it and headed east, boots squishing in the mud as I walked.

I had left my car, a battered 1970 Ford Maverick whose hood was held shut by a knotted sock, parked off a back road no more than a mile east of the cave. I walked at least a mile and a half. No car.

No road, either.

Confused, I continued east another half mile but found no sign of a road at all, dirt, paved, or otherwise, except for a game trail. I turned to head northwest, thinking that I was bound to come across the road if I traveled on a slant. I stopped when I saw the panther.

It was a Florida panther: tan, lean, and looking more like a cougar than anything else. It was three hundred feet away, facing away from me, well-defined muscles bunching along its lean frame as it stalked something in the brush. I stood motionless while it gathered itself, flowing forward, and then a gray rabbit sprang out of the bushes and the panther bolted after it. The tall grass hissed with the pursuit, and they were gone.

I frowned. The other day I'd heard on National Public Radio that there were an estimated seventeen Florida panthers left. Those few were almost all in the Everglades, four hundred miles south of me, though one or two had been seen in Ocala and just north of Orlando. To the best of my knowledge none had ever been seen this far north—not around Gainesville, anyhow, and certainly not within a twenty-minute drive of the university.

Curiouser and curiouser.

I headed northwest, keeping a weather eye out for the panther. I unsnapped the case at my belt that contained my folding Buck knife. Not that it would do me a great deal of good against a panther, mind you, but it was better than bare hands. A little.

I stopped short of a web strung between two trees a few feet apart. Centered in the web, waiting patiently, black-and-orange-banded legs splayed wide, was a banana spider three-fourths the size of my hand. A banana spider packs a bite that is no fun at all, and this fine specimen was splayed about six inches from my face. I backed up and went around the trees, giving my eight-legged friend a respectful berth, and trudged on.

Something buzzed loudly by my head, circled, and zoomed off. I bent down and picked up a branch to use as a spider stick, holding it before me as I walked. I waved it up and down as though giving some rustic papal benediction to the woods, hoping that the stick would part the strands of any spiderweb I encountered before the resident beastie had a chance to wrap its loving legs around my face and make me do the funky chicken.

A crane stared at me as I passed it, decided it didn't like my looks, and took wing.

There was no sign of a road. No ranger towers poked through gaps between the trees, no microwave relay stations, no telephone poles. For all the civilization the terrain revealed, I might as well have been a Spanish explorer in the fifteen hundreds, seeing the Land of Flowers for the first time. I was confused, even a bit panicky, but there was really nothing to do but push on until I found a road, a house, a pop-top, anything. I wasn't in an ideal position to quit in frustration. I wanted to get home in case I got sick again, I needed to let Albert out before he crapped on the carpet, and I'd have to call Nicole to cancel our date, because there was no way I could be ready in time.

After I'd spent an hour and a half communing with nature, the brush thinned and finally cleared. Ten yards of open ground lined a riverbank. It *might* have been the St. Johns River. It could have been one of the canals of Mars, for all I knew. I followed it anyhow, adhering to the time-honored maxim that civilizations tend to form along riverbanks, and hoping that if I followed it long enough I'd run across signs of same. College kids out tubing. Bass fishermen. Alligator poachers. I didn't care.

What I saw were a lot of manatees in the water. Manatees—"sea cows"—are so ugly they're. . . . Well, they're ugly. In a half hour of walking, I saw six of them, which was peculiar since manatees were on the endangered list because boaters kept running propeller blades over them, chewing up their backs. They fed on water hyacinths, which, illegally imported to Florida, had proliferated and threatened to choke the canal network and river constrictions. I saw not a single water hyacinth.

What I did see was much more anomalous.

It was late afternoon and shadows were lengthening. I was tired. I had been walking for hours and I had no idea where I was. Spelunker I may have been, but closet survivalist I was not, and I didn't relish the notion of spending the night in the open—not with panthers and creepie-crawlies running around. I had eaten my last granola bar and had decided to ration the rest of my meager food supply until things sorted themselves out. Which I hoped would happen before too long.

I had just decided to call a rest stop when I saw a fat man sitting on the riverbank in the distance. He seemed to be wearing a long-billed cap and a long, gray coat, and he was leaning back against the steep bank with a fishing pole in his hands. I grinned, feeling renewed energy, and headed toward him.

A minute later I was hiding behind a pine tree.

Thirty yards away, sitting on the riverbank, clasping a fishing pole made from a branch, occasionally tugging on it halfheartedly, was a raccoon.

2
Narrative of James Bentley

(continued)

IT WAS HARD to tell because it was seated, but it looked to be about five and a half feet tall. Proportionally, it was a touch thinner than a normal raccoon, not quite as roly-poly, and its head was a mite bigger in relation to its body, and broader. Also, its arms and hands were longer than those of any raccoon I'd ever seen.

It was fishing.

I watched it for about five minutes. In that time it got a nibble, and it stood hurriedly and played the line a bit. There was a tug on the line, and the raccoon began pulling back on the branch, trilling softly to itself. Its catch surfaced, then dove with a splash. The line slackened.

A tickling at my neck made me brush away what I thought was a branch of pine needles. My hand came away with a five-inch banana spider on it. I yelped, jumping out from my cover behind the tree and flapping my hand as if I'd stuck it into a fire. The spider fell off. I heard a screech: the raccoon had jumped up at the sight of me and raised its fishing pole protectively. The loose rocks of the riverbank gave way beneath it, however, and it splashed into the water. Its trilling became shrill, where before it had sounded vaguely like the cooing of a pigeon. It took advantage of its position in the water and swam away from the bank, floating on its back with its eyes on me the whole time.

For my part, I approached the river's edge and simply stared at the raccoon. It stared back. I got the impression it was as frightened and uncertain of me as I was of it. I thought about running away, then thought better of it: there were panthers in the brush, after all, and I wasn't about to try and climb a tree. And it had been *fishing!* That thought ran through my head again and again: it was fishing! Not standing in the shallows and swiping at fish, but, you know . . . fishing. Like on *American Sportsman*.

I got on my knees and retrieved the pole from the edge of the water where the raccoon had dropped it. The pole had been cut from a young tree. The line was a thin, rough rope tied to a hook made from a piece of bone. I grasped the pole by the thin end and held the other out to the raccoon. It eyed me suspiciously for a moment, then grabbed on.

Slowly, unsure whether I was frightened of it becoming alarmed or of becoming alarmed myself, I pulled the huge raccoon toward the bank until it let go and clambered onto the grass. I stepped back and offered it the fishing pole. It shook itself as dry as it could, eyes on me all the while, and began vigorously ruffling its fur with long, curled fingers. Standing, the raccoon came up to my throat. I hoped it was as smart as the fishing pole implied, but who knew? I'd seen films of monkeys stripping the leaves from a branch to make a "tool" for catching termites; the monkeys simply inserted the stripped branch into a termite hole, waited, and withdrew it when it was covered with crawly things. Voilà—lunch. It was a tool deceptive in its simplicity, one I doubt I'd have thought of making under similar circumstances, and I regarded myself as at least a little smarter than a monkey. So maybe the fishing pole was an incidental tool, the product of sophisticated hands, and the furry thing—sure, it was a huge raccoon, but it looked vaguely like a little guy in a Disneyland suit—was going to try to hurt me.

"Hi, guy," I said.

It seemed puzzled when I spoke. It clamped the fishing pole under one arm and began manipulating its fingers with the goddamnedest fluidity I had ever seen. It was a short burst of gestures, punctuated by a few trillings and grunts.

I have seen deaf people signing, holding a conversation with their deft fingers. Once, riding a bus, I watched a husband and wife conduct a disturbingly silent argument for seven miles, until she ended all further conversation by looking away and folding her arms. There was no doubt they were arguing; I could almost "hear" the emotions conveyed.

There was no doubting this, either.

Researchers into primate communication had taught chimpanzees to communicate in Ameslan, American Sign Language. For a while Washoe the chimp had become a celebrity of sorts. If primates could do it, why not a dexterous raccoon?

A dexterous, five-and-one-half-foot-tall raccoon. I'd have been laughing if it hadn't been chest high and standing in front of me.

Where had it come from?

It seemed to have finished signing and was looking at me through narrowed eyes, head hunched down. There was a long, fresh scar across its stomach, a few more, shorter, along one flank.

I shrugged elaborately—don't ask me why I thought the gesture was universal, but I did it anyway—and pointed to my throat. "Can you talk?" I asked, feeling more than a little foolish.

A furrow appeared between its black eyes. It signed again, more rapidly this time, as though agitated. Then it stopped, wrung its hands, and slowly repeated the signing. I shook my head. "I don't understand," I said, mentally cursing myself for never having taken the time to learn Ameslan. A college friend who had a deaf sister I had thought about dating had once offered to teach me, but I had never gotten around to the lesson or to her.

Then the absurdity of this situation struck me and I found myself stifling a laugh. *The amazing thing about a dancing bear is not how well it dances, but that it dances at all.*

Slowly I stood and extended my arms, palms up, but evidently the human gesture indicating "Look—no weapons" didn't mean the same thing to it. It backed up, trilling, and raised the fishing pole to guard position.

"No, no, it's okay," I said.

It feinted at me.

I didn't want to alarm it further, but I also knew I was not exactly in the best of positions here. So, still holding out one hand to placate it, I reached back with the other and drew my Buck knife from its sheath.

The raccoon's trilling grew louder, and it jabbed air with the pole.

Was it about to attack, or was it warning me to put away the knife?

Hell with it. Either way, I wasn't going to put away my only weapon and face a giant, frightened, and armed... animal.

I unfolded the knife.

The raccoon swung and struck me on the wrist. Whether accidentally or by design, the branch hit my radial nerve and I dropped the knife.

"Hey!" I yelled. "Goddammit—"

It poked me in the solar plexus.

I huffed and doubled over. The raccoon rushed forward, grabbed my hair, and yanked me backward onto the grass. By the time I hit, it had laid one end of the branch across my throat and set one foot atop it. I tried to sit up, and the raccoon applied pressure. For a moment I could not breathe. I remained still, and the pressure eased up. A little. The raccoon bent down and picked up my knife. It spun the blade in its hands in a manner too fast for me to follow, but when the motion stopped the blade was four inches from my face.

"Okay, okay," I managed, voice thin and squashed. I stifled an urge to again show it my empty hands, another human submissive gesture it might misinterpret.

The raccoon continued to warble. It lifted its foot from the branch across my throat, grabbed my arm, and tugged. I understood and rolled onto my stomach.

It tied my hands behind my back with the fishing cord. If I had been harboring thoughts of this creature being a dumb animal, they flew in the face of my captivity.

The raccoon had me sitting propped against a young pine, arms behind me and around the trunk, hands tied palm-outward. My shoulders ached. Pine needles poked my butt.

The raccoon was playing with my knife. It turned it about in its hands, examining it from every angle. It closed the blade, then flicked it open with an assist from one finger, trilling in seeming delight when the blade locked out. It tested the blade for sharpness by shaving a little patch of fur from one arm, then hunched down and began tossing the knife from hand to hand.

After a while it returned its attention to me. It untied my hands, removed my daypack, and retied them—tighter than they had been, as I had managed to work them a bit slack.

The raccoon was quite taken with the daypack's zipper. It opened it, closed it, and opened it again. It set one eye near the tab to watch the teeth meshing together and separating as it yanked the tab to and fro. Soon it grew tired of this and opened the zipper all the way. It upended my pack and dumped the contents onto the grass, then tossed the pack aside. Since my lamp helmet was the largest item, it turned its attention to that first, turning it over in its hands, running fingers along the dirty rim. It brushed one hand over the switch and inadvertently turned on the lamp, though the light was hardly noticeable in the sunshine.

It examined the extra batteries a moment, then tossed them away. Likewise the foil granola bar wrapper and two books of matches. It fingered my glasses a moment, smudging the lenses, then tossed them aside as well. Then it discovered my contact-lens case. It tapped at the plastic, ran a thumb along it, unscrewed the white cap with the raised "R" on it, then the blue one. Thank God I was wearing my contacts. It tossed aside the case and continued to inspect my pack.

I worked on loosening my bonds, wondering how I was going to explain this to anyone. (See, it's like this: I got lost and met this huge raccoon, and it poked me with its fishing pole, tied me up, and robbed me.) The rope was loosest around my left wrist. My hands were bound palm-outward, but if I could bend left fingers down to left wrist and tug up just a little bit. . . .

If I could do that, I'd be double-jointed. I'm not, so I watched slack-jawed as the raccoon went through my belongings. While it sniffed at a foil packet of dried apples, I noticed some things about it that hadn't been apparent before. Its spine was straight, its hips were flattened, and its legs were longer than those of a normal raccoon. The feet were broader, thicker, and arched. It had a ringed tail, but it was small and seemed vestigial.

There was room for plenty of gray matter in that skull: while not as large as a human being's, it was nevertheless proportionally larger than a normal raccoon's; the back of the head was rounded and bulged out a bit. Brain *size* isn't an intelligence indicator, anyway: it's the ratio of brain weight to body weight, along with the abundance of convolutions.

Of course, debates concerning its intelligence were academic: it had taken my knife, and it had tied me up. *Quod ergo demonstratum*.

After about fifteen minutes of this the raccoon dropped everything and returned its attention to me in order to check my bonds. It discovered the loosened left side and chittered loudly. It stepped in front of me and began signing with complicated motions. I shook my head. "I don't understand," I said. Vocalization was automatic; I knew that it didn't know what I was saying.

A crease appeared between its eyes, as though the raccoon were frowning. It signed again briefly, then pointed to my bonds, made a sign, and pointed again the bonds. I nodded, then realized that the raccoon might not interpret a nod as an affirmative. Well, what the hell else could I do?

The raccoon seemed satisfied though: it stalked off into the woods.

In half an hour it was back, a dead quail in either hand. It plucked them, cleaned them with my knife, set them aside, and gathered dry branches for a fire. It went back into the woods again. I resumed my efforts to loosen my bonds. No go.

The raccoon returned with two flattened rocks. It knelt before the branches and began striking one rock against the other. When I was a Boy Scout I used to attempt this, but I could never get it to work, though some of the boys could—but not without a *lot* of patience. Who had taught it to do something I'd given up on as hopeless?

And how on *earth* had it learned to cook meat?

As the raccoon worked I sneaked a peek and observed that it was a she. I cleared my throat. The raccoon looked up at me, then returned to trying to start a fire. "Uh, excuse me," I said. She ignored me. "Yoo-hoo. Look, there are some matches on the grass not two feet from your foot. Hello? Knock-knock." She wouldn't look up. All right: I took a deep breath and then yelled hard enough to rasp my throat: *"Hey!"*

The raccoon jumped back, one hand cocking up to let fly a rock.

I did my best to indicate the kindling with my chin, then nodded toward the book of matches.

Her arm remained poised.

I nodded at the branches, tugged exaggeratedly at my bonds,

then nodded again toward the branches.

The raccoon lowered the rock. She bent down, picked up my knife, and walked toward me.

I tried not to flinch as she stepped behind me and squatted. She untied the rope but held on to it, then quickly stepped away from me. She tossed away the knife and raised the rock partway to her ear.

Why didn't she just hold on to the knife? Maybe she liked rocks better; how would I know? Slowly I flexed my fingers, keeping an eye on the rock. I stepped away from the tree, knelt, and retrieved a matchbook. Taking care to keep my movements slow, I opened the cover, singled out a red-tipped match, and tore it from the book. With match against striker I bent to the branches and looked back at the raccoon. She was peering forward and looked more curious than suspicious—if I wasn't anthropomorphizing her expression, that is.

I lit the match and held it to the branches. The flame didn't catch, and in a few seconds the wind snuffed it out. It would have been nice to have had a Bic to flick. Ah, the simple joys of a high-tech world. Oh, well—nothing to do but try again. This time it caught, and I nursed the flame along until a half-decent fire was going, and then I added dried leaves. *Thus Spoke Zarathustra* didn't play, but it should have.

I looked back to the raccoon. She signed something I took to indicate approval, then handed me a quail carcass impaled on a stick. Yum. Quailsicle. I glanced at the knife on the grass, five yards away. The raccoon didn't seem very concerned about it. Maybe she was testing me—go for the knife and I'll bust your skull with my rock, fellah. I decided to play it safe for now.

It grew dark as we ate our quail, which tasted good, though I yearned for my knife so that I could at least cut off the bird's head. I washed down the quail with the last of my water. Seeing what my canteen was and what it held, the raccoon reached forward tentatively and pointed at it with a long, dark finger. I upended the canteen and shook it to show that it was empty. The raccoon signed something and pointed again at the canteen, so I shrugged and handed it over. With a curious, waddling run the raccoon dashed to the river some ten yards away, knelt at the low bank, and dunked the canteen. She returned with the full canteen and began to drink, spilling water all over herself because the canteen mouth wasn't really shaped to accommodate her narrow jaw. She offered the canteen to me, but I declined. Yellow fever ain't my idea of fun. The raccoon seemed happy with her water, though.

After eating I got up and stretched, touched my toes, and shook the stiffness from my legs. The raccoon didn't seem to mind, so I headed toward the riverbank. En route I deliberately stepped by my knife on the grass. If the raccoon noticed, she gave no indication.

I sat on the riverbank, hugging my folded legs. In the darkness the river was glossy black. I heard a fish break water downstream. I tossed a rock, it splashed in with a hollow *plunk*. I stared at the black water where the rock had disappeared.

I was worried about Albert. He'd be howling if I wasn't back soon, and I wasn't allowed to keep a dog at that ratty apartment, so I couldn't have him doing that. If I could at least get to a phone, I could call Nicole and get her to check on him. I sighed. I'd left Albert alone all night before, of course, but not without first discharging my obligations toward his care and feeding. That was my part of our symbiotic relationship: I fed him and petted him and let him mangle my old socks, and in return he occasionally lent an understanding ear and did not judge me harshly.

I lay back in the grass and looked up. The overcast was heavy, as if a gray lid had shut across the sky.

A shape blotted out half the sky.

I got up hurriedly. The raccoon stood before me. My folded knife was in her hand. The raccoon signed something with her free hand, then held the knife up to me. The expression on her face was that of a solemn child.

I took the knife. "Thank you," I said.

The raccoon signed something else, then turned and walked back to the fire, her shape depicted in chiaroscuro by the flickering orange background: spade-shaped ears, tapering nose, and fat-rat body. She banked the fire and sat before it, staring at the flames.

I watched for a few minutes, but the raccoon only sat still, hunched near the fire like an old man warming himself on a sunny park bench. I put my knife into the case at my belt and left the riverbank to revise the primal scene and join the raccoon at the fire.

And that is how I met Truck.

3
Narrative of Truck

(translated by James Bentley)

THIS NIGHT I dream. I shape the dream, the dream shapes me. Dreaming, I meet [Bentley]. I fish and he finds me. There is something special about him, something apart from his odd appearance. In some way he is important to me.

I am searched for. In the distant cities, the nearer Outback towns and countryside, they look. I will return.

The day after my True dream, I make ready. I am stronger now; my leg cuts and stomach cuts heal, though the fur does not grow back. I learn and survive. I take the eggs from the nests of birds, I kill the birds. The [teraton] is good eating but hard to kill. The panther leaves me alone. The alligator does not, but I can climb, can throw rocks. The capybara bothers me at night. I stay near the water, though, to fish, to swim. Today I know it is time to move on, in order to be where [Bentley] will be, and I am ready for this. I break up my hut of grass and dried mud, and I bury the pieces and scatter other pieces so no one will know of me being here. The sticks and ashes from the fires I scatter also. The fishing pole is all I bring; it is all I need.

The sun appears as I walk along the riverbank. At midday when the time of our meeting is near I sit down at the bank. I smell the cool from the water and see the fish beneath. The sun is not yet high enough; [Bentley] is not due. But soon.

I fish.

Today I do not feel like wading in and catching the fish

with my hands, and anyway the river and the riverbank here are too steep. The fishing pole I make from a branch broken off by my weight as I hang from its end. The hook is a bone from a bird I am eating. The bait is a cricket.The cord is the one I am taking from my captors when I escape, the cord that is binding my hands.

I remember this as I fish. Bad memories, but I am free and alive, and surviving. There is something to be signed for this.

My reverie is interrupted by a fish tugging for attention on the line. I give it to him, but poorly, and he escapes. I am thinking this funny when I hear a noise, the bark almost of a dog, and I turn, thinking perhaps it is a Stripe's fighting dog, but it is [Bentley] who leaps out from behind a tree. I expect him, I know, but he is bigger and more frightening than I am dreaming, and his appearance in this loud and flapping way startles me. Jumping up, I slip and fall into the water.

And here is the strange thing, the departure from the dream-thing that renders True dreams untrue, for it does not happen as I envision: [Bentley] does not jump into the water after me, does not sign that he is come to aid me, but instead lowers to his knees and holds out my fishing pole to pull me in. This disturbs me, for it is unexpected, and I am suddenly uncertain how to proceed. I dream of you, [Bentley], but I am not sure that I trust you.

As I dry myself he begins making noises at me. "I am dreaming of you," I sign. "I know of you and am waiting here for you."

He makes more noises.

"Together we will travel," I continue, "and find the towns and those who can help."

And here is another odd thing: he ignores my signing and holds out his stubby hands as if to offer grapple. True dreamer or not, I am no fool, and will not grapple with a giant of uncertain civility. He ignores my refusal, though, and brandishes his knife.

All is going wrong, here, is not as I am dreaming, and so I act with no True dream to guide—as most act throughout their lives.

If being tied to a tree serves to calm him, the sharing of food smooths ruffled fur even more. Things are a little more correct now, a little closer to the dream. Still, I am wondering if I am interpreting this dream correctly, and this disturbs me.

Well:

The sleep is good this night, and dreamless, and when I wake I awaken [Bentley]. Since the untying of his hands he is lighting a fire with an odd portable firebrand, and is accepting the formal return of his captured knife and showing other indications of civility. He does not understand my signings, and this is a problem to which I shall attend later—assuming he is capable of signing in a sophisticated fashion. I shall watch him for a time to determine how best to approach this. For now, though, I gesture as though I attempt to sign to a kit attending library for only a few years, telling him that we are to move on, and we go. For a while we follow the river northward. I study [Bentley] as we walk. He is odd, to be walking so thin and high on two long legs. And the noises from him! Unceasingly, the noises. Like the birds in the trees, but deeper.

I throw at birds for lunch, and he acts as though this is a new thing to him. Imagine: throwing rocks, new! How is he to help me at all if the casting of a stone is a marvel to him? Still, it is a True dream—I think!—and I trust that.

But what will everyone make of us?

4
Narrative of James Bentley

I LIVED WITH a raccoon once.

His name was Truck and he belonged to my friend Paul. The three of us shared an apartment while Paul and I stumbled our respective ways through college. I brought home my bacon by working the graveyard shift at a 7-Eleven. My schedule was such that the bulk of my spare time was spent in a zombied-out torpor. Diversions were few and welcome; Truck was one of the main ones. When Paul brought him home Truck was six weeks old and about the size of a large, plump rat. He shit on everything in sight until we taught him to climb up to the toilet seat and flush it afterward. Thereafter, accidents only happened when one of us left the bathroom door shut.

Truck reached adolescence somewhere around seven months. As is the wont of adolescents the world 'round, he became rebellious and experimental. He grew enamored of the top shelf of Paul's sizable bookcase and took to hiding things there—things like razors, unwashed plates, and paperbacks left lying about. He also developed an inordinate fondness for the silverware drawer. I don't know why. But there I'd be on the living-room carpet, listening to the stereo, and I'd see motion out of the corner of my eye. Beginning with the bottom drawer and working slowly toward the second from the top, which held the silverware, the drawers would open and close seemingly of their own accord. It was Truck, climbing up the backs of the drawers until he reached the silverware, and more often than not the way one of us discovered him was when we were looking for an eating utensil. Scoldings were to little avail during Truck's adolescence, but they did teach me and Paul that the little fuck was able to hold his own, if need be: One scolding, on the heels of a silverware-drawer escapade, led to the discovery that Truck was capable of exuding the most ungodly aroma I have ever had the ill fortune to smell. We had to wash the silverware four or five times.

He cut loose on my neck once when a dog barked at him.

I had no doubt that Truck was smarter than a dog. He listened attentively, though not always docilely, while being lectured; he seemed capable of gathering meaning from inflection; he was more curious than a cat; and he had particular tastes in music. He liked Traffic and Genesis, seemed ambivalent about Brian Eno, and steadfastly refused to remain in the room while one of my Tangerine Dream albums played. Doubtless this will seem an anthropomorphism on my part. I think otherwise, but how else can I convey it? I felt sure that if we had allowed him to mess with the stereo controls he'd have demonstrated his musical preferences a bit more concretely.

It was hard to get used to living with an animal that had hands. Well, not hands *exactly;* he had no opposable thumbs—but Truck could unlatch, unscrew, or pull open just about anything that could be unlatched, unscrewed, or pulled open. A closed door, drawer, or box was a direct challenge. Hell broke loose when he discovered how to open the refrigerator.

Though it got him into mischief, it was nevertheless this specialness—his hands—that set him apart from any other animal with which I have cohabitated. Sure, he got into trouble, and broke things, and pried apart things that wouldn't go back together—but you could play tug-of-war with him, or you could hand him a drinking glass and watch him lift it and tilt it to his mouth like a child with a too-large tumbler. When his water jug was empty he would tug on your pants leg and indicate it with a forlorn expression. He pulled on the ears of visiting dogs with malicious glee, and took pathetic delight in pulling on the fingers of visiting human beings with the goddamnedest hey-mister-can-you-help-me? look on his face. He liked to eat raw eggs from the shell, and one afternoon Paul drove him half-crazy by handing him a hard-boiled egg and smirking as Truck continued to bang it on the floor in frustration. I retaliated by allowing Truck to begin nosing into my mouth so he could lap up saliva, which is nowhere near as disgusting as it sounds. Really. Truck was a clean little guy.

But in the end it was his specialness, the quality that set him apart from being just another pet, that killed him.

One day neither Paul nor I were home, so Truck, in his typical swashbuckling way, went exploring. Atop Paul's dresser he found a bottle of Vivarin stimulant tablets. The pills were mine; I took them on work nights when I hadn't managed to get any sleep during the day. I'd have sworn Truck lacked both the intelligence and the dexterity to do it, but somehow he managed to unscrew the childproof cap and pull out the cotton stuffing, and he ate every chalky yellow tablet in the bottle.

Paul found him when he got home from school. I got in to find Paul standing in the bedroom, bathed in a stripe of afternoon light, hands in his pockets, staring down at Truck with the blankest expression I have ever seen. There was just the smallest streak of dried blood on the carpet beside Truck's mouth.

Paul insisted on burying him without any help, so I watched as he shoveled away a two-foot-deep square of rocks and dirt. I kept trying to find something to do with my hands while he lowered the small body into the hole, and then, red-faced and crying, he looked down at the grave and choked out a single "Sorry." Then he picked up the shovel again and filled in the hole. I don't think I ever felt more helpless.

I only hope it happened fast, after the acidic pills began to eat out Truck's stomach lining and the pain began to lance his insides, but I can't convince myself that it did.

It probably hurt a lot, and he was all alone.

Alone here myself, as I write in my small chamber with its warm fireplace and cold wood floor, I reflect on an existence fraught with attending college and working at a 7-Eleven, with going to movies and vacuuming the carpet on weekends, and I feel sharply aware that I am the only human being in this world. That other life seems so far removed from me now, and my recollection of it is obscured by the intervention of time, of geography and events. But still they happened to me; the expression on Paul's face when he'd open the door to find Truck half-buried in my mouth was one I won't soon forget.

All this is by way of saying that I at least knew *something* about raccoons when I met Truck—the newly dubbed Truck, whose real name is an untranslatable hand gesture, and whose title is what this account is all about.

• • •

For two days we walked along the riverbank. That first night with Truck I had removed my contacts, which were soft, daily-wear lenses that Vanity had compelled me to purchase and Practicality had made me regret, and I hadn't put them on since. Our circumstances were less than ideal for soaping my hands and poking myself in the eyes at least twice a day, so instead I wore my glasses, a prescription sadly out of date. I was half-blind with them on, and I'd been meaning to update the prescription for over a year, but the money always seemed to get allocated to more immediate and pressing needs such as books, records, movies, and late-night munchies. Still, half blind is better than three-quarters blind, and three-quarters blind is what I am without contacts or glasses. I am about as blind as a person can be without blundering into trees. I am extremely myopic; things are pretty clear to me until they get about arm's length away. Farther, and reality begins to blur. From ten feet on I am free to improvise about the nature of the world in front of me.

Truck insisted on following the riverbank for the time being, which was fine with me. If my mutant raccoon friend had a destination in mind—and she *did* have a mind, there was no denying it—it was better than my absence of one. (Destination, that is, not mind.) I followed her, and when I lagged too far behind she waited for me to catch up, then turned and plodded on.

Food had not been a problem. Truck had this facility with a rock that worked like addition: two rocks + two targets = lunch for both of us. Thus far I had dined on rabbit, bluejay, cardinal, and quail. She followed the same simple pattern twice a day: gesture us to a halt, point to her throat to indicate that I should shut the hell up (I had taken to providing my own constant monologue as we walked), peer toward a branch where an unfortunate avian perched, and select a stone. The rest seemed automatic: she gauged distance, cocked her arm slowly so as not to alarm the bird, and then, almost faster than I could follow, let fly. The rock hissed away and, more often than not, there would be a dead or dying bird on the ground.

I had seen her miss. Once.

I still carried my daypack, though by now it was nearly empty, containing only a flashlight, a coil of rope, a small first-aid kit, two books of matches, my contact-lens kit, and my canteen (for convenience sake). On the first day of our trek together Truck had carried the pack, but the straps wouldn't tighten enough for her nearly nonexistent shoulders, so she had since relegated the privilege to me.

I'd begun lagging behind again, and Truck waited for me. When I caught up she pulled imploringly at my sleeve like a five-year-old wanting an ice-cream cone.

"What now?" I asked—rhetorically, of course.

She tugged on the straps of my daypack.

"No," I said, and added the sign I'd learned meant "no"—thumbs touch middle fingers, hands together and then drawn apart as though tautening a string. She thought the pack was slowing me down, and she was offering to carry it for a while. The problem, however, lay not with the pack but with the fact that I simply was not built for overland travel the way she seemed to be. My stride was longer than hers, but she could walk almost all day with only a few rest stops, and my feet wouldn't stand for that.

At my refusal she lowered her hands and hunched over morosely. I laughed at her and she narrowed her masqueraded, flat-black eyes, then turned and walked on. I trudged along behind her.

And where the hell were we going? Wherever our destination was, we seemed to be in a hurry to get there.

The sign language was not proving easy to learn. I had been trying to pick it up by context, but beyond a few basic signs—"eat," "stop," "go," "yes," "no," "me," "you," and the like—its nuances seemed beyond me. What little I knew of American Sign Language, though, reminded me that gestural languages rely heavily on facial expression, body position, and different "inflection" of basic signings to broaden their meanings. One of the few for-instances I am able to give of Ameslan: to sign "house" you steeple your hands in very much the image of a child's drawing of a house. If you want to sign "town," however, you make the sign for "house" several times to indicate several houses (it can also mean "neighborhood," depending on context). For "city," you sign "big," then "house" several times, though again the meaning can change contextually. Understanding these permutations opens up a lot of new meaning. For Truck's particular language—and language it was, make no mistake of it, even though the word "language" itself is prejudicial, for its root word "langue" means "tongue"—I would have to learn the root signs before I could branch out.

It did me no good to continue puzzling over Truck. Who she was, where she came from, where she was leading me, I hadn't the slightest notion. My conjectures regarding her origin were vague and incomplete at best: escaped lab animal, mutation, whatever. She was only a part of the strangeness of the last few days—though by far the strangest part—but I was looking for people, and she was looking for *something,* so I followed. I wanted with something exceeding desperation to see another human being. I'd have traded my soul for one Chicken McNugget. I couldn't possibly be *this* lost; something was very wrong here, and I couldn't account for it. Thinking about it made me want to pull my hair out, so I tried not to think about it much, trusting time and more information to provide me with the answers I needed in order to retain my sanity.

Truck and I walked along the riverbank until sunset. Just before dark she signaled a halt and waded into the river. The bank was less steep here, and the river less deep. Truck stepped out until the water was up to her abdomen. She hunched over and spread her arms out as though imitating a swooping bird, and then her hands knifed into the water with a splash. They emerged clutching a wriggling bass. Trilling triumphantly, she tossed it toward me. I was so startled I only stared as the squirming fish arced toward me and slapped against my thigh. It flopped on the grass a few minutes, spasms lessening. Before it was still, another writhed beside it, drowning in the air.

Truck stood in the water, trilling, signing, elated.

I shook my head and then shrugged off my pack. I unzipped it and began rooting around for a book of matches.

Later, lying on my back and staring at the cloudy sky—a sky so overcast there was only a pale gray patch of moonglow—I continued to worry about Albert. The back of my head rested against my right forearm, which was growing numb. Finally I gave up trying to relax and eased into a sitting position, then slowly stood. I picked up my glasses, unfolded them, wiped the dusty lenses clean with the tail of my T-shirt, and put them on. Remembering the sensitivity of a raccoon's ears, I tiptoed away from Truck, who lay beyond the ashes from our dinner fire, then walked more normally for the remaining twenty yards to the river.

Two days now. Christ, I hoped Albert was all right. When I had failed to show up to take Nicole to the movie, perhaps she went by the apartment to see if everything was all right. Though she didn't have a key, my apartment was hardly burglar proof, and she might have been able to get in and take care of Albert. If not, he would have soon begun to howl when nobody showed up to take care of him. If the apartment manager had heard him, he would have unlocked the apartment door, discovered him, and called the pound to come take him away, which at least meant he'd be *eating*.

Nicole and I had been living together in another, better apartment for about six months when she decided she wanted a dog. I wanted one, too, but I was adamant about not having one; I didn't want to lose our lease. Unfortunately, we went to the bookstore a lot. Unfortunate, because next door to our favorite bookstore was the Animal Shelter.

"Let's just go in," Nicki would say each time we emerged from Goering's with a bagful of books. "Let's just *look.*"

Well, you know where that leads.

Actually it was my fault. One afternoon we went in, "just to look," and Nicki seized and took instant maternal charge of an eight-week-old puppy brought in only hours before. It was black with tan highlights, as I remember, a mutt that looked mostly Labrador. Nicole fondled it and made nonsense noises, and I walked around the small Shelter, looking heavenward and shaking my head.

"Hey," came a conspiratorial call from a nearby cage. "Hey, you. Psst."

I frowned and looked around. Surely that was a dog I'd just heard . . .?

"Hey—I'm talking to you!"

I located the voice and its owner. Two puppies were vying for attention at the grillwork of a cramped cage against the wall. Their food bowl had been overturned and Puppy Chow littered the wire-mesh floor. One of the puppies was a long-haired, black-and-white terrier mix.

"C'mon," I distinctly heard him say. "Get me outta here. There's been some kinda mistake."

I bent and looked closer at his bright eyes.

"C'mon, c'mon," he said. "You're taking me home."

I glanced at Nicole. She sat on a white Formica table at the other end of the shop, still cooing at the younger puppy. I looked at the attendant. "Um . . . do you suppose I could just look at this one for a minute?" I asked.

His hair grew long, and turned gray at the ends, and was in constant disarray at the top of his head. The fur on his nose grew into a dandy moustache. Face on he was a dead ringer for Albert Einstein, so that's what we named him.

Albert was a master of passive resistance. I'd yell at him for getting into the bathroom garbage can and dragging Nicole's tampons all over the apartment, and he'd obligingly roll onto his back and pee on himself. This was also how he handled the neighborhood's dominant male dogs, and when they ignored him for a wimp he trotted off and screwed every female he could get his paws on—though he was a neophyte at this and kept going at it sideways. Albert was a lover, not a fighter.

When he was a puppy he used to sleep between me and Nicole. After she moved out he took to sleeping on the carpet. I tried explaining to him how hurt I was by this, but he just sneezed on my foot and walked away. I think he was worried about what the neighbors might say.

Nicole left me because I wouldn't—or couldn't—commit myself to our relationship. Albert stayed, and soon I found myself committed to him. You figure it. I gave up trying to. I suppose it doesn't speak well of me that I missed him more than I missed Nicole.

I never saw Albert again after the morning I set out for Bat Cave. Sometimes at night I dream of him. Bright-eyed, he sits by his food bowl, patiently waiting for me to come home.

I really hope someone let him out of the apartment.

Truck was up when I finally looked away from the river. Her back was to me and her head was raised. I realized she was sniffing the air.

I tiptoed up to her. "Boo," I said. She whirled, and my knife was in her hand. She swung and I blocked, ducking, and caught the inside of her wrist. I attempted an aikido disarm I'd learned 'way back when—

—and discovered her joints didn't yield the way my body, my set of trained reflexes, expected them to. Not only that, but her center of gravity was about eighteen inches below mine.

So while I stood there, stupidly holding her wrist like a

nurse taking a patient's pulse, she punched me in the stomach with her free hand. It didn't hurt, but I wasn't expecting it. I whuffed away the worst of it and attempted to redirect her arm. She stepped in, raising the knife-wielding hand I held in order to upset my balance, and goddamn if she didn't slide a foot behind mine and wham me on my ass in a classic judo *osotogari*.

Still, reflexes are reflexes: I kept hold of her weapon hand and pushed up on her elbow as I went down, so that a hundred and thirty pounds of raccoon sailed over my head, assisted by my foot.

I held her wrist and rolled with her until I was on top. This time I bent the wrist correctly and her hand let go, and the knife was mine again. Truck bucked and slid out from beneath me—her wrists were *much* more supple than a human being's—and I dove and rolled, coming up with the knife ready. She stopped in the midst of getting up, staring at the point I held leveled at her head. She shook her head the way a cat does when you blow into its ear. Her eyes widened, and it seemed as if she had just realized where she was, had just awakened. We stared at each other for perhaps half a minute, and then, eyes on my knife the whole time, she lowered herself onto her back, relaxed visibly, then tilted her head up and rested her arms at her sides to expose her throat and stomach.

I stared a moment before I understood that it was a gesture of supplication.

"Oh, for—" I tossed aside the knife and turned away. Had she been sleepwalking? With a knife in her hand? Right.

Maybe she'd awakened, found me gone, and was about to come looking for me, armed, when I'd snuck up on her. I had startled her; possibly her actions had been reflexive. Maybe she had thought I was. . . . What? Something else. A bear.

I looked back at her. She remained on her back, vulnerable, eyeing me.

We didn't understand each other, this wonky raccoon and I, but I nevertheless felt we'd come to . . . to trust one another after a few days of traveling together and living off the land. So what now? I thought I knew.

I retrieved my knife and went back to her. I bent and set the flat of the blade against her throat. She regarded me without blinking. I pressed firmly for a moment. Later it turned out I got it wrong—I was supposed to nip her fur. I folded the blade and handed it to her. I stepped away and leaned my head back, exposing my throat and staring at the sky. Dark clouds hid the stars.

I heard her getting up and forced myself not to look. In a few seconds a cold line of steel pressed against my throat, and then my knife was pressed into my palm and my fingers were being curled around it. I looked down at Truck. She signed something. I only recognized three of the (four?) words: "Me no [ ] you," she signed. She repeated it, then changed it to, "You no [ ] me." She signed "yes." The motion was a sort of reversal of "no"—the tautened string held between thumb and second finger is released, and the fingers press each other at right angles.

If I was any judge of her expression, she was waiting for a reply.

Haltingly I did my best. "Me" (both hands curled toward my chest) "no" tauten the invisible string) "[ ]" (I didn't know what it meant, but I could still emulate the sign: the backs of the two large knuckles of one hand stroke from mandible to chin, then both hands clench while separating, as though pulling apart one of those Joe Weider, pectoral-pumper springs) "you" (both hands palm-up toward the addressee, as though offering an invisible tray). I added a "yes" and tried to look definite about it.

Truck seemed satisfied with my response. I was all for it, too, if it would prevent getting my throat cut in the middle of the night, but for all I knew we had just married each other.

Four days later we found civilization.

I was a bit worse for the wear from traveling. My clothes were filthy and torn, I had fleas in my hair even though I'd made a point of bathing in the river each day, my shoulders were raw from the ceaseless chafing of the daypack, and my feet were blistered and sore.

I was having the time of my life.

Truck continued to hunt for the two of us, and nearly always managed to provide us with two meals a day.

Caught in a typical Florida toad-strangling storm one day, we had collaborated on the construction of a shelter from branches, palm fronds, and whatnot, and together we huddled under it until the rain cleared in that quick way Florida rain has of wandering off as though suddenly discovering something better to do. That same night I caught sight of a four-foot-long rat—a capybara. It must have weighed a hundred pounds. It poked its bullet-shaped snout from the brush, curious about our campfire, I think, and then loudly scampered away when I moved. I didn't get much sleep the rest of that night.

Truck had been teaching me more of her sign language, so my vocabulary was expanding, but I still lacked a large enough repertoire of hand signs to question her about herself. I'd developed a few notions of my own—entirely unsatisfactory ones, but you work with what you've got. More than willing to convince myself of *something,* despite an excess of anomalies, I had decided she was a refugee from an experiment in non-primate communication and was the ursine equivalent of Washoe, Nim Chimpsky, and their compatriots, or of John Lilly's dolphin Elvar. Never mind the fucked-up geography of the region; never mind the surplus of manatees, lack of water hyacinths and pollution, the incongruity of Florida brown panthers and South American capybaras—Occam's razor wouldn't slice here; I had only one hypothesis, and I consoled myself with beating it about the edges until it fit at least a few of the available facts.

Truck signed on, threw rocks, fished, and built shelters regardless.

Today had been typical: wake up and break camp—she was adamant about destroying signs of fire and dinner—then start walking, me to eventually lag farther and farther behind Truck. It was midafternoon and she was about two hundred yards ahead of me. I was watching the high grass part at my shins, rasping my jeans, and looked up when I heard a high-pitched yell that sounded like an enraged bird of prey trapped on a belt massager. It was Truck, warbling as she jumped up and down, one hand rapidly describing circles in the air above her head.

She had found a road. It consisted of two well-worn tire ruts, typical of Florida back roads, and it curved from our left to parallel both the riverbank and the path we had been walking.

Truck was a bit calmer by the time I reached her. It took me a few moments to realize she was not agitated but elated. Is this what she had been looking for—civilization?

It didn't matter—I sure as hell was. "All right, which way?" I asked, and pointed: turn right, or keep going along the riverbank?

Truck chittered to herself and wrung her hands. For her this was the equivalent of an "uh . . ."—that unconscious glottal stop we humans use while gathering our thoughts. She put her hands on her hips and looked up at me, head cocked to the side, and the posture was so human I had to laugh.

Her eyes narrowed. I half expected her to begin tapping her foot in exasperation, but no.

"Which way?" I repeated. I pointed to where the road curved to our right. "Go?" I signed. The gesture was vaguely like a slow-motion version of a boxer's uppercut to the stomach. I pointed to the twin ruts following the river. "Go?" I signed. I pointed down. "Stay?" I signed. (It either meant "stay" or "wait," I hadn't been able to figure out which.)

Truck ducked her head and clapped her hands, a gesture I was to learn indicated surprise. She did it a lot around me. Finally she pointed downriver. "Go," she signed. "There go [ ] you I yes."

"Whatever you say. Whatever you sign, rather," I amended, and signed "yes." Together we followed the rutted back road, I in my rut and Truck in hers.

I had done some thinking about what I was going to do with Truck when we got back. Certainly she belonged to *some*one, and she had to be pretty valuable. Maybe there was a reward offered for her return. But perhaps Truck was something new, something not bred by human beings; an accident of nature. That would be nice, too: my name in the papers, appearances on *The Tonight Show,* la de dah.

I glanced at her, striding along determinedly in her rolling, oh-so-serious, Japanese warlord sort of way.

Sell her out? That's what it amounted to, really: turning her over to strangers in exchange for money, for notoriety of the talking-dog, three-day-wonder sort. No, I couldn't do it. Truck and I had become a sort of . . . team, I guess, living off each other's talents—mostly her talents and my living off them, but that's not the point. Somehow it seemed we trusted one another, had formed a kind of bond between us, and to turn her in to whatever authorities might be appropriate, or to sell her, or to make a show of returning her to whatever lab she may have escaped from, would be to reduce her to nothing more than a curiosity, to be poked and prodded, photographed and gawked at. Still—I could make a fortune exhibiting her, selling her to a . . . zoo, or something, licensing stuffed-toy rights after her picture made the cover of *Life*.

I dissipated the cloud of my pipe dream. No, I would do

none of that. I'd feel as if I had accepted thirty silver pieces for the creature who had—astoundingly—kept me warm and fed while I was lost in the woods. But maybe, just maybe, when we got back, I could wrangle a way to keep her.

I've had worse roommates, I can tell you.

I went on in this vein, conjuring scenarios behind my eyes, for hours. But then these daydreams burst like a darted balloon at a sound behind me: the plosive blurt of a horse, but higher-pitched and tremulous.

Truck and I turned around. A small wagon headed toward us, its progress punctuated by the soft, irregular clop of the hooves of the two llamas pulling it.

The sight of llamas pulling a wagon was incongruous enough that I stared at them a moment before looking behind them to see that the driver—

—was a raccoon.

5
Narrative of Truck

SHE IS A good sort, this farmer. Once I assure her that [Bentley] will not harm her she consents to give us a ride into town, which is named Wait-No-More, and which the farmer signs is not far away. I show her that I am teaching [Bentley] several signings, and this helps to make her overcome her initial fear of him.

We are quiet for several miles, the only sounds the cloppings of the llamas and honkings of [Bentley], which I think are incidental sounds like the rubbing together of a cricket's legs. These Outback folk are polite and reluctant to interfere, and that is kind of them, but I know she is brimming with as many questions as the river has fish. Before long, as I am expecting, the questions begin. She shifts the reins to one hand and with the other asks, "Nip me if I intrude, but may this one ask how you come to be here in this outlying place, and what *that*"—she bends a work-gnarled thumb toward [Bentley], whose bald hide is grown pale, and who is noising to himself—"is, and how you come to be traveling with it, or it with you?"

I wave a laugh and lean forward, wanting her to know I am not displeased. So careful, these Outbackers! So exaggerated and ponderous their signing, to keep from offending! "I am a hunter," I sign, "and a trapper of exotic animals and curiosities. This, my 'traveling companion'"—she laughs at my parody of her signing—"is an ape from [Africa], a rare sort of hairless ape. You are seeing of these things, these apes?"

Her head, just beginning to whiten with age, turns to regard [Bentley] before she signs further. "Of these apes, yes, I see rumors, though belief is a thing I withhold until that tree bears fruit. Seeing it, though, I pluck the fruit from the tree and hold it before me!"

I laugh. It costs little to wave a laugh, and can return much.

"It is such a size, though," she continues, "and a small amount frightening, I will not hide to admit. Why does it wear such odd coverings, and spectacles? Does it read?"

I laugh again. "Of course not, goodbody. The spectacles are a joke, yes? For to me it looks quite funny with them, a parody of ourselves. The coverings are a matter of consideration for those who would view the creature, for in truth the sight of its naked, pink body would be deemed by many as grotesque." I do *not* sign that [Bentley's] spectacles and coverings are made of materials I am never before encountering. There will be time later to learn about these things.

"You sign it is trainable, and smart like a dog?"

"Smarter," I sign, and am thankful for her ignorance. I shall rely upon many ignorances before this tale is through."He is capable of simple signs. Notice his hands."

She twitches the reins before signing further. This is also an Outbacker sort of thing, a way of searching for the proper way to sign when they either do not agree with you or when they look sideways from how you look. "Yes. Still . . . it is a beast, yes?"

"Oh, yes—a beast! But even beasts may learn, yes? Do you own a dog?"

"Several dogs."

"Well, then, you know as well as I do that a dog will paw a signing for food when it is hungry. But a dog is a beast. It is much the same with him, with this ape. It imitates, that is all. Only he has more signs, and can grasp with his hands. Nothing more."

"One leans into agreeing winds," she signs. (Outbackers and their clichés!) "But this one still wants to smell your fruit a bit before she bites it." She glances back at [Bentley]; his chest convulses and moisture rims his reddened eyes. Is he ill? "Still," she signs again, "I would strike myself with a stick before I would get too near this one. Its size makes me nervous."

"He does nothing he is not taught," I sign, and the matter

rests there. Lying, here, is flipping the coin: I hope [Bentley] does not prove me wrong!

We make no further conversation the rest of the way into the small town, and I think this farmer regrets her offer of a ride but is too polite in the Outbacker way to indicate it.

Many times I glance back to [Bentley], who sits convulsing amid the straw. His face is wet with water leaking from his eyes. A sound tears from him many times, as though the life rips from his throat. Is he sick? No matter: we are soon in the town of Wait-No-More, and if he is ill I shall find what doctors are for the finding there.

6
Narrative of James Bentley

THIS IS WHERE it gets hard. I have lived it, am still living it, and nevertheless I find it difficult to relate. Confronted with an entire town occupied by intelligent, bipedal raccoons, my state of mind became such that much of what occurred for a while afterward is vague to me, a blur as consciousness went on "hold."

I am only able to report the events of the rest of that day and night as if I were some detached, reportorial observer. About the time I saw *another* too-large, hand-signing raccoon—driving a two-llama wagon, yet—a good part of my rational mind ran for the hills and left the rest on automatic pilot. Like some vacant automaton I climbed into the wagonbed and sat amid the hay. Truck and this new raccoon chittered and signed as we drove along the road. Within a few hours we made it into town. Need I say it?

I was Charlton Heston. This was *Planet of the Raccoons*.

The rutted road broadened into what became a main street. To either side were low, squat structures too small to contain more than two or three rooms each, most of them made of . . . mud? adobe? clay and dirt? Whatever, it was the uniform gray of wet concrete, and the structures were Spartan blocks with harsh gashes cut for windows and rude rectangles for doorways, most of which were blocked by a hanging, rough-woven rug or curtain. If houses they were, they were generic gray cubes. Some had wooden porches along the front. Up the road and to our left a raccoon was hitching a llama to a post in front of an ugly gray cube. I gaped at it as I lay low in the hay-filled back of the wagon, but the raccoon didn't notice me, paying us little attention beyond a passing glance as we clopped and clattered by. *1984* meets the Wild West. Swell.

To my right a door curtain parted, and out came two very young raccoons—kits, I guess I should call them. Their heads would have come to about midthigh on me. One was running from the other, and the pursuer threw something—it turned out to be a ball of rags—and hit its quarry square on the back. The stricken kit turned around and signed something quickly, then picked up the rag ball and ran, and pursued became pursuer.

They looked as if they were having fun.

It had become obvious that what Truck had been using to communicate with me had been baby talk: Truck and our driver resumed their dexterous conversation, and if I bothered to watch, I could pick out an occasional word, but not enough to glean any real meaning. I didn't bother to watch much. Mostly I sat back and stared as the impossible glided past, and I listened and let it all happen to me and cried as my brain turned into a Q-tip.

(A raccoon, goddammit, it's a *raccoon;* they're *both* raccoons; *they're all raccoons!)*

I clenched my eyes and silently prayed, but when I opened them the raccoons were still there, a bunch of furry Zorros going about their quotidian business. I pinched myself hard on the arm. It hurt. I breathed in deeply to calm myself. The smell of hay filled my nostrils, tinted by the musty smell of the llamas. I thought about jumping from the wagon but laughed at myself. Where would I go? (Officer, you gotta believe me—the town's been taken over by giant, intelligent raccoons!) A thought chilled me: Had I gone crazy? How could I really know if I had?

We passed through the small town and were soon back on the open road. Eventually we halted before a small, low-roofed, log cabin. Behind it stretched a freshly plowed field of about ten acres.

From behind the farmhouse came two dogs. They resembled each other enough to seem from the same litter, and though they belonged to no breed I had ever seen before, their similar characteristics gave them the look of finely bred dogs. Both were tan with black highlights and were thin, long-legged, loping dogs with long, pink tongues hanging from axe-shaped heads. Their ears were long and floppy, hanging to midthroat, and they pricked up when I climbed down from the wagon. First one and then both dogs lowered their heads and began growling. It was an odd growl, high-pitched but somehow still menacing. I stood still and tried to avoid meeting their eyes as the farmer waved exaggeratedly for them to go away. A ropy, dirty-looking bracelet danced along the farmer's left wrist whenever she signed.

The farmer signed to Truck and unyoked the llamas, then led them toward the small stable behind the house. Truck followed the farmer, and I numbly followed Truck.

The stables were clean, as stables go, and smelled earthy but not unpleasant. There were four stalls made from pine planks, rough cut but sturdy. Typical stalls, no different from a thousand others. Straw was scattered on the earthen floor of each, and a wooden trough occupied one corner, a wooden bucket beside it.

The farmer gestured from me to an empty stall. I glanced at Truck, since she was my only source of translation.

"There go you," she signed.

I shook my head. "No," I signed. Aloud I said, "I'm not a goddamned horse. *Or* a llama."

The farmer signed something to Truck, who ignored it. "There go," she repeated. "Small wait, no more." She added the injunctive I had learned was a polite but firm "please."

I debated a moment, then shrugged and walked into the stall. The farmer shut the door behind me and secured it with a cord. Since the door was only stomach high to me and I could easily climb over it without bothering to untie the cord, I elected not to worry about it. Truck signed something to me I couldn't quite comprehend, but the gist of it seemed to be, "Wait here; I'll be back." Then she turned and accompanied the farmer toward the house.

I watched her go and then picked up the bucket beside the trough and examined it. It was octagonal, made from eight tapering sections of what looked like pine. They had been connected by metal nails, and the joints were filled with resin. The wood was sanded, and strips of metal banded the top and bottom. I shook my head and thought about all the effort that had gone into making this primitive little bucket—and then I stopped.

I stared at it a moment longer. Could I, twentieth-century man standing atop a high pyramid of technology, construct a primitive little bucket like this from scratch?

I didn't think so. I set it down, and then I sat and waited. What the hell—it was the only party in town.

But now I was alone with my thoughts, and that wasn't particularly comforting. I didn't understand this. That was what kept running through my mind, reeling across it like a special-bulletin notice you see on the bottom of a television screen: I just didn't understand this.

I continued not understanding a large part of it until dark. It had been late afternoon when we passed through the "town," and I was in the stall only a little over an hour before night fell. In another hour Truck returned, this time minus the farmer. In each hand she carried a clay bowl. One was filled with water, and the other contained three eggs. She set them on the doorsill and left before I could say or sign anything.

I picked up the water bowl. The clay was cool to the touch. I sniffed at the water, smelled nothing, and assumed it was just plain water. I'm not sure what I was expecting. Kool-Aid, maybe. The three eggs in the other bowl were small. I picked them up and turned over the bowl, then tried to spin one of the eggs on the bowl's flat bottom. It didn't spin worth a damn, which meant it was raw. Did they expect me to crack 'em open and whip up an omelet? I returned the eggs to the bowl and set it beside the feeding dish in the corner. I might eat them if no other food seemed imminent, but I'd have to be fairly hungry to slide raw eggs down my throat.

A few minutes later I heard the farmer feeding the llamas in their stalls. They bleated and clopped, and I heard food being poured into troughs, then heard stall doors being shut and secured. The farmer looked in on me, but only for a few seconds. She was a bit afraid of me, I think; I must have looked to her the way a hairless gorilla would appear to me.

The llamas loudly munched their meals and then settled down. After a while there came the prolonged and rather awesome sound of one of them urinating onto the dirt.

I sat huddled in a corner of the stall and murmured: "I don't get it. I just don't get it."

A little later Truck returned, carrying an oil lantern made of glass and metal. She opened the stall door and entered, then hung the lantern on a peg driven into a beam near the low ceiling. We regarded each other. Her fur was whitish orange in the lantern glow. Finally she indicated the bowl of eggs in the corner. "Eat no you," she signed, adding an interrogative to make it a question.

I hadn't the slightest idea how to convey that I liked my eggs scrambled, poached, sunny-side up, even powdered—any way but raw. I grabbed an egg and mimed cracking it against the side of the bowl, then stood and held the bowl above the lantern flame, miming stirrings with an invisible fork. She didn't seem to understand, and I gave up and returned the bowl to its corner.

Truck hunkered down a few feet from me, squatting like an old Japanese man, and she slowly reached out and grabbed my hand. Her hand felt odd against mine, I think because it was so disturbingly human and articulate. I remembered having a Woolly Monkey grab my hand at the zoo when I was a kid. It had amazed me because of its . . . *volition,* because the act was so intrinsically *human* (or so we in our chauvinism think) that, coming from a nonhuman animal, its very familiarity felt alien. Truck molded my right hand until it looked as though I were pretending to shoot someone standing to my left, but with middle finger extended also, and then she guided my hand horizontally to my right, level with my chest. She patted the fur at her chest and then made the sign herself, much more rapidly, and then repeated it. Her eyes were bright points in the lantern light, shining with something like . . . enthusiasm?

I thought I understood. I leaned forward and patted the wiry fur at her shoulder, then made the sign. She signed "yes."

She leaned forward and patted me in the same manner, then signed an interrogative.

How to do this? I pointed at her hands, then pointed to my mouth, hoping to indicate that, for each of us, the two served the same purpose. "Jim," I said aloud.

She leaned forward, patted me, and pointed at my hands, then at her mouth.

Damn! She thought the *gesture* had been my name, and not the vocalization. "No," I signed. I repeated her name-sign, then pointed to my mouth and said, "Jim. Bent-lee."

I think she understood this time. Her eyes widened as if it had just dawned on her: Shit—those sounds, those stupid, irritating grunts he makes all the time—they're how he *talks*.

So much for "Me Tarzan, you Jane." And so began my first formal lesson in conversational raccoon.

It's really a very frustrating thing that a language based on hand signing is of necessity conceptually different from one that is spoken. Truck and I—and every *über*-raccoon I shall introduce in this account—were completely incapable of expressing each other's names in the other's "tongue." Truck's name is a hand motion, as is that of every other raccoon. Consequently I am unable to write it down—for though the name has a graphic analogue in their written language, it, too, would mean nothing if I wrote it down; it would just look like streamlined Chinese. Therefore I must keep referring to Truck as "Truck," and I am forced as well to assign human, spoken names to the rest of Truck's kind who will appear later in this account, which makes me guilty of anthropomorphizing them. My rule in writing this account, then, will be to introduce raccoon names in brackets the first two times they appear, in order to make it clear that this is a name I am assigning to an untranslatable gesture. The same applies for certain objects, dates, cultural references, and so on, that I cannot directly translate, and for which I must substitute an English word. Certain gestures I interpreted incorrectly will appear in brackets until such time as I learned their true meaning. I find this distressing, but it is unavoidable, so I can only hope that, when you meet Doc Holliday, Dr. Zorba, Fagin, Captain Squint, Baby Huey, and all the others, I will have given them names to fit their personalities.

The converse was of course true of Truck: not possessing highly developed vocal cords, she was physically incapable of articulating my name. So rather than pick a sign myself (given the English alphabet, would you as an ignorant foreigner grab random letters and arrange them to form what you wanted people to use as your *name,* knowing full well that there was a possibility, however slight, that you had forevermore christened yourself Glxlatc, or Cretin, or something worse?), I left it to Truck to give me a name. It consists of a nullifier, followed by a grooming motion, both hands smoothing back the fur at the sides of the head, and then by another sign made by hunching the head down and curling both arms forward. In reference to me, that sign in this account is written as [Bentley]. Later

I would discover its literal meaning, and I would laugh long and loud. It has since become my title—but I shall refrain from telling that until the time is right.

Truck taught me basic grammar until quite late. I was still nonfunctionally illiterate when we called a halt, but at least I had a grasp—sorry!—of the principles involved, the mechanics employed in how the language worked. I learned how to sign, "What is this?" and, "How do you sign this?"—two of the most important questions to know in a language you want to learn, for from then on I could point to things and sign, "How do you sign this?" and Truck would tell me. I had to be careful, though—pointing to the wall, for instance, could yield the sign for wall, wood, pine, plank, or stable. But holding up an egg and asking was pretty safe.

I even managed, with agonizing ineptness, to ask Truck a few questions that night, but my ignorance kept me from asking them with the precision necessary to make the specific *meaning* of my questions understood. I felt the frustration I sometimes felt in those dreams when I would be trying to reply to somebody, to tell them something important, but the rush of possible things to say and ways to say them became a log jam in my throat and nothing comprehensible emerged. I felt as if I were beating my head against a brick wall, and I wanted to cry.

"Here I where?" I asked. "Place what this?"

"Kept two-llamas place," Truck replied, ever patient. "Outside you, inside not. I-am-sorry." The apology was one sign. "Know-not farmer me. Think dog-with-tricks you. I-am-sorry. Not long."

Her answer was hardly even that comprehensible to me, but after much reflection I managed to put it together at least that much. But she hadn't understood the nature of my question—not her fault—and I lacked the "vocabulary" to make my meaning clear. *Later,* I promised myself.

We halted when the lantern began to sputter. Truck stood and stretched, and the act was so human that I was startled. She wished me a good sleep, then lifted the lantern from its peg and headed back to the house.

Watching her walk toward the farmhouse, the flickering light bobbing in time with her roly-poly walk, I caught myself asking the same question I'd asked about the bucket: could I manufacture a lantern, if I had to? My God, the questions that entailed: How do you blow glass? How do you forge metal? From what animals did you get oil, and how? Shit, man, I was a lit major; if I wanted a lantern, I got in my car, drove to Sears, and *bought* one.

Alone again, I found that my mind seemed to be working on two levels at once. One was questioning and skeptical, and urgently needed to know what the fuck was going on here so that I could retain my sanity. The other was pragmatic and urged adaptability. While my mind was screaming to know where I was and what had happened to me, I was also practicing signings while speaking their meanings and trying to put signs together in various combinations to form different sentences.

It wasn't long before I realized I was exhausted. I yawned, stretched, and breathed deeply the smells of hay, of pine, of llama (imagine an old, wet carpet), and of urine. I decided to get a breath of fresh air and do some toe-touches before surrendering to sleep, so I swung my legs over the stall door and stepped outside.

Florida in midsummer—assuming I was still in Florida, and assuming it was still midsummer—can rarely be called invigorating. It was stuffy, humid, and dense; there was an almost tangible oppressiveness to the night. The breeze blew but did not cool, though it was better than the stall. I touched my toes with my palms a few times, twisted sharply to crack my back, and stepped around to the side of the stables. I unzipped my pants, stood a few feet from the wall, and urinated. I glanced up at the night sky as urine puddled before me.

They skimmed thin slivers of silvered cloud, one large, the other small; one apparently closer than the other; one silver and bright, the other yellowish and a bit dull; one three-quarters full, the other a slim crescent.

Pissing against the stable wall, urine splashing on my boots, I gaped up at the two moons that rode silently through the dark.

7
Narrative of James Bentley

(continued)

YOU'D THINK THAT would be the final blow. That, upon seeing two moons in an otherwise ordinary sky, the camel's back would break and I would turn into a gibbering lunatic. Quite the opposite happened: things became clearer. I realized with the sort of undeniable reality that accompanies a punch in the stomach that, somehow, I was someplace *different*. In retrospect it seems obvious, I suppose, and should have been apparent to me all along, but I was so busy going through it that I had had no chance to step back and view what it was I was going through. The forest for the trees, and all that. But now, shining above me in silver and grayish yellow, was incontrovertible evidence that something had *happened,* that I was *somewhere else*. It was—and I laughed when I thought this—it was in an odd way *reassuring,* for I knew now that the problem wasn't with *me,* or even necessarily with the world. It gave me perspective. All right, said that level that required information and urged adaptability; all right, this was something—some*place*—new; now I could get on with it. I could unload my mental and emotional luggage and set to finding out the what and why of it all. Having accepted, I could now learn.

I realized that for several minutes I had been standing with my dong in my hand. I shook it, tucked it away, and zipped up my jeans, then went around to the other side of the stable and sat with my back against the door leading to a stall where one of the llamas was kept.

I stared at the moons and asked myself a lot of questions.

I even got a few answers.

—Where am I?

Not in the world you knew, pal. The cavalry ain't coming over the hill in this one. You're on your own. The thought brought a rush of tears, but I fought to suppress it. You have to deal with this right now, I told myself. Misery is a luxury you can afford later. On with it, then. I wiped my eyes dry and went on.

—How did I get here?

An image came to mind: me on my knees in the dark, vomit puddled before me.

Something had happened to me in that cave, and it sure as shit hadn't been salmonella. The onset of the sickness had been too abrupt; salmonella gives some warning. This had been more like the quick, queasy, unsettling feeling you can get when you step out from an air-conditioned room to a blazing July afternoon, a coldness and then heat, as though I had stepped from one clime to another.

And suddenly I realized that I had.

Somehow, in that unexplored bit of cave, I had found a . . . a *doorway,* a tunnel from there to here. Wherever *here* is. At this realization a question rose in my mind: *Did the door open both ways?* I vowed to find out as soon as I could. First I needed to learn enough of the sign language to be able to ask for help finding the cave. One thing at a time, Bentley.

The entire notion, the reality of my situation, seemed to tower before me, and it struck me as wonderfully terrible, terribly wonderful, and the thrill of it all scared the hell out of me. It was epiphanic: I felt able to view my life from outside its framework.

And it's a shitty feeling to take inventory of your worth and find yourself lacking.

I had gone to college as a humanities major, had been on the verge of receiving my B.A. in English, of all the useful things, had quit for reasons I am still unsure of, had shared an apartment with Paul and his raccoon, moved into an apartment with Nicole and fucked *that* up rather thoroughly; she had moved out because she found me lacking in certain emotional respects. I had moved into a box of an apartment, taking Albert because Nicole couldn't keep him in the trailer she moved into;

I had taken a graveyard-shift job at a local 7-Eleven that got held up only occasionally. Around four o'clock every morning the carrier delivered the paper and I read alone in the dead hours of the night, turning first to the Local section to see which convenience stores had been held up the night before, who had been shot, who had been stabbed, who had been blinded in one eye by a man wielding a screwdriver, as had happened to one employee. Martial arts training or not, I knew that sooner or later I'd end up as a couple inches' worth of notoriety in the Local section, and I had been on the verge of quitting. No matter what I had done, at whatever moment of my life I pondered over, it seemed I had always been on the verge of quitting something.

The one exception was my martial arts, and I couldn't figure out why I'd stuck with that. I'd started because at twelve I'd been a pudgy, undermuscled kid who hated team sports, and whose idea of a simply ripping good time was to stay in his room reading a book. I must have been the only kid whose parents insisted he put down that book *now,* dammit, and get out there with the other kids and hang around a street corner or something. But at twelve, on a whim, I'd begun tae kwon do lessons, and for some reason it had gotten into my blood. I received my black belt during my first year of high school, and in college began training in aikido, a very odd, *very* effective art about which I had long been curious. Aikido and tae kwon do, respectively "soft" and "hard," seemed to balance very well for me, and I had been maintaining their equilibrium ever since.

But there had persisted a nagging feeling. . . .

Dammit, it did no good for me to harp on my martial arts training; it had helped me to better myself, and might even help save my ass someday, but the truth was that, viewing my life as a whole, I was just no use to anyone but myself. My sex life had not exactly been the sort of thing to inspire a steamy biography, and my romantic near misses—what few I'd had—had caused me to view love and passion with more than a touch of skepticism. Being smart enough to know how to slide by in the Dade County public noneducational system meant that I had managed to receive almost no training in "hard" sciences such as chemistry, physics, biology, or things mechanical. Instead I read a lot of books on my own apart from school, and as a result knew a little about many things and a lot about nothing, though I derived lots of pleasure from "soft" sciences, such as most fields of psychology besides behaviorism, contemporary evolutionary theory, and cosmogony. I was something of a hermit who didn't develop lasting friendships and couldn't hold on to a job because of my antagonism toward authority. Yet at all these things I tried so hard. I felt myself to be a creative person, a person with a drive for self-expression, so I hung around artists and dissected and watched and listened to their songs and paintings and books and plays with the notion in the back of my mind that perhaps the talent so displayed would enter me through some mystical osmosis. I tried to learn to play the guitar. I tried to write a book. I tried acting. I tried singing. I tried painting. And then one day it hit me, in one of those simultaneously blissful and heart-rending moments when the clouds part briefly and you manage to *see* your life for what it is and what you're doing with it. It hit me that I could play, or write, or act, or sing, or paint all I wanted to, and it wouldn't make a bit of difference—because I wasn't an artist. Now, this is hardly the most profound of revelations, but it floored me. There I was: I had the drive, I had the need to express myself, the urge to communicate; I had the creativity—but I had not one ounce of talent. I had no medium. I could try my hand at being an *artiste* anyhow, I supposed, just for the fun of doing it, but my innate Calvinism would cause me to think of myself as a martinet and an also-ran if I tried, because I would have been trying to fool myself, and probably fooling only myself. So I worked at the 7-Eleven and mopped its terrazzo floors at three A.M., and went home at seven A.M., and slept all day and woke up in the late afternoon, and went to either tae kwon do or aikido, depending on what day it was, and came home sore, and took long, hot showers, and went to work and started it all over again. Or, to put it more concisely: I had a routine and I really didn't like it very much. Not that I was powerless to change it, but all my best efforts seemed so much pissing in the ocean. Besides, a cynic gains a certain solace from failure: the ability to say I Told You So. I was happy as a clam, and for the same reasons.

And now it was gone, all of it. No more obsessive infatuations, no more romances, no more sex—no more women. No more late-night, coffee-guzzling conversations on What It's All About. No more lying on the floor listening to my favorite music with the headphones on, conjuring intense images and oblivious to the world around me. No more restless driving along silent streets in the middle of the night. No more fireworks on the Fourth of July. No more reading a novel by a favorite writer at two A.M. on a dead Sunday night behind the counter at the 7-Eleven. No more holiday calls to Mom and Dad ("Well—you'll go ahead and live how you want no matter what I say. I guess you need to make your own mistakes." "Are you warm? Are you looking for another job?") No more badinage with Nicole, whom I loved despite my ambivalence about commitment. No more tug-of-war with my quirky dog, Albert.

I felt cold inside.

The moons were a lot lower in the sky. The breeze had grown a bit brisk. Behind me the llama shifted in its stall, snorting derisively. It bumped twice against the door. I stood and headed for my own stall, thinking, *no room at the inn*. I swung over the tied door and went to the far corner of the stall, where I drank the remainder of my bowl of water and then curled up on the hay.

The alien moons sank in the sky as I cried myself to sleep thinking of Nicole and all that I had lost.

Early next morning Truck woke me by banging on the stall door. She wore my ill-fitting pack and carried a rough-woven bag in one hand. She glanced at the bowl of uneaten eggs and signed, "No eat you?"

I shrugged. "No eat I," I signed. My eyes were puffy from crying, and I had a headache.

A crease appeared between her black eyes, and her head bent down and cocked a little to one side. She reached into her bag and pulled out a small biscuit. I sniffed it, salivated immediately, and popped it into my mouth. It was a hard biscuit, but still warm and tasting freshly baked, though a bit flat. Truck handed me another one, and this time I broke it in two and offered her half. She seemed surprised and eyed the biscuit for a moment, then looked at me. I refrained from eating until she took a bite herself. After she had swallowed I took a bite. She stared at me a moment longer, then wolfed down the remainder of her biscuit. I did the same with mine, and she laughed—it's a fluid motion with one hand that's hard to describe; it looks vaguely like a pantomime of a butterfly in flight. She tossed me one more biscuit and ate another herself, and we left the stall and walked to the rutted road. Truck led us back toward the small town through which we had passed the day before. Along the way I received my second lesson in conversational raccoon, and I learned enough to ask Truck where we were going. It seemed that the town was named Wait-No-More. She had to sign the name four or five times before I caught on; the individual signs were linked by a short, punctuative gesture indicating that the signs were connected to form a single unit. If there was any special reason the town was named Wait-No-More, I never learned it, but having since traveled through towns named Three Big Dogs, Quite-A-Lot, Good Rats, Large-Fight/Small-Fight, and a host of others, I'm sure there was a good story behind it.

The day grew bright and warm as we walked, and there wasn't a cloud in the sky. I thought about the two moons I'd seen last night and realized that I hadn't sighted them earlier because circumstance had hidden them from view: when Truck and I had been camping in the wild, we had either slept under trees or under cover because of rain, or else the night had been overcast. But today there wasn't a hint of rain, and I was surprised to find my spirits light as we walked toward Wait-No-More, despite the puffiness of my eyes and the ache in my head. The walk wasn't very long—no more than a few hours—and, in our fragmented, disjointed way, we conversed as we hiked along.

"Today [ ] day in Wait-No-More," Truck signed. "Understand you [ ] day?"

"No," I replied. "All else, yes. [ ], no." I repeated the unknown sign as best I could.

"[ ] is happy-day, day-of-joy. One every year." She inserted her thumbs beneath the pack straps and pulled forward to relieve some of the rubbing; tighten them though she might, they were still a bit too large. She removed her thumbs from the straps and asked, "Understand you?"

"Yes. Understand small." I made a mental note that "[ ]" in this case meant "festival" or "celebration."

"Good. Two, three things in Wait-No-More need I. I sign, you do. No-questions you. Understand?"

I wiped sweat from my brow. It couldn't have been much later than eight-thirty, and already the day had grown muggy. I swatted at a mosquito hovering near my ear. "Understand small," I signed. "Things need you. You sign, I do. No-questions me. Yes?"

"Yes."

"You sign, understand no I—can-do no I. Yes?"

Truck appeared to think this over. She had to concede my point—if she signed for me to do something, I'd be glad to do it—after all, she was running the show here. But if she signed me to do something and I couldn't understand what she was signing, how was I to do what she wanted?

"Things I sign you before Wait-No-More," she decided. "In Wait-No-More, [ ] are you. Understand?"

"No," I signed, and repeated the unfamiliar gesture. "'[ ]'?"

"'[ ]' is that-which-does-not [ ]."

I shrugged, frustrated. "Understand no," I signed.

Truck appeared equally frustrated. She halted in the middle of the rutted road and looked around. She pointed to a tree, and then to the high grass beside the road, and then at a gray rabbit watching us a hundred yards ahead. Then she pointed at the top of her head and grimaced—I was learning how to read her facial expressions—as though making a physical exertion, and signed a nullifier—a negative that could mean "no," or "not," or "less," or "subtract." The meaning changed contextually.

"Understand no," I repeated.

She frowned—I might as well call it that—and stalked off the road, swishing through the high grass. She stopped before an oak tree, pointed to it, then pointed to the top of her head. She grimaced again and signed "no." She pointed to the grass and repeated the gesture, then came back to the road and pointed to where the rabbit watched us warily, and repeated it again.

A light bulb turned on above my head: the second unknown sign was "think"; Truck's pointing at the top of her head and grimacing was the same as a human being tapping on the temple. Elementary, Watson. Okay, how about the rest? Well, the nullifier negated the symbol for "think"; it equaled "minus-think" or "not-think." So: "'[ ]' is that-which-does-not [think]." In other words, plants, animals, or inanimate objects. She must have meant, in her original statement, that I was to act as if I were a dumb animal when we reached Wait-No-More.

I wondered what she had up her metaphorical sleeve.

"Understand yes," I finally signed. "In Wait-No-More, animal I. That-which-does-not think."

She seemed satisfied. No doubt she didn't want anyone knowing I was anything more than a deformed monkey; it was easier to explain me as a freakish animal—and her my owner, I suddenly realized—than as an alien entity capable of rudimentary conversation and actions indicating cognition. But why? Why deceive them? Was she trying to hide me for something later on? I felt a stab of irony at the thought of Truck selling *me* off to a lab as an object to be poked and prodded. To judge by the level of technology presented by my previous glimpse of Wait-No-More, though, I needn't worry about the existence of an experimental lab somewhere.

Just outside town Truck shrugged off my pack and removed the length of rope with which she had bound me at our first meeting. Now she held it out in front of me, a bit timidly, and gestured for me to extend my hands.

Dammit—how much did I trust her? She noticed my hesitation, and she lowered the rope and stepped closer. She grasped one of my hands in both of hers, stroking lightly, then let go with one and stroked my hair.

Well, hell—if she was going to pass us off as owner and pet, she probably required a leash. Maybe there was a town ordinance requiring her to curb me or something. I held out my hands.

In about two seconds she had my wrists wrapped and secured. I had never seen anyone tie a knot so fast. She held the remainder of the rope coiled in her right hand, and she had left plenty of slack between us, I think to reassure me, for it meant she wouldn't jerk me along. We headed into Wait-No-More.

The street was dotted with peddler carts whose owners were selling or displaying citrus fruits, breads, shoes, bowls, pots, and various handmade goods. On one cart was arrayed a variety of wooden items, sturdily if not finely crafted. I studied them as we walked past. The owner stared back openly with an expression I could only interpret as dumbfounded. The function of some of his wares was incomprehensible to me, though one that caught my eye caused a pang of childhood memory. It was a child's wagon made of pine, wooden-wheeled and unpainted, though stained and varnished, with a peg-hinged handle that reminded me of my Red Racer of long ago.

Hitched to posts along the street, behind the vendors, were llamas. They came in several shapes, sizes, and colors. There were no horses.

It's still hard for me to look at a llama without thinking of it as half a Pushmi-Pullyu.

A group of perhaps twenty raccoons was gathered before one of the few two-story buildings in town. They were watching some local notable or other give a "speech." I noticed that, like the farmer yesterday, this "speaker" and her audience all wore a similar, knotty, ropy, dirty-looking bracelet on the right wrist. The "speech" must have been a doozy; said notable stood on the highest step leading to the narrow porch along the front of the building and gesticulated wildly, signing with exaggerated movements. Her body language and posturing were almost a caricature of a Nō player's, and her facial expressions also seemed a bit histrionic.

I took her for a politician and left it at that.

There was a bit of a stir when they caught sight of Truck and me. In a crowd of human beings you can hear a sort of ripple spreading from an event as discussion of it moves in relays from the epicenter like the transmission of a nerve impulse. Here you could *see* it—raccoons nudged their neighbor and signed, and the neighbor nudged another, and so on. The crowd looked like a casting call for a goddamned muppet movie. I would have laughed if I hadn't been as nervous as a plate of Jell-O in an earthquake.

Truck just waltzed on up, bold as you please, with me tagging along behind. The dumb-animal shuck was not hard to pass off when confronting a bevy of intelligent, upright, bandit-masked raccoons, for the sight caused an odd sensation inside my skull, as if my brain itself were cringing. Truck alone I could accept without too much difficulty, but a town meeting full of Trucks was proof that *I* was the anomaly here—so I gaped and allowed myself to be gently pulled along.

The politician concluded her "speech" and walked down the steps. The crowd did not applaud—later I learned that raccoons never indicate approval in this manner—but instead seemed to wait expectantly while the politician shouldered her way through them and stopped a respectful distance from Truck—though I think I had more to do with the "respectful" part than Truck did. They held a quick exchange that I was unable to follow, with the politician—whom I dubbed "the Mayor," though I later learned her role might more accurately be translated as "police commissioner"—often gesturing toward me.

Truck launched into what seemed a lengthy explanation. The Mayor seemed a bit skeptical. At Truck she hurled a series of signings all ending with interrogatives. Truck answered patiently. All I could glean from the exchange was the "tone," the way you might glean the gist of a verbal conversation held in a language foreign to you from tone of voice and inflection.

Finally they finished whatever they were signing, and Truck turned to me and signed, slowly, as though to a child (her body hiding the signings from the Mayor and the crowd, I noticed), "(+)think things do." She hesitated, then added a "please."

Well. If there was a sign "(−)think" that meant "dumb," I had to assume that "(+)think" meant the opposite. The pressure was on.

Truck sure had a lot of faith.

I looked around for something I could use, some way I could indicate that I was smarter than the average bear—raccoons being ursine. The sight of a vendor's cart containing oranges gave me an idea. It had been a long time, but it was worth a try. . . .

I indicated to Truck that I wanted my hands untied. She complied, but not without a glance toward the Mayor and what I took to be an accompanying reassurance that I wasn't going to go berserk and start mauling kits and other innocent bystanders. I wrung my hands and massaged my wrists a moment to get some circulation back into them, then went to the orange cart. The vendor eyed me as I selected three ripe oranges, but he did nothing to stop me. I tested the oranges' weight and then gave it a try.

Among the many useless things I had taught myself just to see if I could learn them was juggling. I had practiced with beanbags and apples until I could do a simple cascade or shower with three objects, plus a few more simple tricks, then left it at that. Now I held two oranges in my right hand and one in my left, tossed one of the two, and began a shower. Shower is harder than cascade, but it looks easier, which is why I did it first. It's simply the act of throwing the objects in an arc from one hand to the other. Right hand throws, left hand catches and passes to the right, which throws again, and so on. It's important to duplicate the arc as accurately as possible each time so as not to screw up your timing, and you sort of stare at a point about eighteen inches above your head. From shower I switched to cascade, where the objects move in what seems a lopsided figure-eight, and where both hands toss and catch, alternating roles. I added a few passes behind my back and over my head for good measure, then caught the oranges with the notion of quitting while I was ahead. I looked at the crowd for their reaction.

The crowd was looking back. Not a sign, not an excited chitter. So he juggles, so what?

I glanced at Truck. She signed for me to go on.

Yeah, well, okay. I had taught myself other tricks with oranges. I replaced two of them on the vendor's cart and stepped away, hoping the vendor wouldn't be too pissed about the loss of one orange. I straightened my legs, put my feet together, bent, and touched the dirt street with my palms. Not bad. I could be more limber, but considering I hadn't stretched or worked out in some time, plus taking into consideration all the recent walking, not bad at all. I hitched up my jeans so they wouldn't restrict my leg movement quite so much, settled into a good back stance, and tossed the orange experimentally a few times. Okay, now or never. . . .

I tossed the orange and jumped as it reached its apex. Jump, tuck, spin, extend, and the side of my boot thunked into the orange. The force of the jump-spin crescent kick sent juice and pulp spraying from the burst orange. I stumbled a bit on landing and looked again at the crowd.

They were reacting this time. Oh, yeah. I'd recognize consternation anywhere, raccoons or no. The Mayor seemed agitated, and Truck appeared to be trying to placate her.

I cursed myself for an idiot, suddenly realizing it had not been particularly wise to reveal a martial arts skill, demonstrate what could easily be interpreted as a hostile or threatening act, spray the townsfolk with orange juice, and destroy a vendor's orange all with one kick. The cutesy animal act was souring rapidly.

Okay, one more try, out of simple desperation. Vaudeville time, folks. I began mouthing a little tune—Ya da-da da, da-da da *da* da"—and launched into one of the *worst* routines I had seen since elementary school. As I mouthed the irritating tune I showed the crowd my left hand in an "okay" symbol, then repeated the same with my right (thinking, as I did, that I had probably just unwittingly insulted the townsfolk's parentage in raccoon). I put both hands behind my head and brought them forward again, this time with both "okay" symbols linked.

They loved it.

Their hands waved in laughter and they chittered among themselves. Even the Mayor permitted herself a small wave of the hand, which I took for a giggle.

I exhibited the linked fingers for a moment, then put them behind my head again and brought them back unlinked. More silent laughter.

"Ya da-da da, da-da da *da* da. . . ."

I held out both fists and banged them together, popping up my right index finger. Bang, and lower that finger and pop up the left one. Bang: drop it, and pop up two fingers on the right hand in a peace sign. Bang: "shift" them to the left hand. Bang: and so on, until all fingers were up and then reduced one at a time.

I tell you, they were going wild. They looked like furry asylum inmates competing to see who could best mime a butterfly on speed.

I continued through another half dozen equally silly "magic tricks," then decided enough was too much and called a halt with a "ta-daa!" I could have gone on for hours—God help me, my repertoire was extensive enough—but I half expected a cane hook to appear out of nowhere and snatch me away.

There was no applause when I was finished—and it's a bit disconcerting until you're used to it—but many raccoons were still chortling away, hands all aflutter. Several of them purchased oranges, grapefruits, and small breads from vendors and gave them to Truck, who accepted them graciously and stuffed them into the daypack.

We were, saints preserve us, an act.

8
Narrative of Truck

ALL THAT DAY we wander around the Festival in Wait-No-More. A good time is had, though [Bentley] quickly tires of questions, requests for tricks, and requests for him to sign, which particularly delights the townsfolk. He is tired as well of so much staring and hesitant touching. We do well by it, though: the traveling pack of odd material is full of food—good fruits and small breads and cheeses that will last us many days on the road north to the town of Three Big Dogs, where I hope to enlist the aid of an old compatriot, a teacher and friend.

I upset [Bentley], I think, when I tie him to a hitching post and go into a small building to consult with the local physician. They have little in the way of sophistication, these Outback physicians, but they have a knowledge of root and plant, leaf and berry, that one does not find as often in larger towns and cities. The services of a good physician are appreciated in a town as far removed as Wait-No-More.

This physician receives me amicably enough, though his curiosity about me and my injuries is apparent. I show him the healing scars across my stomach and my leg where the fur no longer grows. "Do these look healthy?" I ask. "Will they heal well?"

The physician is an older male. His workspace is clean and well ordered. A few books, valuable things here, rest on a shelf. I find this encouraging, for an inept physician cannot afford books.

He offers me a cup of water, and I accept. He spreads the fur on my stomach and examines the scars. "They are clean," he signs, "and will heal well, but they could be cleaner and could heal faster. Wait here half a finger." I rest in an ugly but comfortable chair while he steps into the other room in the small house—the only sort of house there is in Wait-No-More. Before long he returns bearing a thick, green leaf wrapped in an oil-soaked cloth. Green sap oozes from the end of the leaf where it is snapped from the mother plant. "This is the leaf of an [aloe vera] plant," he signs. "It is from [Africa], and is taking root well in these parts—though it is hardly common yet. The sap heals wounds quickly, and is useful for many other things besides." He washes my scars and then rubs the leaf across them. I am keenly aware that he notices I wear no umbilical bracelet, but he signs nothing of it, as is proper.

"Tell me," he signs after setting the spiky leaf on the table, "how do you come to be so cut? Those are deep wounds, and fairly recent."

Though this sort of bluntness is uncommon among Outback folk, who are circumlocutious to the point of obfuscation, it is not unusual in a physician, who needs what facts s/he may gather in order to treat a patient. But here I sense there is more to his asking than mere medical curiosity. I ascribe it to my strangeness in the town of Wait-No-More. "I am cutting myself as I travel on the road south of Wait-No-More." I answer with both exactness and obviously deliberate vagueness. "Why do you ask?"

Equally obvious and equally vague is the physician's response: "No one reason. Still. . . ." He regards me flatly, then signs, "I am seeing rumors of Stripes in the woods to the south and the west."

"That is unusual for here," I sign after a moment.

"Yes."

"Do you ask, goodbody, if my wounds are caused by Stripes?"

Unsubtly he picks up the [aloe vera] plant and leaves the room. He returns empty-handed. "I do not think to presume this question," he finally signs, "for I feel certain that if your wounds are caused by Stripes, you could not tell me of it because you would be dead."

"I am seeing Stripes in action in the past," I reply, "and I know this to be true." I stand. "Well, I thank you for your attentions, goodbody. I have no coin with which to pay you. Is there some service I may perform for you instead?"

"I am only using a bit of leaf and a bit of my time," he replies graciously. "I would not think to ask for payment for these small things."

"You are kind for this, and I thank you again." I make to leave, but he stops me with a sound. I turn to look at him.

"I am not seeing Stripes here, myself," he signs. "Yet. But if I do, I will not tell them of treating any cuts." He pauses. "Not the sort of cuts, I mean to sign, as might be caused by a Fighting Hand. I know that the Stripes are necessary, and accomplish much that is good, but I do not love them. And so if you are cut, and heal well, that is enough for me."

"Thank you. You are kind for this, also."

"Perhaps." He begins a signing, but hesitates.

"You wish to know about my pet."

"Yes." He seems relieved that it is I who broach the subject. "I am curious. Where does one come by such a creature? It is an odd blend: at once grotesque and charming, repulsive and intriguing."

"A ship returning from Africa founders and wrecks not far off the coast a transit ago," I sign. "The crew and many animals drown. Many others reach the shore alive. This one is able to swim, and survives. I am sent to retrieve him, for he is quite rare and valuable. You are seeing of such?"

"No, never. Tell me, why are you collecting such a strange creature? And what of finding and capturing it? I am curious: surely this is a difficult and dangerous occupation."

This is more than idle curiosity, and I must be careful in my lie. "Of the finding and capture there is in truth little to sign. I know something of the habits of such creatures, and they are not so dangerous as they look. His predictability allows me to slip a rope around his wrist while he feeds at insects from the bark of trees. He comes along easily enough."

"This surprises me. But who sends you for him—you have a look, if I may sign so, of one far from native lands."

"You see much." I study him a moment. Though there seems nothing amiss in his queries, I decide that there is also no reason to avoid answering him—or to tell him the truth. "It is my privilege," I sign, "to be designated a Trapper of Exotics by Architect [Louis XIV] in Seaport [Jacksonville]. He collects such for his own pleasure and for educational purposes."

Skeptical, he turns away a bit. "You see the Architect?" His signing is hurried.

"I am seeing the Architect. I am not meeting him. My orders come through an advisor only."

"Still, to serve the Architect. . . ."

"One might sign that *all* serve the Architect. But it is a job, and not half so exciting as you must think it is."

"The excitement I feel is memory. I am glimpsing the Architect once, when I am a much younger male, as she passes our street with her Stripes and advisors. A glimpse only, yet even this young kit feels the power. They are not like us, those dreamers."

"This must be true. Of course, the Architect you are seeing is not the one who now holds the Chair, for [Louis XIV] is a male, and rules for seven years now."

"Yes. But let us hope there is always an occupied Chair in Seaport [Jacksonville]. Though for all I know there could be a steady stream of Architects since the one I am sighting as a kit; we get so few reports here."

"Sometimes that is best."

I bid him a good Festival day, thank him again for the treating of my wounds, and depart.

[Bentley] sits on the hitching post to which I am tying him—to which he is tied no longer, I note. He dangles his feet and blows air through his mouth in a way that produces interesting melodies, though simple. What does he know of music? I wonder.

He holds the cord out to me in his untied hands.

"You do well this morning," I sign. Slowly and simply, because it is new to him.

His mouth spreads oddly: the ends turn upward and he shows teeth. The mobility of his mouth is repugnant at first, and this latter motion I have to accustom myself to, for it is a common thing with him. At first, though, it terrifies me. "Good animal me," he signs.

Is this a joke? "Smart animal you," I counter experimentally.

"Sign you it so."

I take the cord from him and loop it around one wrist. "Eat?" I sign, and indicate the traveling pack I wear.

"Yes. Please." He fumbles a bit on the politeness gesture,

but I am no less impressed. No matter what he does, I am continually surprised because I persist in thinking him an animal.

"Let us find a hostel, and eat and sleep," I sign. "Between us perhaps we may barter food and bed."

"Understand no," he signs.

"Come." I lead him along the street, inquiring of a Festival-goer after a hostel. It turns out there is only one, and that turns out to be nothing more than a wooden home atop which are built two small rooms that are rented out. We attract stares as I strike the bell outside the curtained door and wait for the owner. In a moment she pulls aside the curtain.

"Good Festival day to you," I sign. "My charge and I—"

She interrupts me. "You want a room." Her gestures are curt, her posture yields nothing.

"Yes."

"I can take no coin, if that is what you offer as payment. Money is little use to me here."

"I have no money with which to pay you, but thought to either trade or perform a service or two for you or your household in exchange for a night's lodging. My charge"—I gesture toward [Bentley], who stands behind me, not out of sight, but neither overtly attracting attention— "is quite entertaining, and I fancy myself a competent musician. Perhaps your boarders would find us amusing? We do not require a room, merely a floor for the night, and we will go in the morning."

She cannot have failed to notice [Bentley], of course, and is still for a moment. Then she signs, "I am seeing signings of this creature. I am not completely believing them until now."

I step aside. "This is [Bentley]."

She stares at him. He stares back. Recognizing the signings that refer to him, he bends forward at the waist and straightens.

"Why does it wear spectacles?"

"So that it may see," I answer soberly.

"Is it not dangerous?" she asks.

"Oh, no; not in the smallest way. He is perfectly trained in all respects, and fit even for the politest company."

"It is ugly." Shave these Outbackers! One expects circumlocution, one receives bluntness. "Does it shit on the floor, or make loud noises? I will not have that."

"No, and I have no fear in accepting responsibility for him."

"That is good, for you are."

This coarseness makes me ache, I tell you! One is not missing more refined conversation until rougher—and thus more abrasive—sorts of intercourse take its place. "What is more," I sign, regaining my politeness out of simple pride, I suppose, "he is strong, and helpful. If you prefer labors performed as payment—"

"We shall work that out. You may stay the night, and your pet as well—but the night, and no more; and you will sleep on the downstairs floor, for there are legitimate guests upstairs. And if *it* screeches about, as I see these things do, or shits upon my floor, then into the street with the two of you."

"I find myself incapable of sufficiently expressing my gratitude." Allow her to chew on that, if she may.

She leads us into the cramped interior of the house. If [Bentley] appears too large outside the walls, he seems gigantic within. I am taller than average myself, but he must bend to enter the doorway, and slump to prevent his head from grazing the ceiling, and control the direction of his arms and legs so that they will not send things sprawling into other things, which I fear he will do frequently until he adjusts. He is not often inside houses, I think.

The hostel owner glances back fretfully, but [Bentley] behaves admirably. He looks about with a kit's curiosity, stopping to stare at the storm door beside the door curtain, at the long dinner table, the cold fireplace, the unpolished wooden floor. At times he must be firmly tugged along and treated like the dumb animal I know he is not, not only because I am seeing that this is so, but because of the True dreams.

To our left is a staircase I am sure will not take [Bentley's] weight. The room in which we are to sleep is small, with a few simple chairs, a dining table, and barely enough space for [Bentley] and myself to lie down.

The windows are slits that contain no glass—an expensive luxury to these folk. The floor is uneven. At the same time I wonder how they can live like this, I think of my existence this last transit and do not complain. Not where anyone can see, anyway.

The hostel-keeper, who signs her name as [Brunhilde], leaves us to ourselves. I remove the traveling pack and bring forth the envelope of odd little sticks [Bentley] uses to light small fires. I sign to him that I would like him to teach me to use them, but he does not respond. In a moment I realize he is not seeing me sign; the next moment he gropes out with his stubby hands until he encounters a rough wall, and I realize he cannot see at all in the dimness. I press the envelope of sticks into his hand. He opens it, removes a stick, and slides it across the bitter-tasting part, the rough strip that chills my spine when I slide it across my teeth. The stick flares, and I lead [Bentley] to a tallow candle in a clay container on a low table. He lights the candle, which sputters a bit, and smokes a bit, and smells more than a bit.

I point to the fire sticks. "These learn you me?" I ask.

His mouth curves up in that odd way. "Yes," he signs. "Not-many them. Gone they, no more."

"Understand me. Wait, later learn me."

He bobs his head.

"Eat," he signs. "Eat you?"

I refrain from laughing at his phraseology. He knows no better. "Eat we," I counter, and from the traveling pack remove two oranges, two bananas, and a grapefruit. I remove [Bentley's] strange knife. Though it is formally returned to him, I keep it for the time we are in Wait-No-More. I do not want to have to explain [Bentley's] facility with tools, especially a knife the likes of which no one is ever before seeing. I unfold the knife, then cut the grapefruit in two and offer him half. We eat. I notice he does not eat the rind of the orange or grapefruit, or the skin of the banana, but instead piles them together in a corner of the small room where they will rot. I empty the traveling pack of fruit and [Bentley's] odd containers, then put in the rinds and skin to feed later to animals. I close the teethed opening of the pack and set it in a corner, then sign to [Bentley]: "Festival go we."

He wipes his mouth dry against the back of one long arm and bobs his head, then remembers to sign, "Yes."

[Brunhilde] is not in sight. I wave out the candle and then hold aside the door curtain for [Bentley], and he ducks out ahead of me.

Conversing with a shop owner in front of a building across the street is [the Mayor], with whom I am signing earlier. She signals me to her and concludes her exchange with the shop owner, who regards us curiously but leaves politely.

"Enjoying our Festival day?" [the Mayor] asks.

"Yes," signs [Bentley].

I try to hide my amusement at this. "I, too," I sign.

The Mayor stares at [Bentley]. "It is a strange one," she signs. "How do you control it so well?"

"It is not difficult." I am nervous, signing to this raccoon, for though Wait-No-More is too small a town to warrant a Stripe contingent or even a Magistrate, she has the power to summon Stripes from nearby towns if she feels the need.

"I am thinking to tell you of the Pull Contest tomorrow at midday," she signs. "It is an annual event with us, a pull after Festival day. We hold a llama pull to see whose beast can pull the most weight. There is a prize of a [mandolute] this year."

"That is a good prize," I acknowledge. "I expect there is much competition for it."

"Yes, I suppose, for a town such as ours. Few here know how to play such an instrument, but it is beautiful. It would be fetching on a wall, or would bring a good price in a larger town. But I tell you of it because the pull attracts many farmers who do not often come to Wait-No-More, and they enter their llamas. There is much betting even among nonentrants, and this in turn attracts entertainers from nearby towns. It is fun, and there is much chance of increasing that pack of food you are garnering yourself today."

"It is a kindness to tell me of it," I sign. "I shall plan to attend."

"It will begin on this street." She waves a small laugh. "It is hard to miss."

We bid each other good Festival and part company. I think: Many will attend tomorrow—I do not need to attract attention to myself, and with [Bentley] this is unavoidable. But also I think: *A [mandolute]!* If I were to wear a mandolute, it would hide the worst of my scars. Besides, it is too long since my fingers are touching the strings of a mandolute. I look at my hands: the old calluses are gone from the tips of my fingers. New calluses ridge my palms from the work of surviving in the wild. I eye [Bentley], gauging his strength, his endurance, his physique. There is no doubt he is strong, stronger even than he looks. But strong enough?

I should not think such things.

On either side of the street peddlers sell fruits and vegetables, meats and breads, cheeses, popcorn, moccasins, spices, cooking implements, children's toys, fabrics, coffees, herbs, liquors. This Festival day must be well known in these parts;

there are nearly as many peddlers as there are customers. The Festival is also an opportunity for peddlers to barter among themselves, for it is common to see them storing away the wares of other peddlers in their own carts. I head toward one cart that belongs to a peddler who sells oranges, limes, and huge lemons, merely to view his fruits. Behind me I tow [Bentley], though it is not really "towing," for the cord is slack and he remains but a few paces behind, the rope loosely knotted about one wrist in order that he may sign. Dirt covers the tops of my feet, and I stamp a small cloud as I walk. I am wearing out my moccasins in the wild, and I look at my dirty feet and think I resemble a poorer sort of trapper than the sort I pretend to be. Soon, though, if all goes well, we shall head north, and so I shall need new moccasins. Survival I am learning, and challenging the hard time of it I am willing to do, but not at the cost of my feet! Is it worth it, to attempt to trade my pack of food, plus some time of entertainments by [Bentley], for a new pair of moccasins? I need to be a shrewder bargainer than I am, to do that.

I stop in front of the fruit seller and sign a greeting. He does not respond, but looks from me to stare hard at [Bentley]. I turn to [Bentley], who merely stands and looks around, curious as a dog. I wave to get his attention. "Before, orange-trick you," I sign. "Not-work it."

He bobs his head, and I wait until he makes the proper sign to indicate that he understands. He will never learn, otherwise, and many are not so tolerant as me.

I wave a laugh. "Look," I sign, and select three oranges from the fruit seller's cart.

I begin to juggle, beginning with cascade and switching to shower, then to over-the-head-and-catch-behind-the-back, to toss-from-behind, to catch-on-the-inner-elbow, to two-up, one-down, and then I catch the "two up" and replace the oranges on the cart.

[Bentley's] facial expressions are so confounded unfathomable! Is he chagrined, as I intend, or is he angry, or something else? I wave another, stronger laugh to put him at ease, to let him know that I am being jocular and nothing more. "A kit's thing, this," I sign. "Enjoyment. Play."

He begins to reply, but stops and points behind me. I turn. The fruit seller looks at me with narrowed eyes. "You owe me an orange," he signs.

"I, goodbody? I am only juggling three, and return them undamaged. I am not—"

"Your pet. The ape-thing. It is kicking my orange this morning."

"You are the one? A pardon, goodbody; indeed, I owe you an orange." I turn to [Bentley]. "Go you, orange get from pack."

He bobs his head—confound it!—and slips the cord easily from his wrist, then turns and jogs away. I look back to the fruit seller, intending some pleasantry or other.

"I do not like your pet," he signs.

I am still for a moment, regarding him. Hostility—and perhaps liquor?—dulls his eyes. Though not as tall as me, this fruit seller is a muscular sort, and from the patches and scars on him a veteran of more than a few flyings of the fur. "Why not?" I finally sign.

"It is too smart. If I am wondering, I am to wonder which is the master—you or it?" The fur at his neck begins to bristle. This I do not need.

"He is but a pet," I sign calmly, "a kind of freak. Intelligent, yes, for an animal. But do not let his appearance frighten you."

"Little frightens me."

By now I see that this one wants not to reason but to provoke. So much for my skills as a diplomat. I try to frame a placating—even conciliatory—reply, when [Bentley] returns, orange in hand. He picks up the cord from where he is dropping it in the street—I still hold the other end—slips it back onto his wrist, and tightens the knot a bit. He steps beside me and holds out the orange to the fruit seller, a bit proudly, I think.

The fruit seller stares at the offending orange and then bats it from [Bentley's] hand. [Bentley] snatches back his hand, and his large, pale eyes grow wide. The orange lands and rolls in the dirty street. By now I sense many others staring at us. [Bentley] bends and retrieves the orange. He dusts it off and again holds it out to the fruit seller.

"I do not like your pet," repeats the fruit seller—only this time he signs to [Bentley] and not to me. The fur on his neck stands out, and I faintly smell his fight readiness. I tug on the cord to get [Bentley's] attention so that we may leave, and this is all the provocation the fruit seller needs. He scurries around his cart with a bludgeon in his hand. I fall into readiness as he comes toward me—

"Hrrrrrr!" It is [Bentley]. He steps past me, arms curved like those of an actual ape, fingers spread. *"Arrrrrr!"* He growls like a dog. I glimpse his face as he passes: it is darkened to a reddish purple, eyes narrow, nostrils wide, lips drawn back to show his large, square teeth and pink gums. Somehow he looks twice as big as before.

"Rrraaahhh!" and the long arms raise as though casting a net. The fruit seller stops and gazes up stupidly at this maddened ape-thing, and at [Bentley's] final, menacing step forward he tosses down his bludgeon and runs away. The fur on his back is flattened.

[Bentley] turns to me. He is still dark-faced and showing his teeth, but there is something different about it. An odd, high-pitched, choking sound comes from his throat.

I think this is what he does in place of laughter.

9
Narrative of James Bentley

WE HAD TO sing for our supper. I felt like an organ-grinder's monkey, and in a way I suppose I was.

After the incident with the fruit seller we returned to our "hotel." We sat out front, squatting on the narrow wooden porch, and Truck gave me another language lesson. The porch was merely a row of wooden planks nailed together to form a low platform along the front of the inn, with a woven mat in front of the door to keep guests from tracking in dirt. Passersby ogled us and dropped food and, occasionally, hand-carved trinkets into a large bowl Truck had borrowed from the innkeeper. Occasionally I was requested to do simple tricks—a handstand once, basic addition using oranges and grapefruits another time. I felt the urge to demonstrate that I was more intelligent than they gave me credit for, but Truck deterred these efforts with negative signings whenever I started appearing too smart. She seemed determined to have me appear as little more than a talking dog to the townsfolk. I wondered why. Did she plan to continue exhibiting me as an organ-grinder's monkey? It was certainly keeping her well-stocked in food; there was now more than either of us could eat or conveniently carry. I was still shell-shocked, though—too much change for little Jim Bentley, and too quickly—and at the moment it was easier to play dumb than act smart. Mostly I did nothing but learn signings from Truck while other raccoons came by, stared, and dropped things in the bowl. Truck would wave her thanks and continue the lesson. For a while we had a crowd, but I guess the novelty of my language lesson got old fast, and they soon wandered off, signing among themselves and cocking their heads in wonder. Or maybe they didn't hang around because it was dinnertime, for I have never known a raccoon to skip a meal without good reason. Your own death is considered a barely adequate excuse. Another lesson I would learn: never stand between a raccoon and lunch.

The raccoons who did remain behind to watch were the kits. They were miniatures of their parents, but tended to plumpness. Their fur was softer than that of their elders, and would not grow wiry until adolescence, which they reach in eight or nine years. Save for one older kit, a near adolescent, none of them wore a bracelet.

The kits watched me and nudged each other, tentatively stepping toward me, stopping when I looked at them. Even seated I was taller than any of them. Their cautious steps toward me, along with their constantly fluttering hands, proved too distracting for me to concentrate on the language lesson, and I signed a halt to Truck and beckoned to one of the kits. "Come," I signed. "(−)bad me. Come."

Truck signed to the kits and they seemed a little more at ease. One of them slowly approached me. She was about two and a half feet tall, dark gray, with large eyes and a white-flecked bandit mask. I held still while she reached out a long-fingered hand and touched my shoulder, then snatched back her hand as though shocked. I wanted to grin but suppressed the urge, for they backed off whenever I showed my teeth.

She touched my shoulder again, then pinched it and jumped back. Behind her, her companions waved laughter. I waved a laugh along with them, leaned forward, slowly extended my arm, and pinched her lightly on the shoulder. Gradually the others approached, and soon we were all pinching and tickling and examining one another. Once their curiosity was unleashed they were uninhibited and unmerciful: I was stroked, poked, tugged, squeezed, and tickled just about everywhere. The sensations grew quite sexual and I felt embarrassed, then foolish, then even more embarrassed about feeling foolish.

The kits were fascinated with my hands. They moved my fingers to see what directions they would go, and they played finger dexterity games with me that I could not hope to equal—for they could hold their hands beside each other in a line, fingers straight, and bend their fingers in sequence, and the effect looked like their hands were boneless and could ripple at will. The game was for everyone to line up, hands out, and fold fingers in order down the line. Whoever messed up was out. When they did it right it traveled in a wave like a line of falling dominoes. I couldn't do it at all, and the game kept breaking up as they waved their laughter.

Truck and I gave out fruits and sweetbreads until it was nearly all gone, for the kits seemed to be able to put it away forever, but I didn't mind and neither did Truck. If this afternoon had been any indication, we would have no trouble acquiring more food.

The kit who had first approached me gave me a teddy-bear hug, so I hugged her in return, pressing her furry body close to my chest, and I stood. She trilled in delight and batted at the others as I held her high and paraded around the porch.

I felt her go rigid in my hands, and I turned to see a knot of adults running toward me from up the street. Some carried bludgeons. Irate parents?

Slowly and exaggeratedly I hugged the kit to my breast and lowered myself to my knees, then lowered the kit to the street.

Truck had risen to her feet, and she stepped in front of me. An argument began, ending with the parents collecting their kits and stalking away with them tucked under their arms. The little one I had been carrying was slung butt-forward in the crook of her father's elbow. She forlornly waved good-bye to me as the grown-ups huffily stomped away.

"Well, so much for the local P.T.A.," I said to Truck. "What now?"

But of course she didn't understand.

Paying guests at Brunhilde's Inn (there were three; it was, after all, a rush week in Wait-No-More) were entitled to dinner; Truck and I earned ours while the guests ate theirs. Dinner was thick slabs of bread and a stew that smelled so good it made my mouth water.

Brunhilde, it developed, was custodian of the musical instrument I later learned was the prize for the next day's llama pull, and Truck apparently sweet-signed her way into borrowing it. The instrument was four-stringed, with a long, wide, and fretless neck that bent at the head. The back was rounded. The different woods of which the instrument was made were finely lacquered, including the tuning pegs, which were driven through the head and wound perpendicular to the strings, rather than entering through the side of the head as was more familiar to me. The hole in the body beneath the strings was unusually large; it and the rounded back deepened the timbre of the high-pitched strings, which were strummed with a pick that might have been made from a tortoise shell. Though the instrument looked very much like a lute, it was played in a staccato style more similar to that of a mandolin, so I dubbed it a mandolute. Truck constantly had to retune the instrument, and I suspected it was because of the placement of the keys. A year later I would change that, creating quite a stir among musicians by having a mandolute constructed with the pegs entering through the side of the head.

The music took some getting used to. At first it sounded atonal and without melody. The eight-note C scale had never been utilized here, and consequently the transitions from phrase to phrase lacked the inevitability I expected. Traditional musical patterns, I am loath to say, tend to follow mathematical sequences: the sine waves of notes either blend—what we call harmony—or don't. Thus we have learned to expect certain notes to follow certain others—not on an overall theme basis, of course, but at the note-to-note level. But anyone raised on Western-cultural music experiences the same out-of-synch sensation when first introduced to Oriental styles: at first it just doesn't sound *right*. Later, of course, the consistency of tonal progressions and the ability to recognize alternate patterns allow a listener to develop a different context in which to place the music, and this revised frame of reference lets the music sound like *music*.

Once I was used to it I realized that Truck's playing was not noise but was in fact subtle and complex. To my unaccustomed eyes the strings looked inverted: bass string on top and highest trebel string on bottom. Truck maintained a steady, almost hypnotic beat with the bass and developed a simple melody on the remaining three strings that varied gradually as it repeated. It reminded me a bit of Philip Glass's variety of minimalism and was a bit monotonous until you allowed yourself to become caught up in the gradually shifting web of rhythm, and you felt the changes and went with them.

As Truck played and the melody grew more and more complex, the rhythm intensifying, I brought in an empty half barrel from in front of the inn. I inverted it and sat beside Truck with the barrel between my knees, and I played percussion. At first Truck seemed surprised by this, and the guests amused, but she continued to play and they continued to eat. I attempted to emulate her style of nonintrusive rhythm that gradually shifted. Soon she began giving way to my makeshift conga, her mandolute at times becoming accompaniment rather than lead. There were passages where I was banging solo on the half barrel, and so skillfully did Truck lead into these that I didn't realize she had stopped playing until she resumed. Soon she guided the melody back to what I realized was a restatement of her original theme. I eased off on the barrel until I was no longer playing, and she finished as she had begun.

There was no applause, no indication of either approval or disapproval. The three guests and Brunhilde just went right on ladling stew into their narrow mouths and sponging it up with torn-off hunks of bread, occasionally setting down bread and utensils to pick up a spouted mug and drink, or to sign something to the others. One of the obvious drawbacks to signing as communication is that it's hard to talk with your hands full. But then, no raccoon ever choked to death trying to talk with food in his mouth, either.

Occasionally one of the guests, and often Brunhilde, would glance my way, I think to be sure I was staying put. Often these glances were followed by a few short signings and the waved laughter of all.

Truck struck up another melody, and this time I just sat back and listened. It was a jaunty tune, it seemed to me, sort of airy and bouncy. She hunched over the mandolute as she played, intent on the strings, a furrow of concentration between her eyes. Occasionally she glanced along the length of the neck to study the workings of her long and nimble fingers as though they belonged to someone else.

She played until dinner ended, when the guests retired to their rooms and Brunhilde beckoned Truck to the table, indicating a bowl of stew and a slice of bread that were not exactly a lion's share. I was given an unwashed bowl of leftovers and no ladle, and I was actually hungry enough, since we had been so foolish to give away most of our food earlier that day, to be willing to eat it—but not with my fingers. The wooden forks were two-tined; spoons were narrow and deep. I grabbed a used spoon, set my bowl on the table across from Truck, wiped the spoon clean against my jeans, and commenced eating. I couldn't tell if the raccoons were amused or alarmed; furthermore, I didn't give a damn. I might be regarded as a pet, if that was how Truck wanted to play it for now, but I was no dog.

The stew didn't taste any different than I expected: the meat was a bit too rare for my palate, and the whole thing could have used some kind of seasoning, but stew is stew. As I ate I reflected that if our circumstances were reversed and Truck was an intelligent raccoon suddenly finding herself in *my* world, I would probably try to pass her off as a pet as well. In fact, I had been planning on it.

But how long was I going to have to act dumb?

One of the guests had hung back and attempted to strike up a conversation with Truck. Truck's terse replies—all of them pointedly followed by her resumption of eating, indicating that no further reply was forthcoming—discouraged the guest enough that he soon gave up and retired to his room.

Brunhilde stared at us throughout our entire meal.

By the end of dinner it had grown dark and I could make out little inside the tiny inn. I kept expecting someone to light a candle, but no one did. Soon it became obvious that their night vision was far superior to mine, and when Truck and I had finished our meager meal she had to guide me by the arm to our sleeping places on the floor. Apparently the streets rolled up early in Wait-No-More. I lay beside Truck, who seemed to have no problem at all going right to sleep, and I fell asleep listening to the night sounds of crickets and barking dogs, and to the occasional hollow clop of a passing llama. I dreamed not of Nicole, who could take care of herself, but of Albert, who could not.

In the middle of the night I woke to the sound of soft strumming. Truck was no longer beside me. I patted the floor until I found my glasses, then unfolded them and put them on. The plastic frames were cool at my temples and behind my ears. I got up and groped in the dark until my fingers touched the rough, unfinished wood of the wall. I patted along that until I encountered the door curtain. I pulled it aside, ducked my head, and stepped outside.

It was hot out, but cooler than inside the stuffy inn. A warm breeze stirred. The town was quiet. Down the street I could hear the plaintive bleats of llamas in their stalls. The larger moon was setting in the west, its dimmer companion a handsbreadth above it. They had been farther apart when I had first seen them, which indicated that the smaller moon was also the nearer. I gazed at the larger moon for a while. It seemed about a third the diameter of the moon I had known, though I could not be sure. The pattern of craters on the silvery-gray disk was alien to me, and try as I might I could not make it form a Man in the Moon. I shook my head. *Pete,* I thought, watching the larger moon touch the horizon. *Pete and Repeat.* I suppose I could have been poetic and scholarly, and christened them Romulus and Remus, or perhaps Pollux and Castor, but Pete and Repeat is what came into my head, and the names stuck.

I went behind the inn and urinated in the dirt, then returned to the front porch. With one moon now invisible below the horizon (though a dimming afterglow remained), the night was darker, and the scene before me could almost have been an amber-lighted town in the Old West, closed up for the night and waiting for tomorrow's stage. Almost.

The door curtain was pulled aside and Truck stepped onto the porch, mandolute in hand. She cocked her head at me, and I signed a greeting. She looked away, gazing at the town, at the starry night sky, at Repeat, the remaining, sulphur-yellow moon, and then she carefully set down the mandolute. The body made a hollow, wooden clunk as it touched the gritty porch. Truck leaned the neck against the wall. A bass string reverberated when she removed her hand.

She turned to look at me. "Good," she signed. She pointed at the sky, at the moon, at the quiet street. "All good."

"Yes," I replied. I mimed her playing the mandolute, then pointed to myself and added an interrogative. Carefully she lifted the instrument and handed it to me. I strummed the strings experimentally while Truck watched. I tried to form what would have been a D chord on a guitar, but my hand would barely wrap around the neck. I have mentioned that her hands were unusually long, but it wasn't until that moment that I was stunned by *how* long they actually were. Were she a pianist, her hands might have bridged a double octave; had she been a basketball player, each hand would wrap nearly halfway around the ball; a baseball pitcher, and any team in the league would have signed her on, at whatever price she cared to name—especially after they saw what she could do with a rock.

I returned the mandolute to her. We regarded the quiet night a moment longer, and then we went inside.

I woke knowing it was bright daylight outside because of the stuffiness of Brunhilde's Inn. Truck was already up, sitting with her back against a wall. A widening tape of dusty sunlight shone through the window slit across from her, curving to follow the contours of one furry leg and rippling along the opposite arm as she peeled our last grapefruit. Seeing me awake, she offered half, and I gratefully accepted. A bracelet of sunlight slid from her furry wrist when she handed me the grapefruit. I scooped out a pale yellow wedge, stuffed it into my mouth, and bit down. Tanginess flooded my tongue. I spit seeds into my hand and showed them to Truck, then signed an interrogative with my other hand. The gesture looks something like an upside-down question mark. Truck indicated a large wooden bucket in one corner, and I tossed the seeds into that. Normally I like to mash the pulp in my mouth, swallow the juice, and spit out the slimy remains, but this time I chewed and swallowed. In the absence of a toothbrush and toothpaste I was grateful for the acidic juice.

I wondered what time it was and realized that, short of making a sundial, I had no way of knowing. It *felt* like ten o'clock, whatever that means. Sometimes it feels like a Friday, sometimes it feels like midnight. That day felt like a Sunday, around ten o'clock.

I put on my glasses, leaned back, and drew aside the bottom corner of the door curtain, squinting in the sudden brightness. The peddlers were on the street again. There were more today than yesterday. I looked for the one who'd tried to start the fight with Truck, but if he was there I couldn't tell which one he was—an anthropocentricism on the order of "All Orientals look alike to me" that would eventually vanish.

There were also many more llamas than there had been yesterday. Some were shorter-necked than the kind of llama I knew. They were sturdier and stouter, and most of them were dun-colored. It seemed that this variety was used mostly as a draft animal. They stood between three and four feet high at the shoulder, though with their long necks they could easily stare you in the eye—and spit in it, likely as not, for they are related to the camel. A few pulled curious, boxlike, two-wheeled, one-raccoon affairs rather like Roman chariots. They were yoked on and were steered by a halter arrangement that fit over the nose and well behind the nostrils, secured by leather strips around the long ears. There was no bit because of the construction of the llama's mouth; a bit would ruin its teeth and be quite painful. The reins led from either side of the muzzle through wooden collars in the top of the yoke, and the llama was steered Indian fashion.

The same arrangement was used for draft llamas pulling dogcarts, and with a double yoke for llamas in tandem pulling four-wheeled wagons and larger peddlers' carts. These clopped along the streets mundanely, driven by raccoons who started and stopped them with sharp handclaps rather than a *"hyah!,"* and the sight was so extraordinarily everyday, in its Glenn Ford way, that I wanted to scream and pull out my hair. For a moment I understood what it is to be mad, to have the world you see not jibe with the world that is.

The most prominent sort of llama I saw that day was one used both for riding and as a pack animal. It was darker than the draft llama and was taller-necked, slender and a bit more graceful—though there is little of grace in a llama. Those being ridden were not saddled as a horse would be; instead they wore a leather collar around the base of the neck, and on top of this collar was something like an ox handle or a saddle horn. Sewn to the top of the collar was a thick leather pad upon which sat the rider, and toward the bottom of the collar were stirrups. The halter arrangement was the same muzzle affair used with the draft llamas.

I got a glimpse of a breed I would later come to know a little better: the Pony Express model, known as the racing or messenger llama. One rode quickly past as I stared through the doorway at the bustle on the street. It was tall, long-necked, long-legged, ivory-colored, and fast. Later I would learn that it is also a gluttonous, capricious creature fully capable of eating itself to death if given the opportunity, and rather more enamored of spitting than most llamas. I was to develop no great love for it.

Not only were there more llamas and peddlers on the street, there were many more raccoons as well, and today seemed a much more active day for Wait-No-More. I wondered how long this Festival was to last, and what, exactly, they were celebrating.

It had become obvious to me that this was not Truck's native village, and I wondered if she would be leaving before too long—and whether she planned on taking me with her.

I released the door curtain, stood, and went to the "kitchen"—really just another corner of the large downstairs room—where I filled a clay bowl from the half barrel of water in the corner. I went back through the door curtain and onto the porch, sipped water, swished it around in my mouth, and spat it into the dirt. Startled raccoons glanced at me from the street. I tried to ignore them. Perhaps spitting was a breach of etiquette for which I could be hanged or drawn and quartered. Mark Twain once wrote that "Laws can be evaded and punishment escaped, but an openly transgressed custom brings sure punishment." It was something to keep in mind—for later. Right now I didn't care; I wanted the sour morning-taste out of my mouth. I gargled, spat again, and brushed my teeth with a finger as best I could. It would be a long time before I was able to brush my teeth in anything close to normal fashion. I removed my glasses and splashed my face with the remainder of the water. It felt good, and I finally felt something akin to alert. Working graveyard at a 7-Eleven gets you easily hooked on caffeine, and for nearly two weeks after my inauspicious arrival here I was to wake up with the headaches symptomatic of caffeine withdrawal. Satisfying the speed monkey on my back would not take long, however; I did not know then that I would be drinking coffee again in a matter of weeks, and that I would be back to my usual high consumption level in no time. The coffee here makes Jamaican Blue Mountain taste like instant.

I dried my face on my T-shirt. By now I was attracting a crowd, and I was beginning to feel like the village idiot. I put my glasses back on, shook the bowl dry, and gave my audience a theatrical bow. I farted loudly for good measure and said, "Next show at five, folks." They backed up a bit, waving agitatedly.

I was going to have to learn to discipline my smile.

Brunhilde had apparently softened a bit and given Truck two eggs for breakfast, which Truck offered to share with me. Maybe our performance last night had won over the innkeeper, a bit.

Raccoons tend toward two meals a day, one upon rising in the early morning and one a few hours after sunset. As with humans, the evening meal is usually the heavier of the two.

As a result I went around hungry much of the time, and lost, at a guess, fifteen pounds during my first two months—and I was fairly thin to start with.

Truck broke her egg into a bowl, sprinkled in shell fragments, and began slurping it up, crunching up the white wedges. Not about to follow her example, I scrounged around for something like a frying pan. I knew that the raccoons cooked their meat, which meant that they probably cooked it *in* something. I mimed what I wanted to Truck and she seemed to understand. After rummaging in a small cabinet against one wall, she produced a small iron skillet. I used the remainder of one book of matches getting the fire going in the stone fireplace, which left me with one more book. Truck pointed from the skillet to the fire and added an interrogative. I pointed to the egg in my hand, to the skillet she held, and at my mouth, then patted my stomach for good measure. The familiar furrow appeared between her eyes, but she signed nothing.

Brunhilde came down the stairs and stood watching us. Truck asked her a question, to which she responded with one of her own. Truck indicated the fireplace with the skillet, pointed to me, and spread her free hand.

Brunhilde answered curtly and went to a cabinet beside the one in which Truck had found the skillet. She opened it and pulled out a little stand made of thin iron bars. She gave it to Truck and folded her arms across her chest, matronly despite her nonhumanness. It's funny; I remember her now as wearing a white apron bordered with a red rose print, though of course she wore no such thing. Truck handed me the skillet, then knelt at the fireplace and gingerly pushed the stand over the fire and turned to face me. I signed that I understood, then added a thank-you to Brunhilde for good measure.

I rapped my egg against the lip of the skillet, separated the halves, pulled a small wedge of shell from the sticky fluid, and dropped the eggshell into Truck's bowl. She munched it absently as she watched me fry my egg.

I am fond of remembering that breakfast I cooked myself. In retrospect it seems somehow to take on an aspect of epic proportion, but at the time all I was thinking was that I was damned if I was going to slurp up raw eggs when I had the means to cook them, no matter how much of a spectacle I made of myself.

The skillet took a while to heat, and the iron stand supporting it wasn't exactly a Rangemaster; I had to take care not to burn myself. My experience with camp cooking was borne out when the skillet heated up all at once and my egg began to cook—and, just as quickly, to overcook.

How did I ask for a potholder?

Did they even *have* potholders?

I growled in frustration and removed my damp T-shirt, folded it, and wrapped it around my hand, then grabbed the hot handle of the skillet and lifted it from the cooking stand. I could feel the shirt growing hot against my palm. I looked around hurriedly for a place to set the skillet, cursing myself for not thinking of this beforehand. My gaze settled on the half barrel of water in the corner.

The handle was getting rather warm.

"Gangway!" I shouted, and quick-stepped across the room, dodging Truck and weaving past the picnic-style dinner table. I dipped the bottom half of the skillet into the barrel, and it breathed at me to *hush*.

I had already slipped a wooden spoon from last night's stew into my back pocket, and now I removed it and attacked my fried egg.

Brunhilde bolted outside and threw up on the front porch.

The edges of my egg were burned brown and crisp, and the white was hard and rubbery. The yolk had broken and cooked solid. I downed it in about five bites.

I think it was the best egg I ever ate.

10
Narrative of Truck

IF I AM knowing then that this is the last unfettered fun I will have for quite some time, would I do anything differently?

I cannot know. It is moot. Dreamed or not, the future is unavoidable. What I do know is that I can scarcely restrain my mirth as Brunhilde dabs her face with a towel and glares at [Bentley]. She signs nothing.

"Truly, all is well," I placate, for I see that she is on the verge of ordering us from the premises. "He does this all the time."

She is not amused.

11
Narrative of James Bentley

AT BRUNHILDE'S INSISTENCE I went with Truck to the well at the edge of town—a three-hundred-yard walk—to refill the half barrel because I'd dirtied the water. Only fair, I guess.

There was raccoon puke on the front porch. I washed it away with the dirty water.

I held one barrel handle and Truck held the other, and together we walked down the street to the well at the south end of town, collecting stares and a gaggle of furiously signing kits. We passed the shop of the town blacksmith, who paused in his shoeing of a huffy llama as we went by. Again I was stricken by the most immediate sense of the surreal, for to me the sharpest incongruities lay in the similarities between Wait-No-More and a human frontier settlement. Thinking about it, though, I realized that certain similarities were probably endemic to particular levels and kinds of civilization, especially civilizations whose constituents are as anatomically similar as humans and the raccoons. In few ways are they truly *alien;* they are, after all, bilaterally symmetrical, upright, bipedal, five-fingered mammals. Contrast humans and dolphins when comparing civilizations, and suddenly you get a sense of something foreign to human experience, for not only do dolphins not have hands, they have entire sensory apparatus humans don't possess. And we have yet to encounter something truly, completely *alien,* something entirely removed from human experience—last I heard, that is.

So it was really quite natural, upon reflection, to discover a smithy among people using domesticated animals for draft and riding purposes, to encounter physicians, to find regularly practiced celebrations of harvesttimes among agrarian peoples, to find inns and restaurants in towns regularly receiving itinerants, to find gambling in an economy based on barter and tokens, and to encounter all manner of other things I found disturbingly alien in their humanness.

But I had a ways to go yet.

At the well I juggled three rocks for the kits who had followed us. I tickled one of the smaller kits for a minute, then drew four or five buckets to fill the barrel. The water table in Florida is high, and so was the well.

Truck and I wrestled the barrel back to the inn and set it in its place against the wall, which seemed to satisfy Brunhilde—or at least, if she was still pissed off, she signed no comment.

Truck collected her few possessions and handed me the daypack. "This day go you me," she signed. It was as I had suspected, then: we were not to stay in Wait-No-More but were to push on. I hadn't the vaguest notion where to, but I guessed I'd see when we got there. Again I wondered if Truck was some sort of vagabond who planned to exhibit me all around.

Truck thanked Brunhilde for her minimal hospitality and bid her adieu, or whatever it was raccoons bade one another when they didn't want to see each other again, and we left.

A crowd was forming outside the smithy, lining both sides of the street, while on the street itself at least two dozen draft llamas were being yoked.

There was a carnival feel in the air, a sense of . . . I don't know, of *aliveness,* the sort of invigoration you feel at the first whiff of winter. Odd here, in this ninety-five-degree heat and stifling humidity, but present nonetheless. I almost expected to see Victorian gentlemen walking slowly past the adobe dwellings and shops, parasoled ladies at their elbows. I found the lack of crowd noise a bit unsettling, but the constant flurry of hands and acting-out of conversation seemed noisy in itself. There was such a normalcy to it all: crowd members jostled for a better view, munched on fruits, sat kits atop narrow shoulders with their short legs wrapped around broad necks, conversed exaggeratedly, wagered on favored llamas, and in general seemed to be having a good time.

You haven't lived until you've seen a family of oversized

raccoons sitting at the front edge of a furry gray crowd as if waiting for the front of a parade, ogling llamas and munching baskets of popcorn. It could almost have been a Norman Rockwell painting.

I saw one very pregnant raccoon, her six breasts swaying in time with her walk, and I reflected that if there was such a thing as a raccoon bikini, it would have one bottom and three tops.

On the street the llamas complained about their yokes. It seemed that what they were to pull were two simple wooden platforms onto which had been loaded a number of logs—more than I would have thought a llama could pull. The logs were secured to the platforms with rope, and the platforms themselves had two wooden runners along the bottom to make pulling easier. Poles on either side of the platforms were to be attached to the llama's yokes. Apparently the contest worked by simple elimination: llamas ran two at a time, winners to be pitted against each other after the first elimination. The llamas looked around in what seemed a constant state of consternation, heads turning back and forth like befuddled chickens, huge eyes black, gold, or green. Beside them stood their owners, adjusting their yokes and soothing the beasts with gentle strokes.

In a few minutes they were ready. The Mayor stepped into the street and delivered a short "speech," swiveling back and forth on her hips while she signed, so that raccoons on both sides could see her. An aide handed her the mandolute and she held it aloft for a moment, then gave it back. Then she stood to the side and the aide put a rock into her hand. She raised it slowly, then dropped it. The pull was on.

I realized I had been half expecting cheers to commence with the start of the pull, but of course there were none—none to be heard, anyway. However, hands waved encouragement, urged favored competitors, and nudged aside neighbors' opposing urgings in what I took for well-intended chiding. The only sounds were excited trillings on the part of spectators and llama owners—a fast, high-pitched warbling that rose and fell—and the bleating of llamas, a sound like neurotic laughter. The beasts strained in their harnesses, kicking up dirt and doing everything in their power to drag the overburdened platforms. The llama nearest us got its sled in motion first and maintained its lead to the end of the race, which was a line drawn in the dirt fifty yards up the street. The winning owner was awarded a green cloth, which he tied around his arm to mark him for the next elimination. Apparently many wagers had been made, for at the awarding of the green cloth raccoons grudgingly gave up goods to other, elated raccoons—fruits, crafts, kitchen implements, other small but useful items. I wondered if there was a favorite among the llamas, and whether the raccoons saved their heavy betting for the final contests.

The Mayor came out again, made another short speech that seemed largely a repeat of the first, stood aside, and dropped another rock. The second pull commenced.

I noticed Truck in animated conversation with a large male standing to her left, a kit perched on his neck. The kit waved to me and signed something. I waved back and repeated her sign, and she waved laughter so hard I was afraid she would fall off. Her father held her tightly, however, with the kit's feet gripped under his armpits so that he could sign. He studiously ignored me while conversing with Truck. I wondered if he was one of the irate parents from yesterday.

Truck pointed repeatedly to a llama being readied for the next pull. The father raccoon signed a "no," pointing from that llama to one beside it. Truck asked a brief question. Father raccoon seemed to be considering, then asked a question himself. Truck's reply was to remove the pack from my back and draw out the remaining book of matches. She opened it, removed a match, and struck it alight. Father's eyes widened. He put a finger over the flame and then snatched it back. A breeze blew out the match. The father reached for the matchbook, but Truck put it back into the pack and zipped it shut—at which, I noticed, the father stared in amazement—and then returned the pack to me. Truck signed something to the father that ended with an interrogative. The father looked down at his moccasined feet, looked at Truck, then at me, and finally signed an affirmative. Truck seemed satisfied, and they turned to wait for the next elimination.

The llamas were hitched to the sleds; the Mayor stepped out and repeated her speech, was handed a rock, and dropped it—and the owners of the llamas began prodding their charges. Truck's favorite was the nearer llama. It got off to a late start but promptly caught up to its competitor and passed it, beating it across the line by a good ten feet. I suppressed the urge to cheer, for it might have alarmed the raccoons around me.

Father raccoon narrowed his eyes at the wide margin of

Truck's llama's win, but he removed the child from his shoulders, bent down, pulled off his moccasins one at a time, and handed them to Truck with obvious reluctance. Truck thanked him expansively and promptly put on the moccasins. When she straightened, father raccoon had found a different spot in the crowd.

A raccoon who had observed this exchange with some amusement tapped Truck's elbow for attention and began signing to her, with many references to me and to the llamas on deck for the next heat. Truck turned to eye me speculatively before replying to the other raccoon. Their conversation continued until the start of the next pull, when the raccoon left Truck and went along the edges of the crowd until she stood beside the Mayor. She signed something to the Mayor and pointed to me and Truck. The Mayor seemed startled, signed briefly, and then began waving laughter. She signed an affirmative, and the other raccoon darted back to Truck and signed excitedly.

Truck turned to me. "Strong you," she signed. She pointed to the two llamas straining toward the finish line, loads scraping in the dirt of the street behind them. "(+)strong?" She pointed to me, then to the llamas again. "You, llama. (+)strong?"

I swallowed. She couldn't be serious. I pointed at the llamas. "(+)strong," I signed. I mimed straining at a rope, attempting to pull an invisible and immobile burden. "Me no." I pointed again to the llamas. "(+)strong," I repeated as firmly as I knew how. I was damned if I was going to play *The Call of the Wild* to satisfy Truck's curiosity.

But she pointed at me again. "(+)smart you," she signed, and she waved a laugh and tugged at my leash. "Come."

"Truck." I signed her name. "Truck. Me no! Please." But she kept her back to me to blind herself to my pleading, and I followed her without resisting because I was afraid to force a showdown here among so many creatures alien to me, who were also obviously strangers to her. All right—at worst they would harness me to a sled and I would just stand there and let the goddamn llama I was supposed to be competing against win. I was tired of being an organ-grinder's monkey, tired even of my thinly veiled dumb-animal pose. I was a human being, dammit, and even if I was foreign to their experience, I was nevertheless intelligent, and I was tired of Truck's unwillingness to allow me to fully demonstrate this. I didn't have to fight back, but I didn't have to go along with this, either.

The current heat ended and the two llamas were unhitched from the sleds. Truck led me to the Mayor, looping her end of my leash about one wrist so she could converse more freely. I glanced about while they signed, since it was useless for me to attempt to follow their conversation. We were being stared at by nearly everybody there, and they signed amongst themselves and held their kits up to see. I got angry—here I was again, another curiosity, and I felt as though I were trapped in some kind of geek show. I glanced at Truck and the Mayor, then at the cord around my wrist. I untied it and dropped it to the street. I turned my back on Truck, walked away three or four paces, folded my arms across my chest, and simply stared back at the crowd. What could I do to prove I was more than a talking dog?

And then I understood: the pull. Truck had pointed from the llama to me. "More smart," she had signed. And I had not understood, was in fact resisting even now, which tempted me to put her observation about my intelligence somewhat in question. If I wanted to prove I was intelligent, I had to win the pull—but with brain instead of brawn. All right, then—*Call of the Wild* time, folks.

I tried to ignore the crowd and concentrate on the log-laden sled. It was obvious I could never pull the weight of the five huge logs on it; even if I could get it in motion—which I strongly doubted I could do—it was virtually impossible for me to drag that much weight a distance of fifty yards. Perhaps I could utilize the old tug-of-war trick and kick indentations in the street at intervals, using them to brace my feet and take advantage of my leg power. But I discarded the notion almost as soon as it occurred to me, for even if I could pull the weight by doing that, I could never beat the llama once it got its burden moving.

Then I looked at the logs themselves and realized the simple way out, and was delighted because I would win, and because it was obviously cheating, and obviously a sign of intelligence, and because it ought to piss off just about everybody.

Truck concluded her conversation with the Mayor and gestured for me to follow her. I walked with her to the sled. Truck argued with two of the handlers, apparently about how best to hook me up to the thing, while the Mayor stepped into the street and delivered another speech—apparently a doozy; hands began to flutter wildly. It seemed the betting was on.

A llama was led to the sled beside mine. Its owner turned a few times while harnessing the blue-eyed, nervous-looking beast and delivered what I guessed were disparaging remarks toward me and Truck. Truck ignored them.

It was decided that I was not to wear any kind of harness, which was fine with me. Instead Truck and the handlers removed the poles and passed a strong rope through the two holes in the forward corners of the sled, and then the free ends of the rope were tied together and given to me. I signed a "no" and untied them, then tied a knot into each free end and took up the slack in the center until the knots were snug against the holes in the sled. I doubled over the middle section and tied a square knot, which left me with a loop through which I could hook one arm and pull.

The llama's owner signed that he was ready. I glanced at Truck and dropped the rope to sign, "Good animal me."

She waved a small laugh. "Smart animal you," she countered, and she picked up the rope and handed it to me, patted me on both forearms, turned, and walked toward the sidelines.

The Mayor concluded her speech and picked up her rock. For some reason she always used the same one. She raised her free hand, held out the rock, turned it over, and let go. The race was on.

No time to waste: I dropped the rope and scurried to the rear of the sled, where I untied both cords securing the logs to the platform. I grabbed the top left log and yanked. It slid out a few inches. "Bullshit," I muttered aloud, and I tugged sideways until the log rolled from the sled. I squatted, lifted, and firmed my grip, and then I turned and began dragging the log as fast as I could to the finish line. *Please, God,* I prayed, *no splinters*.

Fifty yards isn't too fearsome a distance to drag a log that weighs, at a guess, one hundred twenty pounds. But I was going to have to do it again, and then run back and try it with the sled and the remaining logs. I crossed the line and dropped the log. It landed with a solid thump and kicked up dirt. I ran back to the sled, following the line I had dragged along the street. I passed the llama and its owner, barely away from the starting line, the latter chittering wildly and signing as if his hands were on fire. I ignored them and pushed the second log from the sled.

The irate llama owner ran at me as I drew abreast of him with my burden. I grinned at him and made a moderately gruff growl, and he stopped short. He turned to the Mayor, signing furiously, I think trying to get somebody to do something, but a quick glance at the crowd seemed to indicate that everybody was having too grand a time to interfere.

I dropped log number two across the line and ran back. By now I was covered with sweat, and the inner side of my left forearm was scraped and bleeding where I'd been clamping the logs. At the sled I tied two quick granny knots around the three remaining logs to keep them from rolling off while I pulled. I took a quick breath and glanced ahead. The llama owner had just given up his ministrations to the Mayor and was returning his attention to the llama, not even halfway to the finish line. I picked up the rope, put my arms through the loop, and *pulled.* Grudgingly the platform slid forward.

Even cheating, it was going to be a close race.

I pulled, and my arm muscles knotted and my thigh muscles bunched, and my back ached and sweat streaked my glasses—and I crossed the line a good fifteen feet ahead of the llama.

I collapsed in the dirt and lay there panting, squinting at the sun in the cloudless sky. All around me were chittering, warbling, and ratchety noises, punctuative sounds raccoons make to emphasize their gestures. I lifted my head and saw the farmer signing furiously at the crowd, and the crowd waving their laughter all around. Well, at least the mob thought it was funny, instead of being angry enough at my cheating to lynch me. When I caught my breath I stood and dusted myself off as best I could. The llama owner, seeing me stand, stalked to me and began signing. I waved for him to stop. His eyes were bright and he was chittering in agitation. "Understand I no," I signed.

He narrowed his eyes, seemed to momentarily size me up, then stepped closer and began kicking dust all over me, dragging his foot in the dirt, lifting it toward me, raising a small cloud in the warm and still air, further dirtying my already filthy blue jeans. The deprecating gesture was so like a baseball coach furious at an umpire that I began to laugh—a bit hysterically, I realized, but I could not stop myself. I doubled over, clenching at my side, hurting all over and unable to help myself. Apparently this consternated the raccoon, who kicked one final clot of dirt at me, turned, and stalked back to unharness his llama.

After I had stopped laughing and she deemed it safe, the Mayor approached me and ceremoniously tied a green cloth around my arm. If this meant I was to compete in the next round of eliminations, they were doomed to disappointment.

I looked around and saw raccoons reluctantly paying off other raccoons. I was mildly surprised there had been many takers on my side of the bet, but I realized I was a good foot taller than most of them, and much more massive, and to them I probably appeared powerful and somewhat brutish.

I looked for Truck, who should have been easy to spot because of her height, but she was nowhere in sight. Where had she gone? I hadn't seen her since the start of the race—which, I realized with some surprise, had ended only a few minutes ago. Maybe she had gone to take a leak; I didn't know. Hell with it—I was hurting from that spectacle we had just made, and I wanted to sit down. She could find me when she wanted to; I wasn't hard to miss, in this crowd.

I sat on the sidelines at the front of the crowd, even with the starting line. Raccoons approached me and signed incomprehensible things, to most of which I replied, "Understand I no," as politely as I could. It didn't seem to matter; they continued until they had finished whatever they had to sign and walked away. Some were thankful for my part in their winnings. Some had obviously been on the other end of the deal. Parents were now less reluctant to allow their kits to approach me, which surprised me—somehow it seemed my display of intelligence (or perhaps they took it for cunning) set them at ease rather than alarmed them. Whatever the reason, before long I found myself with a kit on my lap, and I was scratching her stomach and tickling her ribs, and letting her feel my fingers and bend the joints. I had cleaned my glasses with the green cloth, the only nongrimy article in my possession, and I let the kit wear them. She found this especially funny and waved her laughter with both hands. Her parents stood a cautiously close but nevertheless complimentarily far distance away, Dad drinking a mug of something that may have been beer or wine, or perhaps moonshine made from corn liquor, Mom wearing what looked like a Chinese coolie hat with holes cut for her ears, a popular sun hat among agrarian raccoons. They seemed amused by their daughter sporting my thick-lensed glasses. The glasses kept slipping off, though; the kit's head sloped, and I couldn't get the stems to tuck behind her ears.

The kit and I watched the next heat, and we picked our favorite with insistent pointings and cheered it along in the silent way of her people. It lost, and I had a grand old time.

The next two llamas were being readied. I saw by the green cloths tied around both owners' arms that it was the first elimination of the second round. Someone tugged on my hair, and I turned to see an adolescent raccoon, waist high, which made him eye-level with me as I sat with the kit on my lap. As with most raccoons, he wore no clothing save moccasins, a flat leather bag worn at the hip with the strap across the opposite shoulder, and the bracelet on one wrist. He signed something to me.

"Understand me no," I signed.

He stepped beside me, crouching a bit and glancing to be sure that no one was watching. He lifted the flap of his purse, reached in, and drew forth something that he kept concealed with his long, curled fingers. Slowly he brought the hand near my face, turned it over, and uncurled his fingers. A book of matches lay in his palm. I took it from him.

He formed a make-believe, two-fingered pistol with his right hand, pointing left, and drew it to his right: "Truck," he signed. "Come. Come you. Truck."

I caught myself nodding a reply. "Truck," I signed. "Yes."

I tickled the kit on my lap once more, then lifted her to her feet—she weighed maybe forty pounds—and scooted her along to her parents. I turned to the adolescent. "Truck," I signed.

He signed something and began to pick his way through the crowd. I followed.

It was impossible for me to just walk away from that crowd without being noticed, yet that was obviously what the adolescent wanted: he kept glancing furtively at the people looking at us and tried to appear casual as he led me along. When I realized what he was doing, I forced him to play a game of catch with a rag ball I found in the street in front of one of the featureless gray dwellings comprising most of Wait-No-More. When he understood what I was doing, he began to run with the ball after he caught it, and I would chase him down, tag him, and force him to stop and throw it to me so that I could run—sort of a two-person rugby, raccoon rules. One time I let him fake me out, dodge past me, and dart behind one of the buildings. I turned to give chase, and both of us were far from the madding crowd.

He was waiting for me behind a building. He dropped the rag ball when I rounded the corner and saw him. I signed a simple interrogative, and he pointed up the street to what I recognized as the rear of the blacksmith's shop. I followed him to it.

Behind the shop were two llamas yoked to a two-seater wagon, the back of which was full of hay. The llamas stood patiently in their yoke, munching contentedly on whatever it is llamas munch on—I think I'd rather not know, considering their other habits. One of them swiveled its long neck to regard us as we approached. It dipped its head and spat. Everyone's a critic.

The adolescent slipped the halters onto the llamas and turned to me. "There," he signed, pointing to the back of the wagon. "There you. Under." He mimed covering himself with hay.

I hesitated. Obviously he *had* seen Truck; he'd had my matchbook, and I doubted there were a great many more of those to be found in these parts. But had Truck sent him, or was something else going on?

"There," the adolescent signed again, more insistently. "Truck. Fast you."

I decided I had to trust him. Maybe Truck was in trouble. I climbed in and covered myself with hay, wedging my head in the crook of one arm so that I could breathe without getting straw up my nose. I heard the adolescent climb into the seat, and in a moment we were jouncing along. The ride was rough. I reminded myself to reinvent the shock absorber when I had the time. How *did* you make a shock absorber . . . ?

We rode for perhaps fifteen minutes. The trip was uneventful: only the clopping of llama hooves and their owners' plaintive bleating, the occasional, incidental warbling of the adolescent raccoon, and the clanking of the wagon. I wanted desperately to peek through the hay to get at least some idea of what I might be headed into but couldn't do so without taking the chance of making myself visible.

We stopped, and the adolescent scampered back and began clearing hay from me. I stood and brushed myself off, spitting out straw and shaking it out of my hair. We were in the woods and had pulled off the rutted road. There were pine trees, ivy,

Spanish bayonets, the vaguely mildewy smell of Florida wild—and little else.

"Truck," I signed to the adolescent.

He turned and clapped his hands sharply twice.

From behind a tree stepped Truck. She waved broad laughter with the hand holding the tortoiseshell pick, then brought it down and struck up a tune on the mandolute she had somehow acquired.

12
Narrative of Truck

I WORRY ABOUT the boy as [Bentley] and I watch him drive the llamas back to Wait-No-More. He is a good boy, it seems, though something of a loner and more than a little idealistic, but these are not bad traits and I think he will tell no one of our leaving.

I play my new mandolute as we walk north. It is not the finest such instrument I am owning, but it is suitably crafted and carries a tune or two. I am expecting to be elated at getting away with the instrument but find that the tunes I play as we walk are sad tunes. When I realize that I play the plodding melody that accompanies the death of the Oldmother in *Wax from a Slow-Burning Candle,* I stop the tune and bring out my feelings that I may look at them.

I am thinking that having a mandolute again will cheer me and serve to remind me of better times and the goals ahead—yet that I am taking this thing from a town so poor shames me, and the shame is knots in the thread of my music. A regret, but one I cannot now act on: I can little afford to return to Wait-No-More. North, then, we follow the road that follows the river.

Giving up the moodiness of my music for a later time and a better mood, I cease playing and set the pick above my ear. I return to [Bentley] his knapsack of odd material and odder closures, and his knife, and before he puts on the pack he places into the bottom of it the cord I am using as a leash for him in Wait-No-More. From the top of the pack he pulls out an orange and sets to peeling it with his pale and stubby hands. I move the mandolute on its strap until it is slung on my back, and it pats my fur in rhythm with my walk. [Bentley] offers me a section of his orange, which I accept with thanks.

"The pull," I sign as I chew on my tangy wedge of orange. I mime tugging on a laden sled. "(+)strong you?"

He tucks the partially peeled fruit beneath one arm to reply. "(+)smart me," he signs, and he waves a laugh.

Though his answer is amusing as a reference to the way I am getting him to enter the pull, it is seeing him laugh that makes me laugh in reply.

He hands me another wedge of orange, peels another for himself, chews, tucks the orange again beneath his arm, and spits out seeds. "Go . . . we . . . where . . . ?" he signs in his halting way. He improves, though, and in truth impresses me with how rapidly.

"North," I sign, and point the direction when I see he does not understand the sign. I use the opportunity to teach him the directions of navigation, which concept he grasps readily enough. "Town there, bigger than Wait-No-More. Understand you?"

"Understand I yes."

"Friend there mine."

He nods, but at least he accompanies this with signings to tell me he understands.

"Dumb-animal there north I?" he asks. "Dog-with-tricks?"

"Know-not me. Seeing-you I not want others. Hiding you difficult. Yes?"

He considers this, then signs, "Grow me fur." After a moment I laugh. He cannot know, I think, that "grow me fur" is a double-meaning sign, an idiomatic thing that refers to something one considers most unlikely, and it takes me a moment to realize that I am supposed to take this signing literally, and that this is intended to be a joke.

We walk a few more miles without conversing. It is difficult for him, I know, for I sense many things he wishes to sign, to ask, to see from me, for which he does not have signs—just as there are many things I wish to sign, to ask, that he is not able to understand. Time will cover this. We will be friends, this [Bentley] and I.

I am grateful for my new moccasins as we walk. They are better than those poor coverings I am making from rabbits in the wild, and I hope they shall keep me walking longer and without pain. Time will cover this as well.

After a while I hear the bleat of a llama on the road behind us, and I motion to [Bentley] to step off the road and crouch behind a stand of bushes. I hide behind a tree and hope it is not the folk of Wait-No-More come to claim their mandolute. I berate myself for being so foolish as to make myself obvious in what has become hostile territory, in a province not my own (though I am hunted in both), and for being so stupid as to follow a road, for doubtless there are few cart-worn paths in this sparsely populated area. But I am so weary of working my way through the brush!

This sort of laziness may be my undoing someday, I think.

Unseen behind my tree, glancing to be sure [Bentley] is not visible, I watch the llama come into view around the bend. The rider holds the reins of another llama that follows as docilely as any llama ever does. Rather than being rigged as a pack animal, though, the second llama is saddled and riderless. In a moment I recognize the nearer llama's rider as the physician who is treating my cuts in Wait-No-More.

I think quickly, crouching behind my tree. From our brief conversation I trust this physician; he strikes me as a perceptive, insightful sort. So I motion to [Bentley] to remain where he is for now, and I set down my mandolute and step out from behind the tree.

The physician pulls up short on the path and lowers the reins. His llama regards me askance with bright blue eyes. The physician takes his time wrapping the reins and looks at me a moment before waving a small laugh. He looks back the way he is coming, toward Wait-No-More. "You are making good time," he finally signs.

"I imagine so. I am a bit hurried."

He laughs again. "I imagine so," he signs. His llama spits into the tall grass at the side of the road. "Where is your friend?"

I motion to [Bentley], and he steps out from behind the bush where he is crouching. He brushes burrs from his leg coverings and signs a greeting to the physician. The physician glances at me and then signs a greeting back to [Bentley]. "My name is [Doc Holliday]," he signs to me.

"I am [Smith]," I reply.

"And your unusual charge there?"

"I sign him [Bentley]."

[Holliday] regards [Bentley] a moment, then looks back to me. "I am but a mediocre physician in an Outback town," he signs, "but it is not the only place I am ever living, and I am no longer a kit. Though I am not seeing such creatures as are brought back from Africa, I am reading about them and seeing drawings of them. This is no ape."

"What else is he to be, then?"

Holliday cocks his head to the side. "I do not know," he admits, "but he is more than he seems. As are you."

"What causes you to sign this?"

"I have eyes. More important, and distinguishing me from the majority of my townsfolk, I have a brain and am capable of hammering a nail through two facts to see what they form together. You are no trapper; certainly you are no trapper for such as Architect Louis XIV. You are poorly equipped, you come into Wait-No-More without even a pair of moccasins. You possess no gear to control your [Bentley] save a leash. You possess only an interesting story and a more interesting beast. You are dressing your own wounds in the wild, yet you do not know the land. Your conversation is broad, expansive, and wordly—yet is also a touch too intelligent, too subtle, and showing signs of quite an education for a simple trapper."

"And what am I to be, then, Holliday, if I am to be no mere trapper?"

"I do not know," he admits again. "Perhaps an actor? For you do carry yourself as such. Is this the thing? Are you a great actor from the east, studying for a role in a play? I am watching a play once, as a youngster in Seaport Jacksonville. I shall never forget it."

The hindmost llama snorts. [Bentley] coughs, yawns, and watches us, obviously interested, equally obviously not understanding our exchange.

"An actor, perhaps," I sign, "though this scarce suffices to explain the presence of my 'charge,' as you sign him." I pause and deliberately cock my head as he is doing a moment ago. "Goodbody Holliday, what is your interest in us?"

It is his turn to pause before signing, and I sense he composes a proper reply. "My interest in you is that you are interesting," he finally signs, "and little of interest happens to me. This, plus I cannot help but feel at the roots of my fur that you and your [Bentley] are important in a way I cannot sign. And I feel you need help—in fact, I know this, as you are so unkind as to be absconding with the well-valued prize for the pull contest. By the by, where is this instrument to be found? Are you managing to sell it already?"

"Selling it is not my intent. I note that the item in question bears the mark of the House [Gibson], a well-regarded but nonetheless mediocre wright, and it is my chagrin to admit that I am yearning for it at the pull because I have a long trip ahead and am thinking to play it as I walk. It reminds me of past times. Better times."

"I see. Well, the people of Wait-No-More are none too happy at having no choice in being so kind as to present it to you. They feel slighted—and well they should, I must add—and many look for you even now."

"As with yourself."

"No. I seek you out that I may ask to accompany you."

"Goodbody Holliday, you do not know who we are. You do not know our destination. You know only that I am not a trapper, that I am a thief, and that my traveling companion is a freakish sort of creature who might snap you in two on a whim. You wish to accompany us?"

"Is this so odd a thing? I am helping you, back in my shop where I am keeping my practice for eight years now, and have more than a little reason to suspect you are tangling with Stripes to receive such scars—which fact also tells me that you are tangling with Stripes and are still able to tell me of it. An impressive thing, this notion."

"If true," I add.

"Certainly. But little interesting is happening to me, as I am signing, and I am not young anymore, and I feel an urge I am not feeling in a good long time—the urge to simply leave everything behind, to go where the pollen may blow. Surely you feel this at times? You seem fairly young; surely you are not so old as to be losing this."

"I feel it," I acknowledge. "At times. But tell me, you sign that you feel we are important. Why do you think this? Someone tangling with Stripes is likely a criminal."

"It is but a feeling. Sometimes I get them. Sometimes they are true. Often they are not, but I know the true ones when they bristle my fur."

"Few are so fortunate."

He gestures with what I see is feigned indifference. "It is rarely useful," he signs.

"It seems it is bringing you here. Tell me, Doc Holliday, how are you knowing where to find us?"

He laughs broadly. "You are the victim of the nature of towns the size of Wait-No-More," he signs. "Everybody knows everybody. The boy who is helping you leave town is a kit I am fathering not long after taking up my practice here. I and his mother are becoming friends over the years, and he is an intelligent boy who often confides in me—and with candor."

I sign a motion of mock disgust. "My fortune is always such," I sign.

"It is of no consequence. It brings me to you, and that is my good fortune. Or, I hope this is so."

"You surprise me, Holliday," I sign, and it is my turn to laugh. "To claim to be seeing some small part of the world in your time, and yet to be so quickly trusting. As I am signing, you *know* I am a thief, you suspect I am tangling with Stripes, and yet you deliver two good llamas, what seems a good traveling pack, and your naïve self directly to us!"

"And that is fine with me, for I am bringing them for you. They will assist you greatly in your flight from the townsfolk, who search for you even as we sign."

"A point well taken! But my charge cannot ride such beasts as these. He is too large."

"His legs are quite long. Surely he can lope alongside with ease?"

"I do not know. But he is certainly capable of walking a good distance without rest, and his stride is quite difficult to match. Very well, Doc Holliday, you shall accompany us—for a time, anyway—and I shall ride and my . . . [Bentley] . . . shall walk beside us. And . . . I thank you for this."

"It is no great sacrifice, as I sign. I long for the new."

"There is rarely safety there."

"Of course I respect your privacy," signs Holliday as we ride alongside one another on our llamas. [Bentley] walks to my left, a hand constantly ruffling the fur of my mount. He ceases attempting to follow our conversation and seems to settle into watching the countryside. It is nearly sunset and a breeze stirs the trees, ruffles my fur, cools my nose. The road is only two wheel ruts worn into the grass, barely discernible this far north of Wait-No-More. "But," continues Holliday, "since I know your charge is more than he seems, as you are signing yourself, I wonder what he is in actuality, if not a freakish sort of ape."

Though Holliday interests me, only half my mind is on my reply. I think of the town toward which we head, the town of Three Big Dogs, which Holliday signs is three days away at the speed we now travel, possibly four. I know someone there and can set in motion a process I am certain will be long in the undertaking. But though I think this, my signing shows nothing of it. "He is something of a puzzle to me as well," I admit. "I have only ideas on it. Being a physician yourself, I assume you know the notions of inheritance of family traits?"

"Yes. They are intriguing."

"In heredity, each of us carries a combination of traits which interact with those of our mates. A negative balance may be tipped, if negative traits are so predisposed, and a malformed or moronic kit is the result. Reckoning on the next finger, however, there is also the favorable offspring, who is intelligent in an almost inexplicable way—who composes symphonies and adds any quantity of seven-digit numbers on [her/his] hands years before adolescence, who begins to sign even before [her/his] vision clears as a kit. Such, according to this notion, are produced in the same manner as the malformed and the moronic—but under favorable predispositions rather than negative."

"And you believe this is the case with [Bentley]."

"I *believe* nothing. I speculate. Possibly he *is* descended from apes and is somehow the culmination of a continuous handing-down of traits—a consequence of random interactions working in his favor."

"An accident, then?"

"In a manner of signing, I suppose, yes. And an accident not to be repeated—for what are the odds, I wonder, against the random combination of traits leading to one such as he?"

"Impossible to know, of course," signs Holliday. "But such improbabilities are producing our entire world, and"— he tugs the fur at his chest, where it is grayest—"ourselves."

I think on this a long time.

My hands are slick with sweating in the late afternoon heat, and I drink much water and am thankful that Holliday is foresighted enough to bring along two filled waterbags of a good size. It is a while since I am riding, and my back and the base of my tail are sore. The three of us bat at the gnats that assail us in a cloud, and after we pass through them we laugh at one another as we spit them out. Holliday and I brush them from our fur. [Bentley] is fortunate in this respect—though, thinking of it as I ruffle my fur to rid myself of the gnats, I wonder how he gets along in the wintertime. Perhaps the coverings he wears do him service then, but they are so thin! I will see him in winter several times since this time of gnats and wondering, of course, and will discover that he does quite poorly indeed in the cold and snow and wind—further proof, I think, of his descent—ascent?—from mothers-before in Africa, which from all reports is always hot.

"The way to settle this speculation of [Bentley's] origin," signs Holliday long after we pass the storm of gnats, "is to ask him. He seems to sign rather well."

"Rather well indeed. But he is only just learning to sign, and does not yet know the signs to understand the question, let alone answer it." *But,* I promise myself, *someday I shall ask, and he shall answer.*

In the cool evening we eat fruits from [Bentley's] pack, tossing out the rinds I am placing in the pack earlier, at the inn. They are beginning to rot. Some we feed to the llamas. Also we eat breads and meats brought along by Holliday, who is managing to bring much, for someone leaving his town in such a hurry. We water the llamas from a scum-covered pond and hitch them to pine trees for the night. After our meal Holliday brushes down his mount and soothes it. I ignore mine. Though I am grateful to Holliday for bringing it, truth to tell it is a cranky beast—even for a llama—and I am not fond of it. It tries to bite me once and to kick [Bentley] once. It shits where it will, in the manner of llamas, but there is something almost of malicious delight it takes in the act—braying and kicking about, sending its excrement flying. It does not endear me.

To [Bentley] I teach language again this night, after the manner of teaching to kits: I mold his hands to shape the words, point to what they represent, form the word myself, and encourage him to independently form the sign. I have little to offer as reward for his quickness save encouragement and enthusiasm, but this seems more than enough. I think him nearly as smart as a raccoon, to watch the speed with which he learns, and to see the initiative he takes with what he is taught—

sometimes to disconcerting effect, as he is demonstrating in Wait-No-More. My notion of entering that town unobtrusively and learning with equal subtlety (what subtlety I can muster, that is, for I am not generally known for it) proves fruitless, and the fault lies not entirely—or even largely—with [Bentley]. Of this I think: I am too used to attention, even when it can do me little but harm.

Late this night, asleep, I dream a True dream.

I lie on the grass and watch the stars watching the turning of the earth. [Repeat] rises as the slit of a cougar's eye this night, and is toward first quarter when at last I close my eyes to sleep and dream. It does not catch up to [Pete] this night in their constant, headlong flight and chase, and will not be in transit for a few nights yet. And this transit of [Pete] by [Repeat] becomes the harbinger of my True dream, and I yield to the turbulence and flow with it:

—The moons move quickly across the sky. Repeat passes Pete, then passes again, and again, until nine transits occur. On the last transit the moons stop moving. They hang motionless in the sky.

—I look down upon a large bucket of water resting upon a dining table laden with fruits, vegetables, and many meats. Several raccoons sit conversing at the table. I cannot distinguish their faces or their signings.

—A stone plummets into the bucket of water. It is only a pebble, really, but the splash it makes is huge, and the water hisses as if the stone is quite hot. The ripple that spreads from the splash rushes to the side of the bucket and spills over the edge. The water splashes onto the table and flows across the platters. It ruins the food and knocks over mugs.

—The bucket continues to overflow, and the water spills from the edges of the table onto one of the seated raccoons. He jumps up from his chair, and I see now that it is [Napoleon], the Architect of Sleep for [the Union] province to the North of me.

—Another raccoon is wet, and it is Louis XIV, Architect of Sleep for [Florida/Cuba] province.

—Yet another raccoon is wet, and it is me.

—The water flows from the bucket for a long time before it stops.

• • •

These images disperse like steam from a kettle boiling in the wind, and I ride the remainder of the night in the hold of true sleep, dreamless and without wake. Thinking, that dissection by the brain, is not for now. Thinking will come with waking, tomorrow.

In the morning we continue north, Holliday and I on our llamas, [Bentley] trudging beside us. I play my mandolute and ponder and puzzle the dream of last night, while Holliday, riding ahead of me, attempts what conversation he may with [Bentley]. I only half pay attention, and if I am not so preoccupied with my analysis I would find it funny. As I recollect it, the signings are something like this:

"Who are you?" asks Holliday.

"[Bentley] me," my odd companion signs, and my ears twitch with a kind of pleasure that he uses the name I am giving him.

"No," signs Holliday. He takes a drink from his water flask, which I know is to delay conversation while he frames his question more accurately.

"Drink me?" signs [Bentley] as Holliday corks the flask.

Holliday cocks his head to the side. He loops the flask on the long saddle horn and signs, "What?"

"Water," signs [Bentley]. "Drink me? Please?" The politeness he adds is a moderate one, signed slowly as though making a request of a child.

Holliday glances at me. I continue playing my mandolute and sign nothing. He looks back to [Bentley], then unwinds the cord from around the saddle horn and passes the flask. [Bentley] uncorks it, squeezes out many swallows, recorks it, and hands it back. He wipes his mouth with his arm and signs gratitude. Holliday replaces the flask. "Where are you from?" he signs.

"I-am-sorry," [Bentley] replies. "Slow and easy, please?"

Holliday shakes his head a moment, then scratches at the fur on his shoulder. "From you?" he signs, elaborately forming the interrogative.

"Other place me. Different. Many differents. [Bentleys] there . . . same raccoons here."

"I do not understand, [Bentley]."

[Bentley] clenches his fists and looks around himself. He looks at me, but I just play, only half watching, thinking about my dream and thinking as well that he must learn to not always rely on me.

"Many [Bentleys] there," he finally signs to Holliday. "Many me's."

"You are from Africa, then?"

"No understand I."

Holliday turns in his saddle to face me. "How do you learn anything from him at all?" he asks. "I barely understand him, and what little I figure out makes littler sense."

I think it is rude to interrupt the playing of a musician in this way, but I set my pick above my ear, clamp the mandolute between one leg and the warm fur of my mount, and answer with deliberate formality. "I grow used to it. You shall do the same if you persist." And I lift up the mandolute and retrieve my pick from my fur.

Holliday turns back huffily and attempts to continue his conversation with [Bentley], who by my reckoning is a great deal more patient than Holliday.

I ignore them and play.

There are many modes in which I like to play. Today I puzzle, for I must interpret my dream, and thus most appropriate is a patterning mode well suited for the unraveling of problems. I pick at the strings (which are old and need replacing), concentrating on the simplicity of the melody and letting the theme echo my dream. I begin with a gossamer thread, a single strand, and slowly add more threads. Playing, I weave and interweave, and listen to my playing. Listening, I am drawn into the pattern and am amazed at the mathematical interlocking of all the parts. I trill at the discovery of a thread of color running a contrasting path through the web of music. It is a randomness in the order, and the web shifts and alters. . . . It is as though I am in a cocoon of music, and I do not realize it until I am looking out from within the unfolding layers of sound.

I have seen it signed that this is an unnatural kind of music. Many do not like it. It is described as the music of machines, a music of artificial patterning and order that does not occur in nature. But the universe—worlds turning, orbiting around their sun, moons orbiting the worlds—*is* a machine. It is patterned and ordered, and so the music of order is the music of nature, even including this strand of chaos, this color of randomness. So I let the melody carry and shift and become something it does not sound like when first it begins, and I let it grow disjointed and then cohesive, and soon it is simple again, and it is decaying as it seems it should, and I allow it to slow and it lets me go.

I set the pick above my ear and sling the mandolute, and I think on what this tells me of my True dream.

It is bad, this dream. Few will believe me when I tell what it portends, unless it is dreamed by others as well.

In nine transits a stone will fall from the sky. It will be a huge stone, and hot, and it will land in the ocean south and east of Seaport [Savannah], capital city of my province of [the Confederacy]. From this impact shall come a huge wave. It will wash over the land for kilospans inland, destroying crops, flooding villages, rendering many thousands homeless and drowning many who are unprepared. This wave will extend almost as far north as [Napoleon's] province of [the Union], and as far south as Louis XIV's province of [Florida/Cuba]. Seaports [Savannah] and Jacksonville must be prepared.

After the wave will come rain. Many days of rain, perhaps as long as half a transit. This will worsen the flooding and ruin the attempts of farmers to salvage their crops and livestock. The shipping trades will be ruined. All ships at sea when the wave comes will be lost. Many buildings will be destroyed. The Keep in Seaport Savannah is sturdy enough that I do not think it will collapse, but it will nevertheless be unsafe to inhabit until after the rains. The bodies of the drowned will be many, too many to collect and cremate, and disease will spread. There will be plague.

This must not be. I cannot allow this; the provinces must be warned or thousands will die. It will be years before the provinces recover, perhaps even a lifetime.

And now I have only nine transits in which to accomplish my goal.

And me here on the road in Florida with an Outback physician and an intelligent ape!

I look up from my ponderings. Holliday signs something to [Bentley], who replies, and both wave broad laughter.

I cannot tell them of this True dream. To do so would be to reveal more about myself than I dare. [Bentley] would not understand, but Holliday would immediately know who and what I am. I like him, but I cannot reveal myself to him or anyone. Not yet.

I have learned that it is impossible to interfere with a True dream. One simply prepares; the knife is already tossed, the forces of circumstance are at work, and either the point or the haft lands, as it may. One dreams which it will be, but one does not redirect. There is fate and there is will, and will cannot alter fate, though indifferent fate can act upon the most impassioned will.

This resignedness embitters me, but what am I to do? I can only concentrate on the particulars of the True dream, interpret it and draw what conclusions and make what plans I may.

I have much thinking to do.

13
Narrative of James Bentley

I LIKED DOC HOLLIDAY. He had a simple, direct sense of humor that I had little trouble understanding, even with my quite limited knowledge of the gestural language, and he was curious about me for my intelligence and uniqueness in his universe rather than for my freakishness and talking-doggishness. He went out of his way to communicate with me, even though it was obviously a frustrating, time-consuming process that little enlightened him about my nature. Still, he was curious in an open and likable way, and I was more than willing to attempt to answer his questions in my fumbling manner. I named him Doc Holliday because, obviously, he was a physician, and because he practiced in an Outback town.

Doc and I traded questions that mostly went unanswered and an occasional attempt at humor, while behind us Truck remained intent on playing her mandolute. Sometimes her playing sounded like music. Sometimes it sounded like she was trying to pull the mandolute apart. Once I interrupted Doc by looking at Truck when her music echoed the sound of Tangerine Dream so closely I'd have almost sworn she was imitating their style.

A surprising number of Doc's questions concerned Truck. From what I could gather, he was nearly as curious about her as he was about me. At least, the questions were much the same: Who was she? Where was she from? How had we met; how had I come into her hands?

I'd have given a lot to be able to answer any of these except how we had met, which of course I already knew.

He stopped me after I had signed Truck's name a few times and informed me that Truck had given him a different sign for her name, one in which the closed fist patted the chest twice and then opened palm-up toward the observer. Doc told me it was a common name, so I mentally tagged it as "Smith."

Doc wanted to know why Truck had given herself a different name to each of us. I could only spread my hands.

We whiled away the afternoon in this manner, querying each other while Truck provided ostensibly musical accompaniment. Near sunset Truck urged her mount beside Doc in order to converse with him. She had slung her mandolute across her back, and I interrupted her signing to ask if I might borrow it for a while. She drew it over her head and handed it to me, then removed the tortoiseshell pick from the fur over her right ear, gave it to me, and resumed her conversation with Doc without any further acknowledgment of me. Well, fine. She had been silent—I mean, she had not *signed* anything—almost all day, and maybe now she felt like signing to someone in something more than baby talk.

I loosened the mandolute strap as far as it would go, drew it over my shoulder, and clasped the pick in my right hand. Though I am left-handed, I have always played the guitar in right-handed fashion, neck pointing to the left. For what it's worth, I also bat right-handed, shoot a rifle right-eyed, shoot a pistol left-eyed, throw, write, and paint with my left hand, and pull a bow left-handed (which means you pull with the left hand and favor the left eye). If these favoritisms mean anything, I'd be curious to know; mostly it just meant I was clumsy when trying something for the first time. Perhaps I was latently anti-ambidextrous: equally inept with both hands.

I fiddled with the mandolute—pardon my phraseology—as shadows lengthened and dusk settled in, until I could find my way around the C scale, which was not easy with a fretless mandolute tuned to a different scale. Once I had an approximation of the C scale, though, I was in business. Sure, there were chords I couldn't strum—most of them, in fact—but I could pluck out melodies and get two-string harmonies. So I went through an awkward version of the first few bars from *Duelling Banjoes*, as much of *Stairway to Heaven* as I could manage—or as much as I cared for, anyway—and then just began improvising simple, monotonous melodies that helped make walking easier.

Later we ate quail—Doc turned out to be every bit as good a rock thrower as Truck; the ability was innate in the raccoons—and then Truck and Doc unceremoniously unfurled bedrolls, flopped down on them, and were soon sleeping away. Truck was perfectly motionless in her sleep. Doc chittered a little bit and "talked" in his sleep, hands flowing in lackluster gestures as he presumably held dream conversations.

The night was cloudy, but not overly so. Though tired from walking all day, I found I could not sleep—an understandable problem, considering what I had gone through, what I was *still* going through. So I leaned against a palm tree, water flask beside my hip, and stared up at the moons I had christened Pete and Repeat as they dipped horns in the night sky. Right now the little moon was about the breadth of an extended finger from the larger. Last night it had been about three finger-widths distant before moonset, so I expected that by the end of the night it would be beginning its transit. Tomorrow night, if the sky wasn't too cloudy, I would get to see it as a mote in the center of Pete's crescent, then as an emerging star cradled in the cusp, just like that line in *The Rime of The Ancient Mariner* describing "The hornèd Moon, with one bright star/ Within the nether tip." I frowned. Upon reflection, I wasn't sure what it would look like. Astronomy had never been my strong suit; I had a romantic rather than hard-science interest in the field (not, I should point out, that the two are mutually exclusive, Walt Whitman poems about learned astronomers to the contrary). It seemed to me, from what little time I had spent watching the strange, new moons, that their phases changed rather rapidly. How rapidly? I wondered. I had always been amazed at how people learned to figure out that sort of thing. I had, after all, been a lit major.

I was still wondering when I fell asleep.

The next day was pretty much a replay of the day before. Truck nudged me awake. She and Doc rolled up their bedrolls, tied them to their respective llamas, unhitched them from the palm trees to which they had been tied all night, and mounted up. Truck asked me if I wanted to play her mandolute. I signed that I did not.

She seemed even more petulant and moody today than yesterday. She also seemed in a hurry, and I was hard-pressed to keep up with the llamas. These were draft animals, really, not the leaner, swifter, riding variety, and though their speed was not great, their endurance was admirable, and they bore their loads with grace and dignity—for llamas. Which meant only a moderate amount of complaining whines and snorts. But not only did the beasts smell like a clothes hamper, they also had a disconcerting habit of staring directly at you with the snottiest I-Told-You-So expression while pointedly dropping llama patties behind them. I have come to rely on llamas, but I do not believe I shall ever develop any great fondness for them; they're smart enough to know how to be mean.

I tried to ask Truck what was wrong, but she only flurried her fingers in a small, polite gesture that meant, "It is nothing," but really meant, "I don't want to sign about it." I gave up and conversed haltingly with Doc. Behind us Truck began playing the mandolute.

"Smith has much beneath her fur," Doc signed to me.

"I don't understand," I replied. Each day my "grasp" of the sign language grew a little better, my "grammar" more proper.

"More Smith than Smith I see. Yes?"

"I do not know. She . . . signs me little. And I . . . understand so little."

"Yes," acknowledged Doc. "Smith signs me little, also. [Bentley], more she is than a trapper. Yes?"

"Think me this, too. But know me so little."

"Know you what of Smith? Sign of her, and perhaps we may piece from it many small things that we may see as one thing. Yes?"

"I know she knows hunting. I know she knows the Outback. I know she is . . . good, and helps me much. I know I. . . ." What was the sign for "trust"? It was hard to ask what the sign was for an abstraction, which wasn't something I could point to and ask about. "I know I hold to her fur. Yes? I . . . follow her."

Doc turned to regard Truck before signing. I glanced back as well. Truck was lost in her playing, eyes closed, hands caressing her mandolute. "I hold to her fur, also, [Bentley]. I [trust] her. Why, I do not know, but she grows this in me. Yes?"

Doc had taken to automatically asking "Yes?" at the end of every statement to be sure I was following. Sometimes a conversation had to occur in painfully slow stages while I learned a new sign, or metaphor, or concept, before I could progress to the next, and the intermittent queries were an efficient way of checking to be sure I hadn't become mired somewhere along the way. What I give here is a cleaned-up version of my conversation with Doc, and the case is much the same with my early converse with most other raccoons, including Truck, for the simple truth is that my dialogue with Doc lasted for hours, and this is only the part of it I managed to understand. The false interpretations, inabilities to contextualize, and just plain ignorance on my part firmed a wedge between Doc and myself and effective communication. Most of what he signed I did not understand, or if I did, I did not know how to reply; most of what I signed was incorrect goggledygook to him. Such was the case with virtually all "conversations"—if such they can be called—of which I was part until I had the chance to spend a bed-ridden month saturated in sign-language and culture tutelage. But I'm getting ahead of myself. Again.

I took Doc's sign "grow," in telling me Truck "grew" trust in him, also, to mean "inspires." It was a quality I thought I could perceive in Truck—something about her inspired trust. She was confident, and intent on something. It seemed she had a mission, though neither Doc nor I could figure out just what it was, but obviously we both had enough faith in her to accompany her toward a goal the two of us found vague at best.

Doc was certainly no slouch when it came to inspiring confidence, either. Though he didn't have quite that . . . *charisma* . . . that Truck possessed, he nevertheless went out of his way to be friendly to me, and I sensed that there was more to his friendliness than just his interest in grilling me about Truck and my own peculiar nature. I got the feeling, though I am unable to express exactly why, that Doc liked me, plain and simple. Which is why it saddened me so much when he died.

It was evening, and for a change the breeze was cool. We had not lit a fire for dinner, so our meal consisted of hard breads and dried beef Doc had brought along. The night was clear and the moons rose bright above the horizon. Repeat was a growing bite in the outside edge of Pete's waxing crescent.

Truck did not play her mandolute after dinner, as had become her custom, but instead sat straight-backed against a tree, eyes hard and bright and alert in the moonlight. I asked her if I might play the instrument for a while, and she refused without explanation. She seemed sullen and reserved.

Though my muscles were tired from walking, I was not sleepy in the least, and it was no more than a few hours past sunset—call it eight o'clock. Doc had seen to the care and feeding of the llamas and was off at the edge of the small clearing we had picked for our evening's encampment, brushing down the beasts' thick fur with a bristle brush.

I decided it would certainly do me no harm to stretch out a bit. I had not truly worked out since my arrival here, and the long marches each day were pulling my hamstrings into steel cables, my calves into knots, and tightening my back muscles so much that it hurt to lie down and relax. Normally I am quite flexible, so I was horrified when I attempted to touch my palms to the ground with my legs straight and found I could come no closer than six inches without pain knifing up the backs of my thighs. I took it slow and attained what flexibility I could. It would certainly make walking easier if I stretched out each night before I went to bed, but I could hurt myself if I pushed too hard. A few years earlier I had severely strained my left hamstring by overstretching it, and it had taken a year to heal to a condition that was still less than healthy. In cold weather it makes its presence known a few inches above the back of my knee.

Aikido is not too strenuous—that is, the simpler exercises are not; it's getting up from the mat after anywhere from fifty to a hundred breakfalls a session that hurts—so I ran through standard aikido preliminaries to loosen my wrists and ankles, and for the relaxing fluidity of the movements.

After he had finished with the llamas Doc watched unobtrusively as I worked through a toned-down version of my old routine. The night was hot despite the cool breeze, and I took off my T-shirt long before I had done much more than basic stretching. Doc trilled as I removed my shirt. He pointed to my hairless chest, scratched at the fur on his own, and laughed. I waved a laugh in reply, laughing out loud as well, and he ducked his head sheepishly and signed a friendly apology.

Soon Truck had joined him in watching me, and I was keenly aware of their presence as I kicked, punched, *ukemi*ed, and practiced forms in the tall grass. I kept glancing their way, for though I was accustomed to working out in front of strangers, I had seldom exercised in front of anyone stranger than two giant, intelligent raccoons. Truck and Doc looked on without comment as the evening deepened, and soon it was easy to ignore them altogether because of the growing darkness. I became aware of their chittering, though, and by then I had been around them long enough to know that this is a sound of agitation. Dripping sweat, brushing wet hair from my eyes, I retrieved my glasses, pushed them back on, and went to Truck and Doc. Doc was leaning with his right hand against a tree, absently scratching his sheathed penis with the other hand and looking a bit perturbed. Truck had her arms folded across her chest and her head lowered, regarding me as an old man might peer over the tops of his spectacles. She seemed quite upset.

"Wrong do I?" I signed, remembering the consternation my jump-spin kick had caused in Wait-No-More.

Truck unfolded her arms and signed. "Taught this, you?" She mimed grappling motions and threw a few looping, exaggerated punches. Because of her long hands, her fists were huge.

"Learned this, me," I answered. "Wrong what is?"

Doc pushed himself away from the tree against which he had been leaning. "[Bentley]," he signed. "Are you [ ]?"

"I do not understand. [ ]?" The sign was a curt motion across the top of the head, as though indicating to a barber where you make your part.

"[ ]," signed Truck, repeating the new gesture. "One-who-fights."

I bit my lower lip. How to answer that? Was I a fighter? Well, yes, I had been taught two martial arts and could technically, I suppose, be considered a fighter. But "[fighter]" could also mean mercenary, or soldier, or even bully. I mulled it over for a few minutes while Doc regarded me worriedly and Truck kept glancing at the moons. Finally I signed, "Fight-knowing me. Fight-taught me. '[Fighter]' no me. Yes?"

Neither responded. Truck glanced again at the sky, and I followed her gaze. Repeat was just emerging into the cusp of Pete's waxing crescent. Truck looked down at her feet. She still seemed extremely agitated, though Doc appeared to have relaxed a bit when I had denied that I was a fighter.

Truck turned and sniffed the air, looking . . . pensive? I motioned to get Doc's attention and asked, "Wrong what is?"

"[Fighters] bad," was all he signed.

And then Truck's and Doc's ears pricked up. Doc's eyes

went wide. Truck turned to him and they signed a brief exchange that was too fast for me to follow, ending with Truck dashing off to our campsite. Doc and I watched her go, then Doc turned to me and signed, "Stay here, in the clearing. Understand?"

"Yes. Wrong what is?"

"Wait."

Then I heard the barking of the dogs.

It was a high-pitched, choppy, almost complaining kind of bark that I associated with small dogs of the sort generally smothered in the arms of rich, fat women—the yip of a Fifi, a Poopsie, a Babykins. The barking came toward us.

Truck returned in a hurry. She had her shoulder bag in one hand and my knife in the other. Before I could ask her anything she pressed the knife into my hand and then opened the bag, reached in, and pulled out a handful of rocks. She gave them to Doc, then reached in again and pulled out a single rock for herself—a fossilized scallop, by the look of it, though it was difficult to tell in the darkness.

The yipes of the dogs were near now, and Truck and Doc turned toward the sound of them crashing through the brush.

I smelled something musky and heavy. It came from Doc and Truck. A glandular excretion.

For raccoons, the "stink of fear" is an actuality.

The dogs emerged into the clearing, racing toward us, and then they were on us.

There were two of them, white, big, and fast. One headed to my right, toward Truck or Doc; I was suddenly too busy to know which, because the other one ran straight for me.

Fighting a dog is no big deal. People generally get hurt by dogs either because they surprise the dog and it snaps at them unexpectedly or because they hesitate when the dog attacks—and a dog interprets prolonged eye contact as a sign of aggression. The fact is that one swift, well-aimed kick ought to end your dog problem real fast.

One swift, well-aimed kick almost cost me my leg.

The dog leapt at me without breaking stride. I kicked just as its front paws left the ground, aiming for beneath its lower jaw or for its throat; I wasn't fussy. Curse the night, curse my poor vision, for though I wore my glasses, they were, as I have said, a prescription sadly out of date. In the darkness and in my blindness I did not see the spiked collar it wore, and I sliced open my left leg at midshin. I didn't feel a thing as the spike that slid into my flesh cut through nerves and opened up an artery. The kick slowed the dog, and the animal twisted aside, landed on its back, and wriggled to its feet. I kicked it again as it got up, hearing ribs crack, and a streak of blood, the color of chocolate syrup in the darkness, splashed onto its white fur as my severed artery gouted, and *then* I knew I had been cut. Not only could I not feel the wound, I could no longer feel anything below it. The dog yelped as its ribs broke, and it curled in on itself and snapped at my foot. I kicked it again and heard its teeth *chok* together as its head snapped up and it flopped backward. I squatted, jumped up, and landed on the dog, thrusting down with both heels just before I hit. It grunted as the air was forced from its lungs, and then it breathed no more.

I stumbled off the dead dog and fell to one knee. I pushed up my pants leg and clamped both hands around the cut. There was a lot of blood, and its warm slickness on my skin made it hard to stem the flow. If I can't stop it, I thought, I'll die.

I looked at Truck and Doc. The other dog lay several yards in front of them, its head a darkened mess. Doc was fishing another rock from Truck's purse. Truck saw me and hurried over. She knelt before me, saw the extent of my wound, turned around, and signed quickly to Doc, who hurried to the tree where I had hung my shirt. Truck forced my hands out of her way and clamped her own long hands around the cut. Doc returned with my shirt; I gave him my knife and he cut the shirt into long strips. Truck let him begin bandaging my leg and then turned, rock in hand, to survey the thicket of avocado trees from which the dogs had emerged.

Doc made speedy work of the bandage, firmly tying the knot opposite the wound. He could not sign to me while his hands were busy, and I couldn't sign anything to him while he worked on my wound. I cursed aloud while Doc worked quickly, and when he was finished he returned my knife and helped me to my feet. Foot, actually, since I could only set my weight on my right leg. I was shaking. "What was that all about?" In my fear and confusion—and shock—I asked the question aloud. "What's going on?" I tried to walk on my left foot, and my weight made it feel like an overinflated balloon that was about to burst, a burning sensation that red-edged my vision. "God-damn," and my breath hissed in.

Doc looked frightened. His furry arm around my naked waist trembled as he helped me walk.

Truck chittered excitedly. I looked at her and a chill went down my spine.

The fur at the back of her neck was standing on end and bristling down the length of her back. I turned to see what she was looking at, and I saw them emerge from the copse at about the same time I heard the *whoo* as a rock shot past my ear. Truck twitched her arm and her own rock hissed away, striking one of them on the arm with a sharp *thock!*, as if it had hit wood, and spinning him completely around.

There were two of them. They were raccoons, and they were nearly my size. They stalked toward us. The one on the right let fly a rock, and I heard it hit Doc in the midsection. He crumpled, clutching at his stomach, and vomited, and I was forced to hop on my right leg.

They kept coming.

Truck threw another rock when they were fifty feet away. Her target twitched an arm and the rock was batted aside with a sharp report. Neither of the two huge raccoons broke stride.

I glanced at Doc. He was struggling to catch his breath and regain his feet. I bent and pulled him up, almost falling down myself in the process, so I missed it when the raccoon on the left threw his final rock. I felt it, though: it felt exactly as if a car door had slammed on my right biceps. I screamed in surprise and pain, and spun around, letting go of Doc and clutching my arm. The pain rasped behind my eyes, so intense I entirely forgot about my wounded leg. I whirled to face the two approaching raccoons—thirty-five feet away now—and drew my knife. I flicked it open with one hand and walked forward, not even noticing that I had set my full weight on my left leg. I brandished the knife and stepped over the corpse of the dog that had wounded me. "Motherfuck you!" I screamed—uselessly, of course.

Truck grabbed the waist of my blue jeans and yanked me backward. I glared at her and turned to confront my unknown assailants, but she signed a curt "No." Air hissed behind me and I glanced back to see Doc completing his follow-through, then heard the *thock* as the rock was deflected. I couldn't follow even the blur of the rock in the darkness; the raccoons' night vision must have been incredible. Certainly their reflexes were.

The two raccoons made an odd waving motion with their

right arms that somehow caused them to elongate, and when they flashed in the moonlight I saw that the right arm of each attacker now ended in several metal blades.

Then there wasn't time to look at anything else because they waded into us and the fighting began.

A bladed hand swung for me, and I leaned back and kicked out with my bad leg—better to kick with it than to try standing on it. I connected, my heel hitting the huge raccoon on the hip, but the jolt of contact probably hurt me as much as I had hurt it. The kick stopped the swing, though, and I lashed out with my knife to cut the extended arm. My blade scraped across my opponent's forearm, and it was only then that I realized the blades emerging from his knuckles were part of a heavy coverlet shielding his right forearm. That armored arm attempted to reverse direction and open me up with a backswing; I moved in close along its line of attack and guided the arm and the raccoon's torso in a variation of *tenshi-nagi* that left the raccoon on the ground with a deep cut along his rib cage. His fur was hard to slash through, however, and the cut was not deep enough to put him out of commission. The raccoon jabbed to prevent me from dancing in while he was down, and as he jabbed he got back to his feet—and his eyes widened as the pain of the knife wound hit him. He trilled loudly and jabbed at my stomach. I stepped off at an oblique angle, intending to stab him in the chest as I did so—but I didn't know that Doc was beside me, and my foot caught on his and I tripped.

It saved me.

It killed Doc.

The blades sank into his chest almost to the wielder's knuckles. The raccoon put a foot against Doc's stomach and pushed him off. He turned for me without glancing back as Doc fell away, but I was already behind him. I stabbed him in the back of the neck, and then I grabbed him in a half nelson to immobilize the flailing, bladed arm. Since my knife was now against the side of his neck, I jerked it left and slit his throat. I pushed him away and he fell face first, dying as he hit the ground.

I hurried to Doc. My leg gave out as I reached him.

There was a lot of blood. It flowed from four inch-wide wounds in his chest, darkening matted fur. He lay on his back, limbs spasming. Truck, having dealt with her opponent, was already hunched over him, but there was nothing she could do.

"Doc," I said.

Truck looked up at the sound of my voice. I glanced to where her opponent lay, right arm up in a grotesque salute, pinned in place by the blades that had been shoved beneath his chin.

A liquidy cough made me look back. Blood streamed from Doc's mouth, and his breath rasped. I knelt by him and propped him up, facing Truck. His head was rolling wildly, but suddenly it stopped. His vision cleared and his eyes grew lucid. He looked at me. His arms jerked up. "[Bentley]," he signed. He spat blood and looked at Truck. "Who . . . are you?" he signed.

"I am Truck," she replied, and then she signed something I didn't understand. It brought life into Doc's face, a light that was like a door opening behind his eyes. Then his eyelids fluttered and he coughed up blood and his limbs trembled violently and the door closed and he died in my arms.

We stared at his body for a long time. Finally Truck looked at me. "No dream this me," she signed, trilling softly, a sound like a forlorn pigeon. "No dream this me," she repeated. Her eyes narrowed and she stood. "Hate dreams me! Understand you?"

"No, Truck. Understand I no."

She looked at Doc's body, at the bodies of our two opponents, then at the two moons in the sky. Repeat was ending its transit of Pete and was beginning to slip from the larger moon's curved embrace. Truck looked at me. "Understand you no," she signed, and turned away.

I stood up, intending to follow her, but the blood drained from my head and I passed out.

I woke up to find myself surrounded by fur, coarse and warm. My head was being stroked, and I heard the trillings of a mournful bird: Truck held me in her lap. I was shivering and in shock from blood loss and from a bruised right biceps already so swollen that I could not move my arm. I reeled from the shock of the new, the shock of the lost. Shirtless and cold; seeing murder, having killed; babbling at the small, yellow pearl of Repeat gradually widening the distance from the thickened crescent of Pete; hating this world onto which I had somehow stumbled, into which I had been thrust; hating that I could express this to no one there. Deaf, dumb, and ignorant in a world where I could hear, speak, and think; confused, tired, and hurt, I wanted to just throw up my hands and take my ball and bat and go *home*. . . .

And Truck held me and stroked my hair and trilled and provided an anchor that kept me from drifting too far away, so that, after moons-set and before dawn, I emerged, numb but ready to try and learn what had happened, to understand what was going on here, even though that might take years.

Truck helped me drag myself to an avocado tree, and I leaned against the trunk while she slowly, patiently, and laboriously explained that we had to move on, that, though I was hurt, she needed my help putting things together so she could take me with her, and that the night's events had made it paramount that she hurry. She was being hunted, she told me, and we were in a land that was not her own, and she needed to get away from here and make her way back home. She told me that she was even less safe there, for her own people were hunting her as well. I asked why and she tried to tell me, but I didn't understand. Understanding would come later, she signed, after I had learned more. But she needed my help now. She called me friend. It took her over an hour to explain this to me, and I signed that I would do what I could to help, and she thanked me and turned away to survey the situation. Still feeling numb and wanting only to run away *(to where?)*, I fell asleep.

The sun was its own diameter above the horizon when next I woke. Truck was nudging me with a stick, a branch she had broken off and shaped into a makeshift crutch with the aid of my knife. I grabbed on with my good arm and favored my good leg as she helped me to my feet and handed it to me. I waved my thanks and propped the crutch under my left armpit. The branch was a little too short, but it was certainly better than nothing, and I could stoop if I had to.

I was a mess. A space the size of my palm was black on my right biceps, ringed by purple ringed by greenish blue. The arm was stiff and I wanted to scream whenever I had to move it.

My left shin throbbed. I could not feel anything below it, and never would again. The nerves had been severed and the sheaths never realigned.

Doc's body was where we had left it the night before, locked now in rigor mortis, staring unseeing at the early morning sky. I glanced at him and looked away.

I hobbled to the body of the dog Truck and Doc had killed with rocks. It was a big dog, but not as big as my first impression had made it seem. The thick, white fur had made it look larger than it was. Still, it was quite muscular. It had a large head and a pronounced jaw. The top of the head was flattened and spade-shaped, vaguely like that of a pit bull terrier, though I had to look at the dog I had killed to notice this because the head of the other one was too bashed in. I shook my head at the thought of the power behind those rock throws. I had gotten off lucky with just a badly bruised arm—a rock thrown by a raccoon became a missile that could crush bone.

The dog had a thick body and short, stocky legs. From the way the head was built, and from the lowness of the dog's center of gravity and thickness of neck, it was easy to see that the beast had been bred for fighting—it was built low and it was powerful, and when fighting it exposed little but hard head and backbone. Both dogs were cotton white, and their appearance reminded me a little of the Japanese Akita.

I bent painfully and fingered the dog's collar. It was made of leather, to which had been affixed six three-sided steel blades resembling those tipping a hunting arrow, each about three inches long. I removed the collars from both dogs.

The corpses of the two raccoons we had killed were something of a shock. They were big, only four or five inches shorter than I, which meant they were a full seven inches higher than the average raccoon I had seen. They were quite muscular, and their shoulders were broad—nowhere near as broad as mine, but the typical raccoon is quite round-shouldered, and these most definitely were not.

Each had a shaved stripe, baring the grayish-white skin beneath, that gradually widened from the tip of the nose to midcranium, continuing between the ears and straight down the back. The stripe ended where a ringed tail should have been, but it wasn't. It looked like the opposite of a Mohawk. On both raccoons a line of fur bordering the right side of the shaved strip was dyed a dark cinnamon color.

Suddenly I understood the meaning of the gesture I had interpreted as "fighter," the gesture that looked as if you were indicating to a barber where you part your hair. It meant "Stripe."

And "Stripe" meant "fighter."

They wore no clothing, only the knotty bracelet worn by most raccoons—but one of the corpses wore three bracelets on its free arm and the other wore two. One raccoon had bits of colored string tied into its fur along either side of the stripe. The other wore an earring made from a red bead from which sprouted a quail feather. They carried no equipment save the leather shoulder bag common among raccoons, and no weaponry except what I later learned was referred to as a Fighting Hand.

A Fighting Hand is a steel carapace worn on the outside right forearm. It is covered with leather, except at the elbow, where it tapers to a point four or five inches past the joint, and at the knuckles, where the steel extends to become four straight, six-inch-long, double-edged blades, quarter-twisted to expose the edges for slashing. A bar wraps around the palm for the hand to grip, and the carapace buckles at the forearm just in front of the elbow. The wrist is hinged, with a little swiveling hook that holds the bladed section doubled back against the carapace, which frees the hand for signing and manipulation. At a wave of the arm the bladed section will unhook itself and swing into fighting position to be grasped by the hand.

The Stripes are astoundingly adept with them.

I unbuckled and removed the Fighting Hand from the corpse of the Stripe I had killed, and spent a few minutes examining it. The leather was well cared for, but had seen some wear. It was freshly marred where it had deflected a rock last night. The blades had seen some use as well: they were honed to razor-sharpness and were without hint of rust, but were nevertheless marred and nicked. The leather looked old, but I got the feeling the steel beneath was much older, though I am not sure why. I tried to put the weapon on, but my forearm and wrist were too wide. Still, if I could get hold of a hammer or a vise I could broaden the carapace—it would probably damage the leather, but who gave a damn?

On all four blades were rust-colored smears—Doc's blood. My face went stony and I tucked the weapon under my bum arm. I hobbled to the llamas and dumped dog collars and Fighting Hand onto the bedroll Doc had spread out last night. I stared at the bedroll a moment.

I limped to the raccoon Truck had killed and stared at him. He stared past me at nothing, bladed arm still pinned to his head in a mock salute. How had Truck done that to him? I shook my head. Squatting gingerly, I set my crutch on the grass beside the dead Stripe, unbuckled the elbow strap of the Fighting Hand on the corpse, forced the stiff arm away from the weapon, and looked away as I pried the blades out of the skull. I picked up my crutch and hobbled back to the bedroll, adding the second Fighting Hand to the meager pile, then went back to the same corpse to examine the contents of its shoulder bag. It contained a utility knife, a sharpening stone, a piece of parchment about three by five inches with Chinese-looking characters written in dark blue ink, a lock of raccoon fur bound by a bow of blue thread, a brush, and nothing else.

The contents of the other raccoon's shoulder bag were identical, minus the lock of fur. Most of the characters on its piece of parchment were different. I dumped the lot of it onto the bedroll and commenced looking for Truck. When I found no sign of her after a few minutes, I began to grow panicky—I was, after all, alone in a small clearing with five corpses—and began calling out for her. Maybe she couldn't understand my speech, but she sure as shit knew the sound of my voice, and it carried *much* farther than any signings I could make. It might seem a deficiency on the part of a gestural language that calling to a person not facing you is not possible. In actuality, however, the trillings, cooings, and other ostensibly "incidental" sounds made by the raccoons are not so incidental as one might think. They perform about two dozen specific functions, not the least of which is commanding the attention of those whose backs are turned. They also impart tone, emphasis, mood, alarm, "fight or flight," and even a kind of modifier to the actual content of the signings themselves. The same sign can take on widely disparate meanings against the backdrop of various vocalized cues. For instance, the sign for "Duck!" or "Heads up!" accompanied by a warbling sort of fight-or-flight trilling can cause raccoons to hit the deck without question—yet the exact same sign when cooing in a sort of condescending manner can mean, idiomatically, "Now, let's just think about this a moment, shall we?"

Truck reappeared after I had been calling for a few minutes. Tucked under one arm she held two stripped saplings, each about seven feet long. In her other hand was my knife, unfolded.

She dropped the saplings next to the Stripe she had killed.

I helped her turn the body onto its back. It remained grotesquely frozen in the same pose, as though it had sighted Medusa while saluting. Truck stabbed it in the lower belly, just above the penile sheath, and began to saw upward. The blade made a ripping sound as it tore through flesh and fur. I gagged but was unable to look away, and as I watched in horrified fascination she skinned the huge raccoon exactly as one would skin a rabbit: up the belly and around the limbs, off with the head. Finally I had to look away. I wanted to throw up but was too weak. Hearing it was worse: wet sounds and tearing sounds as Truck freed the skin from the corpse.

Why was she doing this? Was it some sort of ritual, like the taking of a scalp (a custom the Amerinds had learned from the French)? Or possibly a religious rite, part of a burial ceremony? I knew nothing of their religious feeling(s), since the topic had never come up, and later I learned it was not likely to.

In any case, Truck removed the skin, cut so that when spread out it resembled a gray bearskin rug. Quickly but efficiently she scraped the underside with my knife. I tried not to look at what was left of the skinned raccoon.

Seeing that I was queasy, Truck allowed me to sit out the next round while she skinned the second of the two dead Stripes. I lay back on the grass, crutch across my chest, eyes shut, and I felt the sun on my face and did my best to think about nothing at all. It wasn't very hard. The throbbing in my leg had grown stronger, and the wound itched furiously. I dared not scratch it, instead settling unsatisfactorily for pressing the bandage against the cut. I prayed it did not get infected, though in Florida conditions, and doubtless with hair, pieces of cloth, and who knew what else in the wound, it probably would.

I sat up straight and opened my eyes. The crutch rolled off my chest and onto my lap.

It had not occurred to me until then that there was hardly a chance in all the world of my finding anything like a penicillin tablet. Suddenly a cut on my leg was something that could cause me to lose the limb. Or kill me.

I wanted to go home. . . .

Stop it, I commanded myself. I blinked back tears. *Goddammit, stop it!* If somehow I could discover how to get out of this place, a way back, then fine. Until then I was stuck with it, and all the self-pity I could muster would change that fact not one iota, and the slight nudge it would take to edge me from self-pity into apathy would doubtless get me killed.

But it wasn't just a new game anymore, with different rules. Suddenly it was dangerous. Still a challenge, yes, but one I no longer felt enthusiastic about meeting.

I leaned forward, pulled up my pants leg, and lifted my bandage a bit. Blood-matted hair stuck to it. There was a fleshy, reddish smile in the middle of my leg, but at least it seemed to have stopped bleeding. Still, it would require some stitches. . . . I frowned. Stitches, in a world that had probably never known anything like a sterile operating environment. But there was heat, and probably alcohol, and if I had to, I could do it myself. I hoped. Right now, though, I needed to attend to it as best I could, which meant washing it and redressing it so that the flow of blood to my foot was not impeded—with infection a good possibility, I didn't need to encourage gangrene. I lifted myself to my feet with the aid of my crutch, intending to find the water flask and wash the cut. Dull pain pounded in my right arm.

The two Stripes had been skinned and Truck was now working on a third corpse—Doc.

"What are you doing?" exploded from me before I could contain it. Doc had tried to know me, and had liked me, had died as I held him, and Truck was *skinning* him.

"Hey!"

I shifted my weight to my right leg and raised my crutch to point at Truck. Not a threat . . . exactly.

I had taken aikido for five years, tae kwon do for twice that long. I had spent thousands of hours trading blows with high-caliber experts. For my tae kwon do black belt test I had to fight three opponents at once, and win. Watching the effect of my spin kicks on a heavy bag leaves no doubt in my mind that the unobstructed delivery of such a kick to a man's head would kill him. I had competed in tournaments, and won, and lost. I had spent many hours learning precisely how to redirect, immobilize, stun, injure, or kill a human being intending to do me harm. I had lived and breathed martial arts for a decade.

But I had never been in a fight. I had never had to commit violence, nor had violence been committed to me. In ninth grade a guy named Rodney grabbed me by the shoulders and slammed me into a wall, and I punched him in the mouth. A kid ran for the assistant principal, and that was the extent of it. Nothing else, before then or since.

Until now.

I was shaken. My initial, violent encounter with Truck had been the result, it seemed, of misunderstanding and misinterpretation of intent, and thus had left me startled but not upset. But this. . . . This had been silent, efficient, mechanical, impersonal. The Stripes had released their dogs and then casually walked in to clean up, with virtually no other acknowledgment of our existence other than an attempt to end it. I was . . . I was *offended*, no other word for it, offended and shocked. It was brutal, and they had obviously been rigorously trained—perhaps even bred—to do exactly that sort of thing. I had watched a newfound friend dispassionately stabbed to death, and I had been forced to fight for my life and Truck's, and forced to kill—and I hadn't an inkling as to why. For all I knew they had been cops, and Truck was some sort of outlaw wanted for heinous crimes against the state, which made me one of the Bad Guys. It was possible, but I did not believe it. The attack had been completely unexpected and unprovoked. We had not been asked to surrender and come along peacefully. They had wanted us dead, plain and simple.

And if Truck was indeed some kind of outlaw, a hunted criminal—and she had admitted she was being hunted but had not told me why—what did she want me for? It came down to this: I was ignorant, a stranger in a strange land and an easy mark for any soft sell that happened along. So the question was, simply put, Was Truck a Good Guy or a Bad Guy?

My instincts told me she was a Good Guy. Despite the bad foot on which we had started, she had fed me and helped me survive with her in the wild. She had taught me the rudiments of her language and (despite the subterfuge involved, which I suspected she felt was necessary) helped me pass muster in Wait-No-More—and dammitall, there was additionally a quality to her that I was unable to put my finger on, save to say that I trusted her, that I had faith in her.

All of which is to explain why I was so shaken when she skinned Doc like some prize game she had bagged on a weekend excursion. So I pointed my stick and made a lot of noise, and then realized she couldn't understand me and threw down my crutch and began to sign, swallowing the lump of frustration in my throat caused by my communications handicap. "Why do you this?" I asked. I pointed to the thing that had been Doc. "Friend Doc. Why?"

A crease appeared between her eyes. She set my knife down on the grass and slowly signed, "Hurt, you. Travel, us. Quickly, quickly. I make [ ]. Travel on it, you Quickly."

"Understand me no. [ ]?"

For answer she picked up the two saplings and set them about three feet apart on the grass. She picked up one of the cleaned pelts and draped it over the saplings, then mimed tying the pelt to them with rope. She pointed to me, pointed to the llamas still hitched to the palm tree, and lifted the projecting ends of the saplings.

A cold hand spread its fingers in my stomach. I turned, clamping my hand over my mouth, but it was too late. I fell to my knees and vomited.

She had skinned Doc and the two Stripes to build a travois to be pulled behind one of the llamas so that our travels would not be hampered by my injury.

14
Narrative of Truck

FROM MY PERCH in the crotch of an elm tree I peer toward the town of Three Big Dogs. Here the woods abruptly end and the town begins, thickening as it spills to the banks of the river known here in Florida as Dog Piss, known farther north in [the Confederacy] as Broken Spine. Three Big Dogs is a bigger town than Wait-No-More, but not so big that I am in any danger of mistaking it for a city. The houses and other structures are real buildings, almost, built of wood and stone rather than that primitive Outback clay/mud/straw. There is little activity on the streets as I watch through the parted branches: a mother pulls along her kits; a rug seller haggles with a customer; an older kit nails a new plank onto the porch of a shop. The hammerings make me blink. It is late afternoon and most are within, eating their dinners, impatiently tugging their fur in anticipation of the evening's coolness.

A leaf flutters onto my head. I shake my head and the leaf slides down to intrude on the vision of my right eye. I rub my head against my right arm and the leaf is brushed off, wafting to the ground to join more leaves. Seeing this, I feel a nostalgia, for it makes me remember a poem I am first seeing while still a kit:

Crumpled, crennellated, jagged-edged,
a leaf
revolves behind my eyes, scrapes the edges of vision.

I think of you and [see your voice].
You are not dying well.

I stare at the leaf on the ground without actually seeing it, for I look to times inside, to my education and childhood. Carefree playing, hard lessons, lost friends. I am so far from these now.

The sun sets, but it is a while yet before darkness. I will not move from my perch until nightfall. The patch of sky I see framed by the parted branches is darkening gray and cloudless. I glance once more at the outskirts of Three Big Dogs before letting the branches cover my view with leaves once more, then lean back to rest against a broad limb. I pull a black ant from my hip and flick it away.

I am tired.

I am usually able to function well on little sleep—an irony, that!—but I am not used to such deprivation in the face of so much activity. These are four days since the fight with the Stripes that I do not want to dwell upon, and certainly do not want to relive, yet they live in my dreams—quick dreams, memory dreams, dreams that murder restful sleep.

I close my eyes and rub them, listen to my breathing, to my beating heart, to rustling leaves, feel the tree limb against my back. To occupy myself until darkness I summon forth a dodecahedron in my mind. Its panels are each a different color; its lines are black to help me differentiate them. I rotate it on first one axis, then two, then three, keeping the different colors in their proper places. Then I hold it still and unfold it, observing the two-dimensional star that the colored pentagonal panels now form. This of course occupies me only for so long, so I disappear the dodecahedron and summon forth a sphere. I color it red and then spin it, stop it, and turn it inside out. Inside it is orange.

I can only occupy myself a short time before I grow weary of my own simplistic child-playing, however, and I collapse the sphere and open my eyes. The day is darker, but it is not yet night.

And so I stalk the halls of memory. . . .

—I run along a corridor in the old Keep. My bare feet slap upon the cold stone floor. I flee the wrath of my writing teacher, who is catching me as I urinate into the main water clock in the central courtyard. It is an act I am thinking will be funny, upsetting though it will be to the accuracy of the time, but when my teacher discovers me she is not amused, so my own humor regarding this mischievous childhood act vanishes rather rapidly. I run from her, a thing I am never before doing. She catches me within a dozen strides and lifts me by the fur on my neck, and walks up the stairs to the highest room in the Keep, the room that is so windy and cold. I am left there without food or water until the next day, and the incident is never again mentioned.

—My teacher of warfare strategies holds himself skeptically before me. I glance around at the other adepts, who only minimally conceal the wavings of their hands. Having told my teacher I can hand-pick any five students and defeat his senior war-gaming class, he calls my bluff and a demonstration is arranged. The appointed day I and my five do not appear as scheduled at the foot of the mountain for the ersatz battle, and teacher and his army mill around for the rest of the morning, signing of our cowardice, of the reprimands I shall face for wasting his time and the time of his senior class. Finally the class of thirty leaves the field to reconvene at the classroom in the Keep, and there I and my army of five bar the door and take them prisoner. Teacher is furious. In the brashness of my youth I cannot disguise a calculatedly indifferent posture as I sign to him: "Battles I wage on my own time—not that of my enemy."

I am not to graduate at the top of my warfare strategies class.

—I remember the fight with the adolescent Stripe who ridicules me for having no mother, signing that a raccoon with no mother is a deficient and stunted thing. I defeat him by touching his own blades to his throat in front of other Stripes.

(I am as one who sleeps, to remember these things, for they impinge fully upon my awareness now, eidetic yet dreamlike, and I have no awareness of the tree in which I sit, or of any of the things around me.)

—I remember the anxious anticipation as we lesser adepts—we fledgling True dreamers, we hopeful Architects—await announcement of which of us are eliminated from consideration for the Title. Those who are announced shall move on to higher echelons of education and awareness—and responsibility, obligation, and competition. Those who remain shall become Liaisons, or at best Tribunal members, unless they are selected as advisors. My name is announced, and so is that of my best friend, [Puck].

—The day the Tribunal announces my name as the successor to the Title, half a transit after [Charlemagne's] death. Me, from among the remaining three adepts, who are all older than me, all training as hard as me, and all dreaming True dreams as I am. I suffer from a severe cold when the Tribunal makes its decision, and drip from my nose and shake under thick blankets when the news is brought to me by my friend [Puck]. I am to have few true friends now, in the Keep or out of it, for many are insulted, even dismayed, at the choice of me as Architect. According to those who feel slighted, I am unsubtle, I know nothing of tact, I am too full of myself, I am too insecure, I wave a lot of signs but my hands are empty, I am too serious, I am not serious enough, I am not a unanimous favorite among the adepts or the teachers, and most of all I am too young. How can a majority choose me when so many disapprove of their decision? I have seen thirty-two solstices at the time of my announcement; none so young is holding the Chair in any province in living memory. When Puck brings me the news I should be elated, but because of my cold I can only sneeze. Behold the new Architect of Sleep, snot on her fur.

—The day I take the vows, and cut fur at the top of my head, to drop it into the glazed bowl that it may mingle with the fur of the Architects before me.

These last thoughts return me to my surroundings, and I open my eyes and cast off my reverie with a twitch of my ears. It is dark. Repeat will be up before long but is near new moon phase, and Pete, though full this night, will not rise for hours. I retrieve the mandolute from where it hangs on a projecting branch, and I edge out onto a thick limb and lower the mandolute by the strap until it touches the ground. Then I swing down, hang a moment, and drop the remaining three spans. Bending to retrieve the instrument, I regard the leaves at my feet. Which is the leaf I am watching waft down to join the others?

Does it really matter? I do not know.

I shoulder the mandolute and pull the pick from between the strings. I strike up a happy tune—about which I am less enthusiastic than the playing of a jolly melody deserves, but I doubt many will notice—and enter the town of Three Big Dogs.

• • •

I slide the pick above my ear and push aside the neck of the mandolute. Her back is to me as she studies the menu of the small restaurant. The menu is painted in red on a piece of varnished pine nailed to the left of the door curtain. The selection is limited, but the prices are low. Perhaps I can barter for a meal. In outlying regions this is much more acceptable than in cities.

I trill politely so that I may sign to her. She turns.

She is quite attractive. She favors the sturdy side of the tree, perhaps, but this is to be expected here. On her it looks hearty, and her coat is healthy and a good color. Her eyes are large and her face broad; her teats do not have the look of one who has borne kits. She wears an umbilical bracelet, but I suspect she looks older than she is. Nevertheless, I am cordial and sign to her as a peer."Your pardon, goodbody," I sign," "but I am new here, a traveling musician, and this south end of town is unfamiliar to me. Might you know where I may find the inn and tavern known as The Mongrel?"

Her nostrils twitch and I realize that I probably do not smell very good. "Forgive me, minstrel," she replies, "but you . . . how am I to sign it? . . . It is possible that you might seem out of place in a tavern the likes of The Mongrel. If you do not mind my signing so."

"No; in fact, I appreciate it. Nevertheless, I am, as you sign, a minstrel, and must play that I may eat. Do you know if they cater in this manner to such as me?"

"Goodbody, I do not know, for it is not my habit to frequent the place. But perhaps they do." She pauses, looks me over from head to foot, and glances at my mandolute. "It is toward the river. Walk down this street until the sign of the Two Shoemakers, then turn right and pass three more streets. You will see its sign; it is rather . . . prominent."

"Many thanks, goodbody." I begin to turn away, but stop at a wave from her. "Yes?"

"Goodbody—do pardon me, but might I ask you to play me a tune, if you know a brief one, perhaps?"

"The pleasure is mine, for you are helping me." I reach behind me, grasp the neck, and bring the mandolute around. I retrieve the pick and commence without hesitation to play a short piece from the score of a play by [Sondheim]. It is a brief, jaunty tune, written to make the heart skip in time with the dialogue in the play, which is called *Moodbreaker*. She seems to delight in it and slaps the fur at her thighs in time with the music, but as I play I realize a thing concerning the sort of music I am lately playing. *Moodbreaker* is a famous, well-received play—but only in certain circles, among certain crowds—and in a different province from this one. Doubtless it is little known outside my Seaport Savannah, for it is only showing at a single playhouse there. Anyone recognizing this tune will wonder how I know it, how one of my obviously low station is to be attending these plays at (to me) unaffordable places in the capital city of another province. This is quite capable of turning a conversation to topics I prefer to avoid; hence I must pay attention to the tunes I play and the audiences for whom I play them. But for her I play the short tune and she thanks me, and I thank her for asking me to play for her, and she kindly gives me a copper, and I thank her again, and we go our own ways—she to her perusal of the menu of The Foreleg, me to look for an old friend.

The large sign above the door is a garish painting of a half-starving dog with bared teeth. The lamplight shining through the slit windows and door curtain of The Mongrel is bright, and the sounds from within are the scraping of chairs, the clatter of dishes, and a blend of excited trillings accompanying enthusiastic conversations. Intermittently a raccoon approaches the door curtain, draws it aside, and enters; also intermittently the curtain is yanked aside from within and a raccoon stumbles out, to stagger along the street and sign idiotically to no one. While I watch, hand straying to the neck of my mandolute as though some assurance lies there, the curtain is drawn aside and a small, thin female emerges. She pauses just outside the tavern, bent arms spreading wide as she breathes in the night air. She waves laughter to herself, steps from the porch to the hitching post, unties her llama, and swings atop it. Her motion continues until she lies on the street on the other side of her ostensible mount. She rises, llama shit clinging to her fur, and again mounts the beast—this time with more success, though with nothing approaching grace—and rides off, weaving drunkenly in the saddle.

I puzzle, I frown. To drink to light-headedness can be fine, I think, but drinking to this sort of excess I am never understanding, even now.

I tuck a thumb beneath my shoulder strap and head toward The Mongrel. My purse is slung across the opposite shoulder, beneath the mandolute strap, and the thin leather presses into my upper right breast and left shoulder blade. The purse strap is twisted, and I bend back my arm and straighten it. I open my purse and brush my fur as best I am able with the brush I am taking from the Stripe I am killing four days past. The brush makes a ripping sound through my fur, for I am filthy and matted and not properly cleaned even for such a place as The Mongrel seems to be. After I take care of [Bentley], a bath is the first of my priorities. I return the brush to my purse and draw aside the door curtain.

The Mongrel is lighted in a kind of amber dimness I always find comforting, most especially when there is a storm outside, or snow and howling wind. The greatest illumination, of course, is from the fireplace at the far end of the room, though a few lamps gutter on the longer walls. A huge kettle, containing coffee, by the smell of it, sits above the low-burning fire.

The interior of the place is large enough to warrant two tables, each half the length of the room. Along them are seated no more than a dozen raccoons. Some eat, some drink, some both; some study menus. All stop when I enter. I am not one of the more alarming sights to be encountered in a lifetime, however, and am scarce given more than a glance by most of the customers.

An adolescent scampers to me. "A fine evening . . . goodbody," he signs, hesitating before yielding the honorific. "Will you be eating tonight, or drinking?" Though innocently phrased, the question is pointed, intended to guide me to a less conspicuous station should I be there only to get drunk.

"A little of both, I hope," I sign.

He relaxes a bit. "Then you will want a menu and a place at our table." He hands me a torn, hand-lettered, print-smeared menu and turns to lead me to a place at one of the two long tables. I trill for his attention, and he gives it to me.

"Pardon," I sign, "but is the owner or someone in authority present? I wish to sign with [her/him], if I might."

The youth regards me critically head to feet. "There is a manager, of course," he signs slowly, "but she is most busy at present. Might I ask what you wish? Perhaps I—"

"Two things." Now the diners and drinkers are beginning to stare at me. I do my best to ignore them. If only my back is to them so they cannot see me sign! "It is my hope that I might entertain your guests with my mandolute for a time, in exchange for a meal and a mug or two—of water, even," I add hastily.

"The other thing?"

"I seek the services of a physician. When last I am passing through Three Big Dogs I am seeing that one resides here?"

"An emergency?" he asks, evading an answer.

"No, no—at least, I hope not. I have a friend who complains of severe stomach pains, and I think perhaps he is eating bad meat. The last inn we are staying at is not so concerned for the welfare of its customers as is your own, and I suspect he is served meat left out too long."

He blinks a moment and scratches beneath an arm. "Come," he signs abruptly, and turns and walks past the tables. I follow, eyes on his back and not on the diners, past a thick door hanging and into the cramped kitchen, where a small lantern burns on one wall, hardly bright enough to create shadows in the room. There is a cook, full apron tied about his neck and waist, frying venison steaks on a stove barely large enough to hold the pan. Beside the cook is who I take to be the manager or owner. She signs to the cook, but it is apparent that his attention is focused more upon his work than upon his employer. They both look to us when we enter. It is hot in the kitchen; the back door is in place and barred, and there is only a thin window slit and a small, cloth-screened hole in the ceiling for ventilation, and with the four of us in there it is crowded. The neck of my mandolute bangs against the wall. The youth repeats my request to the manager, though without, I notice, my formality of phrasing. I also notice he refers to me as "goody," passing quickly over the honorific. Perhaps I am grown a bit too aromatic. It is hard to tell, yourself, when you have lived with it for a while.

"Your friend is in poor fettle indeed," comments the manager to me, after the youth is finished, "if he seeks the services of our physician."

"I worry for the possibility of his future distress, goodbody," I reply, "for we have much traveling to do yet, and food poisoning is never a good thing to have—especially between towns."

"Doubtless." She indicates my mandolute. "You are good with that instrument?"

"None is ever asking me to stop playing."

"Tactfully signed." She seems to be considering, but I can tell her decision is already made. "Very well. You may play until we close the kitchen, and you may eat whatever remains in the pots and on the plates—as much as you like. I had best take to your musicianship, though, for if I do not like it, or if but one of my guests expresses dissatisfaction, you are to be tossed out on your ear, and your instrument after you. Do you understand?"

"Indeed I do."

"As to a place to sleep. . . . Rooms are paid for here, and you obviously have no money and no trade goods. I am a business owner, not a phil[anthro]pist."

"I understand that as well, goodbody."

With two fingers she twiddles the fur alongside her nose. "I doubt that. You may sleep on the back porch. That will keep you from being trampled by llamas, and from the rain I feel is in the air for later. Check with me in the morning—it is possible my customers may like your music, and if this is so, you may return the next evening. If this works out, I may employ you a bit more gainfully."

"I thank you." I dip courteously.

"You should. Now, I must sign with my cook. Go play for my guests. Sit by the fire, if you wish." She turns to sign to the cook, turns back to me. "Sit by the fireplace anyway."

I do not move. "My friend," I sign. "Might I see your physician?"

"I shall consult him. —Where is your friend?"

"At the edge of town, with some traveling companions." Not entirely a lie, that.

"You will have to bring [her/him] here. The physician's business is his own and I do not order him about, so long as he pays his room and board, but I know him well enough to know that he will not go anywhere—not this night, anyway. I will tell him of your friend; he will be down to see you before long." She terminates our conversation by turning to the cook. I turn and step past the door hanging and into the dining room. I have little choice but to do as I am told, so I sit beside the fireplace with my back against the wall, mandolute on my lap, pick in hand, purse close beside me, and I play. At first the diners stop eating to listen to me, but my music is purposefully bland, and soon they are eating, drinking, or conversing again and I am ignored.

I grow impatient. The physician does not descend the narrow staircase, which I face. It is hard for me to be impatient and yet play unobtrusively, and in a way it is dishonest, for the music must belie my mood. But it is my sadness to write that one may have technique and craft and be totally void of emotion, of feeling toward the art, yet have none present detect any difference whatsoever.

Playing, I worry about [Bentley], but what am I to do? I must be cautious; I must not seem anxious; I must be slow, and even seem a bit careless; I must do the proper things to find medical help, food, and shelter, or none of these things will be found. This is small solace when I know [Bentley] suffers so, alone but for two llamas in the woods, but I take what comfort in it I am able. I must endure this, or there will be nothing.

I think of the manager's prediction of rain this night and hope it is incorrect.

It seems much later when I pause in my playing to drink from the mug of water the manager is so kind as to allow to rest beside me on the floor. Fewer customers patronize The Mongrel now; most who remain are filled with their draughts. Corn liquor is the favored drink here, for it is local and therefore cheaper than the vodka and beer and barley liquors imported from the western provinces.

I lower the spout from my mouth and see him descending the stairs with unsteady deliberation, a vision from my childhood.

I set the mug beside me, wipe my mouth, and watch him come slowly down the steps toward me. My left hand clasps the neck of the mandolute, my right holds the pick above the strings. I do not play.

He is so much . . . *older*. I am, also, and the differences in me are certainly even more distinct than in him, but nonetheless it is a shock, for the memory I carry, though a long-ago thing, is as fresh as if I am last seeing him but a week ago. He is shorter than I remember, and thin. Fur is grayed almost to white in a fringe around his head, just below his ears. His coat is dull, thinning, and coarse. His eyes, so bright I remember them, and so close together, regard me with a peculiar flatness as he nears. His posture, so impeccable as to be a source of laughter and parody among the adepts (myself among them), is changed: his back is slightly bowed, his shoulders hunched, his gait plodding.

So far a fall! Seeing him again in these first few moments I grow sad—for sadness is nostalgia, a symptom of change and yearning for what no longer is.

He halts before me. His gnarled hands shake a bit as he signs, "I am told you wish my services?"

I look down at my mandolute. His look is changed, perhaps, but the manner of his signing, always held in high esteem by me, and which I am told by those who remember is a thing I emulate as I am growing up, is the same: formal, detached, nearly snide—but proper, always so proper. I weave the pick among the mandolute strings and set aside the instrument. I stand and look down upon him.

This is the first time I am taller than him.

"My friend is sick," I sign. It is so hard to keep myself from hugging him, to keep from telling him who I am. "I believe it to be food poisoning, possibly from bad meat he is eating. He complains of stomach cramps, and he vomits and sweats. Can something be done for this?"

"Something may be done for everything that ails. Whether it works is altogether a different matter." He waves noncommittally. "I will look at your friend. Lead me to your room." His avoidance of either honorific or polite injunctive is so like my memory of him!

"I-am-sorry, goodbody, but he is not here. I am fearful to move him. It is not far from here, though, and your services would put me greatly in your debt."

"I do not want to be in your debt. If you will but provide me with a mug or two, I shall consider your obligations fully discharged."

I look at his eyes a moment before responding and grow sadder still. Ever his old vice, I see now the thing I should be seeing from the moment he descends the stairs: his drinking now controls him instead of the other way around. His binges remain notorious among the adepts, but in those times they are a thing he is able to contain, aside from occasional reprimands from tutors and suitors.

Disliking myself both for the compliance and the lie, I sign, "I have no drink and nothing to buy it with—in fact, I play for what I may get, as you see. Unless a copper will buy a mug?" I add hopefully.

"Three coppers is what they charge here, the brigands."

"Then I regret that I cannot buy you a mug of corn liquor. But I believe a flask or two is kept warm with my friend, and the favor you do him is surely worth that."

"Then lead the way."

I tell the youth that I shall return—the manager is nowhere in sight and is doubtless upstairs signing in her sleep—and sling my mandolute.

I exit the door curtain first. There is, as the manager says, a crispness in the air and a massing of clouds above, hiding Repeat and muting waning Pete. "I feel oncoming rain, goodbody," I sign. "I shall wait here if you wish to get your poncho."

He hesitates, and I know what he thinks: he weighs the possibility of rain against my promise of liquor. I also see which way the scales tip: "I will only be a moment," he signs. "Have you a poncho as well?"

"No. It is all right." I rub fingers along my chest. "A rain will do me little harm, I think."

He waves a small laugh, then goes back into The Mongrel to fetch his poncho. I glance again at the cloudy night sky. Grayness blows across the translucent silver patch that is Pete, and reluctantly I remove my mandolute. Inside The Mongrel again, I extract the youth's promise that the instrument shall be put away safely until my return. "It is my food, my drink, and my shelter," I sign. The things I hate most to do are always those I most have to.

The physician my old teacher returns with two ponchos draped over one arm. Both are treated deerskin. To me he hands the more weather-beaten and torn. "It is old, but keeps out the larger part of the rain," he signs after giving it to me and draping his own across one shoulder. He adjusts the strap of his purse, which is bigger than most, and steps again through the door curtain. I follow.

He turns to regard me as I emerge. "There is something familiar about you," he signs. "Something about the way you sign."

I sign nothing.

"Tell me, what is your name?"

I glance around us. No one is in sight, but I should take no chances, not as yet. "Smith," I sign.

"'Smith.'" From the way he signs it I see he does not believe me. It is a common sign, I admit, but not suspiciously so. "Do I know you, Smith?"

"It is possible," I acknowledge, "for I meet many raccoons. Do you travel much?"

"Hardly at all." He spreads his hands. "Perhaps it is just that you remind me of someone. You certainly do not look familiar, and my memory for faces is quite good, if I may sign so."

I spread my hands as well, heart pounding in my ears, and we walk along the streets.

"How much farther?" he asks as we pass the menu board of The Foreleg.

"A few more streets, in this direction."

He stops walking. "A few more streets in that direction and we shall be out of town. Where do you take me, Smith?"

"Please, goodbody. It is as I sign: to an ailing friend who requires your skills."

"You are a criminal . . . ?"

"No. I am not. Nor is my friend."

He stares into my eyes a long moment. "I should know better than this," he finally signs. "If asked while more sober and in the light of day, I would scoff at the notion of accompanying an itinerent named 'Smith' to the edge of town allegedly to treat her friend." He pauses a long while, then signs, "But something in you makes me believe what you sign, Smith. And there is that familiarness about you that nags at me." He glances back the way we are coming, looks again at me. "Very well, Smith—lead on." I note that he places his hand casually on the flap of his purse, and I do not doubt that there is more inside it than herbs and medicinal plants.

A fine mist begins to fall, dewing my dirty fir. A dozen paces and the mist is light rain that patters us; a dozen more and it is a downpour, and we run for the trees at the end of town, wrapping our ponchos about us and tying them shut as we run. We halt beneath an elm tree, the one from which I am first regarding the outskirts of Three Big Dogs.

"Where do you lead me, Smith?" the physician asks after poking his arms through the overlipped slits in the sides of the poncho and raising the hood to cover his head.

"I must tell you a thing, truly," I sign. "I cannot bring my friend into town because he is not a raccoon."

"Not a raccoon? I am not a veterinarian."

"He does not require one."

"I do not understand, Smith."

"It is hard to explain. He is civilized . . . I think . . . but not a raccoon, and not an animal."

"You are drunker than I am." Lessened by the leaves of the tree, rain patters the hood about his head and runs off in rivulets.

"He is badly hurt," I continue, "suffering from an infected leg wound. He is feverish, and the wound swollen and full of pus." Patches of my fur grow damp through rents in the poncho.

He looks around us as if measuring avenues of escape. "And he is not a raccoon, you sign, and he is not an animal—yes?"

"That is correct. But he needs your help. He is an odd creature, new to me—new to anyone, I venture—and I am fearful he may die."

He looks at his moccasined feet. "This is madness," he signs. He looks up, over my head, squinting at the cold rain that dampens his face, looks to me. "How much farther?"

I point ahead to a thickening in the bush. "In there."

He regards me a moment. "If you mean to rob me—"

"It will already be so by now, and me long on my way." I hesitate, come to a decision, and then sign the things I am holding back since seeing him in The Mongrel. I sign his name—the long-ago name I know him by, regardless of whether it is the one he now uses, and his eyes widen. "How do you know this thing?" he signs rapidly. "I am not—"

"I know you," I sign. "And you know me. Though it is a long, long time since last we are meeting." This time it is I who look up to feel the rain pat my fur. I snuffle out droplets from my nostrils, blink my eyes, and look back at him. I flatten my facial hair with my palms.

"I am a kit of fifteen," I finally sign, "and you walk with me outside the Keep. You hold my hand. You are much taller than me, and I look up at you often and my eyes are teared by the sun. Along the road we see two llamas. They are copulating—"

He withdraws his arms into the side slits of his poncho as he remembers.

"—and their respective owners try to pull them apart, without much success. 'They mate?' I ask. 'Yes,' you answer. 'Your lessons teach you this—explain it to me.'"

He brings his hands back out so that they may find and knead each other.

"And so I answer: 'The male llama inserts his penis into the vagina of the female llama, until he ejaculates and impregnates her with his sperm.'"

I see a dawning memory, a flicker of candle flame behind his eyes, memories not stirred since his retirement, I think.

"'That is correct,' you sign, 'though a bit impersonal, if you ask me.' And we turn to look at the llamas mating and their frustrated owners, who pull at their beasts' reins, straining to get them apart."

His hooded face is fixed ten years in the past as he remembers what I sign.

"I tug at your hand. When you look down at me I release it and sign, 'I imagine they shall be glad when that is finally over.' 'Who,' you reply, 'the farmers, or the llamas?' And you laugh with both hands in the way I remember so well, and the rest of that day with you is fine and good, and a joy of learning and joking, and we walk outside the Keep until sunset and suppertime, and when we return late you accept the reprimands of the gate-warden without a motion, and for that I will always love you."

I stop, for I am finished.

He blinks, drawn out of the past, and looks around: at the trunk of the tree a little behind and to the left of me, at a branch higher up, at the rain falling through the cover of the leaves, at his leathered feet, at me, away, at me again. His hands shake. "Can this be?" he signs. "Is it you, here?" And his hands move to form the name I know they are not forming in a long time: *"Truck . . . ?"*

"Yes, old friend. It is me. And I am never forgetting the one who teaches me to catch well-aimed facts before hurling ill-aimed signings."

"How? How are you here? Truck, my Truck, I am. . . . You are. . . ." He stops, and the full impact of what and who I am registers in his eyes.

"I know what I am, old friend, and I am that no longer—unless many measures are taken. Now, more than at any other time in my life, I need my friends. I need the demonstration of the belief you are always placing in me." I step forward and reach through the front slit of his poncho, and I feel his old, coarse fur, and I tug it and ruffle it and hug him as I am not tugging, ruffling, and hugging in such a long time, and for the first time since my usurpation I feel that my optimism is well founded—that I have a chance.

15
Narrative of Truck

(continued)

"IT IS NOT good, Truck," signs [Dr. Zorba]. "He will not die, but he may lose the leg. The infection is bad. I have herbs, I have plants. But I know nothing of him! You must tell me: what he eats, what he drinks, how often he urinates, defecates. . . . Where is he from? Where are you *finding* such a one? The questions, the questions! They dam up; I cannot get them out fast enough! No, no; I know: patience, and you have a long story to tell. But I must know, and know all, though this old one is not sure he can stand the suspense of the telling. But tell, tell!"

We are in his room in The Mongrel and are toweled dry. The ponchos hang on pegs on the far wall. The night rain cascades outside, sounding like the crackle, almost, of a fire in the hearth. I sit on the floor with my back to the wall. [Zorba] sits opposite me. Between us lies [Bentley], sleeping restlessly on the mat.

"[Bentley] first, please," I reply. "He must be cared for, and then I will sign as freely as I dare in this place. So, please—what of him?"

He spreads his hands, Zorba does, and looks to the wall, on which are shelves on which are books. "Time," he signs. "I will do what I can, and time will determine the rest."

"That is not very helpful, Zorba. Nor reassuring."

"Nonetheless. . . ." He spreads his hands again.

Sneaking [Bentley] in is not an easy thing:

I wait behind The Mongrel, on the porch under the narrow overhang. [Bentley] is covered by my poncho and lies beside me, facing the wall. He is huge, yes, but when he lies down this is not so obvious. I lie beside him, pretending to sleep, and wait for Zorba, who is inside pretending—or perhaps not pretending—to drink beside the fireplace, until the way is clear and the opportunity exists for us to walk [Bentley] up the stairs to Zorba's room. [Bentley] sets no weight on his injured leg and seems only dimly aware of his surroundings. The odd, smooth skin of his arm is hot on my palm. We treat him as one who is drunk, letting him lean against one or the other of us, depending on which way he totters. At the top of the narrow staircase I am mortified when the hood of his poncho falls back, but no one sees him—in fact, we reach Zorba's room without seeing anyone. We remove the poncho and lie [Bentley] on Zorba's sleeping mat. Unlike the previous few nights he does not vocalize incessantly, which is good. I have no assurance he will not begin this again, though, and this worries me. But there is no choice for me but to leave him in Zorba's room for now and help Zorba with our llamas. We lead them down the muddy street to a stable. Zorba rouses the stable owner by pounding on the wall, and the sleepy female agrees to board our mounts for the night. Apparently she owes Zorba a favor or two. There are advantages to being a physician in a small town.

Two kilospans north of the place of our fight with the Stripes I am finding their messenger llamas hitched to a tree. I let them loose; I would like to keep them for their speed, but with their braided and beaded neck hair and tooled saddles they are too conspicuous. Also too conspicuous are the captured Fighting Hands, and it is with much regret that I bury them in the woods.

Considering that I must drag [Bentley] behind Holliday's draft animals, we are making good time heading north. Outside Three Big Dogs I break apart the travois and scatter the pieces. The pelts, though, I tie to rocks and throw into the Dog Piss River, since two of them are Stripe skins, and therefore damning.

Now, though, we converse in Zorba's room as [Bentley] sleeps fitfully between us after a cursory examination by Zorba. There is little moonlight to see by on this rainy night, so a tallow candle tosses its small head in the ever-changing wind slipping through the narrow, woven-screened window. The shadows move constantly. In this shifting light the nearly white fringe around Zorba's head is a pale amber.

In his posture Zorba is his old self—spine nearly flat against the wall, legs crossed before him—but his belly intrudes onto his lap a bit more than I remember. No matter: I am here and he is with me, and we are together: my old friend and teacher; my strange, new friend, and me. In the midst of my fear I am content. It is the last contentedness I will know for quite some time. Thinking on it now, as I write of it, I wonder if, indeed, I shall ever be so content again as I am at that moment, for the times now are interesting and strange, and change faster than I would prefer.

Zorba leans forward, causing me to retreat from the corridors of memory and slam shut the door of reverie, and he commences to examine [Bentley] more thoroughly. Earlier I am washing the wound after shaving off the blood-matted hair and cutting away the covering material to which it sticks. The wound is yellowish green in the wavering light. Zorba presses it with his fingertips. Whitened imprints remain when he lifts his fingers, then slowly fade. The cut is in the shape of a number two [a "V"], ridged with scab crusted over with blood thinned by pus. The region around the cut is inflamed. Zorba looks annoyed and attempts to push up the remainder of the leg covering, but it is too tight and will not go. Zorba pulls at the heavy material and tugs it at the waist, but he cannot figure out how to remove it. I do not know how it is done, either, and so I open [Bentley's] pack—which itself is a source of amazement to Zorba—and remove his knife. I further compound Zorba's amazement when I unfold it. I hand him the knife and he examines it—only a moment, to his credit as a physician—and turns with it to [Bentley]. Carefully he cuts at the material until we are able to remove it. [Bentley] wears still more material beneath it—a smaller, lighter, grayish thing that covers his genitals. We leave this on. Zorba presses his fingers against one pale thigh, which is less furred than the lower part of the leg. The fingermarks disappear quickly. Zorba looks at [Bentley's] face, a furrow appearing between his eyes, and lowers his hands to press below the wound at the ankle. The marks linger a moment, then fade.

Zorba sets down the knife. "Not good," he signs. "Not at all. There is still circulation in the lower leg; otherwise it would have to be removed before it could rot the rest of the limb.

Still, the circulation is poor. I have work to do."

"I understand, Zorba. Catching-up things may wait; this cannot. How may I help?"

"You are always knowing better than to volunteer for tasks when you are younger, Truck. But yes, there are things you can do—hold him down while I bathe the cut, and then when I lance the edema to drain the serous fluid. The cut should be stitched, but it is beginning to scab over. If he can stand the pain, though, I may cut out the scab and sew it anyhow; otherwise it will heal poorly, and be prone to heavy bleeding in the meantime. I must get fluids into him to fight his fever. Without fur—see him shake?—I believe he must be kept warm. Have we something with which to cover him?" He scratches between his eyes. "So much. You must answer many questions and tell me things you think are pertinent to the recovery of this . . . beast. '[Bentley],' you name him?"

"Yes. For so he appears—to my eyes, at least."

"I suppose." He regards [Bentley] a moment. "Yes, I suppose I can see that. When and how is his cut occurring?"

"Four days past," I sign, knowing as I do that my answer can only increase the flood of questions. "Just north of the town of Wait-No-More, we encounter two Stripes and their dogs. They are killing the physician accompanying us. [Bentley] is gashing his leg on the collar of a fighting dog."

"Stripes, Truck? Louis XIV's Stripes, or your own?"

I look away from him. "Louis'. But it makes little difference. I am hunted by my Stripes as well."

"Truck," he signs, forcing me to look back to him, "old pupil, best pupil—always you make me proud, when you are young. You challenge my questions. You demand proof. You let me get away with *nothing!* Always I am knowing you will be more than a failed adept, and more even than a successful advisor. And in Seaport Savannah, when I am standing with the other teachers to watch you add your fur to the urn and take the vows of the Title, I am proud that day—for my investment and my faith are justified. But Truck . . . old friend, old pupil. . . . " And here it is his turn to look away. He shuts his eyes. His hands lower a moment, then raise and sign, "It is my shame to sign that I am not what I am before, when you are knowing me as your teacher, your physician. I am out of touch with affairs these days, especially those of our province, and that is as I am willing it, for this is my home now. And I am slower, my mind a bit foggier—yes?—and what I feel is a quick and empowering year for you is for me a length of monotony, of little in the way of change or challenge. It ages me and leaves behind nothing of benefit. I am perpetually tired these days. So forgive me, Truck, but you must sign it to me from the beginning, and tell me as you would a kit: *What is happening?"*

"The story is long, Zorba. I will tell it after you attend to my friend."

"Your 'friend'. . . . He is a part of the tale?"

"A recent part. And, I dream, an important future part."

Zorba regards [Bentley]. Then he stands, stretches exaggeratedly while yawning, and signs, "Then tell me your story. I must set pots of water to boil at the fireplace downstairs. Bring the ponchos to dry by the fire. Will your 'friend' be all right up here?"

"Unless he wakes, yes, I think so. He seems to sleep soundly now. Doubtless his fever contributes to this."

"We shall do what we may to remedy that, also." He picks up his leather pouch of herbs and roots. "Downstairs, then, and sign to me while I work."

Black iron pots crowd each other for heat on the rack above the flames. Zorba turns to me from the fireplace and sets down the long-handled iron rod with which he opens their lids. "It is a little while yet before the water boils, and I must tend to preparing soups and salves. So tell me, Truck, what needs to be told."

I look around the empty room. It is still and quiet now that all are gone home or to their rooms to sleep. The fireplace provides the only illumination, though that is plenty. The wavering shadows of chair backs sway together on the wooden floor.

My fingers twitch in frustration at how much there is to sign. Zorba sits between me and the hearth; firelight saturates his fur, distinguishes his outline. His wide ears are but silhouettes of two black knives. "There is so much," I sign. "Where am I to begin?"

"The beginning is often best," he signs without humor. So like him!

I twiddle my fingers and crack my knuckles, and for an instant I feel that I am years in the past: Dr. Zorba sitting straight-backed to lecture me before the hearth in the late hours of the night. "There are many beginnings, Zorba. Am I to start with your resignation? With the events following my confirmation as Architect? With my betrayal and—I assume—usurpation?"

"Perhaps I should ask a few questions I consider most important—though in no hierarchy of importance, I assure you—since you already know the tale and it is I who require clarification."

"That seems best."

"Fine. Then: not most important, but about which I am most curious: How are you knowing where to find me, Truck? I am thinking myself rather removed, here, from curious eyes, gossiping hands, and courtly intrigues."

I wave a chuckle. "And so you are, I think. But you are ever one of my favorite teachers, Zorba, and always looking after my welfare. In many ways you are the parent I am never having. I even remember your visits when I am a kit in the crèche. So when I am taking the vows and thus acquire a touch more power, I am sending out queries, sniffing out false leads, eventually to pick up the trail you are leaving behind—and you know the trail I mean—"

He laughs. "Ever one of my vices," he signs.

"And your vices," I counter, "are a tight pouch of mixed contents, for they send you away from me and yet allow me to find you again. Anyway, when I am reasonably sure of where you are, I am sending a small band after you."

"Well, they are not finding me."

I turn my chair so that I may prop my feet upon the long dining table—my moccasins are removed and air out on the front porch—and then I lean back more comfortably in the chair, which creaks like a ship. "Do you remember," I sign with feigned casualness, "a five-member acting troupe entertaining in Three Big Dogs some—let me think . . . four transits ago? I believe you are treating one of them for heat prostration."

"Yes, of course; such actors are unusual enough here that I do—" He breaks off. "You," he signs.

"Me. I am knowing that you will set up a practice somewhere. I am receiving regular reports since then, and leaving firm instructions to let you be—unless you move sometime between reports, in which case your whereabouts are to be discovered again."

He is motionless a decifinger, then signs, "Well, shave me for a drooling llama."

I laugh. He laughs with me.

"A moment," he signs when we are still. He turns to his pots, in which the water is now boiling. He picks up his rod and removes pot lids, sets down the rod, opens his medicine purse, and upends it over the table. Roots, leaves, moss, berries, tied cloth envelopes, and two knives—one small and delicate, the other nearly a span long—spill out. I cock my head speculatively at him. He sorts out thick, green leaves and a root like a fat, tapering, white worm, cuts them up, tosses them into a pot, and replaces the lid. Into the next pot go different leaves and grayish powder from an envelope. He lets the third pot boil while he goes into the kitchen, then emerges from behind the door curtain with a large jar. He kneels before the fire again and removes the lid from the jar, then reaches in and removes a handful of the chunky, dark brown contents, which he sprinkles into the remaining pot.

I sniff. "Coffee?" I ask when he looks back to me.

"Yes." He returns to his chair. "I think this is to be a long night, so I am making it strong."

"Now I know I am away from civilization too long, for I miss coffee."

"I am grown dependent on it. But because of it I am all the time urinating, and if I sleep too long, I wake up with a headache and a thick feeling like a hangover. But it counters my drinking." He glances briefly at the pot. The contents bubble pleasant accompaniment to the fire's crackle. "More questions, then, Truck," he signs as he looks back to me. "The important one—requiring, I am sure, the long answer."

I lean back in my chair so that the front leg comes up. "How am I coming to be here," I sign.

"Yes. What is happening?"

"Zorba, there is much I do not know, and much more about which I am confused. I have suspicions, and I fear them greatly. But I will tell events in order, and perhaps in the telling we shall open new doors."

"It will certainly not shut any," he remarks.

"I am not so certain. Knowledge can be like this: the more one has, the less one is certain of."

"Spare me philosophizing and get on with it, upstart!"

This warms me inside, a bit, and I need this reassurance.

"I am only in the seventh transit of my reign, Zorba," I begin—formally for smoothness' sake, "and in order to maintain our province's uneasy détente with this Florida/Cuba province, I embark on a tour of its northern central regions, accompanied by two of my advisors and an entourage of Stripes, along with two Floridian advisors and *their* Stripes. It is an odd place, the north Florida Outback, to be so sparsely populated yet so resourceful and little utilized. I am curious why, and interested in suggesting remedies, in improving trade."

"Too many bugs. Too hot. Many diseases. And the fishing is better up north."

"Please, Zorba!"

Zorba spreads his hands, then motions for me to continue.

"I decide on a formal tour: one transit, perhaps even two, and I intend to remain well inland rather than opting for the usual comfort afforded by sea travel—for ports are well known, well populated, and their resources obvious. I decide on a small entourage of twelve Stripes, for I do not wish my tour of the Outback to be too conspicuous. I do not like to draw too much attention to myself and my travels. My advisory staff in Seaport Savannah is excellent, I think, and can operate well in my absence."

Here I pause a moment, to find I stare at my feet on the table. My right heel rests atop my left ankle."At least half of my advisors suggest—as is their duty—that I not do this thing. I resist this advice. 'Is anyone dreaming of this tour?' I demand of them. 'Good, bad, or indifferent dreams?' None are, but all the same there is much bad feeling about this. This is, I am thinking, what usually and inevitably results when the Architect vacates the Chair for any length of time, and is to be expected. And I, like my advisors, am dreaming no True dreams of this tour—good, bad, or indifferent. So I decide to go."

The pot on the lowest rung boils over, darkened water hissing into the fire. Zorba moves it higher with the rod, then turns back to me.

I cease tugging at myself. "I am foolish, Zorba. When I am becoming Architect I am taking such care to select advisors I can trust, upon whom I may rely, whose opinions I respect—even if they are not my friends. But no: I am dreaming no True dreams, and feel no hazard. I am so foolish. Just because no one is dreaming a True dream about a thing does not mean it cannot happen. I am an Architect of Sleep, not a creator of the

Real. But I am young and not so wise, especially not so wise as my predecessor Charlemagne. Yet I am not realizing even this obvious thing. I do not know which is worse, Zorba: unwarranted arrogance or unwarranted confidence. I am possessing both." I fall motionless.

Seeing that I want to pause a half finger, Zorba again goes to the kitchen, returning with two large mugs. He hands one to me. I brush a finger along the spout a moment, then look up at the sound of Zorba's trill.

"Tell me the rest," he signs.

I push aside the mug. "It is the southernmost leg of the tour. We are away perhaps half a transit now. There are reports of bison on the prairie south and west of Many Corners, and out of curiosity we leave to investigate. With us are two of Louis XIV's advisors and a complement of Louis' Stripes equal in size to my own. It is a hot day, a slow day. One of my advisors, my friend Puck—"

"I remember Puck. Smart, thin, quick as a fish. Always in trouble."

"Yes, that is Puck. He is ill with incapacitating diarrhea, and remains behind at the inn. The rest of us set out, and we find the bison—huge, ugly, stupid things—and as we return to Many Corners my wagon breaks a wheel. My Stripes get out to see what they may do to fix it."

"Sign no more, Truck," signs Zorba. "Guessing the rest is too easy at this point." Deliberately he turns away, doffs the lid from the lowest pot on the rack, and ladles steaming coffee into my mug.

"My Stripes," I continue, "ask for aid from Louis' Stripes, and when it is given. . . ."

"Truck," signs Zorba after I am motionless a moment. "You need not—"

"When they give aid my Stripes turn on them. Zorba, it is carnage! They slash them with their Fighting Hands. They kill Louis' advisors; they kill my advisor. And then they turn on me. My own Stripes, Zorba! It happens so quickly! I am thrown from the wagon. I try to run and a Stripe blocks my way. We fight. My umbilical bracelet"—my fist strikes the table—"Zorba, the bracelet *you* are giving me on the day of my Naming!—is cut from my wrist. I evade my attacker, I flee, am pursued, must fight, am cut, must kill, flee again, hide from the Stripes, from their dogs—"

"Truck—"

"I hide, I think, I try to piece together facts and understand how it can happen that my Stripes—*my* Stripes!—are turning in this fashion. This is a thing machinated for some time, I am realizing, a thing awaiting an opportunity, overseen by someone desiring the Chair for some time now, perhaps even before I am becoming Architect."

"Who?"

"Many nights I lie awake and try to figure that out, Zorba, and still I cannot be certain. There is . . . a dream . . . that Charlemagne is rumored to be having the night before his death, and I fear it may be pertinent. But I do not know. Nonetheless I am usurped, Zorba. The rightful Architect no longer holds the Chair. And whoever does commands the loyalty of at least some, if not all, of my Stripes."

I sip my coffee. It digs a warm tunnel from mouth to stomach. Zorba is right: strong for a long night. I set down the mug. "There is a river nearby," I continue. "I swim downstream to avoid the dogs, and then I hide in the brush a long while. They search and I bleed, but they do not find me and eventually move on. I do not know the fate of Puck, sick in Many Corners, but I assume he is killed as well. Most of Louis XIV's Stripes are dead, and this can be perceived as nothing but an act of war." I spread my hands. "In the night I venture forth and begin the long process of surviving, of learning the Outback ways. I heal. I think." I drain my coffee and chew on the grounds. "And I dream."

"Of?"

"Of the strange one. Of [Bentley]. And I know your next questions before you sign them, Zorba: What is he? Where is he from? Why is he important? Why do I dream of him?"

"More coffee?"

"Please."

He pours, pours more for himself, glances at me, then adds to the coffee a bit of liquor from a small flask at the foot of his chair, which I am not noticing rests there until now. "Truck, I can tell by the way you sign these questions that you do not know the answers yourself."

"No, I do not. From my dreams I know that he is a stranger here, and that he and I are fated to meet. I know that he is an alien thing to us in many ways, but my dreams tell me that he and I shall be friends."

Zorba laughs with his free hand.

"You find that amusing?" I ask.

"Well, you must admit that it is an unlikely pairing. An Architect of Sleep and an ape!"

"I do not think he is really an ape, Zorba."

"Well, whatever he is, he is as inconspicuous as shit on a dinner table. If you are searched for, Truck, and he is linked with you, there is no place you will be able to hide."

"He fights like a jaguar, Zorba."

"And can he fight four or five Stripes at once, Truck? Can he return you to the Chair?"

I am thoughtful for a moment. "As to the first question, I doubt it. As to the second . . . It is possible. Yes, I feel it is possible he can."

"You are leaving your brains behind you in the woods, Truck. Unless. . . . You know more than you are telling, young one."

"No, not really, Zorba. Not about [Bentley]. I have a . . . feeling about him. It is that vague, I fear, but present nonetheless. I want him around me as much as possible."

"He will be in your way."

"Then let him be in my way. I trust these feelings. Though it will be necessary for me to leave him with you for several days, possibly as long as half a transit."

"With me! I . . . I know nothing for caring for shaven monkeys, Truck. And he is *huge*—to where do you go so suddenly?"

"Seven Answers."

He pushes his mug away from him, then picks up his flask and drinks straight from it. "Seven Answers! That town is a haven for smugglers, Truck! It is on the border between this province and yours, and is sure to be—" He stops. His eyes narrow and he regards me as though trying to pick an answer from my face. "[Lee]," he signs. "You intend to ask for help from [General Lee], that brigand!"

"Do you and Lee keep in contact?"

"Shave me, no!" He offers me a sip from his flask, which I decline. "I have much respect for her . . . " he continues.

"But," I interject wryly.

"But being around her is always making me crazy."

"Perhaps because you are so much alike."

"There is no reason to insult me." And he laughs. "Why do you seek her aid? She lives a comfortable life, or so I see from a few friends who know her. She is even on the Town Council, I believe."

"She is one of the finest strategists the Confederacy, at least, is ever having. She is being instrumental in winning the Battle of Rivers Meeting, you know."

"But the Timberland Stripe Revolt is five years past, and that is Lee's last military action. She is retiring soon afterward." Suddenly he sits upright. "Truck—you intend to regain the Title by *force?*"

"Only if I have no other choice. A Tribunal will be impossible to assemble if there is war, and powerless if, as is likely, the coup is ousting all upper echelons of government—even as far down as the Liaisons-to-Magistrates."

"So thorough a coup?"

"It is not unlikely, Zorba. In any case, the uneasy peace that exists when I take the vows, that I am trying to at least maintain for this short time I sit upon the Chair, is sundered by the manner of my usurpation. I do not even know if Louis XIV knows a coup is taking place! Perhaps he thinks I am the one ordering my Stripes to kill his advisors—which makes war almost a certainty."

"You are not in a good position, Truck."

"Thank you, Zorba. Your insight is always appreciated."

"Chew your tail, youngster. So you enter my life after such a long time and then vanish again."

"You cannot make me feel bad about this, teacher. I have much to do, and must hurry. I will return for [Bentley], or perhaps I may summon him to me in your good company. If you wish to accompany him."

"I . . . I am a physician, Truck, not a politician or a strategist. I am out of touch in this Outback town, and this is a choice I am making. Give me a room in which to sleep and a jug of liquor, and I am happy. Politics, causes—I already have a lifetime's worth."

"Of course, my friend." I reach across the table and ruffle his shoulder. "I am not here to recruit you."

He signs noncommittally. "Why *are* you here? And what is your rush to leave? You will not regain your Title overnight."

I laugh, but it is a mirthless wave. "Another cause, I fear."

I stare at the fire and remember my sleep of five nights ago. "The night before our fight with the Stripes," I begin, "I am having a dream . . ."

As I sign to him I notice a faint lightening through the window slit across the room on the eastern wall: our hands have moved to each other until the dawn. I look from that brightening strip of sunlight to the pots that bubble and hiss above the warmth of the bright flames, and when I am finished I sip again at my coffee and look about the room, savoring this moment and knowing that, desperate as I am, this will be a brighter page in the book of my memories.

Quietly we enter Zorba's room. [Bentley] is still asleep, but I must rouse him in order that we may work on him, for I prefer him alert to chancing the noises he shall doubtless make when we tend his wounds. He flinches when I touch his shoulder, and his eyes open. The skin of his neck is hot. Zorba lights a lantern with his candle. He dips a rag into a waterbowl, wrings it, and gently dabs at the wound. It does not seem to bother [Bentley], but the wound is sickly colored and swollen, and must be lanced. I sign to [Bentley] what we are about to do. It takes a while, for he seems to have trouble concentrating. If he is like us in this regard, then I think he may be embroiled in the quiet and soft of deadly storm that such a fever can be. He seems to understand what must be done, however. Using his knife, I cut a strip from the leg wrappings of strong blue fabric that we are removing from him, and I bundle it up and give it to him, indicating that he is to place it in his mouth when the lancing occurs, for doubtless he shall trill his pain, and this thing may help reduce the noise. We cannot have The Mongrel's tenants investigating Zorba's room.

Zorba sits upon [Bentley's] uncut leg so that it will not flail about. Ready are hot bandages, cloths to absorb the fluids, and a slim knife of Zorba's that he heats above the candle flame. I sit so that [Bentley] cannot see Zorba, and I clench [Bentley's] wrists. Zorba looks at me, looks at [Bentley], and moves swiftly and deftly so that the pain is not worsened by the anticipation of pain: a hand wraps around [Bentley's] ankle. The other glides smoothly and pierces the flesh at midshin beside the wound, sets aside the knife, and applies cloths to catch the profusion of pale yellow fluid that drains, ambers, darkens, becomes thinned blood, slowly thickens toward red, and diminishes.

Zorba wipes. He looks up at me, eyes questioning. I duck my head: [Bentley] bites hard upon the cloth, and growls, but little more. My hold is firm on his wrists; in a way it is fortunate his condition leaves him weakened, for I am not certain I can contain his strength under normal circumstances.

Zorba apparently decides to go another step: he selects a different knife, a slim, small, sharp blade. He looks to me to indicate his readiness, firms his grip on [Bentley's] leg, and cuts out the broad ridge of dirty scab that forms the spearhead of the wound. [Bentley's] back arches, and his mobile lips draw back to expose teeth and gum. Cords stand out on his neck. The color of his skin becomes even more pale. Above my clamped hands his fingers spread, tauten, and curl. I lean forward to bring more weight onto his arms. I glance back. The wound does not bleed, which I gather is a good sign, and seems to be drained well, from what little I know of such things. Layers of skin in the wound yield to a white layer of fat, yielding to a deeper red layer below that.

Zorba waits until [Bentley's] thrashing subsides, releases the leg, picks up the cup of alcohol beside him, and dashes the contents onto the wound.

[Bentley] makes a noise in his throat as though something claws its way out, a sound from deep inside. Not a loud noise, but painful to hear. It does not carry far, and I only hope the residents of adjacent rooms do not inquire as to the goings-on in the early morning. Moisture runs from [Bentley's] eyes and nose. I glance to Zorba: he leans forward and stitches the wound with a curved needle. The penetration of flesh and drawing of string do not seem to bother [Bentley].

The rest is cleaning up: a bandage for the wound is dipped into a bowl containing one of the concoctions made downstairs. This is placed against the stitched wound and covered with another bandage that is wrapped by a clean cloth and tied securely but not too tightly. Zorba absentmindedly tosses the soiled cloths into a corner of the room. He stands, runs fingers through his eternally disarrayed fringe, and signs, "This goes both better and worse than I am thinking it will. We shall watch for further infection, and keep bathing the wound in both alcohol and medicinal poultices. Time is the arbiter now. I am going downstairs to pour him a broth. He must drink it; he needs fluids."

I let go of [Bentley's] wrists. "More coffee?" I ask.

"Certainly. Another cup for myself as well, I think." He turns and brushes aside the door curtain. His footsteps descend the staircase.

[Bentley's] eyelids are closed. They are smooth now, rather than lined from clenching. If I read his expression correctly—and I learn to do this, though I am constantly amazed by the mobility of his features—he looks peaceful. His breath, ragged before, grows slow, smooth, and even. I stroke his hair—such soft, long hair—and rub the bristle along his lower face. The biting rag is fallen beside his head; I set it aside. Though he is too long for Zorba's sleeping mat, it does not seem to hamper him greatly; soon he sleeps again, and I am a bit awed: after such pain, to return so quickly to slumber!

I lean back against the wall and regard him.

Do you dream, [Bentley]? I wonder? Are your dreams such as mine? Or are they the dreams of normal folk, rooted in the events of the day? Or are they something else entirely?

[Bentley] twitches once in sleep, like a dog chasing dream birds. He makes a low noise and is still.

"What are you, [Bentley]?" I sign.

Of course he does not answer.

Zorba returns in less than a finger, bearing a tray on which are three mugs. He sets it on a small stand beside his sleeping mat and signs, "A nice thing about residing in an inn—there is rarely a dearth of dishes." He hands me a mug of coffee and a stirrer, which I accept gratefully. I stir the coffee, sip, and chew the grounds. Warmth spreads through me. I set the mug beside me. "Despite what coffee does to you," I sign, "you should drink more of it and less of alcohol."

"Don't lecture me, upstart. What I do, I do of my own volition. My vices are freely chosen." He lifts his mug to his mouth and sips from the spout.

"Should we wake [Bentley] and get him to drink?"

Zorba regards him for a moment. He sets down his mug. "I think not. I prefer that he rest, for it will heal him faster than any concoction of mine can." He looks from [Bentley] to me. "I will not chase the scrawny chicken here, Truck: his leg is bad, and will have to be cut off at the knee if the infection does not abate. What will you do then?"

I rub my eyes and look around the room. "Right now I plan to go to sleep, for I am exhausted, and staying awake can make not one hair's difference to his leg. When I wake I have much thinking to do, many decisions to make. For now I am tired. You should sleep as well. I would not take your mat from you, but one of us ought to sleep beside my friend, to hush the noises he makes, to guard him from worrying at his wound. If you will sleep beside him, I will sleep on the floor. It will not discomfit me in the least; I am tired enough to sleep on a fire-ant pile without noticing." I drain my coffee mug.

Zorba eyes [Bentley] warily. "Sleep beside him?"

"He will not eat you, Zorba."

He lifts a hand noncommittally.

I wave a chuckle. "Zorba—you are nervous! Are you afraid of him?"

"He is alien to me, Truck. And huge. His feet hang over the edge of the mat."

"Would you prefer to sleep on the floor? I will sleep next to him."

He hesitates, and I laugh. "Then I will sleep beside him," I sign. "I am more used to him than you are."

"Very well, Truck. I think it will let me sleep better."

"Would that I could sign the same for me, Zorba. Can I help you with anything before I go to sleep?"

"No. I have only to put away the knives; I am removing the pots from the fire when I am fetching the coffee. I. . . ."

"Yes, Zorba?"

"It is nothing. I am glad to see you again, little Truck, even under the circumstances. Sleep well. Dream well." He waves out the candle.

"I would prefer," I sign to myself in the darkness, "not to dream at all."

16
Narrative of James Bentley

ZORBA DUCKED PAST the door curtain with a tray in his hands. He set it on the stand beside me. "Morning and waking, [Bentley]," he signed, using the three quick gestures that represented my name. He pointed to the tray, upon which was a plate of cooked peccary ham, two biscuits, and an egg that had been hard-boiled at my request—at my insistence, rather. There was water in a large-handled mug that had a spout like that of a pitcher.

"Breakfast," Zorba signed.

"Gratitude," I replied. It meant that or "thank you."

"Eat, please. Return me in one finger." He turned away.

Feeling a bit foolish, I sounded an attention-getting trill as best I could. He turned around.

"Zorba? Sign you 'return in a finger' why?" I emphasized the sign for finger.

"Length-of-time finger is."

"'Finger' also means." I pointed to a finger.

"Yes. Same thing."

I was confused and literally groped for the right words to ask what I wanted. "'Finger' length-of-time how?"

Comprehension dawned in his near-set eyes. "Sign not-always that, but is coming to mean that—understand?"

"Yes."

"This length on water-time, finger is." And he held his forefinger and thumb a finger's breadth apart.

"'Water-time,' Zorba?"

"Yes. Thing-to-keep-time."

Aha: water-time = clock. They used water clocks! "Understand me, Zorba. Thank you."

"How is it you understand clocks, [Bentley]?"

My God, where to begin? The very concept of telling time, and of exactly *how* the time was divided, was so difficult for me to convey as to be impossible. Plus, the mechanics of a clock—a wound spring uncoiling at a measured rate—entailed a conversation I was not qualified to carry on, for beyond that broad description I had no idea how to build a clock. So I had to content myself with answering: "Clocks my kind have, Zorba. Similar things."

He ducked his head and went out the door curtain. I heard him walking down the stairs.

I shook my head, understanding the expression at last: since the raccoons kept time with water clocks, a "finger" must have been a unit of measure indicating the time it takes the water level to lower approximately a finger's width. They must have had some sort of standardized value if a "finger" was the same everywhere. It turned out that a "finger" was about five minutes.

Satisfied with my deduction, I ate my flat-tasting biscuit, my overcooked ham, my underboiled egg, and sipped tepid water from the huge-handled mug. I had learned not to drink from the spout, because I usually ended up wearing more than I swallowed; my mouth was simply not shaped the same as theirs.

Zorba returned with his own mug and sat facing me against the wall. He sipped from his mug, watching me.

I smelled coffee.

I set down my remaining half biscuit, dusted off my palms, leaned forward, and indicated his mug. A furrow appeared between his eyes. "Hold this me?" I asked.

Cautiously he handed it over. I lifted it to my nostrils and inhaled.

It *was* coffee! I thought about taking a sip but decided against it. Instead I returned the mug. "Zorba," I began. "Many this?"

"More," he corrected. "Yes, [Bentley]. Want some you?"

I nodded and grinned, then caught myself and stopped. "Yes. Please. Much please!"

"Certainly. Wait."

He got up and went downstairs again—taking his mug with him. I sat back and laced my fingers behind my head, reflecting on the events of this last week. It had been goddamned educational.

I had a lot of questions to ask. It became obvious that they did, too, so for six days I had been receiving a crash course in raccoon sign language. It turned out to be amazingly simple to learn, but it was infuriatingly hard to utilize. I could learn an object sign in nothing flat—and then I immediately and invariably used it out of context or improperly. Sentence structure was also a problem at first, until I got it that, for the most part, sentences were constructed noun-verb-subject-predicate. To say, "Truck and I are going to the store," is to sign, "Store go me Truck." Punctuative division is generally accomplished through emphasizing different signs or by brief pauses between signs—for in signed conversation there tends to be no gap between the formation of one sign and the next, just as in spoken conversation there is no cessation of vocalization from one word to the next. This was hardest for me to learn; in order to coherently sign to me, Truck or Zorba had to pause distinctly between one sign and the next, for I interpreted the "null" motion of hands flowing from one sign to the next as part of a sign itself. I would improve as the weeks progressed; you learn a language fast when you're immersed in it to the extent that I was. Am.

My second-biggest problem was dealing with the fact that meanings tend to shift significantly with the use of affirming and/or negating symbols. The phrase "+ [plus] apple I" means "I have an apple." Just as easily, it can mean "I have *another* apple," "I *want* an apple," "I *want another* apple," "I *like* this apple," or (I suppose) "I add apples," depending on context and inflection. Body posture greatly influences this; there is a "sight line" along which much of the correct interpretation relies. The "+" and "−" signs are used a lot; they mean gain/loss, add/subtract, have/have-not, want/don't-want, like/don't-like, yes/no. Thus to say, "I understand," is to sign, "[+] understand." I was helped here (at long last!) by my college training in semiology: in order to operate at a (relatively) high level of conceptualization, a language needs fluid or plastic symbols, transmittable and coherent but flexible rules, and *synonyms,* the latter of which allowed me to substitute signs with similar meaning when asking what a particular sign meant.

It all sounds ponderous, but really it's much simpler than English, because their language is quite pragmatic and, in its own way, utilitarian, and allows little room for excess baggage. The signings lack noncrucial connective words and the vocal null spaces we use to collect our thoughts ("uhh," "like," "y'know," and so on), though of course there is a gestural "pausing" analogue. Though signing is often slower than speech, information is transmitted quickly and without convolution. By and large, if it doesn't carry pertinent, contributory information, it doesn't go in.

In many respects they are empiricists to make a behavioral pyschologist blush. In this fashion Dr. Zorba was apparently the personification of the proper scientist educator. He was elderly—though I did not yet know how old "elderly" was to them. He was short for a raccoon, standing about four feet eight inches tall. (I am six even. The average raccoon stands about five even. The average Stripe stands five six.) Zorba's eyes were small and close-set, and a fringe of hair whiter than the rest ringed his head just below his ears. He looked remarkably like a caricature of actor Sam Jaffe, so I named him Dr. Zorba after the character Jaffe had played on the old *Ben Casey* television show. He was indeed a physician, though he was much else besides. Educator. Political scientist. Cynic. Alcoholic.

I had been under his tutelage a week now. Truck had vanished. He was vague as to her whereabouts, forcing me to content myself with the assurance that she would return "soon." In that time I had learned much about the language, and thus peripherally about the culture that had produced it, and about Zorba himself.

I had mixed feelings about Zorba. He was invariably helpful and quick to answer my questions as best he could. He played nursemaid to me the entire length of my infirmity, bringing me food twice a day, then three times a day when I abashedly told him I needed more; emptying the chamber pot I used; changing my bandages and checking the progress of my wound; removing the stitches toward the end of a week when they became infected.

But Zorba was often drunk and would pound his fist against the floor in the middle of the night until someone banged on the wall for him to stop. Or he would stare dejectedly out the window slit at sunrise, signing to himself. Often he would pace about the room in furious hyperactivity, or—more commonly—he would merely sit on the floor and drink, staring at me, staring at the wall, staring at nothing.

One night when he was drunk he beckoned me to the window slit. I rose awkwardly and hopped to him. He pointed out the window, finger raised to the narrow strip of sky that could be seen.

He pointed from the sky to me and signed an interrogative.

I was stunned. "No, Zorba," I signed. I pointed to the sky. "There no me."

He looked back out the window and signed to himself. After a while I went back to bed.

Zorba had a shelf of books, and I spent a day leafing through most of them. Zorba showed me which way to turn the pages and how to hold the books, since the characters were incomprehensible to me. They resembled Chinese, and I guessed they were descended from pictoglyphs. It turned out the books were read the way our books in English are: spine to the left, pages turned right to left. The writing, however, was columnar, read up to down from left to right. For the life of me I could not tell if the books had been printed or hand-lettered: raccoons write with either a quill pen or a calligraphy brush, and a professional letterer's characters are astoundingly uniform. I was quite curious about this, for possession of the printing press would tell me much about the level of their technology. In many ways a technology may be assessed by its ability to disseminate information speedily and in quantity, and so a printing press is a quantum leap above hand-lettering.

A few of the books had illustrations, and while they looked to be originals, it was still hard to tell: the paper they were on was like vellum, and any printing would take quite readily.

Again I found myself thinking: laugh at the primitives all you want, bucko—but could you make paper if you tried?

Most of the illustrations were not terribly enlightening: line drawings of animals; three drawings of curiously shaped sailing vessels; pictures of several raccoons; drawings of medicinal plants and roots, of medical instruments. One volume was somewhat revealing. It was thick as a telephone book and was obviously a medical reference text, but other than the anatomical depictions of raccoons, most of the illustrations made little sense to me. Those that did reminded me a bit of da Vinci's painstakingly executed anatomical sketches.

Zorba returned with my coffee. I thanked him profusely and accepted the hot mug, into which was set a little wooden swizzle stick. There was no cream or sugar, but I didn't care: it was coffee, it was hot, and it contained *caffeine*.

I stirred the black liquid, which smelled awfully strong, tapped the swizzle stick against the mug, blew on the surface, and sipped. I nearly choked: coffee grounds rasped down my throat when I swallowed. Hurriedly I set down the mug and took a drink of water from the mug on the breakfast tray. Zorba pounded my back while I coughed.

"All-right you, [Bentley]?" he asked when my throat-clearing had subsided.

"Yes. Thank you." I glanced around the room for something I could use to filter the coffee.

"Need you what, [Bentley]?" asked Zorba.

"Cloth?" I replied. "Cloth clean."

Zorba got up and hunted around in the large cedar chest that occupied a corner. He shut the lid and turned to me with a square of cotton cloth like a handkerchief, which was ideal. I thanked him, then poured my mug of water into the covered chamber pot beside my bed (a thin, mungo-filled rectangle ticking similiar to a Japanese *futon)*. I covered the mug with the cloth and poured the coffee through. A good four teaspoonfuls of wet grounds were left in the middle of the dark stain. I bundled it up, leaned forward, and dropped the kerchief and grounds into the trash bucket beside the cedar chest.

Zorba looked exasperated, went to the bucket, fished out the cloth, emptied out the grounds, and banged the cloth a few times against the rim of the bucket. I felt guilty, realizing that he probably wanted to keep the cloth. Things like that weren't as disposable here as I was used to. "I-am-sorry," I signed.

Zorba signed nothing and examined the stain. Some guest I was turning out to be.

I tried the coffee again. It was quite strong and looked like Valvoline, but it tasted almost like espresso, faintly oily and with a bitter aftertaste like Tanzanian coffee. It was delicious and set my stomach to grumbling for hours.

Zorba waited patiently while I finished my breakfast. I drained my coffee, and he finished his. He asked if I wanted more, and I responded with an enthusiastic "yes." He left and returned with an entire pitcher full of the strong black brew.

From then on Zorba and I downed about two pitchers of

coffee a day. This inevitably resulted in each of us having to get accustomed to the other using the chamber pot, and we used it a lot. The raccoons aren't as fussy as we regarding their hygienic privacy.

I thanked Zorba for my breakfast when I was done. I had ceased asking if he cared to share any of my meal, because he always declined my offer. I wondered if he did not relish the notion of eating after me. Eating after him didn't bother me at all—I used to allow a pet raccoon to lap up saliva from my mouth, remember? As long as they were clean and fit, as for the most part these people were, who cared?

And that was when I noticed the shift I had made in my thinking: they were no longer animals to me, no longer qualified by the epithet "intelligent raccoon," either. They had become people.

When I thought this I felt the bottom drop out of my stomach. Taking a neat little trip through raccoon-land was one thing; saturating myself in it to the point where they became people to me, where the sights around me became acknowledged as part of an everyday reality, was a sign I found alarming. Because it meant only one thing: *I accept*.

I had accepted this world. Acceptance meant that I was no longer an observer, but that I was a part of it. That the world—*this world*—was a natural thing, however it may have arisen.

And acceptance signified something else. It meant that I had let go of what I had known. Horribly, alarmingly, in the span of a single month, I had come to regard my previous existence as exactly that—something in the past. In order to accept a new world, I'd had to let go of the old one. It is the difference between the intellectual acceptance I had made that night in the stable when I had seen two moons, and the emotional, heart-wrenching acceptance of *understanding:* that I would never make love, never pet my dog, never ride in an airplane, see my parent, answer a telephone, or any of a million things I had taken as irrevocable, again.

Unless I could make it back. Could I? There was that cave, that doorway, tunnel, whatever the hell it was, back there. All right, I would seek it out. When I got the opportunity, and when I could take someone with me. I would never find it again on my own.

"Signing lesson," announced Zorba after I had moved my wooden tray to the low table beside me. A furrow appeared between his eyes when he saw my face. "[Bentley]? Water from your eyes—why?"

"It is nothing, Zorba."

"Many-things learn you today, yes?"

"Yes," I answered. "Best I try me."

So for two hours I constructed sentences, learned new signs, learned to change the meaning of previously learned signs through emphasis, and the like.

One of the signs Zorba taught me was part of the name Truck had given me. It was a nullifier followed by a quick brushing of the fur at the cheeks with the palms. Because it was familiar and part of my name, I asked Zorba what it meant.

He signed various synonyms until I understood.

Literally it meant "no fur," or "hairless." Bald.

I halted the lesson—sidetracked it, really—and asked Zorba the meaning of the other sign that formed the remainder of my name. It occurred after the sign meaning "bald," and consisted of both arms curved slightly outward, shoulders thrust forward, elbows bent, hands curled in front of the chest like a parody of the human gesture indicating a woman with large breasts.

Zorba seemed hard-pressed to define the gesture. For a moment he rooted around for a synonym. He came up with one that I failed to comprehend. I was trying to think of how to sign to him that it was okay, that I'd learn the gesture's meaning sooner or later, that we could go on with the language lesson—when his head snapped up and his small eyes narrowed, then widened. He went to his bookcase, ran a long index finger along the spines of the cloth- and leather-bound volumes, and pulled one from the right-hand side. Though of course I could not read the title stamped vertically on the leather cover, I knew it was a volume I had not yet perused, simply because I had not worked that far along Zorba's shelves.

Zorba opened the book, standing with his back to me. I got to my feet while he turned pages, chittering impatiently as he did. Finally he turned to me with the opened book, rotated it so that it was right side up, and extended it triumphantly.

I stared.

I looked at Zorba, whose eyes, normally flat and dull, were quite bright. I looked back at the page, and I began to laugh. It welled forth, bubbled up, burst out, rolled from my mouth until it pained my stomach, until I was bent over clutching at my midsection as if to contain the pain and humor of it—for to have it all burst forth at once would surely kill me. My glasses fell from my head, and I inhaled great, wheezing gasps until my throat hurt and my face was hot and tears streamed from my eyes. Zorba pounded my back because he thought I was choking. When I did not stop he hugged me from behind, knotted his hands into fists over my stomach, and began pressing against my diaphragm in the Heimlich maneuver. This made me want to laugh even harder, but the pressure on my stomach made me queasy, and finally my laughter subsided.

I wiped my eyes dry with the backs of my hands. Zorba released me and turned me around. The gray blur of his figure swam before me. I signed that I was all right, but he insisted I sit down. I made no protest as he guided me to the mat and helped me lower myself. I grunted as my weight shifted from my left leg, then asked Zorba if I could see the book again. He picked it up from the floor where he had dropped it, dusted the cover carefully, examined it for damage, and handed it to me. He eyed me warily as I opened it to the page he had shown me.

There was something wrong with it, something I couldn't quite put my finger on, but nevertheless—pictured there, sitting on a tree limb, long-armed, hairy, and open-mouthed, was an ape.

"[Bentley]"—that's me.

"(–) fur ape."

Bald Ape.

17
Narrative of Truck

"SO THE RUMORS I see are true, little Truck?" General Lee shakes her head. "You are deposed?"

"I fear so, Lee. Rumors sign many things, and so some are inevitably correct. But I find myself amazed at you—surprised at your lack of surprise."

"Always I have an eye out for gossip." Lee looks up from the glass of peach wine she pours for me. "Do you remember when you and Puck are adepts?" she asks. "It is just before my retirement, and that Stripe named Limp calls me a relic who represents outmoded and useless military methods—he signs this in front of you all, in your strategies and achievements class." She laughs. "And you two shave Limp's favorite llama and paint it red! Oh, the trouble you get into!"

"We are shoveling that animal's shit for a transit," I sign, and I laugh with her. "I can smell it in my nostrils still."

"Truck, Truck. You are such a good pupil in those days." She falls motionless, remembering old days, better glories. Finally her eyes focus again on me and she signs, "So you are indeed deposed, my young avenger, you are usurped? Tell me of it, then, for I suspect that is part of the reason you are here. It is not a short tale, yes? Yes; here, then: intersperse your conversation with some baked apples and peccary. Quite good. No, no; eat when you pause in your story; not all at once: I want to see this tale, not watch you slop apple onto your hairy face. Now—you are signing?"

• • •

This town of Seven Answers is four days west and north of Three Big Dogs, by one of the llamas inherited from Doc Holliday. It lies on the Scummy River, at the northern boundary of this province, and I am making the journey in a leisurely kind of haste, on the lookout for Stripes, whom I suspect will be watching main roads near the border between Florida and my province of the Confederacy. But the land is large and I am not; there is much ground for them to cover, and communications are not the swiftest here, and I am trying to keep on the move. I feel that the Bald Ape is safe with Zorba so long as he does not venture outside, against which I am cautioning him. Zorba is left with instructions to teach the Bald Ape as best he can—teach him to sign, to read, to write. ("As ever," Zorba's hands sign in my mind as I think of this, "you expect the undoable. Very well, he will be signing when you return. As for the rest . . ." He spreads his hands.)

So the Bald Ape is not a large consideration as I search for General Lee in Seven Answers, and this is a weight from my wagon.

In signing with Zorba I learn that local Stripe garrisons are notified to watch for me, while additional Stripe contingents from Louis XIV's capital of Seaport Jacksonville search the wilds of the Outback even more thoroughly after the discovery of the two dead Stripes and their dogs. While this is not exactly a lightened load, I at least travel more smoothly with the knowledge.

Stripes are good to have on your side and under your control. Not since the Timberland Revolt are they defying an Architect, and now I find that they terrify me. Authority is such a fragile thing, for it relies largely upon the faith of subordinates that you *are* indeed authority. The Stripes heed us because we are True dreamers, and when their faith is somehow shaken, or it is shifted, that authority is no more.

Seven Answers is a larger town than Three Big Dogs. It is renowned for its rugs and its good cloths, both rough and fine, colored with bright dyes. In many respects it is a merchants' town, hampered from larger fame only by the geographical misfortune of not being near the sea. The Scummy River only winds northward into swampland, so Seven Answers' rich fabrics rarely go directly to northern and western provinces. Instead they travel either a week's journey east by cart to the

Dog Piss River, where they can reach Good Rats or Seaport Jacksonville; or they can travel south by boat down the Scummy River and then to Gulfport [Tampa] in Louis' own province, to Gulfport [Mobile] in mine, or to [Tokugawa's] great gulfport city of [New Orleans] in the Frontierland.

In Seven Answers I seek out the location Zorba writes down for me, a house that is situated just outside the south end of town. The house is nice—prosperous, even.

The elderly male who pulls aside the curtain after my ring is not familiar to me, but I sign that I seek the counsel of Lee, being sent by Dr. Zorba from Three Big Dogs, and he indicates that I should wait inside while he fetches her.

I look around while I wait, and feel both happy and sad that Lee is doing so well for herself. Happy, because the Outback is a hard place in which to prosper, and Lee is obviously quite a landholder, a contributor to her community, and —to judge from the paintings and furs and shelves of books on the walls; the expensive rugs on the floors; the beautifully crafted furniture and manatee-oil lamps with globes of expensive, milky glass; the scented rooms, floral arrangements, and many other things that add up to lend an impression of *home*—to judge from these things, Lee is obviously secure in the place she is finding for herself and her family.

But from this derives my sadness as well, for my reason in coming here is to persuade her to leave this for a time, possibly forever. To see the house Lee builds for herself, its trappings and its rich, polished woods; to meet her current suitor; to see her midlitter kits, who visit her for dinner this night—this troubles me, for these are the things I shall ask her to risk, and they are good things, secure things, comfortable things.

Our meeting is very different from my reunion with Zorba. Lee only embraces me, signs a hello, and tells me that we will be more comfortable if we sign in her receiving room. The years since her retirement—albeit fewer than Zorba's—are not as wearing on her. Time only adds to the air of dignity always surrounding Lee, perhaps because she is doing well for herself and is leaving the Keep in pride after her victory at the Battle of Rivers Meeting, rather than in the disgrace attendant upon Zorba's dismissal.

The astounding thing is that she shows no surprise at seeing me here.

Her receiving room is decorated with maps and charts, battle lines and fortress layouts. Her old war helmet hangs on one wall. The few books in evidence are military accounts, histories, and biographies of past Liaison Generals of the known provinces. Though of course not a Stripe herself, Lee understands Stripes. They are bred to fight; General Lee is groomed to lead fighters. In her receiving room we sit in comfortable chairs, savoring peach wine, inhaling the aromas of oiled woods and scented tobaccos, while I tell my story.

"Unfortunate, Truck, that this should happen." Lee's penchant for understatement is not diminished with time. "The current political situation is not good. You sign that you are out of touch for more than a transit now?"

"Yes. I am recuperating until well enough to travel, then spending time traveling."

"Well, Truck, to you I will make no secret that I receive what reports I can from Seaport Savannah. I have friends there still."

"You have friends everywhere, Lee."

She waves this aside, embarrassed.

"So what is the situation now that I am off the Chair?" I ask. "What is my usurper doing?"

A crease appears between her eyes. "I think [her/his] actions may surprise you, Truck."

"Please, tell me. It cannot be so drastic as to exceed my worst imaginings."

"Very well. There are a few odd proclamations, but nothing so drastic as you expect. First, and I suppose most major: All cargo tariffs are removed from ships and boats docking at Confederate seaports and riverside cities."

"What?" I am indeed surprised, and this is indeed unexpected—*this* is one of the major events since my usurpation? It is strange, yes, but not the work of a . . . a despot. "What is the reason for this?"

"None is given, Truck. But now the seaports are jammed. From what I gather, there is virtually no docking space to be had in Seaport Savannah. Balancing this, however, is the fact that exported cargoes are now taxed, and both incoming and outgoing cargo inspections are considerably increased. There are complaints, of course, but nothing severe."

"I do not understand this action, Lee."

"It is a smart thing to do for the short range," she signs. "It brings an enormous amount of trade into the Confederacy in quite a short time, and provides a perfect opportunity for thorough searches."

"What do they search for?"

"Need you ask?"

I sip my wine. It is delicate and cool. Lee must keep a cask soaking in the Scummy River. "My usurper wants to find me so badly? What difference would it make? The Chair is taken; what can it profit [her/him] to find me?"

"I imagine, s/he wishes to keep you from seeking asylum in another province, or from returning to the capital and attempting to summon a Tribunal. Doubtless s/he knows you are escaping, and in some ways you are still a threat."

"Without a tariff the province must be losing a fortune!"

Lee spreads her hands. "You are the Architect. You are a figurehead and a symbol of power. If you are alive and your whereabouts unknown, then you are still a presence in the mind of your usurper."

"Still. . . ." I sip again at my wine. "What else is happening?"

"A new minting."

"My usurper manufactures more *coins?* This is . . . is madness! Is s/he deposing me merely to hand money out to everyone for some altruistic reason?"

"I do not understand it, either, Truck. Minting more coins can only devalue the currency."

I wipe my muzzle where a few drops are spilling. "This action bothers me," I sign. "Even though I do not know its purpose. Curious. Continue, please."

"Naval production is increased."

"Naval production? Lee, the more you tell me, the more perplexed I become. I am coming to you for answers, and they make me feel more ignorant than before I am getting them. What in particular is increased in the shipyards?"

"I know few specifics, Truck. Large vessels are ordered built, several three-masters. Many extant ships are to be refitted and refurbished. All shipwrights are now gainfully employed by the Keep."

"How considerate of my nemesis. Is my usurper trying to deliberately ruin the economy? With no tariff, a new minting, and a huge increase in the fleet, the province could be impoverished within a year, I should think."

"Perhaps. But this all has the feel of a well-thought-out plan, Truck. And lifting the tariffs is bringing a great deal of trade into the major seaports, so that plenty of money circulates—even if it is not Confederate money. Who knows what your usurper may do next?"

"For now I will attempt to puzzle out what s/he is already doing, but I grow afraid to ask. What other good news is there?"

"All town Magistrates are temporarily forbidden to request aid from the Keep. This order is not generally known, of course, so that Magistrates will not be taken advantage of."

"Well, this order, at least, is easily explained," I sign bitterly. "I imagine it is because the Keep is hectic these days, what with a change in upper-echelon personnel."

"It also serves to keep the Magistrates of outlying towns ignorant of events in the Keep. In all probability they know nothing of the coup, and the less chance there is for them to find out, the better for your usurper."

"But surely the Magistrates are complaining?"

"They are assured it is only temporary. And in the meantime, what can they do? Magistrates do not often request aid from the Keep; most of their problems can be handled by the [Police Commissioner] and local Stripes. But there is an odd thing accompanying this edict."

I finish my wine. "And that is?"

"Supporting this order to town Magistrates is a stipulation that their Stripe garrisons remain where they are and assist the local [Police Commissioners] and Magistrates in every way they may."

"Why is this strange?"

"Because they are also instructed to be watchful for a peculiar creature."

"A . . . creature?" I ask, suspecting the answer before Lee signs it.

"Yes. A monstrous thing described as resembling a shaven monkey, if you can imagine this."

"This is indeed most peculiar," I reply. I will sign of Bald Ape when I have the opportunity. "Why are they to watch for it?"

"No explanation is given. But it is to be captured and immediately delivered alive to the Keep in Seaport Savannah. Of all the actions of your usurper, Truck, this is the only unaccountable one."

"Certainly I can make no sense of this, Lee." Is my usurper also dreaming of Bald Ape?

"It is definitely peculiar, young one."

"I am hoping you might provide some insights. You are without parallel at piecing together seemingly unrelated facts to form an image."

She regards my empty wineglass. "More wine?" she offers politely.

"No, no more, thank you." I look at the empty glass, also. "Well, perhaps a little."

She pours me another glassful, then waits until I sip it and set it down again before she casually signs, "It is from piecing together these events I am telling you about," she signs, "that several days ago I am concluding that you are usurped."

Now I am startled. "How so?"

"Because every ruler has a style, Truck, a method of managing a province that is just as distinctively [her/his] own as [her/his] signing, or a fine musician's playing of an instrument. You are only holding the Title . . . what? Six transits now?"

"Seven."

"Very well, seven transits. Yet I know you, and seven transits is long enough to learn to recognize your way of sitting in the Chair. So I am noticing a shift—not a major one, not a drastic one, but a shift nonetheless, and one that is uncharacteristic of you. It occurs uncomfortably close to the time of your tour of the Outback, which itself is a perfect opportunity to oust you. But what is clinching it for me, of course, is Louis XIV's proclamation."

"His proclamation?"

"You do not know of it?"

"I am receiving little news in the swamp, Lee."

She ignores my sarcasm. "Louis is issuing a proclamation that is not only posted in all major towns in northern Florida, but delivered upriver to Seaport Savannah. It declares that your Stripes are massacring not only *his* Stripes, but two of his advisors as well."

"This is certainly true."

"But Louis' proclamation holds you responsible. He demands an accounting by next transit, or he shall assemble a Tribunal. And he hints that he will assemble it at Rivers Meeting, which is strategically wise since it adjoins four provinces—none of which are Florida/Cuba. And Rivers Meeting also has the significant historical attachment of being the site of the Timberland Stripe Revolt and the Battle of Rivers Meeting. The Stripes of all provinces regard that place with something like reverence."

"And the Keep's response to this proclamation?"

"There is none, Truck. No sign whatsoever. Your usurper is making neither public nor private acknowledgment of Louis' proclamation."

"But the threat of Tribunal. . . . Tell me, what of my advisors, what of the adepts?"

"There is not a sign of protest, not from any level of the Confederacy's government. Your usurpation occurs without contest, and from this I can only conclude. . . ." She spreads her hands.

"That my advisors, and possibly the adepts as well, are killed."

"It would be logical. This coup seems a thing planned for quite some time, Truck, to judge by the smoothness of the transfer of power. Few are even aware that the Chair is now warmed by a different hindpart."

"Must you phrase it so indelicately?"

"Apologies. But you see my point?"

"I think so. You imply a thing I am already noticing, a thing that disturbs me greatly: there is a coup, I am ousted, and a usurper holds the Chair, if not the Title—yet the only difference this makes is that trade is increased in the seaport cities."

"The only difference so far. This bothers you."

"Would it not bother you? Who can my usurper be, to be so confident in this coup, so arrogant in [her/his] rule?"

"I do not know enough to do more than guess, Truck. The only thing that is certain is that s/he certainly has the cooperation of many, including the Stripes."

"If several provinces cooperate to assemble a Tribunal, it is an implication that war is only a few steps away. Surely my usurper realizes this."

"Perhaps that is what s/he wants, Truck."

"War with Louis? With the probability that all three of the other bordering provinces will assist Florida/Cuba?"

"I am only suggesting the possibility, Truck. It is too early to tell yet. Perhaps, as you are signing, for some reason the economic ruin of the Confederacy is [her/his] goal."

"This is unfathomable, I tell you!"

"It is the way it is," Lee signs simply.

This only serves to frustrate me further. "What else is Louis doing in response to the attack?" I ask.

"Nothing regarding the Confederacy. He awaits the next transit, which is only . . . ten days away, I think." She glances at the granite calendar on one wall. "Ten days, yes. Locally, though, Louis' Stripes are sent out from Seaport Jacksonville to search the Outback."

"For what? Not for me, not if he knows nothing of the usurpation."

"Again, I am sorry to sign that I do not know. Perhaps he searches for hairless monkeys as well."

"It so happens, Lee, that I know where one can be found."

For the first time in my life I see her startled. "You joke, yes?"

"No. I am discovering him in the Outback. He is a strange creature indeed, and is exactly as my usurper's proclamation describes him. But he is intelligent—as smart as a raccoon, I firmly believe—and I am dreaming of him."

"But what is he?"

"I still am not sure. He is far from his native land, I think. But I feel that he is important, and I feel also that I must keep him near me."

"Where is he now?"

"In Three Big Dogs, under the care of Doctor Zorba."

"Zorba! That old drunkard? You are revealing yourself to him? Truck, I am not sure—"

"You and Zorba have your differences," I sign, "but I would trust Zorba with my life."

"You are, little Truck. You are. And he is fully capable of dropping it and breaking it without even realizing he is doing so while in the midst of some drunken binge."

"The Bald Ape will help prevent this, I think."

"You place great faith in a monster."

"Do not chide me for trusting my True dreams, Lee."

"And do not berate me for my inability to assess a situation full of so many strange and unknown variables, youngster."

"Truly, it is not my intent to seek an argument with you," I sign.

"But you ask questions and then complain when I give you answers."

"I apologize, Lee. I want only to understand what goes on

and how best to proceed. I confess that I am distraught because my usurper. . . . " I stop and regard my hands. I pick up the wineglass and take a long swallow. It burns in my stomach in a way I find almost pleasurable. "I do not know. Perhaps it is merely that this is not what I am expecting."

"You are distraught because your usurper does not appear to be an evil tyrant, I think."

"It is certainly humbling to see that the province continues just as well—perhaps even better—without me."

"Surely you are not so naïve as to question yourself about this, Truck. You are always too apt a pupil."

"I am not in class with you, Lee, and this is not a test."

"But it is, my brash young Architect."

"Then all the more reason to be direct. I need your expertise, Lee. Please."

"Such presumption! Such arrogance! Such—"

"Desperation."

"All right." From drawers in the table between us she withdraws a wooden pipe and a pouch of rich-smelling tobacco. She fiddles with it, tapping the pipe against a black glass cindertray, then filling it, tamping it, and lighting it with a long, thin brand. Lee's way of gathering thoughts is to light her pipe. It is a tactic that infuriates both friends and opponents—and often the two are one—but I am patient, recognizing it for what it is. Finally she blows smoke from around the stem of the pipe and signs, "Your usurper is obviously no fool. S/he will not reveal [her/his] true intentions quickly. I doubt very much that s/he is quite the benefactor you fear s/he may be. Perhaps [her/his] actions are pieces of a bigger thing, and we must wait until more of the pieces are revealed before we may see the thing. Or perhaps they are misdirecting actions that hide another thing."

"What other thing?"

"Do not count the hares in your bag until you are home, Truck. I only speculate."

"If s/he is perceived as a better Architect than me," I sign firmly, "then truly I wish [her/him] well, for I am neither so vain nor so proud that I feel the need to regain my Title purely for the sake of retribution. I have instead more altruistic motivations." I tell Lee my dream of the stone falling from the sky and crashing hotly into the ocean, creating huge waves and long rains, causing floods and crop damage, drowning and starvation. "A small benefit of this dream," I finish, "is that it indicates to me that I *am* more fit to rule than my usurper—for if s/he is dreaming such a thing as this, it is inconceivable that s/he would not be taking precautions even now."

"[Tokugawa] in the Frontierland," adds Lee, "and [Alexander] in the Timberland will be the only ones unaffected. Napoleon in the Union may decide that a helpless Seaport Savannah will be too savory a morsel to resist, for his capital of Seaport [D.C.] will probably be untouched. In any case, the coasts of the Confederacy and Florida/Cuba will be vulnerable after the stone falls."

"Very likely," I sign. "And I cannot have this."

"There is the chance you are interpreting your dream incorrectly, Truck."

"I concede that. But even if that is so, my vows prevent my remaining idle while there is the possibility that the province is maneuvered into war. And my usurper's method of gaining the Chair is insidious. Why is s/he not simply challenging me before a Tribunal of advisors? If s/he feels more suited to rule, this can be demonstrated before a duly elected Tribunal in the Keep. I certainly do not claim to have a monopoly on True dreams!"

"Allowing a Tribunal to decide which of you is the more worthy of the Title would be a gamble at best, Truck. Taking the Chair while you and two of your six advisors tour another province is, in a way, much easier if it is well thought out—for then the outcome does not rest in the hands of others."

"How can such a one replace the entire upper hierarchy of government without sending ripples at least throughout Seaport Savannah, if not through the province?"

"It would certainly take some doing, but it is obviously not impossible."

"To openly send Stripes after me is foolishness; to attack the Stripes and advisors of another province is even more foolish."

"Audacious, perhaps, but not necessarily foolish."

"Can s/he be so secure in [her/his] coup, Lee?"

"It certainly appears so."

"And what *of* my Stripes? How does s/he control them? Shave them, they are bred, trained, and sworn to be loyal to the rightful and proper Architect—me! What is turning them; what is the source of their corruption?"

"Again, Truck, I do not know."

"I must find out. Knowledge is armor, knowledge is weaponry—and I can do nothing in my present, pitifully unarmed state. There is immense information to be gathered before I may act, Lee. I feel so frustrated. The work to be done towers before me; it darkens me with its shadow. The task ahead is arduous, and requires much time, and care, and planning. And I have only nine transits!"

Lee removes the long-stemmed pipe from her mouth, for it is gone out. She tamps it against the cinder tray on the table between us, lights the brand from the wall lamp beside her, and rekindles the pipe. She bites on the stem and blows smoke from her nostrils. Her gaze follows the pale trail of cloud up to the beamed ceiling, follows the heavy beams that line the corners to look at the many rich things on the walls, at the trappings of success displayed here. "There is not much for me to do here in Seven Answers," she finally signs, "and I miss my old work very much."

"Then . . . you will help me?"

"Are you ever doubting this?"

"I am less certain these days than is my custom, Lee. It will be hard to assist me, and dangerous. There is so much to be done, and the risks are great."

She thumps the side of her pipe with a fingernail, her infamous "ready" gesture—known to all who have the misfortune to sit opposite her at one of the many board games at which she is expert. "Then we had best get started, yes?"

18
Narrative of James Bentley

I WOKE UP in the middle of the night. The room was dark; the candle Zorba kept lit for my benefit had burned out and the yellowish moonlight coming in through the narrow window slit was too dim to see by. Zorba slept facing me in the cane chair.

My heart was stammering; my throat felt constricted and my palms were clammy. I had been dreaming. . . .

I had been dreaming about tying my shoelaces. Now what the hell was that supposed to mean?

I got up and emptied my bladder into the chamber pot. The sound of it was loud in the small and quiet room, but Zorba did not awaken. He had been drinking less these last few days, and his sleep seemed less troubled. I think that forcing him to concentrate on teaching me how to sign had been good for him; it occupied his time and prevented him from getting drunk just to relieve the monotony. Monotony was something I gathered he had a lot of.

Shoelaces. . . .

It nagged at me. In kindergarten I had earned a little American flag pin for learning how to tie my shoelaces. The teacher had spent half the day demonstrating it over and over until finally I got it right, and still I wasn't very good at it. The task became no easier as I grew older; my semiambidexterity made me all thumbs—

Holy shit.

I bit my lower lip. I needed the book, the book with the

drawing that had made me laugh so hard that afternoon, but the room was too dark for me to find it, or to examine the picture if I did. Frowning, I stepped into my underwear—the only article of clothing remaining to me, thanks to the medical ministrations of Doc Holliday and Zorba. I put on one of Zorba's ponchos, pulled the hood over my head, and picked up a taper. Out the door curtain and down the stairs. *To grandmother's house we go,* I thought absurdly. Quietly, quietly; remember the second-to-last step that creaks when you step on it.

The fire was out, but a small night-light guttered in the far corner. I lit the taper from it and crept back up the stairs. I had ventured downstairs a few times before; past midnight hardly a soul stirred in the inn, and the risk was not so great. I wasn't sure what I'd do if I was seen. Run away, maybe.

Back in Zorba's room I lit the candle from the taper, blew out the taper and set it aside, then tiptoed with the candle to Zorba's bookshelf.

Next to last book, if I remembered correctly. I pulled it from the shelf and went back to the sleeping mat. I set the candle on the low table to my right, opened the book to the middle, and began leafing past pages of incomprehensible text.

I found the drawing and peered close in the flickering, pale orange light from the lone candle, and I was right.

One of the hands of the ape in the drawing was upraised, depicted clearly. The hand had five digits, parallel and straight. None of them were opposable, which meant that the ape had no thumbs.

Shoelaces. . . .

You can't tie your shoelaces without your thumbs.

You can't do much of anything without thumbs.

I looked at the sleeping figure of Zorba. One of his hands was wedged beneath a leg. The other rested on his crotch. The thumb on that hand was nearly twice the length of the thumb on mine.

Shoelaces.

My God— how could I have been so blind?

In the human world, the main reason primates achieved dominance on the Darwinian chain was because of the development of the thumb. It gave us our tool-making abilities, our facility for delicate manipulation, the capacity to swing a club, hold a bow, throw a rock, paint a picture. In essence, the evolution of the thumb, along with higher brain functions and the development of language (and possibly the thumb had a hand in the origin of these as well), laid the foundation for human civilization.

In the human world, raccoons have no equivalent for the opposable thumb. They have paws. They are dexterous with them, yes—but they are still not "hands," for none of the digits are truly opposable, and the raccoons' environment keeps their status more or less quo.

But what if it had been different? What if, somewhere around a million years ago, the savannas had not opened up in Africa, causing the primates to remain arboreal, preventing the formation of many links on the Darwinian chain: no weapon-making abilities, predatory behavior, group hunts, organization for the hunt—and thus language, and thus improved memory, increased brain size, history, civilization spreading throughout Africa into Europe and Asia, across the Bering Strait land bridge into North and South America during an ice age. What if we had stayed in the trees and become neither dexterous nor smart?

While on the North and South American continents, indigenous raccoons *did* develop opposable thumbs. Tree climbers are predisposed to develop hands, and the hands of these raccoons are much more manipulable than those of a human being. Their thumbs and fingers are half again as long as a human's, and more supple. The leverage afforded by the thumb is dramatically increased. And they acquired upright posture, so necessary to free the hands for tool making. Not possessing versatile vocal cords, they developed a language involving hand gestures and body posture. Their intelligence increased accordingly: with a language and opposable digits, the smart could now outwit—and thus outlive—the strong, and could go on to educate the young. The thumb predisposed intellectual dominance on a high rung of the evolutionary ladder normally reserved for the strongest or the most adaptable. Tool users do not adapt to their environment; they adapt the environment itself as required.

And they had gone on to develop a civilization, to spread across two continents, to domesticate animals, develop large-scale agriculture, build towns, establish trade, form a viable economy, then a system of umbrella government—whatever the latter two consisted of, there was certainly evidence that both existed.

The horse didn't exist here because in the human world it had been brought over by Spaniards in the early 1500s. Here there were no Spaniards; hence the specialized breeding of the indigenous llama—a relative of the camel.

One of the books I had thumbed through had contained drawings of oceangoing vessels. Since it was obvious from the book now in my hand that the raccoons had discovered Africa, it seemed reasonable to assume that they had explored Europe, possibly into Asia. Where, I mused, they might have encountered the onager or the Przhevalski's horse, the only true wild horse—but who knew, by now, with a million years of alternate evolution? Probably they had not yet explored Australia, though they might have discovered it, and almost certainly not Antarctica, either.

My head reeled. The implications, answers, missing pieces—they tumbled down and locked into place.

Somewhere in the past a split had occurred. The road had forked. Did it branch each time a possible variation was introduced, creating an infinity of different worlds, all deriving from the same source, all the result of every possible permutation of a situation, each of *them* branching out as well? The best—the worst—of all possible worlds.

I shut my eyes and removed my glasses, then pinched the bridge of my nose, hard.

The world was still *the world*—but the stream had split. Natural selection had played favorites with someone else.

Raccoons.

We hadn't made it, and they had. It was that simple.

A world of difference, and all because of thumbs.

19
Narrative of Truck

THE STORM DOOR is unbolted and opened a few moments after Lee's ring. "We are closed, goodbodies," signs the short, thin, young male who answers.

"Lee and a friend, to see [Fagin]. He is in, I am sure."

The young male glances briefly at me. "[Fagin] is always glad to receive you, Lee," he signs, "but now is not a good time. I'm sure you understand—"

"My friend is all right," Lee interrupts. "Fagin will want to see us, I assure you. You are never having difficulty with me before."

"That is true; and I do not mean to insult. But I must ask him. If you will wait here?" Not waiting for a reply, he draws shut the door and leaves Lee and me staring at each other.

"Suspicious type," I observe.

"He has every right to be," replies Lee.

In a moment the young male returns, and without a sign he leads us into the crowded room that is Fagin's shop. Bolts of cloth crowd tables arrayed to form aisles stacked to the ceiling. There is everything here from the worst mungo to the finest linen. On the shelves and racks and tables are adzes, abraders, bone needles, books, burning-lenses, exotic brushes, coffees, candies, dinner bowls, dried meats, earfeathers, fantoccini, glassware, hackamores, inks, jars, jarred preserves, kegs, various leathers, moccasins, notchboards, oils, oil lamps, parchment, pots, carved pipes, quilts, razors, room scents, spices, scrimshaw, tobbacos, eating utensils, vases, water clocks, yarns, yo-yos, zori, and many other things besides. If this Fagin's shop specializes in any one item, I cannot determine what it is.

Through another door curtain we are led, then down a narrow, dim hall and into a small room where burns a brass lamp, beside which sits Fagin, brush in hand, open book before him. It seems he is tabulating the records of his shop; occasionally he sets the brush on the edge of the ink block, chisen-bops a column of figures on his fingers, and then picks up the brush and writes down the total.

I count five umbilical bracelets on his wrist.

Lee, the young male, and I stand within the doorway and watch until Fagin blows the ink dry, swishes the brush in a water cup, rests it on a cloth, and turns to us. "Hello, Lee," he signs. "It is a few months since we are seeing each other, yes? How are your suitors, your litters?"

"All are fine, Fagin; and I trust the same is true with you?"

"Yes, yes; the latest object of my affection is nearing estrus, and hopes for one more litter. If not . . ." He spreads his hands. "You may go, [Dodger]," he signs to the male who leads us here. [Dodger] leaves, drawing the curtain behind him.

Lee indicates me. "This is my friend, [Jones]," she signs.

Fagin ducks his head politely. "Goodbody," he signs formally. Then to Lee: "What thing may I do for you, Lee? Surely this is no social visit."

"No, it is not. We would like some things smuggled."

Fagin glances at his ledger. The ink is dried; he shuts the book and sets it aside. "Pity. If you are wanting a nice telescope, just arrived from the Union, I am glad to help you choose one. Or perhaps a bag of one of my many fine coffees, from places on the Southern Continent you are never seeing of. All my smuggling, however—to and fro—is official and in order. This is known as importing. That is my trade."

"Then there are some things we would like imported—exported, actually."

"I am importing things for you in the past, Lee. You never come to me unless it is trouble. Usually more trouble than it is worth."

"Since you are an astute businessperson, Fagin, and invariably charge exactly what a service is worth, I do not understand how anything you do can be more trouble than it is worth. I always compensate you adequately."

"It is easier to move goods unofficially before than at present. From where to where?"

"From here, or possibly from Three Big Dogs, to Seaport Savannah."

"The object in question?"

"Objects. Two raccoons."

"My price goes up as your hands move, Lee. Raccoons, you sign? You and Goodbody [Jones], perhaps?"

"Do you need to know this?"

"No; I would prefer not to. It helps, though, to know if I am exporting contraband. Are these two wanted by the authorities? I assume so, or else you would not require me in this fashion."

"I doubt your cargo will be wanted in any official capacity," signs Lee carefully, "but if it were to be discovered by Stripes, it would be disastrous."

"For you and for me," agrees Fagin. "No, I will not do this thing."

"But you—"

"I am a businessperson. In business ventures there is profit and there is risk. For this the risk is too great. The border is difficult lately. Trade wagons on northbound main roads, and trade boats on both the Scummy and the Broken Spine, are inevitably and methodically searched by Stripes on both borders. The same is true with ships pulling into port in Seaport Savannah. I understand that things have changed in the Confederacy. You are once a citizen of that province, Lee, and are perhaps more familiar in dealing with it. But now is not a good climate for smuggling. Even those of Louis XIV's Stripes garrisoned here act as though they seek something, and this disrupts even my official business. I do not fool with Stripes, Lee. Neither should you."

"I have no choice."

Fagin spreads his hands once more. "Then neither do I."

"We are not necessarily signing about doing this immediately," I sign. "Do you foresee helping us if the cargo searches relax a bit?"

"Possibly. Come to me then and I will let you know. In the meantime, goodbodies, I have much business to attend to. So unless there is some further service I may provide for you . . .?"

"Yes," I sign. "A few things, we hope." From my purse I pull forth a folded sheet of paper. I unfold it, glance at Lee, who signs an affirmative, and hand it to Fagin. He smooths it and then reads it. A crease forms between his eyes. He sets down the paper. "I find this peculiar, goodbodies. The largest riding llama I can find? Letters of intent? A wagon containing a hollow space of six spans by two spans by one? The letters of intent I understand, for you will need such if you are searched. But the rest—why do you come to me for these?"

"As with your 'imports,'" signs Lee, "these must be obtained unofficially. You know how to provide them unobtrusively."

"A giant llama—*unobtrusively?"* He waves a laugh. "A wagon with a space to accommodate a raccoon? Lee, because you live in this province does not mean your loyalties lie with it. I know something of your past."

"Your point being, Fagin?" asks Lee.

"I am not ignorant of some recent events which are not yet common knowledge. Neither, I suspect, are you. And suddenly you want to head north. With a wagon containing a raccoon-sized hideaway."

Lee signs nothing, but steps closer to him. "We are merely asking for your help."

I trill for attention and they look my way. "No, Lee, we are not," I sign. "We are requesting his services, for a fee. He is electing not to do business with us, and that is his right. Let us go. We will do business elsewhere."

Lee turns to me so that Fagin cannot see. "There is nowhere else to go. Fagin has more contacts, more resources, than any other smuggler in Seven Answers. He knows this."

"We will sign about it later. Let us go." I turn to the smuggler. "Thank you for entertaining our proposal, Goodbody Fagin. I am sorry we are not able to reach an agreement."

"Good day, Goody Jones. Perhaps your luck will be better elsewhere."

"Perhaps. I trust our visit here shall go no further than you and your coworker."

"Dodger can be trusted. I am nothing if not reputable, Jones."

"Doubtless. Lee?"

We emerge from the room to find Dodger at the far end of the hall. Again he guides us through the huge and crowded shop. I thank him politely and bid him good afternoon, and we take our leave.

Lee is still in a bristle when we reach her house, a distance of a few miles which we decide to walk, though Lee possesses fine llamas. Inside, Lee stamps about and makes a big show of her frustration as she always does, signing exaggeratedly to herself, ordering her suitor out of her sight, preparing coffee with a loud banging of pots, chewing agitatedly on a rich vanilla bean while waiting for the water to boil. I wait until she calms down, which occurs more from her fatigue than from waning rage, but at last we drink orange-juiced coffee at her table, and both of us stare over the rim of our mugs and sign nothing. Eventually Lee drains her mug, scoops out the grounds with a finger, licks them off, and signs, chewing rapidly, "And what now, Truck?"

"Now we look for a smuggler who can help us. If not in Seven Answers, then in Fallen Tree. If not there, then in another town, until we find one who will help us. We cannot force cooperation, Lee, and I would not trust one whose help is garnered under duress anyhow. We need the willing commitment of individuals and their resources. You know this better than I—why do you carry on so?"

"Because you are usurped! Because the rightful Architect is ousted from her Chair and wanders worthless Outback towns like some common minstrel!" From the way her hands rush with this reply I see that she is containing this for a while now.

"We endeavor to correct that. Pulling out your fur will aid us little."

"It frustrates! We cannot enlist aid without revealing our purpose; we cannot reveal our purpose to those we cannot trust; we cannot win trust without revealing who you are. To reveal who you are to those we do not already trust is suicidal. The Stripes search for you. Florida's and yours. We cannot let them find you, for there is no way for us to fight them. Fagin has no great love for the Stripes, Truck, but he has friends among them—among the local garrison, at least. He must, in order to smuggle continually and successfully."

"All the more reason to hasten my departure from Florida, Lee. I am more powerless here than in my own province. I must get to the Confederacy, to Seaport Savannah, and the Bald Ape must come with me."

"If he is as shockingly different as you are signing, Truck, then it is stupid of you to take him along. For some reason he is already searched for, and if he is linked with you, he will be a sign around your neck proclaiming your identity for all to read."

"Nevertheless. I go, and he comes with me. If Fagin cannot be persuaded, then we shall look elsewhere. But I cannot wait long. I will not seek aid in any official capacity here, for to assist Louis XIV in attacking my usurper will yield me little when all is signed and done; Florida will merely keep what it gains. I must return to Seaport Savannah, and we must delve into the situation more thoroughly, get closer to the source of the province's change. Perhaps we may abet the unrest there, foment rebellion. My friends, my allies, are there."

"This will take time, Truck, time and resources. We have neither."

"This is true, Lee. But do you expect to raise a rebellion overnight? Or even within a few transits? My rule, as you sign, is marked by the faith most others place in me. We cannot use that faith against ourselves. To win friends, allies, vassals, we must be truthful and not endeavor to shape the venting of those allies' belief. We must state our case—cautiously, I concur; slowly, methodically—but state it, and let others *choose* to throw in their lot with us."

"Truck, this is idealistic and naïve of you. What of those who choose *not* to believe, not to throw in their lot—and in fact choose to inform the Confederate Stripes? There is no doubt in my mind, my young Architect, that the reason you are now here rather than in your place in Seaport Savannah is because you are simply too trusting."

"Surely there is some happy medium to be attained."

"Yes! Do not present your rear until you consider that it may be kicked!"

"A tempered trust does not strike me as trust at all, Lee."

She trills angrily. "You make me want to smash your face with this mug in the hope that the pain will wake you up! Truck, you can philosophize with this attitude of yours—but you cannot regain what is taken from you! I may be an outmoded relic, as Limp is signing years ago, but you are coming by a hard road, at great risk, to seek out my advice—the advice of one who is spending all her life learning and applying just what methods you need. To ignore it is to be responsible for that ignorance."

For a long moment I am still. Then I drain my coffee mug, set it on the table, and sign, "Very well. What must we do?"

"That is more like it. More coffee?"

Into the night we sign. We compile lists, consult maps, discuss strategies, argue tactics, and develop what plans we can to get me, Lee, Zorba, and the Bald Ape across the border and as far as Seaport Savannah. Lee and Zorba can travel together openly, but the Bald Ape and I must sneak across.

In the late evening Lee's suitor returns to find us still going at it in Lee's receiving room. He prepares dinner. I hardly even notice; in the midst of our machinations I glance beside the stack of blank parchment on the table and see a cleaned plate an empty mug. I am eating dinner, but do not remember it.

Late at night someone strikes the doorbell. Lee's suitor is upstairs, long asleep. Lee and I glance at each other. Both of us read the same fear in each other's eyes: *Stripes?* Is Fagin informing them?

The bell rings again.

Together we get up and go to the door. I stand to the side while Lee opens the storm door. "Dodger!" she signs in surprise. Out of my sight Dodger signs something, to which Lee replies, "What? Come in, come in, and sign to us, then."

Dodger is polite enough to remove his moccasins before entering. He leaves them on the front porch and enters, ducking his head at me. Lee pulls the door shut behind him, then bolts it.

"I am sorry, goodbodies," signs Dodger, "but there is no time for amenities. Fagin sends me. He wishes to see you, both of you, immediately."

Lee glances at me. "Goodbody Fagin is having his opportunity to deal with us this afternoon," she signs.

"Please, Goody Lee. I am instructed to take you to him." He opens his purse and withdraws an umbilical bracelet. "Good Jones, this is for you."

"You insult me. I will not wear it."

"Please, Goody Jones. It is a difference here between pride and pragmatism: the Stripes know that you have no bracelet, and since there are few adults who do not, it marks you plainly."

"The Stripes?" asks Lee. "How do they know this?"

"Please, Goody Lee. This may be explained later. Now we must leave."

"This suddenly? No; if Fagin wishes to see us now, then he may come to us."

"It is too risky, and will certainly be too late. The Stripes may be here soon."

Fagin's shop again: Dodger leads us through twists and turns of dark hallways with smooth familiarity; by the time we reach the room where Fagin waits I am hard-put to sign where we are within the building. Obviously there is more to it than meets the eye, and thus it reflects its owner well.

Two candles light the room. On shelves are many books. At either end of one bookshelf is a skull. Both are of raccoons; one, from its size, is of a Stripe. A water clock rests on a stand on one wall; in front of it sits Fagin, absently playing with his umbilical bracelets. I note he now wears four, and I try not to glance pointedly at the one now on my wrist. I feel it, though, and do not like its weight on my arm.

"Very well," signs Lee. "We are here. What do you want?"

Fagin leans forward. He is bulky and appears even larger in this small, cramped, oppressive room. His bracelets click together as he signs. "After your business proposition of this afternoon, I am sending out queries—*discreet* queries," he amends for my benefit. "I am learning much."

"How fortunate for you," remarks Lee.

"Please. Sit down. I need clarification; from what I learn, two possibilities present themselves."

"And what is it you learn?" I ask.

"The official sign here in Florida/Cuba is that Truck, the Architect of the Confederacy, is killed by her own Stripes while surveying the Outback with her entourage in the company of Louis' Stripes and advisors. They also are killed, and the assassinating Stripes are escaping back to Seaport Savannah.

"And?" asks Lee.

"Official sign from Savannah, however, is that Truck and her advisors are killed by *our* Stripes."

Lee and I exchange glances. So a reply is now received!

"I know not which to believe," continues Fagin, "for both versions are incredible. But from both sources comes a similiar rumor: that one of Truck's advisors is surviving the attack. If true, s/he can provide the actual details of the occurrence to a Tribunal-elect—and for that reason s/he is sought."

"And your two possibilities?" asks Lee.

"We are dealing with each other several times before, Liaison General Lee," signs Fagin, and Lee starts at the signing of her old rank, which I gather is a thing that few here are aware of. "And though often we clash, I tend to trust you. Your nose is in the right place. You are famous for quelling the Timberland Stripe Revolt in Rivers Meeting, but nevertheless I think you are the sort who might engineer a coup in her old province. But I doubt you would sit here so idly after its initial phases are enacted. Therefore I do not think you or Goodbody 'Jones' here are involved in the killing the way you might easily be perceived to be. That takes care of possibility one, in my mind."

"And possibility two?" asks Lee.

"The obverse, of course: that there is a coup originating in Seaport Savannah, beginning with the killing of Truck and her advisors—and that *you,* Goodbody Jones, are a member of Truck's staff. The surviving advisor. It is only to be expected that General Lee would harbor you, and certainly explains why she wants you smuggled to Seaport Savannah."

"And you believe this latter to be the case." Lee's neck tenses a bit, though Fagin cannot see it from where he sits. Lee is preparing to attack, if need be.

"I do. Though it is beyond me why you would sneak back into that pile of fire-ants rather than hurrying to a neutral province, declaring yourself, and demanding a multiprovincial Tribunal."

"And your intentions regarding us?" pursues Lee, ignoring Fagin's speculation.

"A reward is offered for information leading either to the capture of the assailants—who by now are long going—or to the ostensible rescue of Truck's surviving advisor. Interestingly, this reward is offered by both provinces, though whom they consider the 'assailants' is quite a point of contention—one that could conceivably lead to war. In any case, I do not envy this surviving advisor, for I am certain that she—pardon me, s/he—is to be used as a hostage by our province, and will be killed if captured by the Confederacy.

"I am a businessperson. I am *not* a politician. Nevertheless, Truck's rule is a good one, and my trade prospers under her.

Now it sours, and trade between the provinces sours, and my business sours. While I do not think the provinces revolve around my business, I know that there are things that occur that, on the surface, look like mutually beneficial economic gestures made in good faith. Yet I also know that in the midst of this merchant's freedom is the Confederacy's implied right to seize my cargoes and commandeer my boat or wagon if it so desires. This shifted attitude on the part of the Confederate province affects ours. It is arrogant and assuming, this attitude, and in its own way ruthless. I do not send articles to Seaport Savannah now, if I can help it—officially or not. Too often I cannot afford these searches, and too many times my cargoes are searched."

Fagin tilts back in his chair. "I know you, Lee; if 'Jones' here is of Truck's staff, you will be trying to get her out of Florida to demand a Tribunal. So tell me if she is, and I shall do all I can to assist, so that I may content myself with playing a part in the resumption of my more accustomed business practices. Though first I will try and persuade you to go to a more neutral province—the Frontierland, I think, or even the Timberland."

Lee glances worriedly at me.

"Trust," I sign. "Here, or nowhere."

She ducks her head. "Yes," she signs reluctantly. "Our alternatives are too few."

"I believe we can make do with those we have." I look at Fagin. "I am Truck," I sign simply.

The sound of his chair leg hitting the floor seems quite loud.

20
Narrative of James Bentley

"ZORBA?"

"Yes, Bald Ape?"

"Zorba, who is Truck?"

"Do you never sleep, Bald Ape?"

"I have many questions, Zorba."

"Yes, you do. Too many."

"Will you answer this one?"

"All right; I will try. Truck is many things. She is a raccoon; she is a female; she is my pupil and my friend. She is your friend as well, I suspect. But you ask of something deeper than this, yes?"

"Yes."

"Bald Ape, Truck is a . . . leader. You understand 'leader'?"

"Yes. What kind of leader is Truck? Leading she of whats?"

"'What does she lead,' Bald Ape. Get it right."

"I-am-sorry. What does she lead?"

"Better. She leads an area of land to the north. The eastern part of the continent is divided into several parts. Understand?"

"Yes."

"Truck leads one of these parts. We sign now in the land south of the land she rules. Understand?"

"Yes, Zorba."

"This land is in the southeastern part of the Northern Continent. Understand?"

"Repeat, please. And slower, please. I-am-sorry."

"Watch: This. Land. Is. In. The. Southeastern. Part. Of. The. Northern. Continent. Understand now?"

"Yes. Thank you. Tell me, will you, what it is that Truck is signed? It is a title, it seems, different from her name. I see you sign it before."

"No, no, Bald Ape. Watch: 'I *am seeing* you sign it before.' See the difference?"

"Yes."

"Now, then. You refer to the title Truck is holding, yes?"

"Yes, Zorba. I believe so."

"This, then: Truck is the [ ] of sleep."

"I-am-sorry, Zorba. '[ ]'?"

"You are so frustrating! And I am so tired!"

"I-am-sorry—"

"Be still! ' [ ] ' is that-which-plans. That-which-creates. To design. Yes?"

"Yes . . .?"

"[Trill!] Shave you, Bald Ape! Look!—'[ ]': a designer. A planner. Truck is the [designer/planner] of sleep."

"I must see wrong, Zorba. How can one 'design' sleep?"

"Bald Ape, do you deliberately ask the easy-to-answer questions during the day, and save the convoluted ones for the middle of the night when I should sleep soundly?"

"I-am—"

"Be still! Bald Ape, when you sleep at night, do you not have [ ]s?"

"That last sign is unknown to me, Zorba. '[ ]s'?"

"[ ]s are stories in your sleep. In your head. On your eyelids. Stories that move. Yes? You have such?"

"Yes! Yes—[dreams]."

"Fine. Good dog—do not get angry; I only tease. The [dream] is an important thing. It is a way of regarding the events of your day, or of your recent life. It is the same with you?"

"More or less."

"How can it be 'more or less'? There is same, Bald Ape, and there is not-same."

"It is the same, Zorba."

"Good. I am glad to see it. And are there those among you who, when they dream, dream True?"

"You mean, individuals who dream of what is happening?"

"Of what *is to happen,* Bald Ape. You have such?"

"No. There are . . . signs . . . that such individuals exist, but never proof."

"What an odd world yours must be, Bald Ape."

"What an odd world yours is, Zorba."

"A joke! That is a joke, yes? You must warn me when you make a joke, so that I may grow to understand what you consider humorous."

"You walk a thousand side roads, Zorba! You are signing of Truck, True dreams, and the [Architect] of Sleep."

"Yes. We set great store in dreams, Bald Ape, for some of us dream True, dream of things yet to be. Some True dreamers are more accurate, though, than others. A very few can dream of things-to-come with astounding regularity. These dreams are odd things, different from normal dreams, and are subject to many different interpretations. Sometimes True dreamers may dream the same thing, even down to fine details, but the variations in their interpretations may be great. Those who are determined most accurate in their interpretation are also determined most fit to rule. This ruler is signed the [Architect] of Sleep. There are five of them in the known provinces, one for each province."

"But who determines which raccoons dream more accurately?"

"I sign toward that. When a parent suspects a kit has this ability, s/he brings [her/him] to the capital city of their province, where the kit undergoes a series of tests. If the kit is chosen, the kit becomes an *adept*. Most are turned away, though."

"And Truck is once one of these?"

"Yes, except that she is brought to the capital by the head of the crèche that is taking care of her, and not by a parent. Anyway, these kits are raised in the capital, and are taught how to understand their dreams, how to govern, how to manage an economy, and much else. From these is chosen the Architect of Sleep. Those adepts less accurate about their dreams are usually chosen by the Architect to be advisors. The Architect [her/him]self is chosen by a Tribunal of advisors and high-ranking adepts. Do you fall behind me?"

"It is confusing."

"You will grow to understand. The Architect has absolute power, except in the case of an unanimous vote of advisors and senior adepts against [her/him]. This maintains a balance of power, yes?"

"It . . . seems an odd basis by which to govern a people."

"Why? How is rule determined in your land?"

"There are many kinds of rule, Zorba, for my . . . land . . . is fragmented into many provinces, and most have their own way."

"This seems chaotic to me."

"To me, also, and it is chaotic. The method of rule in the land I am from is to allow each individual a chance to sign yes or no on what actions the ruling body may take, or to suggest alternatives, and the most numerous signs are made the rule."

"This is ridiculous! Are the signings of ten who are unable to dream True to have more worth than those of one who can? Are one hundred? One thousand?"

"Zorba, where I come from, there are no True dreamers."

"How do your rulers provide for calamity? For bad crops, severe frosts, heavy storms, forest fires, unavoidable conflicts, earthquakes in some regions?"

"We cannot know the outcome until it occurs, Zorba. We try to . . . to sight down an unwalked road by extending the one on which we find ourselves. That is the best we can do."

"How unfortunate. How tragic! How do you prevent deaths by hurricane? How do you save water against drought, or take precautions against plague?"

"Our . . . our knowledges aid us greatly in this."

"And so do ours!"

"I do not think we mean the same thing by 'knowledge,' Zorba."

"How unfortunate."

"We do the best we can with our handicap."

"Doubtless, Bald Ape, doubtless. And my intent is not to ridicule your kind; you cannot exceed your . . . limitations. One uses what tools one has. There are many of your kind, Bald Ape?"

"Many."

"How many?"

"I do not know how to sign the number. It is very many. Thousands of thousands-of-thousands."

"We will teach you numbers later, when there is time."

"Concerning Truck, please. She is the Architect of Sleep, and she rules an . . . area, a province . . . and she dreams True. These things you sign me, but their meaning is still vague; it slips my grasp."

"I marvel, Bald Ape, at how quickly you learn to turn a phrase. But all right: more. It is quite simple: The eastern part of the continent is divided into five provinces. Each province is ruled by an individual signed the Architect of Sleep. This title describes the ruler's talent: s/he dreams True, and does so more reliably than any other in the province. It is like being governed by an historian who remembers what is not yet happening. S/he dreams, and makes decisions based on those dreams, and that counsel is heeded unless it is vetoed by a Tribunal. Truck is—until recently—the Architect of Sleep for the province north of here."

"Until recently?"

"That, Bald Ape, entails a longer explanation that any thus far, and I can barely lift my hands now. Go to sleep! You will learn more in the morning."

"I-am-sorry to be so impatient, Zorba. But I have a great need to know these things. To finally express these questions I carry around inside me, and to answer yours regarding me—it is a great feeling of freedom. You understand, yes, Zorba? . . . Zorba?" [Aloud] "Ah, well. Sleep tight, my crusty old teacher. You've certainly earned it."

"No more wine," signed Zorba in his sleep.

"Zorba, what are the things worn around the wrist of many raccoons? Truck does not wear one."

"No, Bald Ape, she does not, and this is a bad thing. It is an [ ] bracelet."

"I-am-sorry: '[ ]'?"

"'[ ]' is the . . . rope-of-birth, rope-of-the-navel. Understand?"

"Yes, Zorba. [Umbilical] bracelet."

"Good, Bald Ape!"

"Why do all wear one?"

"When a kit is of an age, Bald Ape—usually twenty—s/he decides on a name, on what s/he shall be signed for the remainder of [her/his] life. Yes?"

"I understand, Zorba."

"A Ceremony of Naming is held. The friends, the teachers, the relatives, those important to the kit, are assembled, and the kit signs [her/his] new name to all. The mother presents the kit with the cord from [her/his] birth, fashioned into a bracelet. It is a token of adulthood, Bald Ape."

"And why does Truck not wear one?"

"Because she is without parents, and raised in a crèche, as I am signing to you. Though once she is owning an umbilical bracelet that I am giving to her."

"You, Zorba?"

"Yes. It is a long story, and I do not wish to sign of it now. But Truck does not wear an umbilical bracelet now because it is taken from her."

"This is bad, is it not?"

"Bad, Bald Ape. Yes. Most bad."

"Who is doing this to her, Zorba?"

"I will sign of that later as well. Not now. I do not wish to sign of it now."

"Awake at last, Bald Ape!"

"Good morning, Zorba."

"Good afternoon, Bald Ape. You are sleeping the day away."

"It is best I do so; at night it is quiet, and then my restlessness is less likely to lead to my discovery here. I get little exercise, though. Am I to live out my life in your little room, Zorba?"

"I hardly think so. We must wait until Truck returns; I feel we will move on then. Perhaps hurriedly. In any case, I think soon you will have more exercise than you want. Until then, we will exercise your brain."

"I am having more of that than I want, as well. What are you reading?"

"You and your inability to sign tenses! Watch: 'What do you read?' Now repeat."

"'You and your inability to sign tenses! What do you read?'"

"A joke, yes? I learn, Bald Ape, I learn. I read a book."

"Thank you, Zorba. I am glad to see you read a book."

"Panderer! I am taking out this book to show you things, to clarify things. Come here. This is a book describing the history of the provinces. Here, see the map?" He handed me the book.

I looked at the page he had opened it to. It showed a convoluted coastline to the north with a peninsula jutting into the ocean to the northeast, and the map traced the coastline along the east. At the far west were huge lakes. There was something about that map that bugged me.

I looked up at Zorba's trill. "Bald Ape, I am signing to you! Set down the book that you may answer me."

"I-am-sorry, Zorba. You are signing. . . ."

"I am signing, Do you understand 'map'?"

"Yes, Zorba. I understand that sign."

"What is wrong, Bald Ape? If I read your face correctly, you are upset."

"This map. . . ."

"It is quite recent, Bald Ape. It is a map of the five provinces."

My stomach froze. That peninsula to the northeast . . . I rotated the book ninety degrees to the right and felt a sinking sensation as the land mass pictured there transformed into the eastern coastline of North America. The map was drawn with east on top and north to the left. I set down the book. "It is also a map of my world, Zorba."

"Yours? Bald Ape, how can this be? Unless—are you from [ ] ?"

"Which is that?"

"It is not on this map. If it were, it would be here." He pointed east, off the page and across the Atlantic. "It is where others who faintly resemble you are found."

"No, Zorba. My kind sign that place—" and aloud I said "Africa." With my hands I told him, "I am from this place, here." I indicated the Florida peninsula. Sideways it looked like the hammer of a pistol.

"Bald Ape, I do not think you understand. That is where we are now."

"I understand. It is where I am from."

"I find this peculiar."

"Yes." I pointed to north central Florida. "This is where I am living in my world."

"There is a town near there named Many Corners. Half a finger, Bald Ape." He riffled pages until I was looking at a more detailed map of what might have been the state of Florida, except that the northern border was squiggly, not straight, and cut off farther south, at the northernmost point of the Gulf. It stuck out a northern thumb that was delineated by the St. John's River. Like the other map, this one had east at the top, north on the left. Cuba was included on the far right.

"This is a map of the province known as [ ] ." He signed something I have translated as "Florida." Zorba pointed to the St. Johns. "This is the river Dog Piss."

"Dog Piss?"

"Yes." His finger slid left. "Where the river borders Florida and this province, however, it is known as Broken Spine. Where the Broken Spine empties into the ocean is located the town of Seaport [ ]."

That would be about where Jacksonville was in my world.

"Jacksonville is the capital city of [ ] province," Zorba continued. His finger wagged across Florida and Cuba. "The Architect of Florida/Cuba is [ ]." And Zorba signed a name I was to translate as "Louis XIV," though not until after I had met him.

"Where are we on this map, Zorba?" I asked.

He pointed to a dot midway along the length of the St. Johns—the Dog Piss—River. "Here. In Three Big Dogs." Then his finger slid down to the east, at the Suwannee River where it crossed the northern border of Florida. "This is the Scummy River. On it, at the border, is the town of Seven Answers."

"Where Truck is now?"

"Yes."

I turned the pages back to the map of the eastern North America. "What of the provinces, Zorba? Indicate them to me, and tell me of them, please."

"Certainly, Bald Ape." He indicated a large region north of Florida. "Here is [ ]." The area to which he referred was roughly parallel to the Confederate States of the Civil War, so I dubbed it "the Confederacy." "It is Truck's province," he continued. "Her capital is here, at the Keep in Seaport [ ]." He pointed to where the Savannah River emptied into the Atlantic, so I mentally dubbed the town Seaport Savannah. To the left of that—north—was a thin, squiggly line marking the northern border of Truck's province. "The western border of the Confederacy is the Two Transits River, here." He traced the length of the Mississippi until it met the Ohio, where St. Louis would have been in my long-gone good old days. "It is named Two Transits because that is about how long it takes to travel its length. On the other side of the Two Transits is the Frontierland. Western Frontierland is wasteland, and little is known about it. The Architect of Frontierland is [ ]"—whom I called "Tokugawa." "He makes his capital here, at Gulfport [ ]." He indicated the equivalent of New Orleans. "Tokugawa's northern border is this river here." His long finger followed the Missouri to the lower edge of the map. "Do you understand so far, Bald Ape?"

"Yes, Zorba. It fascinates me."

He tapped the region north of Truck's province. "Here is [ ]." This time he referred to an area roughly equivalent to the Civil War's United States—or "the Union." "Its Architect is [ ]"—dubbed Napoleon— "a shrewd ruler and dangerous opponent. He makes his capital at the north end of this huge bay." He indicated the Chesapeake and a point near Washington, D.C. "The Union's western border is this river, Many Turnings." He traced the Ohio down until it met the Mississippi—to him it would be where the Many Turnings met the Two Transits. "Between the Many Turnings and the Two Transits, and bordered to the north by the four lakes known as Dreamers' Lake, Seal Lake, the Lake of Drowned Sailors and the Lake of All Forgetting"—he pointed at Lake Erie, Lake Huron, Lake Michigan and Lake Superior—"is the Timberland. Its Architect is [Alexander], and he makes his capital here." He set his finger against St. Louis' doppelgänger. "This is the city of Rivers Meeting. It is a huge city, an important one, for it connects four provinces. It is a great center of commerce. Five years ago there is a great battle there."

"A battle? Why?"

"Well, the reasons are many and the story is long, but in brief it occurs when Liaison General Lee of Truck's province—the same Lee Truck now seeks in Seven Answers—is leading the Stripes of three provinces to end the Timberland Stripe Revolt after they are slaying Alexander's predecessor, [Catherine the Great]."

"This is all so odd to me, Zorba."

"Why?"

"Because you point to regions I know of as other things. It is . . . unsettling."

"You will grow used to it."

His comment was meant to console me, but of course it did the opposite. My great fear was that I might *have* to grow used to it. "Tell me, please," I signed, to change the subject and get my mind off it, "is Truck the only female Architect?"

"Currently, yes."

"Why?"

"That is just the way it is now. There is no reason for or

against Truck being the only female Architect."

"I see." Odd, how an English idiom such as "I see," which figuratively means "I understand," can mean exactly the same thing in a literal sense: "I see" means "I just saw what your hands signed," their version of "I hear you."

"Tell me another thing, Zorba."

"If I am able."

"Why is east at the top of your maps? My kind draw them with north on top."

"East is on top because that is the direction in which the world rotates, Bald Ape. Why else?"

"Then . . . then your kind know that the world is a globe?"

"Of course, Bald Ape. Any kit can construct a pendulum to prove it is a rotating sphere. Why do you look so surprised?"

"It is a conversation I will attempt another day. But this knowledge implies many things about your people, Zorba, about your knowledge of the world and its place in the . . . in the everything, the all-that-is. Continually your people surprise me, Zorba."

"How is it, Bald Ape, that your kind can exist in what you claim is the same area occupied by raccoons, yet we know nothing of you? You are signing that there are 'thousands of thousands-of-thousands' of you, as I recall."

"There are, Zorba. These areas are the same lands, but they are not the same lands."

"There you go again! There is same, Bald Ape, and there is not-same. Which is it?"

"I think it is both, Zorba. Where I am from the land is the same—but my kind are exploring it thoroughly." I indicated the map. "I can tell you what lies beyond the wastelands in the western Frontierland. I can draw you a map of the west coastline. I can draw you a map of the continent south of here, the one whose southeastern coast forms part of this gulf. I know that there are six continents"—I decided to count Europe and Asia as one land mass—"and that one of them lies at the bottom of the world. My people explore, Zorba. More than you can imagine. We are even sending up people in ships to look at the globe of the world from above, from so high that the shapes of the lands are visible."

"No! Such a thing is wondered at for generations, but none has the capability."

"My people do, Zorba."

"You are only being a braggart, I think."

"No, Zorba. My people are traveling to the moon."

"Joke! This is another joke, yes? Funny, Bald Ape. See: I laugh."

"I do not. I do not joke."

"Which moon, then?"

"Where I am from there is only one."

"Then you are from a different world!"

"No. I lack the signs to explain, and am not sure I am able to even if I have the signs. It is as if each time a decision is made, in history, in the past, or now, a world is created from each way this decision can possibly be made. If you are to slap me now, there is also a world made where you do not slap me, or where you hit me hard enough to kill me, or where I stop you from slapping me, or any of all possible things. And in the past, somehow the decisions, the twinings, that are leading to my kind being present in my world, are not occurring here. Instead the twinings are leading to you. Who is to sign where else they may be leading, what different threads are breaking off to go their own way?"

"I find this notion intriguing, Bald Ape. And most sophisticated."

"My sophistication surprises you, Zorba?"

"Your existence surprises me, Bald Ape."

I was learning a lot, and learning it fast, but believe it or not I was bored. I slept during the day, awakening only when Zorba came in or went out, or when I had to hide in the cramped closet when a patient came knocking. Despite the fact that solid interior doors were uncommon, it was such extremely bad form to enter a room unannounced that such a thing seldom occurred. I thought the custom odd, and entirely too trusting—what about theft?—but there had been odder customs among humans: the Aztecs had used no doors at all, and would even leave a stick wedged in the portal to indicate that noboby was home.

I was in the room all the time, and Zorba forbade me to talk or go outside. It was making me twitchy. I have always been a restless person, an extremely hyperactive person. I pace incessantly and can't even sit down at a desk or dinner table without drumming yacka-ta-tacka-ta-tak-tak, monotonously and annoyingly. The graveyard-shift job at the 7-Eleven had been marvelous only in one respect: it accommodated this small-scale wanderlust, for in the unpopulated hours of three A.M. I could pace, sing, or drum all night long to my heart's content. But here in Zorba's cell—for cell it had become, though my imprisonment within it was necessary and voluntary—I had little room to pace and could not beat makeshift congas into the wee hours.

The effort it required for me to refrain from singing became a hell of a problem. I have always sung, and what I lack in vocal eloquence is more than compensated by volume. I tend to sing unconsciously, perhaps to occupy yet another restless corner of my mind, almost as if I am providing an ongoing soundtrack for my life. Nowadays my communication is almost solely limited to gestures and writing, and singing is just about the only sort of vocalizing I do anymore. But if I got caught doing it at the inn—and such odd stuff would certainly be investigated, for the raccoons had quite literally never heard of such a thing as singing—there would be hell to pay. I couldn't even hum. Zorba reprimanded me more than once.

So I paced, and I stared unobtrusively out the window slit at the impossible mundaneness of this world, and I drank endless mugs of coffee, of which there seemed an infinite variety of flavors. Zorba was disgusted when I requested milk for my coffee, and he refused to bring me any. He drank his coffee with a wedge of orange squeezed into it. I tried it once. No, thank you.

In the late afternoon Zorba gave me signing lessons, after which we could converse, asking each other confusing questions and giving involved and convoluted answers that satisfied neither of us.

Zorba maintained his sobriety with only occasional backslidings, but he was often out late, either socially or professionally. I was not allowed to burn candles while he was gone at night, for fire is something feared by those who live in wooden buildings, and there was a good chance some Good Samaritan would come fan it out—after politely knocking, of course.

So the wonder of it all was beginning to wear thin, to settle into a dreadful ordinariness. In all fairness, though, I was bored not with this world but with my cage, because I couldn't leave it to investigate the New Wide World Out There.

One night while Zorba slept I used a spanstick—a ruler the length of a raccoon's hand span, about fourteen inches—and a piece of charcoal to draw a graph of sixty-four squares onto a large piece of parchment. I shaded alternating squares, then set it aside and began tearing, folding, and shaking other parchment sheets.

When I was in elementary school one of my favorite books had been Joseph Lemmings' *Fun with Paper*. I spent endless hours constructing paper drinking cups, poppers, animals, caps, swords, and geometric shapes. So I shamelessly used half of Zorba's parchment to construct eight triangular "footballs" to represent pawns, four squares for rooks, four lightning-bolt shapes for knights, four up-ended, flower-looking things for bishops, two Japanese birds for queens, and two standing cones for kings.

And then I sat and thought for a good long while. Zorba had been drilling something of their government and caste system into me, so I knew that the names of all the pieces, and the concepts behind them—except possibly for "rook"—would be foreign to the raccoons. So I came up with substitutes:

Pawn, Rook, Knight, Bishop, Queen, King.

Stripe, Keep, General, Adept, Advisor, Architect.

Chess had long been a feudal game, adopted and popularized by the medieval nobility—though evidence indicated it had originated in India. I hoped I could explain the game to Zorba, and that he would want to play.

Zorba pushed a Stripe to Architect four. I responded in kind. Standard opening.

"I still do not understand why you need the board and pieces," he signed. "Once they are fixed within your head you do not need them." He moved his Adept to Advisor's Adept four.

"Perhaps you do not, Zorba, But I am not so fortunate. Remember my limitations, my handicaps." I moved General to Advisor's Adept three, thinking that if he kept pieces trapped in the back rank by his Stripes, in a few moves I could get away with a nice fork on his Keep and his Architect.

"I do not complain—well, a little perhaps. It is a bit frustrating to actually move pieces on a real board. It slows down the game." And he moved his Advisor—the Queen, the most powerful piece on the board—to Architect's Adept three.

In truth I was paying scant attention to the game. Watching Zorba was amazing and distracting enough: this wizened raccoon, hunched over the parchment chessboard between us, signing fluidly and pushing origami pieces around without hesitation, without even having the decency to show the sort of trepidation about committing to a move endemic to the chess novice.

I glanced at the board and decided to go on the offensive. Since my Knight—pardon me, my General—suggested a potential fork on his Architect and Keep, I decided to pound a bit harder and shoved my General to Advisor five to threaten his Advisor and set me up for that fork.

Zorba glanced at me curiously. He seemed about to sign something, thought better of it, and instead picked up his own Advisor. Advisor takes Stripe.

"Finish," signed Zorba.

I gaped at the board. It made no sense, it was just paper shapes on the paper checkerboard, an abstract thing. I shook my head and forced the shapes to pattern themselves into something I could recognize.

Four moves—his first chess game, and Zorba had beaten me with a fool's mate.

Of course I demanded a rematch. And of course this time I didn't lose in a mere four moves. It took twelve.

I looked up from the paper carnage before me. "Zorba," I signed, "your people have a game similar to this?"

"We have many games, Bald Ape, but none like this. I confess I am again surprised at you; this is a novel game, and any kit should like it very much."

"Any kit?" I refrained from telling him that in many respects chess is considered by humans to be the epitome of intellectual gamesmanship, the essence of a thinking person's competition.

"Certainly," replied Zorba. "It seems a good way to teach about interlocking combinations of potential. In fact, I look at the board now and see that it is a good simile for the notion you are signing of earlier, the notion of different twinings created by alternative occurrences."

"Please, Zorba, sign slower. It is difficult for me to understand you when you sign so many abstractions."

"I-am-sorry, Bald Ape. Despite your appearance, sometimes I forget you are not a raccoon."

I took it as a compliment. "Thank you, Zorba."

"You are welcome. The game, you see, is an entire universe of sixty-four squares, and each piece is nothing more than a symbol representing potential directions of movement. Within even the small space of these sixty-four squares, there are millions of combinations of moves—understand? A universe is determined each time a piece is either moved or ignored."

"That is remarkably fitting, Zorba."

"I think so, also. The simile breaks down, though, because of the limitations of the game—it is only flat, after all."

"My people have a version that moves on three levels, Zorba." My human chauvinism caused me to refrain from mentioning that I knew of few people who could play it with anything approaching proficiency.

"Now *that* I should like to play! Let us play this on three levels, Bald Ape."

"I have no means to construct such a board, Zorba—I require three more boards and a means to stack them."

"You have an imagination, do you not? Stack this board in your mind, and we will play."

"Zorba—" I didn't know whether to laugh or cry. "I-am-sorry, Zorba, but I cannot play this. Apparently I cannot move things in my head as well as you."

"That is all right, Bald Ape," Zorba signed diplomatically. "There are other things you do well—signing, for example."

I felt patted on the head. Still, he meant well. "I am always having a talent for . . ." Dammit, there was no sign for "language" in the sense of the spoken word, just as there is no word in English to suggest gestural communication (the phrase "sign language" is technically an oxymoron) "For such things."

"Tell me—you sign that this game is intended to symbolize warfare between the Architects of provinces in your world?"

"We have neither Architects nor provinces as you do, Zorba, but we have similar things. This game derives from them, yes. Why?"

"Well, it seems to me that this game represents not warfare so much as landholding. Inherent within its strategies is the notion of private property, and of defending it. And, I should add, of taking that of others."

"Curious, Zorba."

"Yes, Bald Ape. It reveals much about your people, and tells me that in certain ways you are perhaps more similar to ours than either of us may be realizing. Certain notions intrinsic to this game—landholding, warfare, warrior castes, titled nobility, strategy—are shared by us. And forgive me, Bald Ape, but it also demonstrates that you are smarter than I am perceiving you, for it indicates that you belong to a people with a stratified history and well-developed cultural heritage."

All that from the idea of chess? I was playing with no slouch here, and if I didn't keep reminding myself of that, Zorba would constantly and unwittingly rub my nose in it. "While I understand the truth of what you sign, Zorba, there are many things you mention as similarities that I am not sure I understand."

"You have but to ask."

"Doubtless." I waved a small laugh. "You are a good teacher, Zorba."

"Doubtless. I am having the best students imaginable, Bald Ape. Truck among them. About what are you curious?"

"About everything, Zorba. But in this instance, about the Stripes."

"What of them?"

"I want to know more of them. My people have nothing like them, and they seem very different from the rest of you."

"Yes, Bald Ape, they are. They are a class unto themselves."

"They are those-who-fight?"

"Yes, but more than that. You understand 'breeding,' Bald Ape? As when a farmer wishes to maintain a characteristic among [her/his] cattle, s/he pairs those with similar traits to perpetuate those characteristics?"

"I understand this, Zorba. It seems a thing your people are doing very much with the llama. My people have a similar animal they are breeding for many of the same uses, but I am seeing none here and do not know the sign for it."

"No matter. The llama is a good example. The same applies to the Stripes: they are bred as fighters. The traits strengthened in them are size and speed, and all their lives they learn fighting methods. They train with the Fighting Hand and the Hard Arm, the bolo, the net, the cudgel, and the knife. They also train to fight fur to fur, without weapons. They learn strategy and tactics, and are sworn to serve the Architect of their province, and are taught loyalty all their lives. They are forbidden to mate with any but Stripes, to keep the breed pure, and they prefer to associate with none but themselves and are generally quite reserved. They take great pride in the breeding of their own dog, a beautiful creature, I think, which they train alongside themselves."

"I have some slight experience with these dogs," I signed, meaningfully rubbing my forever-benumbed shin.

"The Stripes love their dogs, Bald Ape. As the Stripes to the Architect, so are the fighting dogs to the Stripes: loyal and obedient."

"But why are Stripes obedient, if they have all the might? They are, as you sign, bred to fight, and so they hold the true power."

"But the Architect dreams True, and it is in the best interest of Stripes to obey [her/him]."

"Then what is causing this Timberland Stripe Revolt you are signing of?"

"A charlatan. A Stripe claiming to dream True, but not in reality possessing the ability. The Timberland Stripes are rallying around her, but she is being a liar, interested only in power and not in the prosperity of her province."

"How do you know she is lying?"

"Because she is claiming to dream of ruling the Timberland as Architect, and the alliance of Stripes Lee is commanding against her are killing her."

"And so this proves her wrong?"

"Her death is certainly evidence that her dream of holding the Timberland Chair is false," he replied wryly.

"What of a Stripe who really does dream True?" I asked.

A crease appeared between his eyes. "There are none such," he signed firmly. "The capacity is not in Stripes, and cannot be cultivated."

"I cannot help but notice," I signed, "that when you refer to the Stripes you take on a [tone] that suggests they are regarded very differently from most raccoons."

"This is most perceptive of you, Bald Ape. Few raccoons like to sign of it, but we are indeed a bit . . . disconcerted by our own creation. The Stripes are very different from us in many more ways than their fighting abilities."

"What ways?"

"They take great joy in life; they revel in it with an intensity paralleled by few normal raccoons. Among the Stripes are some of our greatest poets and painters, musicians and playwrights."

"Why do they shave a stripe on themselves? Is it merely a custom?"

"It is that, but it is also a way to further set themselves apart from us. Louis XIV's Stripes dye a dark red strip alongside their Stripe, while Truck's Stripes leave it plain. Stripes like to decorate themselves, and take pride in the fact that they have no tails. Their manner is calculatedly aloof. Many generations ago it is the aim of provincial Architects to create a fighting caste, a warrior class apart from other raccoons, and this is indeed what is created—a class apart from other raccoons."

"But now you need them to fight your wars, yes?"

"I can certainly tell you that neither fighting dog nor Stripe is something you want to fly the fur with, for they are quick and they are deadly."

"I understand this all too well, Zorba. But tell me—if Stripes are swearing loyalty to their Architect, why are Truck and I attacked by them? Why are they killing Doc Holliday?"

"Those are not Truck's Stripes. They are the Stripes of Louis XIV of Florida/Cuba, who mistakenly thinks that Truck is making war upon him. But the truth is that there is a coup at all levels in Seaport Savannah, and Truck is usurped. Her usurper is turning the Stripes against Truck, and they are attacking Louis' Stripes and killing two of his advisors. Even our best conjecture to explain this happening is insufficient, for there are virtually no grumblings from the Keep, the capital of the Confederacy. It is conceivable that Truck's remaining four advisors are turning against her, though I cannot think why they would do such a thing. There is also a chance that the usurper is some power-mad but extremely cunning adept, though I find this even more unlikely."

"Why do you think it most likely?"

"That is difficult to sign, Bald Ape. Based on what little I know, my feeling is that it is one of the Liaison Generals, for they command the Stripes, and therefore command their loyalty. Liaison Generals, Bald Ape, are not True dreamers, for it would be sheerest stupidity to allow such a one to command the Stripes. It is primarily a hereditary title, and they are constantly under the scrutiny of the Architect, the advisors, and even the adepts, and it would be impossible to keep the ability to dream True a secret for very long. Not being a True dreamer, a General could not hold the Chair very long, for the Title of Architect would crumble without the ability to back it. So if it is a General who is staging this coup, it is possible s/he has an advisor or an adept as accomplice."

"It is all so complicated, Zorba."

"It is, indeed, Bald Ape. It is a puzzle which Truck attempts to resolve in Seven Answers."

"I worry about her, Zorba. She is gone fourteen days now."

"It is four days there and four days back, Bald Ape. We will give her more time before we commence scratching ourselves hairless."

How far along were these raccoons? I wondered. How much progress had they made? They were exploring Africa, Europe, and Asia. Their ships resembled early-eighteenth-century sailing vessels. Did they have a way to determine longitude? Didn't that require at least a spring-driven clock and a standardized shore time? Did they have springs? Was their metals industry that refined, that they could have tempered steel? How did you *make* tempered steel? Had something to do with putting carbon in it. . . . How *did* you put carbon in it? What were their philosophies like? Religious feelings, if any? How did they teach their young? Did they have schools? Teachers? Schools that produce teachers, like colleges? What was the main method of communication? Of transportation? Could I help them improve it? Did their wagon wheels have bearings? How did you make bearings, anyway? Did they know why the sky is blue?

Did I?

What did they know of their place in the universe? They know that the world is a sphere, that the moons are moons and not swans pulling chariots, or whatever. Did they know that the sun is the center of the solar system, that the whole works is only an insignificant speck of a thing called a galaxy in a sea of galaxies? What elements needed to be present in their culture for them to know this? The telescope, no dominant religion bent on repressing findings that contradicted its tenets. What else? How much did they know?

How much could I help them?

So far my role had been almost entirely passive. I seemed to be along for the ride, and I wasn't sure I liked that. Even here, in a new world, I felt that I was just in the way.

Well, all I could do was try to assess the situation and see what I could contribute to correcting it in Truck's favor.

As I understood Zorba, Truck was a . . . a queen, a ruler, the Architect of Sleep by virtue of her prescient dreams, though I wasn't sure I believed in True dreams. Many human cultures had set store by prophetic dreams, most notably the Australian and North American aborigines. These dreams tended to be highly symbolic in nature, and the power in them usually lay more in their interpretation than in the dreams themselves.

The truth about dreams—as I had always been given to understand it, anyway—is that they really *are* symbolic abstractions, and quite deservedly lend themselves to accurate interpretation. Dogs dream, dolphins dream, apes dream. But the content of a dream, the very *abstractness* of a dream, its depth and detail and the sentience it displays, depends on the mental capacity of the animal doing the dreaming. Sleep and symbolic dreaming are the price we humans pay for our intelligence; they are our brain's way of assimilating and sorting the staggering quantity of information taken in by the senses during the course of a day.

To abstract is to express a quality apart from an object. To *be* abstract is to remove or to separate, to consider a thing apart from the way it applies to a particular instance, to view it intrinsically.

"Beasts," declared John Locke, "abstract not."

Raccoons most definitely did. They were as intelligent as ourselves, and it was only to be expected that they dreamed as abstractedly. But in some ways the raccoons seemed . . . closer to their origins, more in touch with their "primal" nature, than human beings are. I wasn't sure why I felt this was so. I think it was because of their hands. Physiologically, their hands seem to have evolved faster than the raccoons themselves. Their hands can build a technology the raccoons cannot culturally grasp or emotionally assimilate.

My first inclination was to dismiss this thought as absurd, but then I thought of the example of my own kind.

We human beings carry ancient religious ornaments on the dashboards of our sophisticated automobiles. We knock on wood before sealing ourselves within our experimental fighter jets. We banish the night with electrical light and are afraid of the dark. We read scripture to the globe of Earth from vessels a few miles above the surface of the Moon. We conceive of universes bigger than we can imagine. We draw diagrams of things smaller than our own minds can realistically comprehend. In this respect we are still fragile monkeys with our machines, emotionally incapable of comprehending the vastness of the very things our own intellect has provided us. We are builders and thinkers in touch with an older self, reduced, and often hampered, by a voice literally in the back of our head.

We dream, and when we dream a door opens that makes

that voice louder. I think that for the raccoons, that door is not yet closed.

Would human beings, were they closer to this older self, govern their lives by the interpretations of those they proclaimed as True dreamers? Given what I knew of dreaming, and of humans and their relationship with technology, it did not seem so ludicrous.

But sleep is a thing I have always resented. Sleep is time stolen from your life, a life too short as it is. It made me furious that if I lived to be sixty years old, a full third of that time—*twenty years*—would be spent unconscious. Most people I knew preferred to hope that they would die in their sleep. I myself was terrified of the notion that one night I could innocently surrender myself to unconsciousness completely oblivious to the fact that I would never wake up again, that I would be totally unaware of the moment of my own death. Someone once spoke of "sleep, those little snatches of death." Contemplating suicide, Hamlet wonders, "To sleep—perchance to dream?" Confronted with the notion that it will cease to exist, Clarke's computer HAL 9000 asks its creator, "Will I dream?"

A fundamental question asked by thinking creatures. An intelligent being would naturally be curious about the power of dreaming, the meaning of dreams. They are issues symptomatic of consciousness itself, and touch upon a thinking being's awareness of its own mortality. And the raccoons were nothing if not curious, thinking, mortal creatures.

But when it came to justifying why the raccoons believed in prescient dreams, I kept finding a fly in the ointment.

The raccoons are very much the pragmatist. They prefer to stick a thermometer up a thing's butt and read its temperature rather than accept its existence on faith. What mistaken beliefs they did have were the result of ignorance rather than superstition. Nobody had burned the Library of Alexandria here; no Crusades had bottlenecked the spread of intellectualism; no Catholic Church had repressed or combated the Galileos, the Newtons, and the Darwins of the raccoon world. Being mammals, the raccoons revered motherhood, and that was about as close to religion as they got. They were not mired in tradition for tradition's sake, and those misconceptions they held that I later took upon myself to correct were quite enthusiastically revised—once I'd offered proof.

Because of this, their belief in precognition stood out like a sore thumb. It didn't jibe with their innate empiricism. Where was its tangibility; how much did it weigh; where did you stick the thermometer? Where was the *proof?*

The proof, my grandmother used to say, is in the pudding.

You didn't need to actually have prescient dreams in order to interpret them as such. I didn't have to accept prescient dreams to accept a government and a culture centered around them. After all, being unable to shove a thermometer up God's butt never prevented millions from kneeling before him, from killing in his name.

And the hard fact was that none of this rumination changed the situation one bit—Truck might think she was as mystical as Castañeda, but she nevertheless *was* the Architect of Sleep and had still been overthrown by a person—you'll pardon the term—or persons unknown. And, more important, she was my friend.

So what could I *do* for her, other than being an observer, a babe in raccoon-land? I felt the compulsion—no, the *obligation*—to become a participant rather than a spectator.

How could I help?

I am a twentieth-century man. Not Everyman, not a Renaissance man, not one of the High or the Low, but nevertheless a man whose culture stood atop an ever-growing pyramid of technological history. Surely there were *volumes* I could contribute—not only in the long run, but right now, for Truck's immediate cause.

My problem was that I stood so high on that pyramid of technology that I had lost sight of its foundation.

I had been a goddamned lit major. I knew from books, from aesthetics, from critical methodology. I lived and breathed in a world where it was possible to make a living studying and teaching something as utterly useless as semiology. I was fully qualified to sign to raccoons about Art-with-a-capital-"A" for the rest of my life, but when it came to things mechanical, to How Things Work—

Shee-it, as my father would say.

In terms of practical value, whom would you rather have in your Bomb shelter: an auto mechanic or Rex Reed?

Well, Truck had gotten Rex. *Ignoramus rex.*

In my mind I held a conversation:

"Truck, you guys really oughta have automobiles. They'd

make life a whole lot easier for you. No more cleaning up llama shit."

"This sounds fine, Bald Ape. What is an automobile?"

"Well, Truck, it's sort of a metal box on wheels that moves under its own power."

"Indeed it *would* make life easier, Bald Ape. How does this metal box work?"

"Why, it has a thing we sign an 'engine,' Truck."

"What a fine sign, Bald Ape! And what is an engine?"

"Why . . . it's . . . a lot of metal pieces that move around, motivated by a . . . very small, deliberately created lightning flash . . . and by . . . burning the remains of dead dinosaurs. I mean. . . . It's pretty hard to describe, Truck. You don't have the signs for much of it."

"Could you draw a picture of this thing, Bald Ape? Of the thing you sign an 'engine' as well?"

"Well. . . . You know, Truck, now that I think of it, a llama *is* a pretty dependable beast. . . ."

Like that.

That Bomb shelter test was goddamned sobering, because in essence it asked: *What is the practical worth of what you know? What the hell good are you anyway?*

I sure couldn't pass it. I wondered how many people could.

Well, I could spend the rest of my life contemplating what I didn't know. What about what I did?

Literature? Aesthetics? Chuck that—for now. When it comes to survival, art is the first thing to get left out of the Bomb shelter.

Martial arts? Well, okay, so I could fight. No problem, then: Truck and I would just waltz on up to her usurper and a bevy of Stripes, and I would strike an impressive fighting stance and let out a hearty "hi-*yaaa!*"

Still, I could act as her bodyguard. . . . But no. I mean, yes, but there had to be more. Bodyguards don't win counter-revolutions.

I could train raccoons to fight, I supposed.

I laughed aloud at this one. Sure—give me five years, and maybe, just maybe, I would be willing to send ten trained raccoons against five Stripes.

Now that I thought of it, though, the Okinawans, the Japanese, and the Chinese had come up with some awfully effective weapons for people who didn't have guns—

Shee-it.

I shivered. In the middle of Zorba's room in the middle of a ninety-five-degree summer day in Florida, sitting with my back to the wall and watching the Sir Edmund Hillary of the fly world scaling the Everest of the chamber pot, I listened to my heart pound and felt the sweat turn chill on my palms and on my back.

They could do it. They could make them. There wasn't a doubt in the world. The raccoons had steel, judging by those Fighting Hands, and probably tempered steel at that. And chemically all you needed were three things. Potassium nitrate you can make from pig dung. And anyone capable of lighting a fire could make charcoal. And sulphur you can practically find on the ground, if you know where to look. I hadn't the slightest idea of the proper proportions in which to mix the three to get gunpowder, but a little experimentation would soon lead to the right way to make a neat little explosion. Or a big one. I may be ignorant, but I ain't stupid. I didn't need to know metallurgy and chemistry for this; the *idea* was so simple that, once I passed it on to them, they'd go wild with it.

How about that. I was good for something after all.

I could give them guns.

At that moment Zorba entered the room, took a look at me, and trilled for my attention. "Bald Ape, are you unwell?"

"I merely think, Zorba."

"It seems to have a dire effect on you, Bald Ape."

"Yes, yes."

"You seem preoccupied. Is something wrong?"

"No, no, Zorba. I merely wish to think."

"I am sorry to interrupt you, then." And he stalked out.

I sighed. Let him stew, I decided. Now wasn't the time to confront him about it. Later. Right now I had a decision to make, probably the most important decision I would ever make.

There was no doubt that if I gave them guns, Truck would win. Hands down, no ifs, ands, or buts. Raccoons might be able to throw rocks like Sandy Koufax, and block like Bruce Lee, but there was only one way to stop bullets.

Truck would win. It was certain, and I could give it to her.

But.

As sure as eggs is eggs, you can bet that the next time a

battle was fought, both sides would be using firearms. A logical progression follows from there to musketeer divisions, wide-scale manufacture of muskets, jacketed bullets containing their own gunpowder, multiple-shot rifles, the pistol, the revolver, the automatic, the machine gun. Gunpowder would give them bombs, grenades, incendiaries, cannon, mortar. With the ball-and-powder musket the first snowflakes in the inevitable avalanche that is an arms race would be dislodged, and I would be the one who had sent it on its way.

I may not be a mechanic's messiah, but I ain't no dummy. The gun had changed the course of human history. The introduction of the musket to feudal Japan had led to the destruction of *Bushido,* the samurai code, and a way of life that had been maintained for centuries. Though the Japanese had attempted to incorporate muskets into their military, the death knell for their way of life had been sounded, and the only course to follow was increasingly Western.

When we think of the king's musketeers we picture swashbuckling figures with flashing rapiers, but those musketeers were exactly what their name implies: military men who used muskets, primarily against the uprisings of peasants who could not afford to obtain such weapons.

The Colt .45 came along in the mid–nineteenth century, and it wasn't called the Great Equalizer for nothing. The invention of the easy-to-use, easy-to-conceal, multiple-shot, large-caliber, personal handgun rendered the gun accessible to nearly *anybody.* Eventually it brought about a culture where deaths from handguns were considered routine, were no longer headline news unless they killed somebody famous or important: our Lincolns, our Kennedys, our Kings, our Lennons. One utter and complete moron with a working eyeball and a bendable index finger could blow out the brains of the finest mind of our age.

Indira Gandhis and Anwar Sadats aren't slaughtered in their own streets in a world where people make war by throwing rocks and fighting with close-quarter blades. You could populate entire countries with the number of people killed by guns.

There was no happy medium I could attain here, because an idea can't be monopolized. If someone sees that you have it, and that it's killing people on their side, before long they'll come up with it themselves, whether they use your methods or not. Necessity is a mother. I couldn't give Truck the gun and have her promise to clamp down on knowledge that was certain to spread. It was either reinvent them or not.

Guarantee Truck's return to her Title, or prevent the death of untold millions.

Put that way, it wasn't a choice at all. Those who cannot remember the past, wrote Santayana, are condemned to repeat it.

I couldn't do it. Hell, the raccoons were smart enough that they might very well come up with firearms before long anyhow. For all I knew they already had gunpowder; the Chinese had used it to make loud bangs for centuries before anyone thought of using it to propel objects into people's bodies. Personally, though, I wondered if the raccoons' psychology might at least hamper this for a long time, for I believed that the reason they didn't have the bow and arrow, a weapon invented independently by nearly every human culture, was simply because they hadn't needed it. Who needs arrows when you can throw rocks nearly as effectively?

I bit my lower lip. *I'm sorry, Truck,* I thought. *I'm so sorry. But I can't give you the one sure thing that would win your fight. I refuse to be the one to set that awful machinery in motion.*

It was an ethical question, and I felt my answer was the right one.

But it didn't make me feel any better. Because if Truck lost her battle, I was going to have to live with my decision.

Then again, if Truck lost, I might not live at all.

Shee-it.

"Zorba, I would like to sign to you about . . . about your drinking."

"My drinking, Bald Ape?"

"Yes. You are my friend, and I worry about your health."

"It is nothing. We will sign no more of it, yes?"

"If you wish, Zorba. I only want to understand the . . . the why of it. I am confronting habitual drinking before, in friends, in family. It is not a pleasant thing, not a good thing. Often it occurs because you try to run away from something inside you, something in the past. But you cannot escape yourself. Otherwise it eats at your insides like . . . like a strong tree rotting from within."

"You know nothing of my past, Bald Ape, and it is none of your concern."

"I do not ask about your past, Zorba. I merely desire to sign my distress toward the . . . frequency of your drinking."

"It is a vice I can live with, Bald Ape."

"It is a vice that will kill you before your time, Zorba."

He waved a laugh that I had learned to recognize as mirthless. "It is not very long before that time. I may as well enjoy myself."

"But you do not enjoy yourself. And why hasten the arrival of that time? How old *are* you, Zorba?"

"You understand what is a [ ], Bald Ape?"

"No, Zorba. That sign is new to me."

"A [ ] is both the longest and shortest of days. There are two. They oppose each other, one in winter and one in summer. Understand?"

"Yes, Zorba. '[Solstice].'"

"Good, Bald Ape. I am seeing fifty-four [solstices] now. This winter shall be my fifty-fifth."

"That is not all that . . ." I stopped. Two solstices a year—Zorba was twenty-seven years old.

"What is your age, Bald Ape?"

"I am seeing . . . forty-six solstices, Zorba. My kind measure by the years."

"Forty-six solstices is not so young, either."

I mulled this a minute. "Zorba, how long do your kind live?"

"I am seeing of a raccoon who is living to see one hundred solstices, though it is an easy thing to lose track of at that age, or to lie about, so I am not certain I believe it. Most do not live past their seventieth solstice."

Seventy. . . . *Thirty-five years?*

"This . . . surprises me, Zorba."

"Why, Bald Ape? What is the lifespan of your kind?"

"I am considered young, Zorba. Most bald apes live forty-and-one-hundred solstices, and two hundred is not unknown."

It was Zorba's turn to be still a minute. Finally he signed, a bit subdued, "Truly, Bald Ape?"

"Truly, Zorba."

"What a marvelous thing, to live two hundred solstices. To learn for so long, to see two lifetimes of change. To love longer, to witness the growth of your grandkits and great-grandkits. I envy you, Bald Ape. Truly I do."

And he fell still.

The door curtain jerked aside and Zorba stepped in holding a large glass jug in one long hand. He bumped against the stand on which the basin sat, and water sloshed over the rim. Zorba stepped away and backed into the wall. He set down the jug. "I-am-sorry," he signed to the basin with great formality. His eyes narrowed and he hunched over, peering stagily around the room. He straightened when he saw me sitting on the sleeping mat with my back to the wall. "Bald Ape!" he signed. I barely recognized my name because he signed it with so much extraneous motion. "Bald Ape, here!" He picked up the jug and waved it around. Its contents sloshed. Zorba hunched and resumed his exaggerated scrutinizing of the room until his gaze settled on my empty coffee mug on the table beside the mat. He straightened, unstoppered his jug, and indicated that I should hand him my mug. I did and he filled it, spilling some of the contents onto his hand. He set down the jug, handed me the mug, and waved a flamboyant laugh. "You drink too much coffee, Bald Ape. Here—drink this. Drink."

I raised the mug and sniffed. I sipped.

Corn liquor. Moonshine! But it was sweet and good, and—as I was about to discover—snuck up behind you and kicked you in the head. I glanced at Zorba.

"Drink!" he signed. "Drink!"

I drank.

Zorba laughed. He seemed enormously pleased with himself, as if he had just pulled off some wonderful prank, and he lifted the long-necked, narrow-mouthed jug to his mouth and drank deeply. He lowered the jug and belched. "Drink!" he signed.

Incredulous, I shook my head at him, but I drank.

Bringing the jug with him, Zorba came to the mat and sat heavily beside me. The fur of his right arm tickled my left biceps, causing a shudder and a wave of gooseflesh. He drank again, wiped liquid from the fur around his mouth, and waved the jug recklessly. "Good," he signed. He unnecessarily refilled my mug, sloshing liquor onto the mat, then leaned his head back against the wall, belched again, and set the jug down between his legs. He shut his eyes, and for a moment we just sat there, me staring at him, him lost in whatever jumbled thoughts he had.

Just to have something to do I raised my mug again and drank. Zorba opened his eyes and turned to regard me, leaning away and cocking his head to the side as though appraising me. "You are an ugly thing, Bald Ape," he signed. "But I like you. Why is that?"

It was hard for me to follow his signings, not only because they were "slurred," but because he sat beside me instead of facing me, and some of the inflection gleaned from posture and the advantage of the sight line was lost.

"I do not know, Zorba," I answered. "But I like you, too."

"I do not know why that is," he signed. I wasn't sure if he referred to my reply, or if he was answering himself. "You are huge, and pale, and threatening. But you have a mind; you—" His hands stopped, remained poised, then fell to the jug and lifted. He drank. I drank.

The stuff really was pretty good.

"Do you know," he signed after he had set down the jug, "that to us it is an insult to be without fur? Grayness is fine, for it is a symptom of age and an indication of surviving the years, but baldness . . ." For a moment he groped. "Baldness is an indication either of sickness or of humiliation, for shaving is a thing we do to criminals—understand, Bald Ape?" He waved a laugh—a private laugh, because he kept it close to himself, apparently thinking it was shielded with his body.

"I understand, Zorba. Do you know that where I am from, we punish physicians who do poor work?"

He trilled. "Then I am safe in your world, Bald Ape! See—your leg heals well." He reached out and grasped my shin, then roughly pulled it toward him. The skin went taut at the wound. I shuddered at his touch, for I could not feel it: from the cut at midshin to my instep, my leg was dead meat so far as sensation was concerned. I could feel pressure, but little else, and I did not like the leg to be touched. Zorba ran his palm across the wound, then pointed to my face and back to the wound. He let go of my leg. "If not for me, you would have one leg, Bald Ape. Punish me? [!]"

I glanced at the wound. It *had* begun to heal nicely; the tissues surrounding the gash were no longer puffy and discolored; the "V" of the cut was scabbed but clean. He had removed the stitches five days before when they had shown signs of infection, and he regularly washed the cut.

"Wounds," Zorba signed, more to himself, it seemed, than to me. "Wounds. Wounds heal, yes? Yes. No. All wounds, all healings. All nothing."

He drank. I drank.

"I am not meaning to insult you," Zorba signed suddenly. "Your baldness is natural for you, and you can do nothing about it. I am sure you are not ugly to others of your kind."

"I am not insulted, Zorba." I clacked my teeth together three times. My molars had started to go numb. "Yes, some females among my kind are thinking me good-looking."

"I would not *want* to insult you, Bald Ape. You . . . you are *endearing,* and it is not right to insult you."

"And I find many females among my kind good-looking as well," I signed. I looked at the circle of moonshine seesawing in my mug. "Women," I said aloud, and drained the mug.

"Yes," Zorba signed. "Endearing. And clever. You stir my curiosity as it is not stirred since. . . ." He looked away from me, but his hands signed on. "It is a long time ago. I am not thinking of it much." He looked at me. "I have a life here now. It is a good life. Yes?"

"Yes, Zorba. But there are no females."

"No females! Bald Ape, there are . . . *many* . . . females! I am no longer a kit, but—"

"Females, Zorba." I thumped my chest. "Females of me. Of my kind," I corrected. I attempted to drink from my mug and discovered it was empty when the back of my head hit the wall. I frowned and extended the mug to Zorba, but he lifted the jug and turned it upside down. A few drops spilled out. Slowly I turned over my mug, shook it sorrowfully, set it down, and spread my hands. "No more," I signed. "How sign it be this drink, Zorba?"

Though seated, it seemed as if he drew himself erect in a huffy show of propriety. "'What do you sign this?' Bald Ape."

"[!] Enough teaching, Zorba! I learn all day, every day. Now I do not wish to learn. Now I wish to be stupid."

"Then I will not sign you the name of this, Bald Ape, and you will not learn and you will be stupid." He laughed smugly with both hands.

"You copulate, Zorba!"

"Yes certainly. Do you not?"

"Ahhh—" I said aloud. Dammit, "Fuck you" wasn't an insult to these furry little shits. That it is to us reveals us in a rather harsh light.

"It is signed [moonshine], Bald Ape. It is made from corn. Understand you 'corn'?"

"Yes, yes, yes. '[Moonshine],' yes?"

"Right, right, right."

"More moonshine!" And aloud: "More moonshine!" I punctuated the sentence by banging my mug against the mat.

"More moonshine," agreed Zorba, and he grabbed the jug and stood up. He wobbled a bit and stepped forward uncertainly. He looked at me, tittered with one hand, and pointed to the jug. Then he clutched it in both hands (though the jug was large, the two long hands spanned it easily), and with great determination and utmost deliberation, he strode across the room and out the door curtain. I heard him walk along the hall and down the stairs, heard him stumble midway, heard the jug *thunk!* against the wall, and heard him trill. I got up and headed for the door, and it was not until I tried to walk that I realized I was already beginning to fly a sheet or two to the wind myself. I had a hand on the door curtain and was about to move it aside when I realized that I couldn't step out of the room to see if Zorba was hurt. I heard him negotiate the rest of the steps, though, and figured he was all right. In any case, it was not late and The Mongrel probably still had customers; somebody would help Zorba if he was hurt. I released the door curtain and returned to my place on the sleeping mat. "Oof," I said aloud when I sat down. It occurred to me that I should not be saying anything because someone might investigate.

Oh, yeah? Well, let 'em investigate. So goddamned what. I mean, what did they think they were gonna do if they discovered me? I could talk if I wanted to. "Fuck 'em," I said. Aloud.

As a drinking man, I have never exactly been the sort who, after four or five rounds, can perform complex algebraic calculations whilst riding a unicycle and singing "America the Beautiful." The truth is, I was and remain both a cheap and an easy drunk. I do not sip—nay, I do not drink. I *guzzle*. I treat it like soda pop and gulp the stuff, and to add insult to injury, I tend to guzzle sweet drinks that I consider more palatable—which meant they were easier to guzzle. Beer, straight liquor—blecch. Give me strawberry daiquiris any day. On top of this was the fact that, though a typical college student in many ways, I actually drank very little, and my tolerance for alcohol was zilch.

The long and short of it is that two drinks and I'm rather effervescent for an hour; three or four and I'm clumsy (clumsier) and my jokes get worse, only I think they get better; more than four and I get stupid and need to be tucked into bed, where I can hold on to the sheets to keep from falling onto the ceiling while the room spins.

I'd already downed two mugs of moonshine. Not small, those coffee mugs.

Zorba returned with another jug. He set it between us and plopped down beside me. I held out my mug and he poured.

"No more," he signed dejectedly. "The manager signs that I may have no more." He hefted the bottle, tilted it above his mouth, and swallowed. He looked sad.

I drank. Did I mention that the stuff was warm? Very well: the stuff was warm. No refrigeration. Not in Florida, anyhow. Good ol' Florida. Land of bugs, all *kinds* of bugs; land of sweltering heat and thick humidity. Land of oranges and alligators. Some things never change.

I belched. Zorba looked astonished, and then began to laugh. I belched again. He stopped laughing and drew himself up in his dignified-teacher pose, then emitted a loud burp himself. I began to laugh out loud. I sipped moonshine, gargled it, and swallowed. I belched with enough force to make your ears pop.

Not to be outdone, Zorba stood up, put his hands on his knees, lifted his tail, and let out a truly impressive fart. I laughed until my stomach hurt, then grew mock serious and got up myself. I hunched over, tightened my diaphragm, and let out a fart that was truly embarrassing in its utter weakness, humiliating in its utter absence of oomph, a sound more like a Lilliputian hiccough than the Brobdingnagian effort necessary to outdo Zorba, who, upon hearing this puny excuse for a fart, lay on his back and pounded his heels against the floor, hands all aflutter.

I felt my face go red. I was embarrassed not for farting, but for farting poorly. "And the llama you are riding in on," I signed in chagrin. Zorba did not see me because he was still laughing on the floor, looking like he was having an attack of grand mal.

I gulped more moonshine. As I drank, the sight of Zorba silently laughing on the floor suddenly struck me as hysterically funny and I laughed, then coughed and sprayed moonshine all over myself. I wiped my hands dry against my filthy underwear and sat down heavily. Zorba sat up and regarded me. He looked far away, like I was seeing him through the wrong end of a telescope.

"You," he signed, "are a sloppy drunk." And then he laughed again.

"There is not a bald ape in all the world," I retorted, "who deals with [her/his] liquor better than me." And I laughed. "In fact," I continued, "there is not another bald ape in all the world."

Zorba signed something in reply, but I was no longer paying attention. A cold grenade had gone off in my stomach.

Not another bald ape in all the world. . . .

It was true. My God, it was true. I was the only human being on the planet. I was alone. I was surrounded by intelligent raccoons, and I was more alone than I had ever been in my entire life. Nothing else like me existed here—not a man, not a woman. . . .

I looked at the mug in my hands. I lifted it to my lips and drank deeply. Liquor spilled down my cheeks, ran down my neck, grew cold at my collarbones, and stopped at midchest.

"Women." I said it aloud. I shook my head at Zorba. "Females," I signed, splaying the fingers of both hands and touching them to my chest to indicate nipples.

Zorba had learned to read my facial expressions well enough to ask, "What is wrong, Bald Ape?"

"Females," I signed again.

"Females again!" He made what I interpreted as a knowing laugh, then raised his jug and drank. Seeing that my mug was again empty, he refilled it and set down the jug. "Females," he signed. "One cannot endure them; one cannot endure without them. Yes?"

"Fuckin' A," I said aloud. And I signed, "I drink to that." And I did.

"Do you know, Zorba," I signed after wiping moonshine from my mouth with an arm that got stickier each time I repeated the motion, "that I will never see another female? Not the rest of my life."

"What do you sign? There are females in abundance, Bald Ape! You have but to look. Even though no kit, I certainly do not suffer from a lack of—"

"No, no, no. Females." I thumped my chest. "Female bald apes." I snorted at the image conjured by the phrase. My head was beginning to feel like it was packed with Styrofoam.

"What we must do, then, is find you a female ape, and shave it, and then you may—"

"I am not an ape!"

"Please, Bald Ape, do not roar! Others will come to investigate. What will happen if they find you?"

"Bring them on," I signed. But again I felt chagrined. "I-am-sorry, Zorba. You just do not understand."

"I understand, Bald Ape. You are not an ape. I know that. Truck knows it. But what else are we to name you? To us you resemble an ape; no insult is intended. When I am signing of shaving a female ape I am only making a joke, yes?"

"It is not a joke to me, Zorba."

"What are the females of your kind like, Bald Ape?"

"They are . . . softer. Softer—less rough in both manner and appearance. They are not as violent as males. Or as crazy." I laughed with my hands. "They are seen as embodiments of beauty, though males are not usually considered as such."

"That is odd, Bald Ape."

I spread my hands. "That is the way it is, Zorba. Females are . . . a joy to look at, to hear. Their . . . their signing . . . is softer, like music. They are stronger than males, in here—" I patted my chest—"for in many ways they must endure more harshness."

"What harshness, Bald Ape?"

"Males, for one thing, Zorba." I laughed, though Zorba did not—for here it was not a joke—and in the middle of waving laughter I realized that my nose had clogged and that I had begun to cry. I sat back and clenched my eyes, gritting my teeth until my jaw muscles hurt. I began thinking about women I had loved, women I had made love with. Shit, sometimes there was even some overlap. The images ran in my head, snipped from the rest of my life and spliced: faces, motions, a smell of perfume, badinage across a table in a restaurant, a certain bend of leg, curve of jaw, brightness of eye; the sheer happiness on Nicole's face when she saw me again after I'd been away; looking down on her looking up at me; the adrenaline rush of meeting the gaze of a woman across the room, and you just knew—call it pheromones or body language or subliminal communication or any damn thing else you want to, but you *knew*—that you were going to end up horizontal with this woman, and you knew she knew it, too, and it was the god-*damned*est sensation and I would never have it again, never wake up to find Nicole there, one leg bent across both of mine, a hand on my chest, and feeling as though we had been on some voyage together through the night—

I opened my eyes at Zorba's touch on my arm. "Bald Ape, are you all right?"

I looked at him for a long moment. "I do not want to live in a world without females," I finally signed.

"I suppose I would not want to, either. But what may be done about it, Bald Ape? It is the cart you must draw. Sooner or later each of us has a cart s/he must draw."

This time it was my turn to come out of my funk enough to feel that something was bothering Zorba. "You are troubled, Zorba?"

"It is nothing."

Human or raccoon, a line like that is a dead giveaway. It means, I wanna tell ya, but ya gotta drag it out of me.

"It is something, or it would not bother you," I prompted.

"I do not wish to sign of it."

"I am your friend, Zorba."

He regarded me a while. Then he sat back on the sleeping mat and took a long pull from the jug, which was now two-thirds empty, and set it down. "There is a thing that eats away at me," he signed, looking not at me but at the space before him. "A long-ago thing. It is the reason for this." He indicated the jug. "Moonshine does not take away the bite, but it makes it less painful." He regarded me with two bright-dark eyes that caught the flickerings of the candle that had begun to gutter in front of the window slit. "I am a fine teacher once," he signed.

"You are a fine teacher now," I replied.

He waved that away. "I am teaching in the Keep in Seaport Savannah. The adepts are a fine group. I am teaching you about adepts, Bald Ape?"

I signed that he had.

"These adepts," continued Zorba, "are bright, eager, wanting to learn, demanding more, allowing no sloppiness, always ready to find the flaws in my claims and feed them back to me. I teach them natural sciences, and about medicines and healing. I teach them about the life around them. Truck is among them, and is the brightest, the most promising. She is my favorite, though I do not show this for it would be improper—and it would lead to questions I would rather not answer. But I am close to the kits, and they are dear to me. All but one."

He fell motionless for a while. I thought he had finished and I polished off my moonshine. Zorba refilled my mug. "I must urinate," he signed, "or I shall burst." He got up and went to the chamber pot, where he hunched over and let loose for an amazingly long time. Male raccoons have sheathed penises, like a dog's, and in order to do something as civilized as pissing into a pot they must bend over it. When he finished I realized with something approaching desperation, that I, too, had to piss, and I added my two pints' worth. The chamber pot would have been recognized instantly in human society: function and form, and all that. Every day in the early afternoon a wagon rolled along the street in front of the hotel, and full chamber pots were emptied into one of several cisterns in the back. Where the shit went from there I had no idea.

I covered the pot and returned to my place.

"There is a student who simply does not like me," Zorba resumes without preamble. "I do not know why, even to this day. But she does not, and at every opportunity she argues with me. She poisons me to the eyes of the other adepts. One day she reports to one of the other teachers that she is having her first estrus, and that I am attempting to force sex upon her. Such things happen in your world, Bald Ape?"

"Too often, Zorba."

"It is not common here, but it happens. It is a serious thing. A male cannot help what he thinks when a female is in estrus, but he can help what he does. And I am doing nothing to this adept—estrus or not, she is still a kit! Still, the accusation is weighty, and is made even heavier by the fact that she is an adept. I am summoned for a review by a Tribunal and called upon to defend myself. My career is at stake, which is exactly what this reptile of a kit desires. But to her dismay each and every one of the other adepts I teach comes to my aid. Truck, the most articulate of the group, though hardly the most eloquent, states flatly that this she-kit wants nothing less than my removal from the Keep, that she is always wanting it and will stop at nothing to attain it. Truck repeats the stories spread to the adepts by this kit, and shows them for the lies they are. But this is the kind of loyalty any good teacher can create in [her/his] students, and hence the signings of my pupils move before blind eyes. The Tribunal members want to believe me, but there is the damning evidence that this little reptile is pregnant, and none will step forward to claim himself the father. In the end I am not found guilty, but my career is in ruins in many respects. My credibility is in doubt."

He drank again. "That night this creature comes to my room to revel in her victory. I . . . I am drunk, it is my shame to sign. Drinking is a thing I do much even then, though much more privately, and this night I only want to be drunk and alone. And so, drunk and confronted with this . . . *reptile*, this manipulative dirt of an adept, I am crazed. Here she is, this thing"—Zorba gestured as though the adept were in fact standing before him—"and she is signing her sorrow that I must go and teach elsewhere, that she will miss me, that I am her favorite teacher. And I . . ." Zorba stood, weaved uncertainly, and suddenly lashed out. "I strike her in the face. Once, only once, but hard, too hard, and she falls backward and her head strikes a table and she is dead." Zorba regarded a space on the floor where her imaginary body lay. "She is dead! It happens so quickly that, Mother, it does not seem real! But there is her body, just the same, and it will not go away, and I am killing her."

"Zorba—"

"Charlemagne is kind. I am exiled, probably the least severe punishment I can be given. He has the right to my life, you know."

"Zorba—"

"And in the company of Charlemagne's Stripes I am led to the border of my choosing, the southern border, and there I walk south and do not look back. And never again will I see my kits, the kits I so love to teach, their eager learning, my Truck, whom I am promising to watch over—"

I trilled. "Zorba!"

This time he stopped at the signing of his name. For a moment he seemed disoriented, and then he signed, "I-am-sorry, Bald Ape. I forget myself."

"It is all right, Zorba. I feel . . . closer to you, knowing these things."

"You are a good sort, Bald Ape." He took a swig on the jug, polishing off the rest of the moonshine. "Truly you are. Beneath that hairless skin of yours beats the heart of a raccoon."

"And you are my friend, Zorba. You know you are." I finished off my mug and held it out for more. Zorba spread his hands dejectedly and thumped the jug. "No more," he signed sadly. "No more."

"Then fetch another, please," I signed. "The night is young and we have much drinking to do. Yes?"

He hunched over morosely. "No. No more drinking. They are signing that this is the last jug they will allow me tonight."

"What? What? They cannot do this. You pay for your moonshine, do you not?"

"With services, with favors, yes, yes."

"Then it is a fair exchange—services for another jug."

"They will give me no more, Bald Ape."

I stood up. The room went fuzzy for a moment, then righted itself. "And how will they stop us?" I picked up the jug and blew across the lip until it sounded a deep note. Zorba looked astonished. I bowed a courtly bow. "Thank you, thank you, one and all," I signed one-handedly. I returned the jug to Zorba. "Let us go downstairs and get another jug, Zorba."

"My friend, we cannot go down there!"

I drew myself up and puffed out my chest in righteous indignation. "My friend, I am the Bald Ape. I am much bigger, stronger, and meaner than any copulating raccoon in this town." I bared my teeth and growled, waving my arms wildly. Zorba shrank back. "I am sick and tired of hiding in this room and seeing the world through a slit in the wall. I want to go out. And I want more moonshine!"

With that I turned and drew aside the door curtain. I stepped out into the hall. "More moonshine!" I bellowed. I stomped toward the staircase, footsteps thudding on the wooden floor. Behind me I heard Zorba, trilling to himself in consternation as he followed me.

At the head of the stairs I encountered a raccoon. He was looking down at his feet as he walked up the steps, and his gaze traveled from my boots to my bare legs, past my dirty underwear, up my bare chest, and stopped at my face. His eyes went quite wide. He fell back against the wall as though I had pushed him. A bright blue peacock feather dangled from his pierced right ear and his umbilical bracelet dangled on one wrist.

I dipped in a most courtly bow. "A fine evening to you, goodbody," I signed.

He merely stared.

I shrugged and brushed past him to clop the rest of the way down the stairs. Behind me Zorba trilled for my attention. I glanced back and waved a laugh.

At the bottom of the stairs I stopped.

The dining room was full. Crowded. Friday night at the raccoon watering hole. Despite the crowding there was little noise: the clatter of dishes, incidental trillings, mugs banging on tables, chairs creaking, sliding on the floor.

All sound stopped within ten seconds of my highly unexpected arrival. All motion ceased as well: conversations stopped, waiters holding trays of food and jugs of wine and beer froze in their tracks. For a few seconds it was a tableau, and then a waiter dropped a pitcher and it shattered on the floor. Everyone in the room winced at the sound.

I went to the waiter who had dropped the pitcher and signed, as though I did this every day, as though nothing at all were out of the ordinary here, "Pardon, goodbody, but my friend physician Zorba and I desire another pitcher of moonshine. Might you provide us with one?"

(Hey, buddy, you serve Bald Apes here?)

(Sure, Mac, we serve anybody.)

The waiter looked around for help. None seemed forthcoming. I heard him swallow. He looked at the pieces of the broken pitcher at his feet as though some answer might lie there, looked back at me, raised his hands as if to sign, backed up a step, and then bolted as if his tail were on fire.

"Moonshine!" I signed. I turned to Zorba, who, if I was reading him correctly, was walking the border between being petrified with fright and being overcome with laughter. "Zorba," I signed, "my friend, my best friend in all the world—where do we get our moonshine?"

One of the raccoons at table stood up. To Zorba she signed, "What is this? What manner of creature is this?"

I answered before Zorba could. "You are not seeing of me? My fame is not preceding me? I am the Bald Ape! I am from another world, and I have powers you cannot guess. *And I want more moonshine!*" I smiled. They shrank back.

Zorba came up beside me. "I would suggest you give it to him," he signed mildly. "Not long ago he is reducing an entire town to rubble merely because they are refusing to allow him to eat at table with raccoons." He clasped his hands together, and I knew it was to keep from laughing.

I scowled and tried to look menacing.

Another of the customers got up. He was an elderly raccoon, his fur gone even more grayish white and matted than Zorba's. A neat three-inch-long furrow of scar speared into his bandit mask above his left eye. "I am seeing this thing before," he signed, looking at me but signing to the others. "It is a pet. It is a creature-with-tricks, and mimes our signings as a marmoset does. I am seeing it on the end of a leash in Wait-No-More during Festival Day. It is an African ape captured by a trapper. A pet. It is entered in their llama pull."

"You are training it to get you more moonshine, Zorba?" ventured one of the waiters. Some of the customers laughed.

"I get my own moonshine," I signed. And with great deliberation I walked to the nearest table, snatched up one of the stiff paper menus, and made five simple folds in it to form a paper cup. I lifted a pitcher of what turned out to be wine rather than moonshine, poured the cup half-full, and drank.

I looked to Zorba. "Zorba, will you join me?" I signed. And I sat down at the table.

Zorba, who was far drunker than I, seemed to have caught the spirit of the thing. He sat across from me and extended the mug in front of him. I poured. We drank.

A raccoon who had been standing by the door curtain leading to the kitchen came forward. In her hands was a straw broom. She tucked it under one arm and signed, "Zorba, I will not have this. Get rid of it."

"Are you the manager of this place, goodbody?" I asked.

She ignored me, though she seemed perturbed by my signing. "Get rid of it, Zorba. And then get yourself out as well. I am enduring a lot from you, but this is too much. It explains the noises from your room late at night, and it explains why my larder is unaccountably low. How long are you keeping it? Never mind; I do not wish to know. Just get rid of it, and go away yourself."

I stood up and looked down on her. "Physician Zorba is worth much to you," I signed. "And you treat him poorly.

There is hardly a night when he does not treat one of your guests. He is an excellent healer. He deserves more than you give him."

She stepped back and raised her broom. I stepped toward her and she swung. Though drunk, my reflexes were still good enough to allow me to duck the broom, grab it, and take it from her. I twirled it over my head and then spun it in a bent figure-eight like a majorette, then stopped with it held in a ready position.

Behind me Zorba trilled. I glanced back. "Bald Ape, this is going too far, I think. Let us go and—"

Movement caught my eye and I glanced left and saw the blur of an object speeding toward me. I dodged right and it whooshed past my head and shattered against the wall. One of the customers had hurled a plate hard enough to crack my skull. I stepped toward him with every intention of doing him severe violence, and then I stopped. I looked at the broom in my hands. I looked at the manager, and then at Zorba. Aw, shit—I didn't want to hurt anybody. I just wanted another fucking jug of moonshine.

I threw down the broom. "Let us go," I signed to Zorba. "Let us go back to our room. These"— I gestured around us —"can copulate themselves."

"We cannot go back up there, Bald Ape. They will throw us out."

"They and whose Stripes?"

There was a stirring around us. "If that is intended to be humorous, Bald Ape, it is not. We must leave before we are forced out."

"They will do this, Zorba? Force us out? Throw *you* out?"

"Yes, Bald Ape. Unless you wish to fight. And I am no longer young, and you cannot fight forever." He turned to the manager. "My books, my things?"

"You may send for them. They will be safe."

"Then let us go, Bald Ape. I need only my medical purse and a few items."

"My pack, Zorba. Will you fetch it? And your poncho? It will be cold for me without coverings."

"Certainly." He turned away. His step was heavy as he trod up the stairs.

I looked back at the patrons of The Mongrel. "Seeing any good jokes lately?" I signed.

No reply. They didn't think I was very funny.

I stared. They stared.

I cleared my throat and everyone in the place jumped as if a gun had gone off. I waved a nervous laugh and apologized.

They stared.

The raccoon I'd passed on the way down the stairs, the one with the peacock-feather earring, ran back down the stairs, trilling loudly. He signed wildly about the big, ugly creature he had seen, and then he turned and ran smack into the big, ugly creature. He fell down and stayed there, regarding me from the floor with the look of unadulterated terror. I bent and extended a hand to help him up. He scampered backward.

My God, I thought, *I'm a monster in a raccoon B movie.* This is how legends are born.

I spread my hands in a shrug at the raccoon on the floor, then signed, "Let me help you, goodbody."

He looked around the inn. Some of the customers and staff regarded him sympathetically, some in open amusement. None offered to help him.

"Hell with it," I said aloud, and I stepped forward, grabbed his arm, and lifted him to his feet. He stared up at me with something approaching awe. Or maybe he was just in shock. His arm trembled beneath my hand, and I stroked his fur once to reassure him, then dusted him off and stepped away from him. He continued to gape at me.

Zorba was back in five minutes. It was a long five minutes. He handed me my pack and a poncho. I thanked him and unzipped the pack, checking to be sure my contacts, cleaning solutions, first-aid kit, and one remaining book of matches were still there, and then I put on the poncho and the pack.

Zorba had on a newer pair of moccasins and his medical purse. Slung across one shoulder was his coolie hat with two holes cut out for his ears. Without further adieu he signed, "Let us go, Bald Ape."

"To where, Zorba?"

He glanced around significantly. I understood and did not press him.

We left.

A dozen raccoons followed and escorted us through the streets as we walked to the western edge of town. We weren't just being thrown out of The Mongrel; we were being ridden out of town. Nothing was ever overtly signed that we were being kicked out, but the presence of the crowd and their inexorable pressure toward the edge of town rudely informed us that Three Big Dogs just wasn't big enough for the two of us. Zorba wanted to detour to a stable and get the remaining llama he and Truck had boarded there, but I told him I didn't think our escort would like it.

By the time we reached the double-rutted road leading into the forest we had acquired quite a procession. We headed it with what dignity and aplomb we could muster.

"Where do we travel, Zorba?" I asked again when our bodies hid our conversation from our unofficial fan club.

"Seven Answers, of course. You and I must seek a friend there. Yes?"

"Yes!" I had been worried about Truck. At least getting tossed out on our ear was leading us to do *something* about finding her.

Despite the circumstances of our eviction and my waning drunkenness, it felt good to be outside. It seemed as if it had been months. I tried to count the days since my injury in the fight with the Stripes and realized I had completely lost track of time. A month, maybe?

I looked at Zorba. "How do you feel?"

"Sober."

I glanced back at the crowd behind us. Some of them carried clubs.

"In the music of your people, Zorba, do you have signings to accompany it? To go along with the music?"

"Of course, Bald Ape. We sign them [songs]."

"'[Songs].'" I repeated the sign a few times until I was sure I had it. "Would you like to see a song of my people, Zorba? Songing with us is done through the throat, with air, the way we sign, but I can song it with my hands, I think."

"I would be interested, yes, Bald Ape."

I cracked my knuckles and tried my hand, humming the tune as I signed. We were at the edge of town where the woods began, and we left the crowd behind and didn't even look back as we walked on into the night.

"Ninety-nine bottles of beer on the wall,
Ninety-nine bottles of beer!
You take one down and pass it around—
Ninety-eight bottles of beer on the wall.

Ninety-eight bottles of beer on the wall,
Ninety-eight bottles of beer!
You take one down and pass it around—
Ninety-seven bottles of beer on the wall.
Ninety-seven—"

Zorba interrupted me. "Does this 'song' continue in this way until you reach zero?"

"Yes, Zorba, that is exactly how it continues."

"What is the point, Bald Ape? It is repetitious. Predictable. Boring."

"It is not only a drinking song but a traveling song. It passes the time."

He trilled. "There are more productive ways to pass the time."

"Such as?"

He glanced around a moment before signing. The tall pine trees rustled in the gentle wind. Crickets chirped, frogs sawed. I was thankful that the night was warm, but I wore the poncho anyway. It pinched at my armpits, gathered by the straps of my pack. Zorba looked back at me. "Stripe to Architect four," he announced.

"Zorba, you know full well I cannot keep up with that." And I signed:

"Ninety-seven bottles of beer on the wall,
Ninety-seven bottles of beer!
You take one down and pass it around. . . ."

Zorba gave up and joined in at ninety-four.

21
Narrative of Truck

GENERAL LEE AND I compile lists of the many things we need. The lists are long and varied, and consist of such items as a boat, a printing press, messenger llamas, a storage house, a room under a false name at an inn in Seaport Savannah, capital, allegiance of landholders, names of merchants in Seaport Savannah, names of social critics and reformers publishing pamphlets criticizing my rule, whose ostensibly covert operations are entirely known to me (such is the advantage of being the Architect of Sleep), secret emissaries to the provinces of Architect Tokugawa to the west and Napoleon to the north, for those two are brilliant strategists. Most important in terms of planning, we need whatever information we can get out of the Keep—for even those who know of the coup know nothing of my usurper, and this knowledge is crucial in dealing with ways to confront [her/him].

The room in which we make our skimpy plans is small and cramped, containing little more than a small table and two chairs, and requires candlelight by which to see even though outside it is bright afternoon. The room is ensconced within the confusing jumble that is Fagin's building. The place is impossible for me to figure out even though I possess a fine sense of spatial orientation. Fagin being the sort that he is, I can only assume this confusing construction is deliberate.

Our needs are provided for as best Fagin is able. Most of them are attended to by Dodger, who is invaluable in passing along whatever information, rumors, gossip, and pertinent hand-flapping he is seeing. Of Fagin we see little, and when we do he is always hurrying on to some important thing or other. Always concocting a thing, is Fagin, always planning. From his resourcefulness I surmise he is careful to have a spoon in everyone's stewpot.

We are here eight days now, by my count. Fagin insists we stay, insists on hiding us here, for eight days ago the six Stripes comprising the local garrison are riding through Seven Answers on their messenger llamas, accompanied by their fighting dogs. They ride through the town all that day, demanding of whomever they encounter whether s/he is seeing a female raccoon with a scarred belly in the company of an odd, naked-apish thing.

They know of me, and of the Bald Ape. Is Louis XIV dreaming of us? In any case, their behavior is unusual, for generally Stripes sign to no one other than themselves if they can avoid it.

Fagin feels they signify that a larger party of Stripes from Seaport Jacksonville may search nearby. He makes preparations for a quick departure, should need arise, and tells Lee and me to be able to leave at a finger's notice.

But they know of me and the Bald Ape. I cannot rid myself of this thought, that we are hunted like deer.

Lee and I look up from the scribbled sheets before us when Dodger rushes into the room without knocking. "Many apologies, goodbodies," he signs hurriedly. I smell his anxiety. "Gather your things, quickly," he continues, "and prepare to leave."

Lee glances at me. "Are we discovered?" I ask.

"Not yet, but soon, I fear. Stripes enter the town."

Lee stands. From the table she picks up her old iron war helmet, which she is bringing along when we are summoned here. "How many, and from where?"

"From the southwest, General Lee. Twenty to forty Stripes. We must hurry."

Fagin is already yoking two llamas to a wagon behind his building. He turns at our approach. "I do not know how, but they know you are here," he signs without preamble. "We must leave, and quickly."

"We?"

"I will drive the wagon. I know whom to bribe, whom to contact, what routes are best. Dodger will remain behind and clear away any traces of you and Lee. Do you have what you need to travel? You cannot take much."

I indicate the hastily assembled stack of paper Lee holds. "This is all."

"What of your mandolute?"

"I am thinking to leave it, Fagin. It is cumbersome."

"Bring it. It is a good cover for the road, and covers your belly as well—though you cannot withstand even a cursory examination by Stripes. And you can wager that they will look." He turns to Lee. "If you bring that war helmet along," he signs, "you must hide it."

"I will fetch your mandolute," signs Dodger, and runs off.

"They will expect us to travel north up the river," continues Fagin. "Or possibly on the western road if they think you may seek sanctuary in Tokugawa's province. The river is now blockaded on the Florida side, and the north and west roads will be guarded heavily. We will leave by the eastbound route, and travel that direction until it meets the north road toward Seaport Savannah. I expect we shall encounter Stripes, but I rely on there being few. You will play your mandolute until we sight them; I shall give you as much warning as I can. Lee . . . it is possible you are known to them, yes?"

"Well, yes, though I doubt they search for me."

"Louis XIV may be a self-indulgent Architect, but he is no fool. Knowing you are here, and that you are once a Liaison General of Stripes for Charlemagne, he will certainly dispatch Stripes to your household. It is too obvious: where else would the Architect of the Confederacy go for aid in the border town of Seven Answers?"

"How do they know Truck is here?" asks Lee.

"I do not know. I suggest we not remain here to pursue the question."

"Louis XIV is an Architect," I remind Lee. "I am not the only True dreamer. Perhaps he is dreaming of me." I turn to Fagin. "Let us depart, then—but there is no reason for you to risk yourself. You are providing more than enough for us, and I am in your debt."

"No offense, Architect, but I do not want to be in your debt. What favors I bestow are pragmatically motivated: I do not want war. It is bad for my business. It is bad for all trade throughout several provinces. Your usurper takes actions that are subtle, but that I think are intended to tool the Confederacy up for war. I feel that if you regain your Chair, you can prevent this, and so I play my small part. It is no large effort for me, Truck."

I see that he is uncomfortable with having to explain himself, so I change the topic. "You are having this wagon ready all this time," I sign.

"Stripes are thorough and quick," he replies. "And I am knowing your stay will be most ephemeral. General Lee, if you would set those papers in here . . .?" We follow Fagin to the back of the wagon, which contains hay. Fagin brushes hay from the right side near the back and uses a bar lying there to pry up two boards. Beneath is a small, shallow compartment. The wagon is carefully built so as to give no hint that this space is there; indeed, the way it is constructed one would assume that to lift out these boards would be to look down onto the road.

Lee places our papers and Lee's war helmet in the compartment. Fagin replaces the boards and sweeps hay across them. Then he clambers aboard the wagon and motions for me to follow him. He squats at the front of the wagonbed, just behind the driver's bench, and clears hay away. "Here," he signs. "Lower this bar"—he lowers a recessed metal bar on the left side that is made to look like part of the wagon frame—"and this bar." He lowers another like it on the right side. There is a click, and Fagin pulls out the lowest of the front boards. I peer closer. There is a hollow space under the driver's bench, running the length of the wagon and large enough—barely—for a raccoon. "Play your mandolute as we drive," Fagin signs. "When I trill to you, *quickly* give the instrument to Lee, open this space and get inside, and draw it tightly shut behind you. The bars to the left and right are accessible inside the compartment; slide them up to secure the board. Otherwise it may fall open." He kneels and reaches into the compartment. I trill in surprise when he draws forth a Fighting Hand. He tucks it under one arm and asks, "Can you put on one of these in the dark?"

"Yes. I—"

"Then do so the moment you shut the board. If we stop and are examined by Stripes, they may discover this compartment. If this board should open without being knocked upon twice"—

he knocks sharply, *tok! tok!*—"come out slashing. *Do not hesitate!* Questions?"

"Why do I not simply hide in the compartment when we set out, and stay there until we are safely out of town?"

"If we are stopped before we leave Seven Answers, there will only be one reason for it—and therefore they will search the wagon anyhow. In which case I prefer you out and able to fight."

"To fight? What chance shall we have against many Stripes?"

"Little to none. Further questions?"

"No. None."

He sets the Fighting Hand back into the compartment and replaces the board, then slides up the two metal bars. He straightens.

"Where are you coming by a Fighting Hand?" I ask.

"Perhaps someday I will tell you."

"I am certain it is an interesting tale."

"It is. Interesting and long." He steps to the rear of the wagon and climbs down.

"Goody Fagin," signs Lee. "I see that your wagons for importing are designed with a certain economy in mind."

Fagin's only reply is a narrow-eyed look.

Dodger returns with my mandolute, and I thank him and draw the strap over my head, then turn the mandolute until it rests against my back. "A favor?" I ask him.

"Yes?"

"There are two in Three Big Dogs who must be informed of my leaving, of the presence of many Stripes. One is once my teacher in the Keep in Seaport Savannah; he is a physician named Zorba. The other. . . . Zorba will know to inform the other himself. Can someone be dispatched to instruct them to meet me in Seaport Savannah? At [Geppetto] the Shipwright's. Zorba will know where it is. Give them the route we shall take, and perhaps they may meet us on the way."

"I will send somebody," signs Dodger. "I regret that I cannot do it myself, but I must act quickly here and then catch up to you on the road, for I suspect you goodbodies will need whatever help you can get."

"I thank you, Dodger," I sign. "I am certain that whomever you dispatch will be trustworthy."

"We go," signs Fagin. "Dodger . . . before you carry out the instructions I am giving you earlier, there are two skulls acting as bookends in my ledger room. One of them . . ." He glances at us momentarily, then spreads his hands philosophically—realizing, I think, that we are already seeing the skulls anyhow, and are doubtless figuring out what they are. "One of them is the skull of a Stripe. Destroy both, and bury the pieces. Otherwise. . . ."

Dodger gives his assent and I complete the unsigned thought: *otherwise the Stripes will stake me to a tree and feed small bits of me to their dogs while I yet live.*

"On the wagon, then, Truck; on, Lee," orders Fagin. "Lee, you sit beside me; Truck, sit comfortably in back and play your mandolute. Keep it across your belly." He opens his purse and glances inside, then shuts it and ties the flap.

Despite his knowledge of who and what I am, Fagin does not defer to me, and this I find I like in him. There is something in his worldliness, in his preparedness, his grace under pressure, and his utter lack of being impressed with me or with anything, that I find appealing. Fagin is not *aloof,* but neither is he *involved.* He directs; he rarely participates. Sometimes I think it is this sort who runs the world, and not generals or advisors or Architects of Sleep.

Lee clambers aboard the wagon and I climb into the back, holding on to the neck of the mandolute to keep it from banging. Fagin sits to Lee's right. He claps his hands sharply and we are under way.

For four or five kilospans I play my mandolute. Usually I find it relaxing, my playing, but the mood of the music comes from me, so my music is of partings before long journeys, unfolding in such a way as to suggest a *going away.* Into this I find I weave two threads: one suggests an assurance that I travel with good companions, and one conveys a tension at the hazards of the journey itself. But the oddness of it is that despite the hazard, the tension, and my fear, I hear the life in my own music, as though it is an actual thing I am wrapping both arms around. Once, my playing falters because in attempting to display this feeling I stagger with the load—but the enthusiasm is there.

The why of this puzzles me. Perhaps it is that you are never more alive than when that life is threatened.

And then Fagin trills for my attention without looking back, and I hand Lee my mandolute, careful to keep it low, and—

foolishly, but I cannot help it—I risk a glance at the Stripes not two hectospans ahead, at the edge of the wood.

There are four of them, wearing their Fighting Hands with the blades hooked back. On either side of the road are their dogs, which sit and stretch and lick lazily in the afternoon heat.

I do not take in any more details, but instead carry out Fagin's instructions as quickly as I can. I am ensconced within the compartment and putting on the Fighting Hand well before Fagin and Lee are made to halt.

The compartment is dark and cramped and smells of wood and hay and llama. All I can see is the thin slit of light from the upper juncture of the removable board. Lee's war helmet presses uncomfortably against my back.

I squeeze the bar of the Fighting Hand across my palm. The blades are unhooked and I hold my arm across my chest. I do not move. I breathe slowly. We are stopped.

I listen.

I watch the slit for the interruption of a body that will signify that the board may be removed.

The wait is interminable. I am frustrated at being unable to see what is being signed. The compartment seems to close in on me, to stifle me; my hands and feet are damp, and I must repress an urge to lash out, to kick at the wood and knock out the board, to claw my way to sunshine and fresh air—and certain death.

I hear the high-pitched bark of a fighting dog, and I flinch.

I feel a slight bounce as someone climbs onto the back of the wagon. There are sounds of brushing as s/he cleans hay away, looking for someone hiding in it.

Thud! and *thud!* And nearer: *thud!* S/he stamps on the wagonbed, searching for hollow places.

An interruption segments the line of sunlight. My right arm tenses across my chest, and I will it to relax. I will strike faster if the muscles are relaxed.

A fighting dog barks.

My eyes are opened wide. The slice of Stripe moving in the slit of light is become my entire world. I feel a need to blink, but know that I must not, though my eyes burn. I hold my breath.

The interruption in the line of light slides to the left. The wagon gives a slight bounce and a squeak, and then there is a muffled thud as the Stripe lands on the grass.

Trillings, and another bark, this one from a different dog, by the sound.

A sharp handclap startles me, and I jerk as the wagon begins to move.

Now I wait in the dark and burn more with curiosity than with fear.

What of the Bald Ape? I wonder. What of Zorba? I hope they do not encounter Stripes. I hope they find me in Seaport Savannah, but more than this, I hope they can catch up to us on the road.

So many uncertainties.

After a few fingers the wagon stops. In a moment come two sharp raps on the board in front of my face. One bar is lowered, then the other. I blink as sunlight floods me.

I clamber out, squinting.

We are in the woods. It is damp, and quiet but for an ivory-billed woodpecker slamming its bill upon a tree beside the road. "Yes?" I ask Lee. "Yes, well . . .?"

"Not even exciting," she signs. And she waves laughter. If only because it is a release of tension, I join her.

Fagin steps around to the rear of the wagon. "We are not out of the alligator's jaws yet," he signs. "It is quite possible that in Seven Answers they will discover what we are doing, and we cannot outrun messenger llamas. So we shall travel at a leisurely pace for now, until Dodger catches up, and we will see what he has to sign."

"And if Dodger does not catch up?" asks Lee.

"Then there is nothing to be done. Our fates are decided, yes, Truck?"

Rather than reply, I unbuckle the Fighting Hand and give it to Fagin. He takes it and regards me a moment, then waves a small laugh and turns away. He climbs back onto the driver's bench and sets the Fighting Hand beside him.

Lee looks from him to me. "We are on our way, Truck," she signs. And she sits beside Fagin and hands me my mandolute.

Well, there is nothing else to do: I sit down and strike up a tune.

The trees are an arch above us. We are nearly at the intersection of eastbound and northbound roads. The path through the woods is a sun-flecked tunnel of greens. A red wolf watches disinterestedly as we pass. In the distance I hear a feline cry. A jaguar?

Not long ago I am a stranger to the woods. No longer.

In alarm I look up from my playing at the sound of thudding hooves on the path behind us. A messenger llama speeds toward us—Dodger.

I trill, and Fagin and Lee look back. Fagin claps the llamas to a halt, and we wait while Dodger catches up.

He dismounts quickly. He is breathing hard. "Fagin," he signs quickly. "They know. Do not ask me how, but they know. They are heading directly for our place and Goody Lee's house, with others going to guard the roads."

"My family—," begins Lee.

"Is unharmed, Goody Lee," signs Dodger. Even in his excitement and fear, I notice, he cannot help but sign the honorific to Lee. "Your house is ransacked, but none there are hurt. I am sure they will be questioned, though."

"And my shop, my building?" implores Fagin.

"Burned down, as you are instructing me."

As Fagin is instructing him?

"And the Stripes?" continues Fagin.

"All within are burned with it. I am escaping through the tunnel to the other side of the road."

"Your shop?" I sign in disbelief. "Fagin, your *shop?*"

"Be still! Dodger, what of the remaining Stripes?"

"As best I can determine, four guard the road to the north, four to the west, three to the east, and three to the south. Two small pole boats guard the river at the north and south ends of town. The remainder of the Stripes are divided between Lee's place and yours, and as I sign, I am taking care of those who break into your shop."

"You are certain none are surviving the fire?"

"I am waiting until they are well within the building before setting it."

"Good."

"In addition," continues Dodger, "I am hiring wagoners to take several different roads out of the town. These will act as distractions; though they will pass inspections, the Stripes will remember their passage and will thus have no certainty of our direction. Knowing we are leaving town, they will realize we could be any one of those wagons. They will be forced to divide their forces still further."

"Yes," signs Fagin. "General Lee—your opinion? How do you think they will proceed?"

"We are already duping them once now," she signs in her slow and thoughtful way. "Though hurried, they will be cautious. I would think that, if they have the Stripes to spare, they will leave behind at least ten in Seven Answers, in case we are remaining. They will also keep guards on the four roads leading out of town. How many depends on their estimation of our strength. The rest will spread equally along the east, south, west, and north roads. Except for the river blockades, of course."

"But it is certain that a contingent of Stripes heads our way," I sign.

"It would seem likely," she replied. Lee is so infuriatingly calm!

Fagin steps beside the wagon and picks up his Fighting Hand from the driver's bench. He straps it on, leaving the blades hooked back.

"We cannot hide," I sign. "They have their dogs—"

"We cannot hope to defeat more than a few Stripes at best," signs Lee.

"We cannot continue to sign about it, either," signs Fagin. He turns away from us. "Dodger, unyoke the llamas. With yours, there is one for each of you." He glances at Lee and me, then looks back to Dodger. "Get them out of here."

I trill. "Fagin, you cannot hope to do this alone!"

He ignores me. I grab his shoulder and pull him around. "Fagin! What of not wanting to owe me favors? You are 'pragmatically motivated,' as I recall."

"My shop is my life," he signs. "It is gone."

"What can you hope to accomplish? You will only be killed, and no good can come of it."

He indicates the four umbilical bracelets on his left, unweaponed wrist—I wear the fifth. "Where do you think I am getting these?" he demands. "I am not winning them at a Festival." His eyes narrow and he turns so that the others cannot see what he signs. "Do not tell me how to save your life, Architect." He turns away and will see nothing further from me. He works his hand from behind the clasp bar and removes one of the umbilical bracelets, then holds it out to Dodger, who takes it and stares at it as though he expects it to squirm in his hands.

"Dodger," signs Fagin. "Long ago I am promising to return this to you when I consider your debt repaid. It is yours."

Dodger looks up at Fagin with glittering eyes. "I—," he signs. "I do not . . ." He stops and thrusts his hand through the bracelet.

"I am sure I will not stop them all," signs Fagin. "But the capybaras will have to eat through a corpse or two before reaching mine, yes?" And he laughs.

"Dodger?" asks Lee. "How long before they are here?"

"Goody Lee, I have no way of knowing." Dodger turns back to Fagin. "I . . . cannot stay with you. I cannot help you here, now."

"No; I understand. Be still. And go! Take them with you; help them to Seaport Savannah. You are free of obligation to me after that. Go—I have much to do right now, and little time in which to do it."

I see that there is no arguing with him, so rather than waste what time remains to him, I help Dodger unyoke the llamas. We prepare them for riding as best we can—they have no leather pads on which to sit, and no stirrups, and the halter is suitable for their tandem yoke but not for riding. Still, we can ride bareback and hang on to their fur. While we remove the halters Lee helps Fagin turn the wagon to block the road, and then they push it over onto one side. From the hidden compartment Fagin retrieves our papers and her war helmet.

Dodger, Lee, and I mount our llamas. I regard Fagin. His look is steady; his eyes yield nothing.

"Thank you," I finally sign.

Is there, briefly, some acknowledgment in his eyes? He turns away before I can be sure.

We clap our hands and are on our way. I look back, once, before Fagin is out of sight. With his Fighting Hand he cuts the reins from the harness we are leaving behind. He removes his purse and pulls something from it. I am too far away to tell what it is. Leaving the object on the ground, he hurries to a tree and begins hacking at a branch.

Then we turn left onto the north road, and Fagin is out of sight.

Nobody signs anything, and we are alone with our thoughts as we hurry along the road. I stare at the back of my llama's neck.

It is not long before Lee trills for our attention. "It is not right to leave him behind like this," she signs. "I will turn around and help him."

"You will do nothing of the kind," I sign. "Leave him to his fate."

Dodger pulls abreast of Lee. "Fagin knows what he does," he signs.

Fagin does, indeed, I think to myself. And he is perhaps the most courageous raccoon I am ever knowing.

Fight well, Fagin, I wish. *Fight well.*

We clap our mounts faster, heading north.

22
Narrative of James Bentley

I MUST HAVE been a hell of a sight as I trudged along wearing my army-surplus boots, a pair of socks grimier than a theater floor, a pair of once white Calvin Klein underwear now beginning to develop a life of its own, my daypack, and my glasses.

Zorba walked beside me and did not sign. He looked at his feet if I met his gaze. If I asked him a question, he answered curtly. When I tried to initiate an innocuous language lesson, he would not be drawn out. Finally I just left him to his funk.

Last night we had slept on the grass near the road. When I awoke I was cold, wet with dew, and hung over. At least Zorba had fur.

We had relieved ourselves and resumed our westward walk. By noon my back was burned nearly enough to attract hungry wildlife. I gave up and removed the poncho from my pack, and I put it on. Immediately I began to sweat.

I was beginning to resent my male anatomy. I'd have scraped off my underwear if it hadn't been the only thing that kept my ding-dong from playing bell-clapper against my thighs.

And there were a lot of thorny bushes around.

Zorba was exactly like Truck when it came to hiking: trudge, trudge, trudge all the doo-dah day, one steady pace, no stops, like a machine. Not fast, because their legs are short, but relentless. I had to force rest stops by unceremoniously sitting down in the middle of the road.

Twice we were passed by wagons, and once by a lone rider on a messenger llama. Each time Zorba made me hide behind trees at the sound of their approach.

We hiked until just after sundown, when I was prevented from going farther by the convenient expedient of exhaustion. Zorba, of course, seemed more than willing to keep walking.

I used the poncho as a blanket and was still cold in the morning, but not wet.

Awake, and up, and walk.

Since Zorba continued to keep his hands to himself—to keep his mouth shut, in a manner of (not) speaking—I ruminated about Truck and her world. And welcome to it, Bentley, a.k.a. Bald Ape.

We were supposed to find Truck in the town toward which we plodded, a place called Seven Answers. (What had been the Question? I wondered.) Zorba knew whom Truck had sought out in Seven Answers—apparently some high-ranking military mucky-muck she had once known, whom I dubbed General Lee.

But what were we supposed to do when we found them?

Ahead on the road a capybara lifted its bullet-shaped head, caught wind of us, and scuttled into the brush. There must have been a river nearby; they tended to hang around waterways and feed alligators—the hard way.

The poncho swished in time with my walk as my knees bumped it. My feet hurt. My back burned. No Solarcaine for ol' Jimbo. The sap from an aloe vera plant would help lots, but did they even *have* aloe vera? Where was it indigenous? Africa? If it was, had they brought it over here? Coconut butter helped a sunburn, though—would coconut milk? Or rubbing coconut over the burn?

Hell, I didn't know.

Just past the intersection of the westbound and northbound roads we came upon a four-wheeled wagon turned on its side and blocking the way. There was no sign of llamas or raccoons. Zorba ushered me behind one of the tall pine trees lining the road.

"What is it, Zorba?" I asked.

He spread his hands. "Brigands, perhaps. Perhaps nothing. But we shall not stupidly walk up; it may be a trap. Let us first watch for half a finger."

We stared at the upturned wagon. There was no motion, no sound save the wind rushing through the tall pines with a sound like the sustained crashing of a wave. In front of the wagon was a small pile of rocks. I pointed them out to Zorba, who again spread his hands.

We watched for a few minutes, but nothing happened. Zorba nudged me, and we began threading our way toward the wagon through the trees at the side of the road. Zorba told me to wait behind a tree while he went to examine the wagon. "If I am attacked," he signed, "run out howling and waving your arms. The sight of you would frighten away anything."

He stepped away before I could thank him properly.

Nothing seemed amiss at the wagon, and Zorba motioned me to join him. I stepped out onto the road and walked around the wagon, puzzled. As far as I could tell it was not damaged, and there seemed no evidence of foul play. "Curious, Zorba," I remarked.

"Yes, Bald Ape."

"Should we right it, and move it out of the way?"

He considered. "No," he decided. "Let us press on. But keep your ears pricked."

We stepped around the wagon, and before we had walked a dozen paces a crashing in the bush sent us scampering behind an oak on the right side of the road. I stared over Zorba's head and tried to keep my breathing from being loud as we watched a raccoon emerge from the brush, dragging a pretty hefty log behind him. He was having no easy time of it, though he managed to wrestle the log to the middle of the road, where he dropped it and sat on it while he caught his breath.

He wore a Fighting Hand with the bladed section hooked back.

I glanced at Zorba. Zorba glanced back. I backed up a step to give us room to sign, then spread my hands.

"He is certainly no Stripe," Zorba signed. He looked back, narrowing his eyes and peering closer. "He wears several umbilical bracelets."

I tugged the fur at Zorba's shoulder to get his attention. "This is unusual?" I asked when he looked back.

"It is almost unknown, and even then it is a Stripe custom. It is . . . vulgar." He did not elaborate.

The stranger, meanwhile, had picked up a sturdy branch lying beside the log, and now he squatted and lifted one end of the log, holding the branch along one side of it. Slowly he rose to a standing position, then raised the log higher until he was able to rest it on one shoulder. He set one end of the branch on the ground and the other against the log, making sure the branch was firmly wedged, and then he shifted until he seemed confident the log was balanced on the branch. He gradually lowered himself and stepped from beneath the log. He regarded the arrangement a moment, stepped to the right, and stared down the road, cocking his head as though listening. Then he bent and retrieved a long leather strip from the grass, and he carefully tied one end around the upper part of the branch supporting the log.

He stepped away and looked down the road again.

"I can watch no further," signed Zorba. "I must know what goes on here. Bald Ape, wait here as before." And he left me there and stepped onto the road. As I watched he stepped toward the strange raccoon, deliberately trampling through the high grass between the ruts to attract the stranger's attention.

The stranger whirled, right arm cocking, blades swinging down to fighting position. Zorba stopped and kept his hands at his sides.

The Fighting-Handed raccoon was not large, as raccoons go, but he was stout and, to judge by the size of the log he had lifted, strong. I estimated he was in middle age, for his fur had begun to lighten and grow coarser, and though he was obviously strong, he had a bit of a paunch. Except for kits, raccoons don't often tend to fat, though they do gain weight just before winter.

The stranger signed first. "What do you want, goodbody?" The honorific seemed a bit forced.

"I want to know what is going on here," Zorba answered bluntly. "The road is blocked, you wear a Fighting Hand, and you build a log fall."

"Do you travel west?"

"Yes."

"Then travel on, and do not concern yourself further."

"In good conscience I cannot do this, goodbody," Zorba retorted. "It seems you construct a trap of some sort, the purpose of which I cannot discern. Are you a brigand?"

Zorba was either more naïve than I gave him credit for, or else he was relying a bit too heavily on my coming to the rescue if he got himself into trouble. I was too far away to save him if this armed stranger decided to carve him up and feed him to the capybaras.

The stranger made no reply, and Zorba pressed further. "Were I to travel on, goodbody, how would you feel about my telling those I might encounter of what I am seeing here?"

I winced. Zorba, you dumbfuck. . . . I withdrew my arms into my poncho and tried to quietly shrug out of my pack. I lowered it to the ground, poked my arms through the slits again, and unzipped the pack, keeping my eyes on Zorba and the stranger all the while. As I did this the stranger signed, "I would not like it at all, goodbody. And I could not allow it." For all the tension he seemed unperturbed.

I fished my knife from my pack.

"You present a problem," the stranger continued. "And I am in quite a hurry, goody . . .?"

"Zorba," supplied Zorba.

The stranger's eyes widened. "Zorba?" he repeated.

"Yes. That is my name. And you?"

I unfolded my knife.

"Tell me," the stranger pursued, ignoring Zorba's question, "your occupation?"

"Why do you ask this, goodbody?"

"No time! Your occupation?"

No longer caring about the noise, I quickly removed my poncho; it would restrict my movement too much.

"I am a physician," Zorba admitted.

"From?"

"Goodbody, I hardly think—"

"From?"

I began creeping forward, hugging to trees and shadows, avoiding branches, stepping on falls of pine needles where possible, but never taking my eyes from them.

"I am from Three Big Dogs!" answered Zorba. "And who are *you*, and why do you ask—"

"You are a friend of Truck," the stranger signed. "Yes?"

I stopped.

The stranger continued without waiting for a reply. "Pay attention, Goody Zorba; I cannot afford even this time. My name is Fagin. I am in the midst of helping your friend Truck. Stripes are after her. She heads now toward Seaport Savannah on the north road, there. I remain here to slow the Stripes who pursue her. She sends a message to you to meet her at the place of [Geppetto] the Shipwright. She signs that you will know where this is, and that you will know to pass this information on to another. The message cannot be reaching you yet; no time. Go now, and you may catch up to her. Stay, and you may help me. *But do not delay me further!*"

Zorba seemed indecisive. "How many Stripes?" he asked.

"I do not know. At least three or four; possibly as many as ten. They will be here any finger now."

"Ten! You are crazy, or brave, or both."

"Perhaps. But still your hands and help me, Zorba, or still them and join the Architect."

"My . . . friend . . . is with me," Zorba signed. "We . . . We will help you."

"Good. Get [her/him]." And without another sign he turned away and began hacking a slim branch off a tree with the blades of his Fighting Hand.

Zorba watched him, dumbfounded, then turned to face where I had been. Anticipating him, I stepped out from behind the tree, wondering exactly how he planned to introduce me.

Fagin took my appearance shockingly well, considering: he turned to regard me, jumped back in startlement and brought up the Fighting Hand, and looked to Zorba.

"Fagin," signed Zorba imperturbably, "this is my friend, the Bald Ape."

"What is it?" he demanded, signing one-handed.

"I am just signing that to you," Zorba signed. "He is a sort of bald ape."

"I am glad to meet you," I signed. "A friend of Truck's is a friend of mine."

"It is. . . . He is . . . ," he signed to Zorba, and then he turned to me. "You are intelligent?"

"It depends on to whom I am compared, goodbody."

Fagin glanced at Zorba again, then back to me. "Intelligent enough," he signed, suddenly matter-of-fact, all business. "We will sign of this later. Right now I can put you to work." He paused. "I . . . hope to know more of you when our little chore is done," he signed. "I gather you have a tale that would not put me to sleep, yes?"

I laughed and replied, "I shall endeavor to be certain that you see it, Goody Fagin."

He cocked his head. "I, too, Bald Ape. For now, you may break these branches in half for me and sharpen one end of each with that knife you carry with such subtlety. Hurry."

Without another sign he turned around and went back to his work, moving hurriedly but not wasting a motion.

More than a little bemused, I picked up one of the branches, set one end on the ground, held the other end, put my boot in the middle, and broke it in two. With my knife I scraped slivers from the broken ends until they formed reasonably nasty points. I made six stakes from three branches, and when I was through Fagin tied them into two bundles of three, splayed them to form a tripod, and pounded them into the road with a rock, one bundle in each rut. He covered them with Spanish moss, and though they hardly blended in with the road, at least they didn't look like the pongee sticks they were.

Fagin regarded the work, trilled his satisfaction, and turned to face me. "This would be better if I am having more line. Perhaps I will use the reins I am tying to the log fall. They are not as essential there."

"Half a finger, Fagin," I signed, and I retrieved my pack and pulled the coil of nylon rope from it. Fagin tugged it sharply, bit it, and trilled in delight. He trotted to the trunk of a tree on the left side of the road, ten feet ahead of the camouflaged stakes. He knelt and tied one end of the rope around the trunk, tugged firmly to be sure it would hold, then dashed across the road with the free end in one hand. The line just barely made it. Still holding the end of the line, Fagin crouched behind a tree, let the line go slack, looked at me a moment to be sure I was watching, and then yanked. The rope jerked taut at thigh level. I looked from it to the clumps of Spanish moss.

"You are not a nice raccoon," I signed to Fagin.

He dropped the rope. "My demeanor is situational," he replied, and he stepped onto the road and worked the rope into the grass, then covered it with dirt where it crossed the wheel ruts.

"You cannot think to fool a Stripe into running beneath that log trap," signed Zorba when Fagin straightened up.

"The log is for their fighting dogs," he retorted. "As many of them as I can get, anyway." He dusted off his thigh and stepped closer to us. "Zorba, Bald Ape, we have little time, and you must do exactly as I tell you." He regarded me for a moment. "Bald Ape, you are large, but can you fight?"

"Yes. I can fight well. But unarmed, against Stripes who wear those—" I indicated the Fighting Hand he wore with the blades again hooked back, then signed an interrogative.

"Then be still and watch. Zorba, take the remainder of this harness and fashion it into a noose. Can you climb a tree?"

"Like a kit."

Fagin eyed him doubtfully but signed nothing. "Bald Ape, fashion yourself a branch of no more than four spans, and sharpen one end. Let me know when you are finished, for there are other things we must do . . ."

The hidden compartment beneath the driver's bench of the upturned wagon was stuffy and cramped. It was meant to hide raccoons, not bald apes, and I had to bend my knees and let the wood support me in a half-sitting position. I held a makeshift spear in my left hand, and I had to be careful not to lean it against the partially shut panel, which would fall open if I did. The branch was nearly two feet shorter than I'd have preferred, for I had been trained to wield a six-foot staff, but it was that or nothing. I had stuck my knife into the ground at the foot of the wagonbed; it was a last-resort weapon in case the branch was somehow wrested away or cut in half. All I had to do was get to it.

I coughed once. I couldn't help it.

I rested my forehead against the rough wood and peered out through the slit we had made by prying apart two boards on the bottom of the sidewise wagon. My glasses pressed against the bridge of my nose. The lenses were slightly fogged at the top because I was sweating heavily, and not just from the heat. I would have liked to put on my contacts, but I had no mirror, my hands were filthy, and it seemed that I couldn't afford the time anyway.

I stared through the narrow gap in the boards at the faint line of the rope on the road a hundred feet away. I could barely make out Fagin's shadowy form where he squatted behind an oak tree. He held the free end of the line in one hand that rested against the trunk of the tree. Motionless, he watched the road, which curved left about twenty feet past him, and he waited.

Across the road from me, above and slightly ahead of the foot of the wagon, Zorba sat perched in the crotch of another oak tree, no doubt staring intently at the same spot Fagin watched. He clutched the lariat he had fashioned from the remains of the harness, and he waited.

A trickle of sweat ran down the right lens of my glasses. I took them off and wiped my brow with my right arm, which was also slick with sweat, then dried my glasses on my underwear and put them back on. The right lens was now streaked, and tears formed in my eyes when I tried to focus on the road past the streak. I removed my glasses and cleaned them again, and I waited.

Alone in that hot, stuffy, cramped, and dark compartment, which was ripe with the musky odor of alarmed raccoon, my mind played tricks on me as I watched the twin ruts that curved away past Fagin. I conjured up the sounds of barking dogs and hoof-beats where there were only bird chirpings and the wind; I saw the movement of llamas and riders where there was only waving grass and an occasional fluttering bluejay or mockingbird. Once a cardinal flew at me, presumably to perch upon the side of the wagon, and it startled me enough that I banged the top of my head when I jerked involuntarily. My left hand, wet, cooled as I removed it from the staff to rub my scalp. My right hand remained slick on the staff. Even my feet were wet in my boots. I wriggled my toes to help keep my feet from going to sleep. Grit ground beneath my boots.

Anything could be coming down that road, anything at all, and in whatever quantity I cared—or didn't care—to imagine.

I'd have traded my soul for an Uzi and a suit of armor made of filled ammo clips. *So much for the great gun hater,* I thought. *Stricken by a case of situational ethics.*

For the dozenth time I surveyed the ambush we had set up, if only to divert my attention enough to quell my trembling.

Ten feet behind the camouflaged pongee sticks was the propped-up log Fagin had been setting up when we happened upon him. It was obvious as hell and couldn't be camouflaged, but by the time it was seen we hoped it would make little difference.

Behind the log was a pile of rocks gathered by Zorba. Between the pile of rocks and my hidden self a sharpened sapling lay in the grass, with the sharp end pointing away from me, toward the bend in the road.

Leaning against the foot of the wagon, on my side, was yet another stick. My water-filled canteen dangled from one end of it, tied on with a strip of leather. If I had to use it, I hoped it would serve as a good mace for at least a couple of blows.

Truth to tell, I hoped I wouldn't have to use it.

Just outside my hidden compartment was another pile of rocks. Beside this was a metal mesh net. I had no idea what it was for, but Fagin had placed it there.

Simple traps, these sticks, these logs, these rocks; crude things, but effective—we hoped. We had spent an hour preparing them, until Fagin decided that it was getting too risky for us to be caught in the midst of preparing our surprise reception, and we had taken our stations.

There is a kind of fear that is sudden and immediate, the kind of jolt you get at night when you're walking down a city street and someone steps out from an alleyway beside you, or when you are nearly run over by a speeding car. I remember the heartfreezing instant when a customer at the 7-Eleven had reached into his jacket for his wallet and I had thought he was going for a gun. These incidents are sudden and unexpected things, and there is time only to react, not to think.

There is another kind of fear, the kind where you have plenty of time to mull over your predicament, to sort through all the possible ways in which you can get hurt, to conjure up the worst possible scenarios. There is nothing of suddenness here, nothing of mere reaction. It's the difference between one situation where some big guy swings on you out of nowhere, and before you have time to size him up and realize you'd be *crazy* to fight him, you're blocking and hitting him back; and another situation where the same neckless musclehead is glaring at you from across the room and making a fist the size of a canned ham and screaming, "I'm gonna mash your fuckin' face in, asshole! Try and leave this place, motherfucker! I'll be out there! I'll be waitin'! An' I'm gonna put you in the fuckin' hospital!" And he leaves and you have all the time in the world to rehearse it all in your head, to picture that ten-pound fist smashing your face to a soggy mess, and you can see that he outweighs you by a good fifty pounds, not an ounce of it fat, and goddamn, you gotta leave *sometime*.

Waiting there, alone in something smaller than a broom closet, clad only in boots and underwear, my only weapon a pointy stick, was like having all the time in the world to wait for twenty neckless muscleheads to come down on me like white on rice, and the cancer of my imagination ate at me all the harder because the Stripes were such an unknown to me—because, of all the things I had encountered in this world, they frightened me the most. In some ways, though, I was more worried about how we could stop their dogs, for they would be on us before the Stripes were. I had been hurt by the dogs before but not by the Stripes, and while the dogs kept us busy the Stripes would strike.

Sweat stung my eyes, and I blinked rapidly. Some terrible war drum had begun to beat in my temples, some relentless rhythm anticipating the onset of action: ba-*bum*, ba-*bum*, ba-ba-ba-ba-*bum*, and the throbbing scored my anxiety and would not go away.

We are never more alive than at our moments of greatest fear, at the height of our anticipation—something you can know intellectually but never really understand until you have experienced it yourself. No wonder soldiers are drawn back to their memories of battle, to relive them again and again, to reenact those moments where life is so vibrant, so chrome-edged. You can become maddened by the inability to get away from those moments, I think, but they are always there, bright, vivid, and alive.

Down the road, hiding behind his tree, Fagin shifted. He raised his free hand a moment, then lowered it to grasp the rope in both hands, and braced himself.

The "get-ready" signal.

I took a deep breath and held it. The wood of the wagon was rough against my forehead and right shoulder. The branch in my hand remained woefully inadequate, but it had a reassuring *solidity*. The day seemed unnaturally bright, the sky as pale blue as a whiff of ozone, the tree leaves green as olives. My heart convulsed in my chest like the spasming muscle it was. My entire body seemed to resonate like a struck tuning fork. In my head the war drum throbbed.

I let out the breath, and it emerged staccato.

Fuck these raccoons, man; fuck 'em. Why did I give a shit whether Truck got away? In the company of an elderly physician and a middle-aged, overweight smuggler, I was supposed to take on an unknown number of armed *Stripes?* Were we fucking *crazy?* Why should I feel any camaraderie, any loyalty, any sense of—

Beyond the curve of the road came the beat of llamas' hooves and the high-pitched barking of dogs.

23
Narrative of Truck

ALL THAT DAY we ride, Dodger, Lee, and I. We follow the north road and stop only when we must. I constantly finger my mandolute but do not play. Lee continually glances behind us.

Riding just ahead of us, Dodger often rubs his newly returned umbilical bracelet, as though to assure himself it is not vanishing. It reminds me of the bracelet on my own wrist, the bracelet I am shamed to wear because it is not mine. To whom does it originally belong? I wonder. Who is nurtured within [her/his] mother by this cord that I now wear? Is Fagin killing to obtain it? For that is usually what is signified by this wearing of several umbilical bracelets.

Though the thing is light, it is an unpleasant weight on my arm.

Curious about the return of Dodger's bracelet to him, and about what this implies, I sign to Lee to remain behind and I nudge my mount forward to pull abreast of Dodger. I wrap the reins and sign, "We make good time, Dodger."

"Yes," he replies. "I am fearful the Stripes may catch up to us, but we can ill afford to be waylaid by a side road."

"Then you think Fagin will not stop them?"

"Let us not sell candles that are not made, Goody Truck. I have every confidence in my former employer—but Stripes are Stripes, yes?"

"Yes," I admit. "He is an odd one, your former employer. I owe him much."

"He is long since ceasing to seem odd to me, Goody Truck. It is the way he is."

"Why are you always so formal in your signing, Dodger?"

He laughs. "It is the way *I* am, Goody Truck. I might as well ask why you, of the highest of stations, are so *in*formal in your signing. I suspect it is because that is the way you are. Yes?"

"Yes. No matter what its color, the chameleon remains the same on the inside. But I am curious about Fagin, about your employment with him. May I ask you about it?"

"You may ask, goodbody," he signs carefully.

I glance back at Lee to see if she watches our conversation, but she regards the road behind us. "I gather you work with Fagin for some time now," I begin.

"Since my early adolescence, yes. He is taking me in after the death of my mother."

"That is magnanimous of him."

"It is not an altruistic act on his part, Goody Truck. Fagin never invests without expecting a return. Being constantly in trouble as a youth, and moving with an unsavory crowd, I am knowing him by reputation and seeking him out."

"You are in servitude to him?"

His look grows wary and evasive. "I am serving him. In return he is giving me food and a place to live. My free time is my own and he is asking no questions about it."

"Forgive my impertinence in signing so, Dodger, but it seems you are bound to him in some way." I indicate his bracelet.

He rubs it thoughtfully. "It is hard to accurately assess or describe."

"Slavery is proscribed everywhere I know of," I sign.

"It is not slavery! It is voluntary! At all times I am free to leave."

"But without your bracelet, yes?"

"You do not understand, Goody Truck. Fagin is, as you sign, a peculiar male. He deals in power, and possession of an umbilical bracelet that is not his own is certainly a symbol of this. It implies that he has many resources, abilities, strengths, and a bit of warranted arrogance. It intimidates, which suits Fagin's purposes in his many dealings, legitimate or otherwise. The fear associated with the Stripes' wearing of several bracelets is conferred upon Fagin when he does so. In giving over my bracelet I am providing him a token of power—but not of ownership."

"But you *are* giving it over."

"He is requiring it of me."

"Nothing can be 'required' of a volunteer."

"Do you deliberately provoke, Goody Truck? I am signing to you that to temporarily relinquish my bracelet is a price I pay, a choice I make freely. Think of it as the token of admission into Fagin's world, if you wish. Either one decides the cost is worth the return, or not. But I am never a slave."

"Pardon my unwarranted assumption, Dodger. I am merely intending to inquire after events you must admit are curious and unusual."

"Yes, they are that, Goody Truck. Though on my part I must sign that all events surrounding you are curious and unusual, and out of habit I am restraining my own inquisitiveness."

I sit straighter on my mount. "A point for you, Dodger! I will keep my hands to myself in the future."

His motionlessness is acknowledgment of his victory. But he is too polite to gloat over an earned point, and by way of letting this topic pass he twists on his llama, one hand reaching out to steady himself against the beast's neck, and regards General Lee. I glance back. As I expect, Lee is twisted around as well, regarding the road behind us. She turns to face us and sees that we watch her. Embarrassed, she ducks her head and spreads her hands. So that she will not feel chagrined I sign, "Better you look for them and they do not show, Lee, than you do not look for them and they do."

"A line of thinking that looks familiar to me, little Truck," she replies.

I wave a laugh and turn back.

"Your General Lee will soon begin jumping from things that are not there," observes Dodger, "if she maintains her vigil so."

"She knows Stripes," I reply. "She knows their thinking and their abilities. She is commanding them, and not so long ago that her edge is not still keen."

"She is your Liaison General, then?"

"Not mine. Charlemagne's. Lee is retiring not long after the Battle of Rivers Meeting."

Dodger's eyes widen and he glances back once more, then

looks back to me. *"That* General Lee?" he asks.

"The same, yes."

He is contemplative for a moment, and I look away from him as we ride past the fly-ridden body of a boar. From the rents in its back and the way the eyes are gouged out, it looks as if it may be killed by a [teraton]. Mother, what birds, to go for such game!

After a finger Dodger trills for my attention. "Goodbody Truck," he asks, "how does one become a Liaison General? How is one who is not a Stripe to be commanding them?"

"It is usually an hereditary position," I reply. "Though in the tumult of recent years this custom seems more disrupted than usual. Lee is being selected by Charlemagne when Lee's predecessor is discovered to be giving birth to a kit fathered by a Stripe. Lee and her then fledgling family are moving to Seven Answers. A new Liaison General is selected by Charlemagne, and she remains my General still." *If she still lives,* I add to myself.

"What of the mother?" asks Dodger.

"Mother?"

"Of the hybrid Stripe."

"Why, she is shaved before an assembly and then executed, and the kit killed as well. Why do you ask?"

"I am merely curious." He waves a bite-fly from his llama's neck. "Tell me, Truck, how one such as Lee—not a Stripe—is able to command them, to win their loyalty?"

"Lee is raised among Stripes, and educated alongside them and the adepts. This is the way for one groomed toward Liaison Generalship, to live in these two worlds. Lee is a master strategist, and she understands and respects the Stripes. More fully than many of us, she realizes their importance as a resource upon which the province may draw."

"A precarious resource, Architect."

Not afraid to fly the fur, this Dodger! "Part of our mission," I retort, "is to determine why they are becoming such."

"And you wonder at your usurpation, Truck!" For once Dodger neglects the use of honorifics.

I ask him what he means by this last remark, but he will sign nothing further of it. "Tell me of Fagin, then," I ask, "since I am telling you of Lee."

"Why are you so interested in Fagin?"

"Because he is helping me, and at the greatest cost an individual can pay—his life. Plus, he is helping me for no good reason, though I am effectively in his power and he would have more to gain by turning me over to Louis XIV."

Dodger signs nothing.

"Do you feel nothing for his loss?" I persist.

"I am done with him. He chooses his own fate; I choose mine."

I sign my derision. "And you assume a stance of worldliness! Here is a thing all Architects and adepts know that those who do not dream True can never understand: that no one chooses [her/his] fate."

"And where are these True dreams leaving you, *Architect?* You ride an old llama in a foreign land, accompanied by a weary old ex-General and a thief. [!]"

I regard him a moment before I answer. "The tale is not yet finished," I finally sign, "and the ending yet undreamed."

"Such conviction must comfort you."

"Do I detect more than a little sarcasm there, young Dodger? Tell me, if you are so cynical, so contemptuous of the Chair, why do you assist me?"

"I am not so young, Architect. I am nearly as old as you."

"And I am young. And you avoid an answer."

"Very well, Goody Truck. I help you not from any naïve notion of idealism, but that I may discharge a final obligation to Fagin."

"Fagin is dead by now, or soon will be. You are free from him, or so you are signing—you choose your own path, yes? He is having no hold on you, yes?" Again I sign my derision. "And he is staying behind to fight alone for me! Leave us, then, Dodger, for your loyalty does not lie with my cause. I would sooner you go your own way than to have your unwilling assistance. We can find our way to Seaport Savannah without difficulty, I think."

"There will be things along the way for which you shall want my help."

"Certainly. But that help must be a thing you desire to provide, not a duty you feel obligated to discharge."

He looks away from me. "Leave me alone, Architect," he signs.

"Whatever your problem is," I sign, "whatever dichotomy you feel, you insist on grappling with it alone."

But he will not see me, and I drop back and ride alongside General Lee.

"That is one troubled young male," comments Lee.

"So you *are* watching our conversation."

"Of course. When one is in trouble, Truck, no thing is peripheral."

I glance at Dodger, but he rides resolutely forward, straight-backed on his fine messenger llama. "He is merely spending too much time keeping things private, I think. Dealing with Fagin can do this, I would venture."

"There is a difference between 'private' and 'secret,'" she signs.

"Everyone deserves some secrets, Lee. I imagine you have one or two yourself."

She regards me a moment before signing. "Not as would affect you, Truck. And not as would affect my helping you. That is the demonstrable essence of trust. This Dodger is keeping things from you that concern you, and I do not trust him."

"He is not our enemy, Lee. He is killing many Stripes himself."

She scratches her muzzle. "One is not required to be an enemy," she signs, "to be untrustworthy."

There is certainly fodder enough in these conversations that I may chew on them for several decafingers before Lee finally brings me out of my reverie. I turn at her trilling and realize that I am so absorbed in my ponderings that I am losing all sense of my surroundings. This happens to me too often, I think.

"Truck," asks Lee, "who is this Geppetto we travel to meet?"

"She is a shipwright, and lately is providing many fine ships for our navy. Her ancestors are shipbuilders for as long as any can remember."

"But who is this Geppetto to you?"

"A friend, really. Nothing more and nothing less. When I am an adept she is letting me watch the building of great and beautiful ships, and explaining much about them." I pull the image from my past and it is as though it exists around me again: me an early adolescent, sitting unobtrusively on a bench while Geppetto measures beams, directs her crews, consults her plans, signs in inarticulate rage at the bearer of a load of knotty, green, inferior wood. "She directs the manufacture of ships to travel the coastlines, and from her yards emerge incredible, three-masted ships to explore Africa and [Europe], ships to bring back new foods and those odd animals we sign [onagers] and [Przhevalski's horses], ships to travel across unsailed seas toward unknown lands. I am spending many a decafinger in that huge place on the rivermouth, watching the tales of odd lands and fantastic creatures. Many afternoons I am watching those ships hoist anchor, watching their sails fill, seeing them shrink toward the horizon, wondering where they go, what they will bring back—if they come back at all. If I am not being an adept, Lee, if I am not becoming the Architect, I think more than any other thing I should like to be a sailor."

"And how do you know this Geppetto will help you now?"

"Shave you, Lee! Is there no romance with the unknown in your heart?"

"It has no bearing on the situation, Truck. Why do you think Geppetto will assist us?"

Lee is ever exasperating—but what causes this exasperation is an unswerving realism that gets much accomplished. "Geppetto remains my friend," I sign. "I keep in contact with her as I grow, even well after the conferring of the Title to me. She is taking me on my first sea voyage, down the coast to Seaport Jacksonville while I am still an adept. The weather is beautiful for that entire voyage, and the sea is calm. Geppetto is also assisting in the training of contingents of my Stripes to become sailors—"

"She *what?*"

"Her loyalty is to me, Lee," I assure her. "Not to the Stripes."

"You are thinking this of the Stripes, too," she chides.

"Is everyone bent on reminding me of my failings? I would rather maintain the naïve idealism of my excessive trust, Lee, than abandon it in favor of the wariness and suspicion all of you so heartily commend to me."

"You do not even realize it, my young one," replies Lee, "but you are already learning better than this. It surfaces often because it is much on your mind."

"Many things are on my mind, Lee."

"As they should be, little Truck. I would worry for you if it is otherwise." And she waves a laugh.

I am at a loss for a reply, but this is made moot when Lee

nudges her llama ahead to sign with Dodger—about what, I cannot see.

Before dark we make camp well off the road. Dodger throws at quails for our dinner, and Lee and I build a fire over which to cook them. Afterward we eat peaches picked from a nearby tree.

Dodger is sullen as he eats, intent on his food and signing nothing. Lee seems lost in her own thoughts, staring into the fire and picking slivers of meat from the quail. I regard her as she delicately eats her dinner, and I think of how good it is to have her with me.

I finish my peaches and wipe the juice from my muzzle with my hands, then wipe my hands against my haunches. It is annoying not to have drying-cloths. To myself I laugh: the refined qualities of the elite life!

Elite life. I think of Dodger's comments of this afternoon, of his derision of the Chair. We are certainly not an elite, we dreamers. The adepts are produced from all endeavors of life, for the talent selects no single type in which to lodge. Adepts are indeed trained for the Title and for advisorhood, but they consist of farmers' kits and the kits of butchers, of landowners, building constructors, shipwrights, bakers, importers, painters, printers, candlemakers. How can we be accused of thinking ourselves above the common when we *are* the common?

Dodger puts out the fire before dark. As the sun sets I pull the pick from my mandolute strings.

"Do not play your instrument too long," warns Lee. "The sound will carry, and in the night it will lead any who search directly to us."

I indicate that I will heed her advice, and I take my mandolute and remove myself from their company. For this playing I want to be alone.

I sit with my back against the trunk of an old mother oak, and I nestle the curve of the mandolute on my thigh, against my belly. I look up at the sky as I tune the strings. Repeat, small and bright, is already rising, half-full in the darkening sky. It will be three-quarters full before the night is ended. If Pete is risen, it is not yet visible above the tree line.

When the mandolute is tuned I place a hand over the strings to still them. I regard the browns and greens of the tortoiseshell pick and remember the beautiful, luminous, finely carved ivory pick that is a gift from my old music teacher, who is long since dying of the coughing sickness. Is that pick still there, in its cedar box in my chambers deep within the Keep? I will endeavor to find out.

I lower the tortoiseshell pick to the strings. *For you, Fagin,* I think, and I play.

There is a language that sound has. A musician loves sound the way a poet loves signing—for the flowing of signs in certain sequences, merely for the images they create by the way they fit together. For the turn of a phrase, or a pun resembling another sign or passage, or the making-up of something new when no old sign will do. The poet and the musician both use their talents to reach into a common archive of signs and sounds to suggest vivid landscapes, strong and often brooding or moody images. In this way sound *is* language, for produced by capable hands it communicates idea, mood, theme, setting, and an almost tactile *contour* even in the absence of signs. In the mind of the listener this creates an eidetic transformation, a translation of sound into sign, hence into image and sensation, and for this reason alone, if for no other, the musician is a poet, a shaper of signs.

For Fagin I play a music of the blood. The music is discordant, but the meter is fixed, like a heartbeat, and suggests the simple vitality of infants, the nakedness of need. This music is not afraid to sound ugly, and is sunk to the roots in a deeper self we all share. In striking certain chords I pluck a cord buried within all raccoons, a responsive cord that I think is uniquely raccoon in its shared immediacy and intimacy. I try to create an imagery that sweeps, yet one that loves life in a deliberately reserved way. My closed eyes watch the sound form shapes in the air. It is a liquid thing, this music, but not at all graceful. It is instead phlegmatic and commands attention in the manner of a cough. But this discordance confers an irony, for it creates a delicacy not possible with the flatness of bald statement. This music affects the pulse because it is written by the blood.

I strike a last cord and open my eyes. The imagery remains; it lives beyond the ephemera of the music.

It is darker now. Pete, pale and also half-full, rises above the dark tops of the trees. I weave my pick into the strings at the neck of the mandolute, then stand and brush twigs from my fur. Once again I need a bath and a good brushing.

I carry the mandolute back to our camp and lean it against a tree near where I will sleep. Dodger attends the llamas, which are tired. I am tired, too.

Lee regards me from where she sits atop a large branch of a cypress tree. She is curiously and endearingly kit-like, climbing up there so, sitting on this branch and swinging her feet.

"Your music is for Fagin," she signs.

"Yes, it is. I can do nothing else for him." She makes no reply, and suddenly I am very sad.

It is late, and Lee and Dodger are asleep. I keep the second watch of the night. Repeat is below the horizon, and Pete is high overhead and beginning to wax. The gray-white form of Dodger's messenger llama is visible through the trees. Difficult things to camouflage, llamas.

It is good that it is my watch, for sleep tonight is a thing that would elude me if I am pursuing.

I am worried.

I am hunted by Stripes in and of a province not my own, a province turning hostile because my own Stripes are attacking and killing its Stripes and several of its officials. Why do Florida's Stripes pursue me so? Is Louis XIV allied with my usurper? All reports indicate the opposite, that he prepares for war with my province. More likely his alliance is formed with Architect Tokugawa, to the west.

The Stripes are an issue unto themselves, and a frightening one at that. Suddenly it seems we are creating an alien thing in our very midst. My usurper is powerful, to turn them against me. Who s/he is I do not know. What actions I shall take against [her/him] are uncertain. I sail into an undreamed future and am unsure of my course. I have no guide but my surroundings of the moment, and it frustrates.

Just what is it I hope to accomplish? Already Fagin and Doc Holliday are dying for me, and I fear this is but the beginning. How many more shall give their lives for me? Is my return to the Chair worth this? Of course it is, for I have the conviction of my dream, and I know how many more will die if I abandon my cause.

I wrestle, I grapple; I push, I pull, but I do not resolve.

A twig snaps. I look: it is only one of the llamas shifting about. Lee signs in her sleep. Dodger does not. Probably he is teaching himself not to, for he cannot afford to reveal himself, even in his sleep. The wind gusts, then calms. The night is cloudless and clear.

I worry also about Zorba and the Bald Ape. I hope they are receiving my message to meet me at Geppetto's, but even if they are, I have much cause to fret. How are they to travel to Seaport Savannah, and through the Seaport itself, inconspicuously? Zorba I admire; he is smarter than a rat seeking food in a pantry. Nevertheless, the Bald Ape stands out like a teraton on a snowfield.

The Bald Ape. I puzzle, I fret. He is a creature without a home, it seems, a stranger here somehow. What is his role in all of this? And how much of my situation is he aware of?

I hope Zorba is teaching him well, for there is much to tell him, much to ask him, much to learn. I cannot rid myself of worry about him. It is true that I am dreaming of him, but only of my meeting him and of a vague, underlying admonition to keep him nearby—which he is *not* now. This thought makes me uncomfortable. If there is any one rule I must live by, it is this: never go against a True dream. It is certain that they may be interpreted incorrectly, but one must not ignore what they portend.

I feel that my watch is ended, for it seems certain that five decafingers are passing by now. I rouse Dodger from his slumber. He wakes quickly and comes instantly to full alertness. As with the suppression of signing in his sleep, I wonder if this is another learned trait.

Dodger takes the watch, and I lie down on the grass where he is sleeping. It is still warm from his body. I look up at the uncountable stars.

Relay this message, you stars, to my friends Zorba and the Bald Ape, I think to them: *Good fortune, and a safe journey.*

Soon I am asleep—and I dream.

24
Narrative of James Bentley

THEY ROUNDED THE bend on their messenger llamas: six Stripes riding two abreast, three fighting dogs running in front of them, and Fagin yanked on the line from behind his tree; the line went taut, the two lead llamas went down, and the two Stripes riding them pitched forward, one landing belly-first on the moss-covered pongee sticks and thrashing there, the other impaled through the lower ribs by one stake, rolling over and snapping it off in his side, then trying to stand and trampled by his companions' llamas

(Two down, four to go, tallied in my head)
while Fagin dashed onto the road, stopped before the confused, bleating llamas and the startled, trilling Stripes, and threw a rock at a Stripe that was deflected by a Hard Arm, though Fagin turned without wanting to see if his throw was good and ran toward me, pursued by the three knife-collared fighting dogs, and he glanced over his shoulder as he rounded the propped-up log, stopped short, fumbled for the leather strip tied to the supporting branch, grasped it, bolted, and yanked when the dogs were ten feet away, teeth snapping, jaws foaming, one dog straining ahead of the other two who were running neck and neck, so that it squeezed past when the log fell and crushed the dog's slower companions, one of them yelping once and falling silent, the other baying in pain as it died while Fagin, bent over and still running, reached the pile of rocks and scooped with his unarmed hand, then straightened and

transferred a rock to his right hand, stopped suddenly, spun, and let fly with deadly accuracy, the rock's impact slamming the head of the remaining dog into the ground as it yiped and spasmed, blood spurting from its head as Fagin let fly again at the Stripes who galloped on the heels of the dog, and though Fagin's throw did not kill the Stripe at which it was aimed, it struck her left shoulder and she fell from her llama as though jerked by a string, causing a pile-up in the left rut when the riderless llama pulled up short and the llama following ran full tilt into it, the rider of the second llama trilling his anger and dismounting while the Stripe riding the lead llama in the right rut urged his mount toward Fagin without hesitation, reining the llama to Fagin's right and leaning out to the left with his Fighting Hand blades extended, his free hand gripping the braided neck hair of his messenger llama, and he straightened his Fighting-Handed arm, pointing the blades forward as he pounded closer to Fagin, who dropped, reached into the high grass, and brought up the long, sharpened branch we had placed there, holding the blunt end firm against the ground and bracing himself as the Stripe saw what was coming too late to prevent it; his llama charged past Fagin, and Fagin leaned away from it but did not move the spear until the Stripe tried to bat it aside, and then Fagin dipped the point slightly and brought it up again, impaling the Stripe as his momentum carried him forward; the Stripe swung his Fighting Hand toward Fagin's head even as he was run through and falling from his mount, causing Fagin to duck and release the spear—and just before the Stripe hit the ground, his llama passed in front of the wagon and blocked my view, and when I could see again Fagin was pulling the spear from the chest of the Stripe, and blood was running from Fagin's right leg where the Stripe had cut him with a final slash of his Fighting Hand.

(Three down, three to go)

then Fagin, seemingly oblivious to the blood darkening the fur of his lower leg, hurled the spear toward the nearest of the Stripes, the one he had unseated with his last rock throw, turned without waiting to see if the spear connected, and ran to the left and out of my view, toward the side of the road where Zorba waited in the oak tree with his noose, having no idea how quickly things were about to turn to shit as Fagin rounded the wagon and pounded toward the compartment in which I waited, and I turned my head so that I could see him through the partially opened compartment lid as he came into view, and I watched as he bent and picked up the metal net from beside the second pile of rocks, holding it by the middle so that the weighted fringe dangled, then waved his arm to swing the blades of his Fighting Hand into place, standing with his back to the wagon, waiting for attack from either side, sparing me not so much as a glance as the blood that glistened in his fur dripped onto the sun-browned grass while he breathed heavily and cooed lowly with each exhalation, so I turned my gaze to see what the remaining three Stripes were doing just in time to hear the high-pitched, tremulous scream and soft thump as Zorba was jerked out of the oak tree by the Stripe he had tried to lasso, the Stripe who had dodged Fagin's hurled spear with a speed that was ominous in its ease, and I peered through the slit between the two boards and saw the other two Stripes dismounting, snatching their weapons ready with amazing speed, hugging their llamas to use the beasts as shields, one of the Stripes armed with a Fighting Hand and a Hard Arm, the other with a Fighting Hand on the left hand and an iron-balled bola dangling from the right; I blinked sweat from my eyes and jerked my head back as the Stripes nudged their long-legged llamas closer, seeing their flat-black eyes and their wary faces as they approached the wagon, and my nostrils flared, for the air was rich with a musky smell, the glandular odor of raccoons fighting for their lives, and I fought an urge to sneeze as the Stripes came on without a sign to one another, and while the burning sensation built in my nose they cautiously surveyed the wagon and the trees, not about to be taken by surprise again, though their attention was momentarily occupied by an altercation out of sight to my left—Zorba being dealt with by the third Stripe—and snot ran down my nose and I dared not sniff as the taller of the approaching Stripes signed to the other to go around to the right while he went left, and they separated, leaving me with a momentary view of several consternated llamas and the corpses of three dogs and three Stripes on the road before I again turned my head to watch Fagin—who still stood ready, poised like some ursine gladiator, Fighting Hand over his right arm, weighted net in his left hand, head metronomically turning left, right, left, right, occasionally glancing over his shoulder as if expecting attack from over the top of the wagon—I watched him and did not know whether to jump out of the compartment now, and maybe give me and Fagin enough time to assess the situation and fight back-to-back, or to rush out just before Fagin was attacked, and use the surprise of my appearance to our advantage, and for all of perhaps three seconds I was paralyzed by this indecision, and at the end of those three seconds the question became moot because I felt the wagon beginning to tip and I realized with a shock that the two Stripes were shoving the wagon over so that Fagin couldn't use it to protect his rear, and I had just enough time to knock open the compartment door with my spear and rush out before the creaking wagon fell over onto its wheels and a rush of air brushed the back of my legs, then I turned with my spear readied to confront my attackers, and if they were startled by my appearance, they sure as hell recovered quickly: the one who had escaped Zorba's lariat was already running for Fagin when the wagon tipped over; she slowed at the sight of me but did not stop, and Fagin was half-turned to engage her when something hissed toward him and wrapped around his lower legs like a hungry python, spiraling inward until one of the iron balls of the hurled bola smacked against another, and the force of the throw buckled Fagin's knees and sent him to the ground, and the running Stripe was on Fagin before he could recover, and I stepped toward the nearest Stripe as he jumped at me from the wagonbed onto which he had vaulted, and I thrust at him as he descended and my spear was batted aside as if it were an irritating mosquito and my legs were knocked from under me and I landed hard on my tailbone and the wind was knocked out of me and I was slammed onto my back so that my skull thudded dully against the ground and straddling me was the Stripe who had leaped at me and he bent closer and I was looking into a dispassionate pair of black eyes in a face divided by a naked strip and I could feel nothing but the four steel blades pressing against my neck.

The fight was over.

They tied me up. The rope bound my ankles, knotted around my wrists, which were crossed behind my back, looped around my throat, and snaked back down to my ankles. The circulation was cut off in my wrists, and my hands felt numb and heavy. The rope was taut and choked me if I moved. I was forced to sit Japanese style.

Fagin was a few yards away, tied in the same manner. He looked furious. Drying blood matted the lower half of his right leg. He met my gaze for a moment, and his eyes were bright.

Zorba was behind Fagin. He was alive, but it looked as if he had broken a leg when he fell out of the tree. The two male Stripes were splinting it while the female watched me and Fagin. The males worked efficiently and without signing, and Zorba made no comment as they wrapped the splint. When they were done they tied Zorba's hands behind his back and then tied the rope around a tree.

The female stared at me, and I stared back. Her gaze was intense, and I was reminded of the "stare wars" we kids used to hold in junior high school, when two of us would simply stare at each other until one looked away. The first to do so was the loser. I had the distinct impression that this Stripe expected me to drop my gaze, and she seemed puzzled when I did not do so after a few seconds, then angry when I continued to stare back with all the calmness I could muster, focusing on the cinammon-colored strip bordering the left side of her stripe. The contest—if contest it was—ended when one of her companions trilled for her attention and signed something that was blocked from my view by her body. She stepped behind Fagin, then knelt and untied his hands, taking up the slack in the rope and leaving the line connected from his crossed ankles to his throat. While Fagin massaged his hands she stepped in front of him, unbuckled her Fighting Hand, and removed it. She squatted and deliberately set the Fighting Hand between them, looking into Fagin's eyes the entire time. Fagin never glanced at the weapon; instead he cast her a smoldering look that he lowered after a few seconds.

She trilled for his attention and his head came up sharply. Behind them Zorba watched what he could see of their conversation. The two male Stripes flanking him looked on as well.

"You are?" the female asked.

"Fagin," he replied.

"Fagin." She glanced at her companions, then back at Fagin. She indicated me. "That is the bald ape?" she asked.

Fagin did not look at her as he replied. "I do not know what he is," he signed.

She casually picked up her Fighting Hand and slapped Fagin across the side of the head with the back of it. The sound of it striking him made me wince, but other than recoiling from the blow, Fagin gave no indication that it had hurt him.

Behind Fagin the two male Stripes signed something to each other.

The female set down the Fighting Hand. "That is the bald ape?" she asked again.

Fagin signed nothing. She picked up the Fighting Hand again, but a trill from Zorba kept her from striking. She went to him and untied his hands.

"That is the bald ape," Zorba signed. "Do not hit my friend again."

She regarded Zorba a moment, then returned to Fagin and hit him again. He fell to the side and began to choke on the rope. He lay there, half-conscious, gagging, and bleeding from the side of his head. None of the Stripes moved to help him; instead the female left him there and went to stand in front of Zorba. Slowly she put her Fighting Hand back on, buckling it at the elbow and hooking back the blades, oblivious to Fagin's choking sounds behind her. I wanted to shout, but it would have done no good, and my hands were tied so that I could not sign.

The female squatted before Zorba. "You are?" she signed.

"Zorba. A physician."

"A physician." She pointed at Fagin thrashing in the grass beside the road as he slowly choked to death. "It is bad for Fagin's health that you order me not to hit him. Yes?"

Zorba looked away from her. "I understand," he signed.

The taller male Stripe hooked back his Fighting Hand and went to Fagin. He loosened the rope around Fagin's neck and held him up while Fagin breathed in hungry gasps. The Stripe held him until he was breathing more normally, then released him. Fagin sagged where he sat. Seemingly disinterested, the other male began to round up the llamas.

"Tell me, physician," continued the female Stripe, "what you know of this bald ape."

"What do you wish to know?"

"Is it wild and uncontrollable? Or will it come along peacefully."

Zorba glanced at me. "It is not wild. Whether it comes along peacefully depends upon where you take it."

She regarded him for a full minute before signing, "Physician, you are an idiot." She stood up and turned her back on him, then came to me and squatted directly in front of me, staring me in the face, her eyes challenging. I pressed my lips together until they hurt and I did not look away.

For a raccoon, and even for a Stripe, her face was narrow and hard. She wore a gold hoop in her right ear. The musk of battle clung to her fur. A scar interrupted the fur at her right shoulder, and her dark gray nipples dotted her torso like three rows of eyes.

Slowly her hands rose. "I do not like the way it looks at me," she signed to the others without breaking our staring match. Her hands came toward my face and I jerked away, even though the rope burned at my throat. "It is freakish," she signed.

"Get fucked," I said.

"It growls at me." She seemed amused.

She turned to Fagin. "What is so special about it?" she demanded.

"I know little of it," he answered. "I am never seeing it before today."

Zorba trilled for her attention. "It is a rare animal," he signed. "If I may ask, how do you know of it?"

She ignored him. "Fagin," she signed. "Fagin, Fagin. We are sent to find you in Seven Answers. But you are knowing that, yes?"

Fagin signed nothing.

"You are killing twenty of us by fire," she continued. "Do you even know why you are doing that?"

"Because you are coming after me," he signed.

"We are coming after the bald ape. We are coming after Truck."

"Truck is rightfully seeking sanctuary with me."

"And do you even know why we are coming for her?"

"No," he admitted after a moment.

"No," she agreed. "You burn us and you ambush us without provocation—and you do not even know why."

"You are trying to kill us."

She waved a humorless laugh. "When? Here, on the road? We are defending ourselves. Who is trying to kill you in Seven Answers?"

"You are coming to kill the ruler of your neighboring province!"

Again she sat down before Fagin, and she reached out her Fighting-Handed arm. Fagin flinched, but this time she caressed his face, smoothing the fur along his muzzle, wiping the blood from the side of his head. Soon she removed her hand from him. "Fagin," she signed, and there was something oddly gentle about the way her hands moved, something reminiscent of the way she had just caressed his face, "why do you wear these many umbilical bracelets? From where are you getting them? Might they be the bracelets of Stripes?"

Fagin looked at the ground. She trilled and he looked up again. "Yes?" she prodded.

Fagin's expression was hateful. "They are the bracelets of Stripes," he admitted, "but for the one that is my own. I am obtaining them in fair fashion and in the same manner that any Stripe would obtain umbilical bracelets not [her/his] own."

She looked at the tall male, and they both waved a brief laugh. "But you are not a Stripe, Goody Fagin. Tell me, which of these bracelets is your own?"

Fagan glanced at the ropy bracelets on his wrist but signed nothing.

"Fagin?" she persisted. "Which of the bracelets is your own?" Fagin did not answer immediately, and she wrung her right hand. The blades of her Fighting Hand swung into place.

Reluctantly Fagin held out his right arm and singled out one of the umbilical bracelets. The female Stripe slid it up to his shoulder, then gathered the remaining bracelets and shoved two Fighting Hand blades beneath them. She sawed back and forth three times, and the bracelets were cut through. She pulled them from Fagin's wrist and flung them to the ground. "It is the act of a savage," she signed, "to take the umbilical bracelet of another—so you may keep the one that is yours." She looked at the taller male Stripe standing beside her, at the other Stripe now hitching the last llama to a tree, at the bodies of the three Stripes lying in the road, then back to Fagin. "Why do you think we are coming for Truck?" she asked again.

"To kill her," repeated Fagin. "Why else?"

"Because Louis XIV wants to help her."

"Then why are you not telling this to us before?" asked Fagin.

"Because," signed the tall male, "you are killing us before we have the opportunity."

"Stripes . . . Stripes should not be so easy to kill," Fagin replied lamely.

"Your work is made easier," countered the male, "when Stripes are under orders to let no harm come to those they seek."

Fagin was motionless, and I could tell that Zorba was shocked as well.

"Do we frighten you so much?" asked the female, and she and the male looked at one another and waved their laughter.

If it was a joke, I didn't get it.

They tied Fagin's hands behind him again, and then they held a conversation that ended with the tall male going off to collect wood while the female and the other male pulled the bodies of their comrades off the pongee sticks. They set the corpse of the third Stripe, the one Fagin had speared, beside the other two, and then the female lifted one end of the log while the male pulled the bodies of the two dogs from beneath it. While the tall male piled wood, the other two Stripes debated whether it was prudent to burn the bodies in the middle of the road, or if it might be better to find a clearing away from the road. The tall one joined in and reminded them that they were in a hurry, and without further discussion they built a pyre for their dead in the middle of the road. The smaller male struck rocks until he got a fire going, and he fanned it briskly while it caught.

"If they are in such a hurry," Fagin signed to Zorba, "why do they not simply leave the bodies behind?"

The tall male saw and turned to face Fagin. "Because our companions are not food for rats," he signed, and turned his back to us.

They placed the dead Stripes on the fire, and then they stepped back and watched them burn. Soon the air was filled with the stench of burning fur and charring meat, and the snapping sound of frying fat. After a few minutes our captors added the dogs to the fire as well. The female tossed on the umbilical bracelets she had cut from Fagin's wrist, then turned to regard Fagin while the bracelets blackened behind her.

The males unhitched two of the messenger llamas and began yoking them to the wagon. They soon discovered that the leather reins had been cut off when we had laid our ambush, and they were forced to untie me and Fagin because they needed the rope.

I sat back and massaged my hands and ankles to restore circulation. The female watched me with what I interpreted as a wry expression. "It is ugly," she signed to Zorba. "I do not like the way it stares back at me."

Zorba finished retying one of the knots binding his splint, apparently tied too loose to suit his taste. "How do you know of it?" he asked again.

"Louis XIV," she replied offhandedly. She walked to me and stood in front of me. "How intelligent is it?" she asked. She was looking over her right shoulder at Zorba for a reply, and she turned her head my way when I cleared my throat.

"Intelligent enough," I signed.

Her eyes widened and she jumped into a defensive stance with her Fighting Hand held ready. The two males had just finished hitching the llamas to the wagon, and they rushed toward us at the quick movement from their companion.

Abruptly the female dropped her guard. The males joined her and asked what was wrong. She spread her hands. "It signs," she told them.

"What signs?" asked the taller male. "The bald thing?"

"Yes. It signs."

"How interesting," signed the shorter male.

The female stepped closer to me while the males watched. "Why do you stare at me?" she asked.

"Because you stare at me," I replied.

"Well, stop it." And then she made her order moot by turning her back on me. I could not follow her conversation with the other two Stripes. To my left, out of their sight, Fagin pointed to his eyes and signed a negative, then repeated the gesture. I was puzzled, until the Stripes' conversation abruptly broke off and the shorter male held my Buck knife out for Zorba and Fagin to see. "Whose?" he asked.

Both Zorba and Fagin watched his hands as he signed, and I noticed that they were careful not to meet his gaze for more than a few seconds at a time.

I thought I understood why my staring at them made them nervous—it was a matter of territoriality. Humans of the same sex use prolonged eye contact to either challenge or acknowledge territory. It seems to be an unwritten rule that you are allowed one unquestioned instance of eye contact. Two, and the person being looked at will start looking back to see if s/he is indeed being looked at. Three, and the object of scrutiny begins to stare frankly to deter the offending gaze. If it isn't deterred, the person gazed upon either acquiesces, in which case the person doing the gazing has won, or s/he challenges: "You got a problem?" It is simple and it is primal. There are other, sexual connotations, much more situational, brought into play in eye contact between men and women.

The raccoons are much the same in this regard, and the Stripes even more so, though without the slew of sexual connotations underlying such eye contact between males and females. For me to meet the Stripes' gaze was an open refusal to acquiesce; it implied that I was willing to hold my territory against them, that I regarded myself as a peer—and they didn't like that. They would, I learned later, stare down anybody who was not a Stripe, and most who weren't Stripes would quickly lower their gaze—the feeling being that nobody who wasn't a Stripe had any business challenging one.

Again I cleared my throat for their attention. "It is my knife," I signed.

And again they were staring at me, and I continued to stare back.

Their ground was uncertain here. I was not a raccoon, and I was not a Stripe, but there I was, locking eyes and questioning territory as if I were every bit as qualified to do so as any goddamned Stripe.

Fagin and Zorba were aware of it, too, and just as the female was beginning to bristle, Zorba quickly trilled for their attention, giving them an excuse to break eye contact. Apparently the ploy was acceptable to them, and the tension broke—this particular tension, anyway; there was a lot of it in the air, and for many reasons.

"Goodbodies," signed Zorba, "pardon my signing so, but how do you know that Truck will trust you? You are, after all, Louis' Stripes, and Truck only knows that you hunt her."

The Stripes glanced at each other a moment, and then the female signed, "Be still"—the raccoon way of telling Zorba to shut up.

They put me and Zorba in the wagon. Fagin rode behind us, guarded by the tall male, who rode beside him on a messenger llama that could probably have supported my weight without difficulty. The shorter male drove the wagon, and the female rode ahead of us. The extra llama trailed behind her. We headed back toward Three Big Dogs and then turned onto the road that led north, presumably toward Seaport Savannah. It took no great effort for the Stripes to figure that Fagin, Zorba, and I had been there to stall any attempt to follow Truck as she made her way northward, and they wanted to catch up to her as quickly as possible. Their messenger llamas were faster than a normal riding llama, but they were slowed by the wagon.

I sat beside Zorba, and we both watched Fagin and the Stripe riding side by side. No one signed. The Stripe driving the wagon frequently glanced over his shoulder to check on us. He held the reins in one hand and my knife in the other, and occasionally he flicked open the knife to examine the blade, running his finger across the MADE IN USA stamped into the base, then closing it and scrutinizing the locking mechanism.

Other than their initial surprise at my ability to sign, the Stripes had expressed no further curiosity about me, and this disconcerted me more than if they had been upset by it. They were inscrutable, these Stripes; I could not tell what they were thinking, what their attitude or intentions were regarding us. I couldn't get a handle on them.

After we had traveled perhaps a mile, I asked Zorba how his leg felt.

"Painful," he replied. "But I do not think it is broken, though they are splinting it. It seems I am wrenching the joint at the knee when I am hitting the ground."

"How is this happening, Zorba?"

He ducked his head. "Bad timing, Bald Ape, nothing more. My throw with the rope is perfect, but I do not tug quickly enough, and she merely grasps the line and steps aside to put me off my balance, then tugs me out of the tree as if I am a kit's wind toy. Perhaps if I am not as—"

Behind us the tall Stripe trilled, and Zorba stopped signing. "My name is [Little John]," he signed. "He who drives you is signed Longfingers"—that was the literal meaning of the sign he used to indicate our driver—"and the female is [Natasha]." He fell still.

Zorba, Fagin, and I regarded him, nonplussed. I think simply because he felt some reply was expected, Zorba signed, "You know our names, yes?"

"Yes." And he signed nothing further.

We rode for another fifteen minutes without further conversation, and then the tall Stripe trilled again. "You are alive because Truck will believe you more readily than she will believe us."

Fagin glanced at Zorba. Zorba glanced at me. I spread my hands. "How do we know, Goodbody [Little John]," asked

Zorba, "that Louis truly desires to help Truck?"

"Because I tell you so."

Zorba waved an indulgent laugh. "That is hardly proof, goodbody Little John."

"Because Truck's advisor Puck is alive," he elaborated.

"Puck?" repeated Zorba. "Puck is alive?" He seemed incredulous.

"Who is this Puck?" asked Fagin.

"He is Truck's friend," Zorba replied, "and one of her most trusted advisors. He is accompanying Truck on her tour of the Outback, and is presumed to be killed by the Confederate Stripes who are turning against Truck. But . . . if our new acquaintance signs truthfully . . . Puck is not dead."

"He is reaching Seaport Jacksonville," continued Little John, "and informing Louis of the true events of the attack outside Many Corners."

"But still we must ask," persisted Zorba, "how we can know this is true. We do not know that Puck is truly alive."

"Puck sends a message to repeat to Truck," countered Little John, "which will convince Truck that her advisor truly lives."

"And this message is?" asked Fagin.

"None of your concern," finished Little John.

"Do you hate us so?" asked Zorba. "We fight for the same cause, yes?"

"We do not hate you at all," signed Little John. "You presume too much. We do not care about you; our 'cause' is merely this: we are ordered to bring Truck and the bald ape back to Louis. In attempting this, more than twenty of us are killed. We need you to help us convince Truck to come to Louis, but we are hardly enthusiastic about your company."

"You only do your duty," I signed. "You follow your orders, and nothing more. Yes?"

He looked at me a long moment. "You are very strange," he finally signed.

"You are very strange to me," I rejoined.

He accepted this without comment, though a crease appeared in the bare, gray flesh between his eyes. Like the other two Stripes, he had a cinammon-colored strip bordering one side of his stripe. "From where do you come?" he asked.

"From a place . . . you are never seeing of."

"There are many such places. Where is this one?"

"It . . . is hard to describe, and the tale is long."

"You have nothing better to do."

I glanced at Zorba, and he spread his hands philosophically. I frowned. Could it cause any harm to tell him about myself? He already knew I was intelligent, and in many respects this was the most important thing he could discover about me. I didn't know what effect it could have on Truck to have others know of my origins, but I confess to having the notion in the back of my mind that being an intelligent creature from Somewhere Else might lend an air of mystique to my presence here. I had become embroiled in what was essentially a political campaign, and for the first time I found myself concerned about my *image*, especially in regard to how it affected Truck. It was not to be the last time I acted with this in mind.

Little John had hooked back his Fighting Hand and was cracking his knuckles one at a time while I deliberated. I cleared my throat and he looked up at me, but he continued to worry at his hands, popping the little finger of his right hand and going on to the index finger of his armored left hand (for he was the Stripe who had thrown the bola and wore his Fighting Hand on the left side).

"I am from another world—," I began.

"Why do you wear spectacles?" interrupted Little John.

"To . . . to correct my vision."

"I see. Continue."

I didn't know if his pun had been deliberate or not, but I waved a tentative laugh just in case. "As I am signing," I went on hesitantly, "I am from another world. . . . " I expected him to interrupt again, but he did not. "A world," I continued, "populated by many such as myself." Fagin was attentive as well. I think he wanted to ask me many questions about what I was signing but felt constrained by the presence of Little John—who was, after all, a Stripe, Fagin's captor, and a good twelve inches taller than Fagin, almost as tall as me. "I do not know how it is I am getting to this world," I continued, "but one day in my world I am exploring a cave—"

"Why?" interrupted Little John.

"For . . . for recreation. It is a cave I am exploring many times, yet this time I am finding a place within the cave that I am never before encountering. . . . "

I went on to sign how I had embarked on my hazardous and technically unexplainable journey to raccoon-land, and the increasingly fluid motions of my hands were watched by the Stripe I had named Little John, the peculiar Stripe who was to become my friend, as the wagon jounced along the rutted road, heading north toward my auspicious but disquieting reunion with Truck.

25
Narrative of Truck

NEAR THE OCEAN is a forest of tall trees made of stone. The trees are gaunt and foreboding, unadorned by leaves. They seem like the skeletons of unimaginable creatures, and they cut into a sky in which dark clouds thicken like ink pouring into water.

Perched upon a low branch of one of the bare trees is a black bird—a raven, perhaps. There is decay in this bird, a kind of rot, as though maggots writhe beneath its dark feathers. With malevolent red eyes the black bird looks down upon a clearing in the stone forest, where many wolves are gathered in a ring. In stillness and in silence they watch two tailless wolves that warily circle each other beneath the darkening sky.

Suspended in the air above the circling wolves are two tablets of graven stone. The writing upon them is indistinct.

The two wolves bristle. Their teeth are bared. They slaver, growl, and snap.

Lightning flashes in the dark sky. It is reflected in the eyes of the bird that watches from the tree.

The circling wolves lower their heads and leap at each other. They clash as thunder rumbles through the stone forest like the crashing of a gigantic wave. They separate, and one wolf now bleeds from a shoulder.

Lightning reveals streaks of rain like countless suspended needles.

The black bird takes wing. It glides through the air without extending its wings, passing silently into the ring of watching wolves.

Out of the ring leaps a fighting dog. It is a white blur among the many wolves as it jumps toward the two wolves in the center of the ring. The black bird descends upon this fighting dog with a joyous fury in its eyes. Its claws grip the fur of the fighting dog, and with its sharp beak it rips at the dog's chest. Blood reddens the dog's fur as the black bird stabs with its beak, tearing away fur and flesh. It is digging furiously for the fighting dog's heart, its body embedding in the dog's chest as it rips deeper. The dog writhes upon the ground as the fighting wolves regard it.

The scene is frozen in the cold light of another lightning flash.

There is a grinding sound from above, and the wolves look up into the rainy sky.

Cracks spread across one of the suspended tablets in imitation of the lightning. The tablet crumbles until there is nothing left of it. The pieces fall to the ground. The remaining tablet floats above the injured wolf, which now chews at the bird in the fighting dog's chest. It tugs its head, it worries back and forth, but the bird will not pull free. It is lodged in the chest of the fighting dog, hungry for the taste of its heart.

I awaken with my heart beating rapidly.

It is after moons-set and the night is cloudy and dark. Dodger's messenger llama is tall and milky beside the draft llamas hitched to a tree. Dodger himself sleeps placidly upon the ground. General Lee squats with her back to me, patiently watching the road. It is signed of Lee that she could outstare a tree, if need be.

She turns to regard me when I rise. I brush leaves and twigs from my fur. My palms are sweaty, and my feet as well.

"It is a few decafingers before your watch," signs Lee as I step toward her.

"I know. But I am not sleepy."

She yawns and stretches. Its strap tied around her throat, her war helmet dangles from her back. "Bad dreams?" she asks.

"Dreams, anyway," I reply.

"Nightmares are always bad, Truck. For such as you they must be worse."

I spread my hands. "There is nothing to be done about them." I do not wish to sign about dreams and nightmares, so

I ask, "Do you think we will have trouble when we near Seaport Jacksonville?"

"Who can sign? We journey on a road less traveled, and I think they will expect us to make our way northward on either the Scummy or the Broken Spine, because it would be faster. If need be, we will take to the forest near Seaport Jacksonville and the border, and keep away from roads until we are well within the Confederacy. For now I feel we are safe—comparatively, anyway—and I prefer to stay on the road." She yawns again and this time cracks her knuckles as she stretches. "I do wish I could light my pipe, though," she signs wistfully. "It is good company on a night such as this."

I regard the overcast sky. "Do you think it will rain, Lee?"

Thunder rumbles a reply before Lee can respond, and we laugh. "Well," signs Lee, "prediction is your occupation, yes? What do you think is the likelihood of rain?"

Thunder again, like the rolling of a heavy stone.

"I think the night will be clear and dry." We laugh again, and she scratches the top of her head and around her eyes.

"You seem tired, Lee—either that or I bore you, for you yawn like a fish out of water."

"It is nothing. I can sleep while we ride tomorrow."

"Sleep now; I shall keep the watch. I will sleep no more tonight."

"You are signing me into it, little Truck." She rises and shakes out first her left leg, then her right. She stifles a yawn with one hand as she pats me on the shoulder with the other. "It is awful to grow old," she signs after yawning, and I look down upon her face and see that she is even more tired than I am first perceiving. "When you are back in your Chair in the Keep," she continues, "appoint me some busy post, won't you? Life is too dull in places like Seven Answers." And she trudges off to lie across from Dodger, leaving me alone with my thoughts.

As quietly as I am able, I walk to the tree where my mandolute is propped, and I turn the instrument face-down to reduce the chance of damage if it does rain.

It would be nice to be able to play the mandolute, to once more use my music to help me unravel my True dream. It is so helpful to have a pattern to help me order my thoughts. But I cannot play my ill-gotten instrument this night, for the sound would carry.

I return to the spot where Lee is keeping her watch. Fifty

spans away an armadillo noses its way along a rut in the road. They are strange creatures, armadillos. Their appearance seems fantastic, and they never quite look real to me.

A stone forest. A black bird. Many wolves.

What am I supposed to make of this dream?

As a young adept I am taught that each raccoon possesses a unique and individual vocabulary of symbols. As adults we are influenced in the way we view the world by the imagery we hold within ourselves, and our imagery is almost always that possessed by a kit, for the bulk of our personal symbols forms in our early youth. Insight into the origin of these symbols is the adept's way to unravel the knot of meaning that is a dream. An adept is taught a formalized introspection, a way to look closely at how s/he interprets the world. S/he is taught to constantly examine [her/his] motivations in an attempt to understand the ways in which approaching a situation with certain predispositions can influence that situation. My most recurrent dream is of a violent shipwreck, and I know that for me the ship being tossed about on the waves and dashed upon the rocks is an image that occurs when I feel helpless against the forces which act upon my life. When I dream of rotting or maggot-ridden fruit, as I am doing before the death of my music teacher, it is almost always because I am fearful for the health of a friend.

And now I dream a True dream of wolves in a stone forest.

Wolves can mean many things to me. They may represent a fear of enemies who attack my exposed weaknesses, for wolves are scavengers. In the past I am having dreams in which wolves represent Stripes. For me a ring of wolves can be a symbol for the feeling of being outnumbered, or an image implying the untrustworthiness of those around me.

I distill the elements of my dream. Wolves that fight. A ring of wolves. A stone forest. A storm. A black bird. Two floating tablets, graven but indecipherable. A fighting dog. . . .

I draw in a sharp breath. I turn to look at Dodger and Lee asleep on the ground. An opossum slinks toward the trees not five spans from Lee's head.

Thunder rumbles, then rumbles louder, and a light rain begins to fall. The opossum abandons its stealth and scampers for the cover of the brush, a glint of reflected lightning flashing in its eyes.

The rain patters the leaves with a sound like crumpling

paper. It begins to bead upon my fur, but I do nothing to cover myself, for I am too preoccupied by my sudden comprehension of my dream.

I know what it means. I *know.* And in my knowledge there is room for the terror of certainty, which is in a way more frightening than my previous ignorance.

Now I understand the role of the Bald Ape, and I am afraid for him.

Now I know something of the nature of my usurper, and it chills me—for if true, it fulfills the last True dream of Charlemagne, the dream he is signed to be having the night before his death:

Within the lifetime of kits now born, a Stripe shall sit upon the Chair, and claim the title of Architect of Sleep.

And now I see the end of the road upon which I walk, and I am afraid.

The rest of that night is a concert of thunder and lightning and rain.